Love an

By the same author

Family Trees
Voices of Song

Love and Duty

Kate Alexander

PIATKUS

Copyright © 1997 by Kate Alexander

First published in Great Britain in 1997 by
Judy Piatkus (Publishers) Ltd of
5 Windmill Street, London W1

The moral right of the author has been asserted

A catalogue record for this book is available from the British Library

ISBN 0–7499–0420–8

Set in Times by
Action Typesetting Ltd, Gloucester
Printed and bound in Great Britain by
Bookcraft Ltd, Midsomer Norton, Avon

For my sisters, Dorothy and Margaret

Chapter One

The marriage room in the Registrar's Office was self-consciously gracious, all cream paint and Adam style mouldings. On the desk there was an arrangement of pink gladioli and white spray chrysanthemums. The late August sun streamed through tall windows tactfully shrouded in white net. As she stood before the Registrar with her hand in Piers', Ella could see golden motes of dust dancing in the sunlight, and thought how strange it was that her attention should be caught by this tiny detail at such a time.

Behind her, the small group of people who had come to witness her marriage were attentive and silent. There were few enough of them: a couple of colleagues from the school where she had taught; Piers' friends, Claudia and Bernie Caldicott; the Secretary of the local golf club and his wife, because Piers and Bernie, and Claudia, too, were fanatical players; and the bridegroom's three children.

The Registrar was speaking. Ella's hand jerked in Piers' grasp as he gave Piers the formula to be repeated. 'I, Percy George Armitage . . .' *Percy*?

She managed to make her own response without hesitating, but, for goodness sake, *Percy*?

In a few minutes the ceremony was over. She was no longer Ella Martin but Ella Armitage, wife to Piers – Percy! – Armitage and stepmother to his three children. There was a flurry of congratulations and kissing and then they adjourned to the grounds of the Registrar's Office so that Bernie could take photographs. There was no official photographer: why waste money when the bridegroom's best friend was an expert

1

amateur photographer with his own dark room?

They went on to lunch at a local hotel, given by Bernie and Claudia as a wedding present. There were no speeches, but Bernie could not be prevented from proposing a toast to the bride and groom, nor from reading out a few of the good wishes that had been sent to them. There was a telegram from Piers' mother and father and one from his dead wife's brother, rather ambiguously worded, in Ella's opinion, wishing them good fortune and sending his love to Verity, Harry and Jennifer. The children were disappointed that their Uncle Toby had not come to the wedding, but he had excused himself on the grounds of duty, which might be true since his work with the Red Cross was likely to take him abroad at short notice. On the whole, Ella thought it had been tactful of him to stay away, especially since she had the impression that Piers was not all that keen on his brother-in-law. To Ella, Toby sounded like an interesting character, an Army officer who had resigned after seven years and taken a post with the Red Cross which took him to some very out-of-the-way places, but Piers had been dismissive when she had expressed an interest.

The lunch was not prolonged because Piers and Ella had a long drive ahead of them. Ella was afraid that the car would have been dressed up, but the only decoration was a large bow of white ribbon, which was easily removed. As they drove away, with the luncheon guests lined up on the pavement to wave goodbye, Piers said, 'Well, that went off very nicely, didn't it, Mrs Armitage?'

'Yes, lovely, except ... *Percy*! You might have warned me. I was afraid I was marrying the wrong man.'

'It's an old family name. Mum insisted on it to please my grandfather. I've always been known as Piers. I suppose I forget about it except on official occasions.'

He sounded quite offhand, but Ella was so sensitive to every tone of his voice that she suspected that he was not quite pleased by her reaction to his proper name. It was of no importance. Something they would laugh about in years to come. In all the long, lovely years to come.

She had been hooked as soon as they encountered one another at a school open day. He had been so endearing:

harassed, conscientious, full of charm, talking eagerly about his young family and the difficulty of bringing up motherless children. Ella had been desperate to see him again, despairing that there was the slightest chance of him finding her as attractive as she found him. She had managed to avoid the temptation to invent a flimsy excuse to go to his house and her patience had been rewarded when Piers had put in an appearance at Sports Day and an end-of-term play and had made a point of seeking her out.

It was after that play that they had had their first date and only a couple of weeks later she had taken him back to the house she had inherited from her parents and they had made love. After that Ella was wholly lost, totally bound up in Piers and her dream of a possible life together, ready to agree to any conditions, to overcome any difficulties, refusing to see the three children as any sort of obstacle.

And now she had got him. He was her husband. Nothing else mattered.

The only thing wrong with the honeymoon was that it was too short. They had three days, and three nights, in the Lake District in a hotel that satisfied every dream. Ella put all her misgivings – three stepchildren – behind her and gave herself up to bliss. She was fathoms deep in love, an authentic enchantment, in thrall to Piers as if to a magician, alive to his every shift of mood, unable to be near him without touching him, living through the days in a dream of remembrance and expectation, waiting for the night to come when they could plunge into one another's arms again.

On the last morning she tried to be practical, but they had breakfast in bed, which was not conducive to an early departure. In a welter of tumbled sheets and crumbs of toast, Ella finally disentangled herself and moved away from Piers.

'We must get up.'

'Mm?' Piers' hand moved slowly over her hip.

'No, we must get up. I'm going to have a bath and get dressed and finish packing. We have to be out of this room by midday and you know we promised to be home by tea time.'

For the children. As she slid out of bed and looked round for the dressing gown that must be somewhere amongst her discarded clothes, Ella felt a twist of nervousness in her

3

stomach. Of course she would manage. She'd have to, there was no going back now.

'Don't fall asleep,' she said over her shoulder to Piers as she opened the bathroom door. She got no more than a grunt out of him, which made her smile. He must be tired, just as she was.

Lying in the foaming, scented water, Ella closed her eyes, drifting blissfully. She was exhausted and exhilarated and happy beyond belief. Piers had been wonderful; they had both been wonderful; everything was perfect. No matter what difficulties lay ahead, and she was not daft enough to believe that coping with three stepchildren was going to be easy, at least they had these few perfect days to remember.

They managed to get downstairs by twelve o'clock, their suitcases chaotically packed, and with a telltale tendency to break into idiotic smiles at nothing in particular. Ella looked round, impressing on her mind the dull gold carpet, the wall-paper discreetly patterned with tiny gold leaves, the armchairs and sofas like well-stuffed aubergines, the tall vases of flowers, the discreet scent in the air. The smell of money, she told herself; make the most of it, you won't get many breaks like this, not unless Piers comes into a fortune.

While Piers took their cases out to the car, Ella sat down on one of the purple sofas and glanced at the Sunday papers they had not bothered to order for themselves. She looked up when Piers came back and sat watching him as he went to the desk to pay their bill.

By anyone's standards she had married a handsome man, tall and long-limbed and elegant, with hair cut short to show the fine shape of his head and a small, neat moustache which defined his upper lip. Rather a nineteen-thirties looking man, she thought idly. When Piers turned from the desk and came towards her she looked at him with such unabashed pleasure that his lips twitched and he gave her a quick, conspiratorial wink.

'Darling, the stupidest thing,' he said. 'I've packed my credit card. Do you have yours handy?'

'Yes, of course.'

As she produced the card at the desk, Ella said, with a trace of embarrassment, 'It's still in my maiden name.'

'That won't matter,' the receptionist assured her. 'As long as you sign the slip correctly.'

4

'We must sort out a joint account when we get home,' Piers said.

Ella agreed without really taking in what he was saying, her attention riveted by the startling total of the bill. Could they really have spent all that on a three night stay? Yes, they could, she realised, at over a hundred pounds a night for a room, breakfast not included, the champagne on ice in their bedroom, the gourmet dinners.

'Dry bread and water for the next three months,' she remarked and then realised from Piers' frown that she had said the wrong thing. Darling Piers, did he think she was criticising him for extravagance? Or did he perhaps want the receptionist to get the impression that they were accustomed to living at this level? Ella slipped a hand through his arm and gave it a squeeze and knew from the answering pressure that she had been swiftly forgiven.

They made good time down the motorway, not bothering to stop for any lunch. They were heading for the Kent coast, for the little town of Kits Harbour, where Ella had been born and to which she had returned to nurse her mother in her last illness. After her mother's death, Ella had intended selling the bungalow on the cliff which had been the family home, then the idea had taken possession of her, so gradually that she hardly remembered making a decision, that she should make her return to Kits Harbour permanent. There was a vacancy at a local school and it seemed pre-ordained that it should be for a teacher of her two specialities, geography and domestic science. She had not regretted the choice she had made, but she had begun to realise that while still only in her late twenties she had settled in to a life that had all the elements of middle age. There were few men in Ella's life and she regretted that. She wanted a partner, preferably a permanent one, with a home and family. Then she had met Piers. And now she was married and had given up her job because she had a husband and three children to look after.

Three children. Well, that was the package. If she wanted Piers – and how she wanted Piers – she had to take his motherless children as well.

5

'It will be all right, won't it?' she asked as Piers turned the car into the Kits Harbour road.

'Still worrying about the kids? Of course it'll be all right. They know you, they like you and God knows they need you.'

'I suppose they do like me,' Ella said. 'I never know what they're thinking. Piers, go by the coast road and stop when you get to the top of Kits Bay.'

They drove past the bungalow she had sold, the place where she had grown up. The estate agents' board with a bold 'Sold' sticker across it was still standing in the front garden.

'The new people don't seem to have moved in yet,' Ella said.

'But the sale has gone through okay?'

'It was completed last week.'

'That's good. I only married you for your money.'

'I knew there had to be a reason,' Ella said. 'Stop here, darling.'

Piers pulled up just short of the old lighthouse, no longer operating, but solid and white, with glittering windows at the top. They got out of the car, crossed a short stretch of grass to the edge of the cliff and stood looking down on the curving bay beneath. The sea was calm. Small waves curled over and broke on the sand with an edge of white foam. Black rocks, with small pools beside them in which she had searched for sea creatures in her childhood, stood isolated on the wide beach.

'Tide's out,' Ella said. She was filled with an immense satisfaction. For her the tide was very definitely in. Her doubts floated away. She, who had coped with classes of thirty children, could surely manage three in her own home. Piers was right, the children needed her. She could give them not just material care, but affection and a strong foundation for their lives. And perhaps, one day, not too soon, but in a year or two, she could have a child of her own and complete the family.

They drove on, past the golf course, making for the sprawling red brick house which belonged to Bernie and Claudia, who were looking after the children while Piers and Ella were on their brief honeymoon. It had been good of them to offer; Ella just wished that she did not have to make a conscious effort to remind herself that it was kind of Piers' friends to solve this difficulty for them. The truth was Bernie and

Claudia made her nervous, especially Claudia, with her golden hair and her unchipped nail varnish, the childless wife of a rich man, with all the confidence of someone who never had to think twice about the money in her purse.

'The garden looks lovely,' Ella murmured as they turned into the drive of Kits View House.

'So it should,' Piers said, which was true because Bernie owned a large local garden centre and treated the garden round his own house as a showcase.

'They'll be by the swimming pool,' Piers said and led the way with the ease of long friendship round the side of the house to the back.

The swimming pool was green and blue and white and all the garden furniture matched. Terribly *Homes & Gardens*, Ella thought distractedly, looking round for the children. Bernie and Claudia were relaxing on reclining chairs. They were both wearing swim suits. Claudia sat up, picked up a length of colourful cotton material and crossed it over in front of her, tying it at the nape of her neck. When she stood up it fell into graceful folds.

'Darlings, you're back!' she said. 'Did you have a fabulous time?'

'Splendid, thank you,' Piers said. He bent to kiss her cheek.

Claudia looked up at him, the corners of her eyes crinkling in secret amusement. 'I bet!' she said.

Bernie, too, stood up. He was a big man, as tall as Piers, but more thickset, with a sprinkling of coarse black hair on his chest, his forearms and his legs. Ella hoped he was not going to kiss her. Not that she had anything against Bernie, it was just that there was so much of him, especially in his semi-nude state. She felt ridiculously over-dressed in her neat wedding suit.

'The kids went inside to dress,' Claudia explained. 'We knew you wouldn't be long. Sit down, do. Would you like tea ... a drink?'

'I think I'll go and see how they're getting on,' Ella said. 'If you don't mind ...?'

'Of course. *Mia casa es sua casa*, even though you wouldn't let us send you out to our villa in Spain.'

'It was too far ... too long to be away ...' Ella said, still making excuses, even though this was something that

7

had been settled long before the wedding.

She went into the house and found the children in the kitchen, their three small bags packed and ready for departure. They were not actually touching one another and yet they gave an indefinable impression of huddling together.

Verity was the eldest, thirteen years old, thin, sallow and black-haired, with big, silver-grey eyes that would always be her most beautiful feature. Her T-shirt showed only the faintest indication of developing breasts and her jeans hung slackly over her skinny hips. Harry was ten, a sturdy boy with curling hair as dark as his sister's, but with more blue in his eyes and much more colour in his cheeks. He was a silent child, but none of them was particularly talkative, not even eight-year-old Jennifer, who was the baby of the family and, Ella suspected, inclined to play on it. She was fairer, sunnier and more out-going than the other two, a real little charmer when she chose. Piers' charm; she was more like him than the other two, who must take after their dead mother.

It occurred to Ella for the first time that she had never seen a photograph of Lucy. Poor Lucy, who had died so young. Perhaps Piers had put away her pictures. It was only two years since her death and the memory must still be painful, to him and the children. Who could tell what they had suffered? Lucy had been having treatment for cancer for a year before she died, and that must have been a difficult, painful time for them, knowing she was ill, not knowing how serious it was, but guessing and fearing.

Seeing them now in Claudia's designer kitchen, all peasant tiles and curlicue wood, Ella recognised the anxiety concealed by their silence and if, when she spoke, the words were mundane, the intention behind them was full of loving kindness.

'Hello, we're back,' she said.

'We heard the car,' Verity said. 'Where's Dad?'

'In the garden, talking to ...' Ella hesitated. 'To Uncle Bernie and Aunt Claudia,' she concluded.

'We don't call them aunt and uncle. They're not,' Verity said. 'We've only got one uncle and that's Uncle Toby.'

'I do call Uncle Bernie uncle because he likes me to,' Jennifer said. 'But I don't call Claudia auntie because she doesn't.'

8

'Are we leaving straight away?' Harry asked.

'I think so. Let's go and see what Dad says.'

'While we're talking about names, we've decided to call you Mother,' Verity said abruptly.

'Even though you're not,' Jennifer put in.

'It'll save explaining things to people,' Verity said.

'We couldn't call you Mummy because that was what we called Mummy,' Jennifer said.

There was a brief, horrible pause and then Ella said, 'I'm glad you've decided on Mother. It was difficult to know what to suggest.'

It was, in fact, an enormous hurdle cleared. Ella felt quite light-headed with relief as she led them out into the garden.

Piers had made himself comfortable on one of the loungers and had a long drink in his hand.

'Hello, chicks. Everything all right?' he asked.

'Yes, thank you,' Harry said. 'Are we going home now?'

'As soon as I've quenched my thirst.'

'Are you sure you won't have anything, Ella?' Claudia asked, not moving.

Part of Ella longed to relax like Piers, to be able to chat easily with these carefree, careless people, but mostly she just wanted to get away, to start settling into her new life. She smiled and refused Claudia's offer of refreshment and tried to catch Piers' eye.

'Are we playing golf as usual next Sunday?' Bernie asked.

'Of course,' Piers said.

'Hey, hadn't you better ask your new wife?' Claudia said.

At last Piers turned his head to look at Ella. 'You don't mind, do you?' he asked. 'It's the only chance I get for a bit of exercise.' Without waiting for her answer he turned to Bernie again. 'What did you do today?'

'We stayed home with the kids.'

'What a sacrifice!'

Piers began to drain his glass as Jennifer demanded, 'What did you bring us back from your holiday, Daddy?'

'Some Kendal mintcake, honey child.'

'I don't like mint,' Verity said.

'And some fudge.'

'I'll have *both*,' Jennifer said.

'You'll be a little butterball,' Bernie said. 'Uncle Bernie's little butterball.' He seized hold of Jennifer and swung her high into the air, laughing as she squealed.

'Jennifer, don't be such a baby,' Verity said.

'Time to go,' Piers said. 'Claudia, it was good of you to have the kids for us. Say thanks, chicks.'

'Thank you for having us,' Verity said. Harry muttered something inaudible and Jennifer, set down on her feet by Bernie, ran excitedly over to Claudia and hugged her round the middle, an embrace which Ella suspected was not altogether welcome.

'Thank God that's over,' Claudia said.

'Seems quiet now they've gone.'

'Blissfully quiet.'

'Oh, come on! They were no trouble.'

'You didn't have to cater for them or pick up after them. I hope the little bride knows what she's taken on.'

'Don't you like her?'

'What makes you think that?'

'The way you called her "the little bride". She seems all right to me, and not bad looking in a quiet way; decent figure, good legs ...'

'A nicely packaged mouse. Oh, she'll do, I suppose. A quiet, domesticated girl with a bit of money of her own. Piers could hardly have found anyone more suitable.'

'He looks well pleased with his choice.' Bernie gave a short laugh. 'I'd guess he's had plenty of exercise, even if he did miss his round of golf today.'

Claudia got up abruptly. 'Bring the towels in, would you? I'll put them in the washing machine while I'm changing.'

'Are we eating out tonight?'

'You can bet we are! I've had enough of preparing kiddy meals and staying in to watch television.'

'Sorry you found it such a bore. When Piers asked, we could hardly refuse to have the kids. He's done me the odd favour or two.'

'The last three days cancel all favours in my eyes.' Stacking glasses on a tray and not looking at him, Claudia said, 'You ought not to throw the little one around like that.'

10

'Why can't you use their names? She's called Jennifer,' Bernie said.

'What about your heart? Did you take your pills today?'

'Of course I did. Little Jenny's no weight.'

'She's eight years old, not a baby any more.'

'She was the sweetest little toddler I ever set eyes on,' Bernie said regretfully. 'I wish she could have been ours.'

Claudia shot a look of acute irritation at him, but she bit back the words that sprang to her lips and went and put an arm round his neck. 'I'm being grouchy,' she said. 'Sorry, darling. I need to be wined and dined and made up to.' Her loose sarong swung open and she pressed herself against his bare torso, looking up at him through half-closed eyes. Her tongue flickered out and moistened her lips and Bernie clutched her to him with a convulsive movement. They kissed avidly, shifting from one bare foot to the other as their bodies moved.

'You do love your Big Daddy, don't you?' Bernie whispered.

Claudia closed her eyes. Oh, God, it was going to be one of those sessions. She opened her eyes again and looked up into Bernie's flushed face. 'As much as you love your Baby Doll,' she said. 'Let's go and take a shower together.'

She glanced at the untidy poolside as she took Bernie's hand and led him into the house. That could wait. First of all she would satisfy Bernie – and distract her own thoughts from bloody Piers and the ninny he had married.

The house smelt musty when Piers opened it up, even though it had only been left for three days. When Lucy had first died Piers' mother had come down from the North to look after him and the children, but she had not been able to stay on indefinitely, neither had Piers been willing to move nearer her home. Then he had employed a housekeeper, who had been vaguely unsatisfactory. In recent months, ever since Ella had known him, the family had been at the mercy of a daily woman who rushed through the house with a duster and a vacuum cleaner, reckoned to do no more than one load of washing a week, and shopped in a haphazard fashion for food which Piers prepared.

Ella was familiar with the house, of course, though she had never spent a night in it or allowed Piers to make love to her there. She had cooked them a few meals, eaten with enthusiasm

11

by Piers and with caution by the children, but she had held back from anything that might have looked like interference until she was sure of her status. Now, as Piers' wife and the children's stepmother, she was going to make them comfortable. Look on it as a new career, she told herself, observing the unpolished furniture, the lank curtains, the washing up left to dry on the draining board since before the wedding.

'I'm hungry,' Harry said as soon as he had dumped his bag in the hall.

'So am I,' Jennifer immediately echoed him.

'Claudia only gave us salad for lunch because she said they were eating out tonight,' Verity said. 'What are we going to have to eat?'

The look she turned on Ella was politely expectant. Ella hoped she was imagining the touch of malice behind Verity's bland face.

'I'll have to see what there is,' she said weakly.

The refrigerator was empty apart from half a bottle of suspect milk, a piece of cheese with mould on it and a few slices of stale bread. The freezer contained a solid block of mince, some chicken joints and an opened packet of frozen peas. There was a large tin of peaches, a packet of noodles and some breakfast cereals in the food cupboard.

'Supplies are scanty, not to say non-existent,' Ella said.

'It'll have to be a take-away,' Verity said. 'What kind of pizza shall I order for you?'

'I don't like that kind with the spicy sausage bits on top,' Jennifer said.

'I *know* that. I'm asking ...' there was a perceptible pause, '... Mother, what she likes.'

'Just plain cheese and tomato,' Ella said weakly. Damn it, she's taken charge, she thought. I ought to have thought about food for our return, but I didn't, and now Verity is having her little triumph.

'I'll order one large Margharita and one large Hawaiian,' Verity decided. 'That ought to be enough between us. Two portions of coleslaw ...'

'Ugh, horrible stuff,' Harry said.

'You don't have to eat it. Does anyone want onion rings or pickles or anything?'

'Onion rings!' Jennifer shouted. 'And Coke.'

'Three large Cokes.' She glanced at Ella. 'I don't suppose you want to drink Coke?'

Ella shook her head. 'I'll have coffee afterwards.' She remembered the suspect milk. 'Black coffee.'

'So will Dad. Just one thing before I order ...' She darted into the living room and Ella followed. Piers had picked up some letters from the mat as they came in and had sat down in an armchair to look at them.

'Everything under control?' he asked.

'We're having a pizza home delivery,' Verity said. 'But before I telephone, have you got enough money to pay for it?'

When Piers felt in his pocket for his cash he stretched out his leg to reach it more easily and Ella, looking at the long, extended line and remembering the bone and flesh beneath the fabric, was overwhelmed by a wave of desire. I must get over this, she thought dizzily, it must fade in time. Oh, Piers, Piers, I love you so much.

When Verity left the room in a bustle of self-importance, Piers stretched out his hand to Ella. She went to him and, in response to a pull from his hand, sat down on his knee. They kissed and she felt him moving his fingers slowly down her spine, but after that one kiss Ella pulled away.

'No,' she said. 'We must be sensible. I've already fallen down over the matter of food. I must unpack, lay the table, assert myself a bit.'

'Start being a little housewife,' Piers suggested lazily.

'Start being a part of the family,' Ella said more seriously.

It would have been easier if the children's holidays had been over and they had been back at school. As it was, Ella felt they were under her feet all day and she had an obligation to entertain them as well as feeding them and starting the clean up the house sorely needed. There were also still affairs of her own that had to be attended to. The sale of her bungalow had gone through and she had to give some thought to the disposal of the money. As Piers had suggested, she set up a joint account with him and paid a thousand pounds into it. The rest of her profit she put into a Building Society account until she had time to decide whether to seek another home for it. She had got rid of most of her parents' furniture, but there were still a few bits and pieces of her own to be rescued from the friends who had stored them temporarily.

It was, of course, Verity who reminded her of another chore to be tackled before the new term started.

'We can probably wear our summer things for a week or two,' she said. 'But my winter coat is *completely* worn out and my school skirt is too short and Harry needs shoes.'

'We'll have a day in Canterbury to fit you out,' Ella promised.

'Have you got enough money?' Verity asked.

'I expect we'll manage,' Ella said absentmindedly.

Verity was fidgeting with the trimming on the edge of an armchair, picking at it with her fingernails in a way that set Ella's teeth on edge. Without looking at Ella she said, with such elaborate casualness that Ella's attention was caught. 'Are you going to ... you know, sort of take charge of things, like Mum did?'

'As far as I can. I'm relying on you to help me,' Ella said, carefully diplomatic.

'I mean, pay the bills and that sort of thing,' Verity said. She cast a look of dislike, almost of fear, at the old rolltop desk in the corner of the room which Ella had not yet had reason to open. 'Dad's a bit ... careless. He stuffs bills and things in there and then forgets about them. Electricity and that sort of thing.'

'I'll talk it over with him,' Ella said. She wondered why, in fact, she had never thought before to discuss with Piers how they would handle the household accounts. Probably because her own limited experience had been that the man of the family, if there was one, paid the bills. So much for the equality of the sexes.

As soon as Verity left the room Ella went and opened the rolltop desk. Inside there was a jumble of paper and, as Verity had suggested, most of it consisted of bills. Water, gas, electricity, Council tax, telephone bills. Reminders, final notices, letters from Piers' bank. Was she intruding into something she had no right to see? No, that was a feeble way of looking at it. This was something she had to share with Piers and, what was more, it had to be dealt with, and quickly.

14

Ella began sorting through the bills, putting them into categories. No wonder Verity had mentioned electricity, that was seriously overdue. They were hundreds of pounds in debt and, the final blow, a recent statement from the bank revealed that Piers was only just in credit. Of course, they now had a joint account and she had put in a thousand pounds, which would help, and presumably Piers' monthly salary had also been paid in, so the situation was by no means hopeless. It was, as Verity had also said, just carelessness. All the same, Ella was shocked. True, Piers had had a lot on his mind, but surely he could have spared an evening to put his affairs in order?

She tackled him about it after the children had gone to bed, in what she had begun to look upon as the one short period of the day when she had Piers to herself, except when they were in bed, and this was not something she wanted to take to bed with her.

Piers was rueful and guilty and, she had to admit, totally disarming in the frankness with which he met her mild scolding.

'I'm hopeless over money,' he said. 'Darling, you will take over, won't you? There's something about bills that makes my mind go a complete blank.'

'Because you don't want to pay them,' Ella suggested.

'Possibly. At least I can put my hand on my heart and say that the mortgage payments on the house are up to date.'

Only because the bank had allowed him to be overdrawn several times, but Ella decided not to point that out. She was not entirely pleased to have to take on another responsibility, but it would be better than spending her time worrying whether Piers had remembered to pay the bills.

'What about insurance?' she asked.

'Included in the mortgage payments.'

'I mean insurance on yourself. What provision have you made for the children if anything should happen to you?'

'Darling, what a morbid thought.'

'Does that mean you've done nothing about it?'

'I'm a young man – comparatively speaking.'

'Lucy was a young woman.'

Ella could have bitten her tongue out as soon as the words

15

left her lips. When Piers said evenly, 'You don't have to remind me of that,' she got up impulsively and went to him.

'Darling, I'm sorry. It's just that you seem to take life very lightly and because you've known such tragedy it surprises me. You're thirty-nine and you have responsibilities. Don't you think you should take care of them?'

'I believe you're trying to persuade me to insure my life for vast sums so that you can bump me off.'

He was laughing, but he was not entirely pleased. The smiling mouth was also obstinate and the hands that held her were not as kind as they usually were. If she persisted he might be seriously annoyed and that was not what Ella wanted. She allowed herself to relax against him and held up her mouth for a kiss. Time enough to work on him about serious things like insurance when they had settled into a familiar domestic routine.

All the same, Ella called in at the bank the next day and arranged to have monthly statements sent to her so that she could keep a running check on their finances. The first statement arrived a day or two later and she studied it carefully. True, Piers' salary had been paid in, but a very large slice of that went on the mortgage payments. A four-bedroomed house in a good situation was an expensive item. Her contribution had boosted the balance satisfactorily, but what was the item of six hundred pounds which had been debited as soon as she had paid in her thousand?

'A six hundred pound payment?' Piers said. 'That must be my annual Golf Club subscription.'

'Six hundred pounds?' Ella said faintly.

'Expensive, I know, but look on it as a necessary business expense. I need to know who's buying and selling a house and who has one to rent or needs to find one. I meet people like that at the golf club.'

'Do you? Why don't they come to the office?'

'They do, of course, but the gossip I pick up at the Club House is immensely valuable to me.'

'And belonging to the Club is part of your image as a successful business man?'

'There's that as well,' Piers agreed in all seriousness.

'I'm struggling to understand,' Ella said. 'But it's difficult

16

for me to see how you can justify paying so much for a game when you're in danger of having your gas cut off.'

'Oh, you can usually do a deal with the utilities. Three orphan children ... they can hardly deprive them of heat and light.'

'That's not nice, Piers. And don't laugh, I'm unhappy about your attitude.'

'Darling, we're not going to spend all our time wrangling about money, are we? Look, I've had a damned expensive time. I paid out a fortune for that housekeeper who was totally useless and the daily woman whose work you despise cost nearly as much.'

'Yes, of course,' Ella said, full of contrition.

'Now that I've got a nice, cheap, unpaid wife, things should look up,' Piers suggested.

'Beast! I know you said you married me for my money, but I didn't think you meant it.'

'I married you for your legs and the way your hips swell out below your waist and those tipped-up breasts and your soft brown hair and the way at the age of twenty-nine you can still blush when your husband pays you compliments.'

It was the sort of reassurance that Ella desperately needed. She did not think highly of her own looks, but she knew she had a good body. The pity was that before she met Piers it had gone unappreciated. She had raged about it at times, frustrated because she had failed to find a man capable of seeing behind her reticence and slightly old-fashioned ways. Until Piers. He had opened the box in which she had been afraid she was incarcerated for life and she worshipped him for it.

The discussion ended in laughter and loving and bliss. It was only later in the month when Ella got her credit card account that she wondered how Piers, with a bank balance of under twenty pounds, had intended paying their excessively expensive hotel bill and a tiny niggle of resentment wormed away inside her because she had, in effect, been forced to pay for her own honeymoon.

Chapter Two

Verity sprawled on the grass, her Walkman plugged into her ears, reading a book that was a holiday task and should have been read weeks ago, so cut off from the world that she was unaware of Ella approaching until she saw a pair of feet in sandals in front of her nose.

She sat up. 'You ought to paint your toe nails,' she said.

'I've never been very good at it,' Ella said. 'Anyway, in a week or two we'll be forced into wearing tights again.'

'Horrible winter. I hate it.'

'You're a real salamander,' Ella said in amusement. 'Harry and Jennifer are going to bring us out some lemonade.'

'That homemade stuff?'

'You like it, don't you?'

'I do, actually,' Verity admitted. She caught a glint of silver in Ella's hand and sat up straighter, staring at it.

'I found this in Dad's desk when I was clearing it out,' Ella said, holding out a photograph in a silver frame. 'I thought ... it's a picture of your mother, isn't it?'

Verity nodded and took the picture from her. 'It used to be on top of the desk.'

'I expect Dad put it away, out of sight. They can be painful things, photographs.'

'Mum used to let me clean the frame. It's real silver.'

'It needs cleaning now,' Ella said. 'I thought perhaps you might like to have it in your bedroom.'

'Yes.' Verity looked up, frowning fiercely. 'I don't cry about it any more,' she said.

'One has to grieve. I've lost my parents, too, you know. Of

course, I was grown up, but it still hurts.'

'I suppose so.' Verity sounded vaguely surprised. 'When you said you'd cleared out the desk, did you mean that all the bills and things ...'

'Everything has been settled and I've arranged for future bills to be paid by monthly instalments from the bank. No need to worry about them any more.'

Except that it was a problem to know how to keep the bank balance topped up sufficiently to cover their expenses. Without breaking into her own capital, that was, and Ella had made up her mind to do that only for a really dire emergency. In the meantime, it was rewarding to see the relief in Verity's face. Piers should have realised that the child was burdened by an over-developed sense of responsibility. Poor Piers, Ella thought, quickly excusing him, he had just had too much on his mind for one man to cope with.

'Canterbury tomorrow,' she said as Harry and Jennifer came across the grass towards them carefully carrying a tray of plastic tumblers and a jug full of the lemonade she had made for them. 'I've made a list, but if there are any desperate needs you might let me know.'

'My knickers are all in holes.'

'I've already noticed that. Winter coat, skirt, underclothes and tights for you, shoes for Harry and Jennifer ...'

'Football boots,' Harry said, managing to put the jug down on the ground without spilling any lemonade.

'Help! Are you sure? Yes, I suppose if your shoes are too small then your boots will be as well. Do you know where to go for them and the right kind to buy? I'm not well up in football boots.'

She was getting through to them, Ella thought hopefully. They were easy with her, not awkward as they had been before she and Piers were married. She understood now that they had been embarrassed by her ambiguous status, not knowing how to treat a prospective stepmother.

If only money were not a problem. Had she been wrong to give up her job? Goodness knows there were plenty of working mothers, but not many of them had plunged straight into a ready-made family and Ella was finding her time fully occupied just keeping up with her new duties.

19

What she needed was a money-making occupation she could carry out at home. And if there was an easy answer to that conundrum then hundreds of women would have already latched on to it.

She did have some special skills, of course. Geography was not likely to earn her anything, unless she taught, but cooking ...? Kits Harbour was not an area that was likely to want directors' lunches or gourmet dinner parties. Besides, both those ideas would take her away from home. She would just have to go on thinking about it.

'Don't let me forget Dad wants us to stop at Bernie's garden centre,' she said, mentally ticking off the list of things to be done the next day.

'Must we?' Harry muttered.

'He's promised us a bag of cut-price daffodil bulbs.'

'Straight in and out, then? No trying out the garden swing and that sort of thing?'

'Certainly not, we can't afford garden swings. Besides, Bernie will be too busy.'

'Uncle Bernie's never too busy to give me a swing,' Jennifer said importantly.

'You suck up to him,' Harry said.

'I'm *nice*,' Jennifer said. 'You're not, you're nasty, you're rude.'

'That's enough,' Ella said in what she privately thought of as her schoolmistress voice.

'"Birds in their little nests agree",' Verity said, prone on the ground once more.

'You've been reading "Little Women",' Ella guessed.

'Yes, I have. Well, actually re-reading it, I read it *years* ago. It's not bad, is it? Smarmy, but you sort of get to like it. Of course, I really prefer modern literature.'

'Of course,' Ella agreed gravely.

Jennifer was still in the local Junior School and would eventually move up to the Comprehensive School Verity and Harry attended, where Ella had once taught. Neither school had a uniform, as such, but the girls were expected to wear grey skirts and the boys either grey shorts or trousers.

'No jeans,' Verity said. 'I do think it's the *pits* not being able to wear jeans.'

'You wear them all the time at home,' Ella pointed out.

She was feeling weary. She had had no idea that buying shoes for children was such a fraught business. Why had she never noticed that they all had such difficult narrow feet? Harry, in particularly, was a nightmare to fit. It had been necessary to pay a great deal more than she had anticipated. That money-making venture was looking more necessary than ever.

'My coat next,' Verity said. 'Of course, I'd just as soon settle for an anorak. A really good one – padded. Or a leather jacket.'

'Forget the leather jacket,' Ella said. 'As for an anorak, is that practical for bad weather, remembering that you'll be wearing a skirt?'

'Aren't you going to take us to school by car?'

'Nope. There's a perfectly good bus at the end of the road and you're all used to catching it.'

'You'll be sorry when we fall victims to drug dealers at the school gates.'

'Are there any?' Ella asked.

'Not that I've ever noticed,' Verity admitted. 'But we're always being warned about the dangers we face when we venture out into the big, bad world.'

'Then you'll know how to avoid them. Where are we going for this coat you need?'

'There are some moderately decent raincoats in Marks and Spencers.'

Ella recognised this as a real concession and closed with it thankfully.

'It's not fair,' Jennifer said. 'Harry's got shoes *and* football boots and Verity's got a raincoat *and* a skirt and knickers and tights and I've only got rotten old school shoes that I don't like.'

'What we're buying today is what we need, not treats,' Ella said.

'I need to have the same as Harry and Verity.'

She sounded whiny, almost tearful. She was tired, Ella realised, and bored with being dragged round the shops. Come to that, Ella was worn out herself.

'Let's go into a café and have tea,' she suggested. 'And you can choose the cakes.'

21

It was an unnecessary expense, but it saved the day and the rest and the hot tea were certainly welcome. It was a pleasant little restaurant with checked table cloths, decent china and a good array of homemade cakes. Cakes, Ella thought idly. I could make those, but where would I sell them? When she went to pay the bill at the desk she noticed a shelf of jellies and jams for sale. Preserves, that would be more practical than quickly deteriorating cakes. Again, the question of an outlet was a problem.

'Don't forget we have to call in on Bernie for the daffodil bulbs,' Verity reminded her.

'I haven't forgotten,' Ella said. Thankfully she stowed the shopping away in the boot of her car. Just as well she had held on to it. In fact, the idea of parting with it had never occurred to her until she had begun to realise how expensive it was to keep a family.

Bernie's garden centre had plenty of customers. It was late in the season, but it was still bright with colour from the pots of chrysanthemums standing in rows amongst the rose bushes, the young fruit trees and the ornamental shrubs. A few bright green lawnmowers and a stack of gleaming garden tools had been pushed into a corner, this not being the time of year when people were into buying garden implements. There was a stand of decorated pots for indoor plants – made locally, Ella noted – and a display of greetings cards next to the packets of seeds.

Waiting for Bernie to be free to speak to them, Ella had an idea. She was still turning it over in her mind when Bernie got rid of his customer and came over to them. He was dressed like a jobbing gardener, Ella thought in amusement, knowing that Bernie's plants came from outside suppliers and most of his work was in the office. He was wearing thick shoes, corduroy trousers and a loud checked shirt, open at the neck and with the sleeves rolled up.

'Open up the car and I'll lift the bulbs in for you,' he said. 'Why don't you and Piers bring the kids over for a swim on Sunday? This weather can't last. Must make the most of it.'

'I'm not sure,' Ella said. 'They start school the next day.'

'A last treat for them.'

'Thank you. I'll speak to Piers. Hey, we only want one bag of bulbs.'

22

'The other one's full of apples. We've got a couple of trees that are absolutely groaning with them. And a few tomatoes. I picked them from the greenhouse before I came to work this morning. Are you into chutney and things? I could do you a nice line in green tomatoes if you are.'

'I might be,' Ella said slowly. 'Bernie, do you sell things like jams and pickles? Some garden centres do, don't they?'

'I've thought of having some sort of local produce stall, but I've never got round to organising it.'

'Would you be interested in letting me supply you, as an experiment?'

'I'd give it a go. Of course, it'd have to be a professional job – good presentation, good quality.'

'And a reasonable profit for you.'

'I wouldn't press too hard over that, but obviously I couldn't do it for charity.'

'I wouldn't expect it. Incidentally, what do I owe you for the bulbs?'

'You can give me a couple of quid. Well, kids, you're very quiet today.'

'They're tired,' Ella said. 'Shopping is an exhausting experience.'

'Claudia thrives on it.'

Drifting into a designer shop and trying on one or two desirable outfits was not to be compared with fitting out three children on a restricted budget, Ella thought drily, but she kept the thought to herself. Could they get out of visiting Bernie and Claudia on Sunday? Probably not.

She commented on the bustle at the garden centre when she was with Piers that evening.

'Bernie does a good trade,' Piers agreed. 'In fact, he's loaded. It's not just the garden centre; he owns quite a bit of property along the coast, not just in Kits Harbour, but Ramsgate, Margate, Cliftonville.'

'And a villa in Spain.'

'Where we could have spent our honeymoon.'

'Not worth it for the few days we could take, although it might have been cheaper than that fearsomely expensive hotel.'

She waited, not very hopefully, for Piers to offer to take on

23

the payment of that bill, but he said nothing.

'You enjoyed it, didn't you?' he asked.

'I did, but I would have enjoyed anywhere just so long as I could be with you.'

'That's nice. Give me a kiss.'

'Too lazy to move. Shopping with the children really wore me out. Darling, let's be practical for a moment. Money is going to be a problem. I've thought up a scheme which might, and I can only say *might* at the moment, earn us some useful cash.'

'Tell me.'

'I want to set up a little business making pickles and chutneys, and perhaps jams. To start with I could test the market at Bernie's Garden Centre.'

'Won't it make a lot of work for you? Do you really want to be tied up in the kitchen stirring jams?'

'The alternative is to go back to teaching.'

Piers shifted restlessly in his chair, a frown on his face.

'Surely we can manage,' he said.

'I've costed everything out for the year and, yes, we could just get by on your salary, but that means watching every penny, not going away for any holidays and not having anything put by for an emergency.'

She watched him struggling with this assessment and knew, with a touch of disillusionment and regret, the exact moment when he decided not to mention her own small capital from the sale of her family home.

'It would be a mistake to keep on breaking into what I've stashed away in the building society,' she said, responding to his unspoken thought. 'I've already taken two thousand pounds out of it and I'll need to take more to start up my little business. Bernie said it would have to be a professional operation and, of course, he's quite right.'

'You talked it over with him before mentioning it to me?'

'Don't look so wounded, you know you don't really mind. The idea was lurking in my mind, but selling through Bernie only came to me when we were with him today and it seemed as well to clear it with him straight away.'

'You could hardly consult anyone better,' Piers admitted. 'Bernie's a whizz with figures and profit making, not to mention milking the benefits system, which he's got down to a fine art.'

'I don't understand. Don't tell me Bernie's claiming DHSS benefit!'

'Of course not, but most of his tenants are.'

'All those rundown boarding houses, full of out-of-work youngsters looking for seasonal jobs, and drop-outs who fancy a summer by the sea,' Ella said slowly. 'You don't deal with those sort of lettings, do you, Piers?'

'My firm's into the high class end of the trade, but I sometimes put Bernie on to a property that's likely to be on the market cheaply. He soon fills it up, believe me.'

'I do believe you,' Ella said. 'I've taught some of the children who live in one room with their parents, or more usually a single parent, with a gas ring and a washbasin in the corner if they're lucky, and a shared bathroom down the corridor. Those who came to school, that is.'

'I wish our kids didn't have to mix with them,' Piers said sincerely. 'But there was no way I could afford fees for private schools.'

'I doubt if it will do them any harm. The population shifts so rapidly that they're hardly likely to form lasting friendships, which is a pity because it might benefit the less fortunate children.'

She got no response to that from Piers, beyond a puzzled frown. The revelation that Bernie's prosperity was based on the bed-and-breakfast trade of Benefits claimants, a trade which Ella knew could, in its worse aspects, be exceedingly sordid, did not make her like him any better. Perhaps she did him an injustice, perhaps his properties were well run and salubrious. She hoped so, because she could see that his activities did him no harm in Piers' eyes and there was no hope of interrupting that long-standing friendship.

'Bernie invited us to take the children to their place for a swim on Sunday,' she said. 'Do you want to go?'

'Sure. We'll arrange to have an early round of golf and join you there around noon. Claudia will give us a picnic lunch round the pool. Do you want to go out in the evening, if we can get a babysitter?'

'If it's just us. I mean, after spending all day with Bernie

25

and Claudia I'd like you to myself for a change.'

'You do like them, don't you?'

Ella hesitated. She was not too keen on what she had just learned about Bernie's business empire, but she might be doing him an injustice since she knew none of the details. 'I find them a bit overwhelming,' she admitted cautiously.

'They're the salt of the earth. My very best friends. I can't tell you how good they've been to me over the last couple of years.'

'Yes, I know,' Ella said. She would have to try to find Bernie and Claudia more congenial, especially if Bernie, with his invariable good nature, was going to give her a helping hand in her moneymaking venture. Just don't expect me to roll on my back with my paws in the air, she thought rebelliously.

In the event, the Sunday passed off better than she had anticipated. It was a beautiful day, warm and sunny, with just a hint of the deeper glow of autumn in the air. The sun had been on the swimming pool all morning, warming the water. All the children liked to swim. They were out of their clothes and into the pool with the alacrity of young ducks. Bernie joined them, romping with a boisterousness which, for once, they did not seem to mind. Ella herself swam slowly up and down the pool, avoiding the splashes and thrashing limbs. Claudia sat on the side looking decorative and talking to Piers until he slipped into the water, smooth as an otter, remaining under for so long that Ella was momentarily alarmed, until he surfaced at her side, laughing and throwing his wet hair back from his face.

'Nice?' he asked.

'Lovely,' she admitted. She turned over on her back and floated. 'Do you know what Bernie reminds me of? A big black labrador.' She watched as Bernie hauled himself out of the water, his black hair gleaming, drops of water glittering on the mat of hair on his body. 'If he shakes himself he'll make Claudia wet all over.'

Fortunately, Bernie contented himself with taking a towelling robe and wrapping it round himself.

'Barbecue's ready,' he called. 'I'm going to start cooking.'

It was all very well done: pieces of chicken laid ready in a marinade which sizzled as they were laid on the grill, fat sausages, little lamb chops which could be held in the hand, great bowls of salad, bottle of squash for the children, a good red wine for the adults.

'Ice cream in the freezer for anyone who wants it afterwards,' Claudia said, lazily waiting for Piers to bring her a plate of food.

'I do!' Jennifer said. 'Have you got my favourite raspberry ripple?'

'We'll go and look together,' Bernie promised her.

'No swimming for at least an hour after you've eaten,' Ella decreed. 'Don't groan, Harry. You'll sink like a stone if you go into the water after all the sausages you've put away.'

'I've only had four,' Harry protested.

They were all fairly comatose after they had finished Bernie's lavish barbecue. Claudia was lying back with her eyes closed, her head shaded by an umbrella, but her body, well displayed by her small white bikini, turning to a deeper shade of gold in the sun. Piers sat on the ground by Ella's feet, supporting himself on one hand while he idly twirled the wine in his glass, watching the colour, and Ella, relaxed and replete, leaned back, looking at the sparkling water. Bernie was sharing a swinging seat with Verity and Jennifer while Harry, restless and full of energy, idly kicked a beach ball round the side of the pool. Watching him, Ella knew that if it fell into the water he would use it as an excuse to go in after it.

'If Harry goes in again after being told not to, you're the one who has to bawl him out,' she murmured to Piers.

Bernie out his arm round Jennifer and gave her a hug. 'How about that ice cream? Shall we go and look for it?'

Claudia roused herself. 'Don't bother, I'll go,' she said. 'Raspberry ripple, wasn't it? I'll put the coffee on while I'm inside.'

'Jennifer and I will come and help you,' Verity said. She got up a little stiffly and Jennifer, surprised at being promoted to a grown-up role, freed herself from Bernie's arm and followed her sister.

'There's no need ...' Bernie said, but Claudia interrupted him. 'You've done all the work. Take a rest, busy man.'

He sank back on the seat, Harry's ball fell into the water, Harry jumped in after it and Piers said in a voice of unaccustomed severity, 'Harry, come out at once. I'm damned if I'm coming in to rescue you if you get cramp.'

'I was only getting the ball,' Harry protested. To show his independence he climbed out with the brightly coloured ball under his arm and gave it a careless kick which carried it high into the air and landed it in one of the choice bushes with which Bernie had surrounded the pool.

'Right, that's it,' Piers said. 'No more swimming today.'

'But, Dad, it was an accident!' Harry cast a harassed glance at the bush. 'It hasn't done much damage,' he said optimistically.

'I can see two broken branches. Apologise to Bernie and then sit down and try to behave like a civilised human being.'

'Sorry,' Harry muttered. His face was flushed and he kicked the ground, looking down with his lower lip jutting out mutinously.

'Don't worry, I can tidy it up later with the secateurs,' Bernie said.

Harry looked hopefully at his father, but for once Piers had decided to assert his authority. 'I told you to sit down,' he said.

As Harry reluctantly did as he was told the girls came back from the kitchen carrying bowls of ice cream, followed by Claudia with the coffee.

'Something wrong?' Claudia asked.

'Harry being a bit obstreperous,' Piers said lazily. 'No more swimming today, I think, not for any of them.'

'That's not fair!' Jennifer exclaimed. 'I want to go back in the water! Just because Harry is silly ...'

'No more swimming.'

'Eat your ice cream,' Ella said, hoping to avert the storm which Jennifer's pout and brimming eyes seemed to threaten.

'Don't keep telling me what to do. You're not my mother.'

It had to come, Ella thought, in the moment of frozen stillness that followed. One of them was bound to say it sooner or later. But Jennifer ... little, sunny Jennifer? Spoilt Jennifer. Younger than the others and less inhibited because of that. She knew she had gone too far, her flushed, mulish face betrayed that. She looked sideways at her father and her lower lip trembled.

Ella hurried into speech because the last thing she wanted

was a full-scale scene; not here, not now, in front of Claudia and Bernie, especially Claudia, with that amused look on her face. Not gloating, surely? Not gloating over the naughty remark of a small child?

'I'm your horrible bullying stepmother,' she said. 'And I condemn you to finish your ice cream. After that I think we'll all get dressed and go home. Dad and I are going out this evening.'

'You're an idiot,' Verity said fiercely to her sister.

'I'm not,' Jennifer protested, on the verge of tears once more.

'Yes, you are. A stupid, snivelling idiot. I told you over and over to be nice to her. I told you before they got married she was the best we were likely to get.'

'You'll only make her grizzle,' Harry said, hovering at the door of the bathroom where the girls had gone to shower and change. 'She's been smarming up to Bernie all day. She's got above herself.'

'No, I haven't,' Jennifer said. 'I only said what was true. She's *not* our mother.'

For a moment Verity hesitated, then she put an awkward arm round her small sister. 'Look, Mum's not coming back. There's nothing we can do about that. Ella's been good to us. Think what it was like before she came. When Gran was living with us it was chaos, you know it was, and horrible Mrs Hugo wasn't even *clean*. And Leah ... you know how awful it was when Leah met us from school every day and took us home.'

'They're going to go out and leave us alone this evening and Leah's coming in to be babysitter.'

'Yes, I know.' Verity looked bothered.

'You ought to tell her about Leah,' Harry said.

'I didn't think we'd have to have her again.'

'If she starts telling us any of those horrible stories I'll go upstairs and put my head under the pillow.'

'I'll lend you my Walkman,' Verity promised. 'Then you can shut her out. I will try to tell her, Harry, honestly I will, but not today when Jennifer's already upset everything.'

Jennifer gave a disconsolate sniff. From behind Harry Ella said, not trying to hide her exasperation, 'Haven't you started to get changed? Get a move on do. Harry, you can go and use the shower in Bernie and Claudia's room.'

'Where's Bernie?' Harry asked.

'Downstairs, talking to Dad. Come on, girls, get moving.'

'Jennifer would like to apologise,' Verity said.

Jennifer gave another sniff. If one listened closely it was possible to hear an anguished whisper, 'Sorry.'

'All right, sweetheart,' Ella bent down and put her arms round the damp, disconsolate little figure. 'I know it's hard to accept me, but give me a chance, I'm doing the best I can. Just look at the beautiful towels Claudia's put out for us. Pale mauve!'

'It's her lavender bathroom,' Verity said. 'Everything, all the soap and talc and that, smells of lavender.' She looked round disparagingly. 'A bit twee, if you ask me.'

Ella suppressed a smile. Briskly, she set about getting Jennifer out of her swimsuit, towelling her dry and putting her back into the cotton dress she had worn earlier in the day. Verity, of course, was wearing her invariable uniform of jeans and a T-shirt.

'Have we got to have Leah to be with us this evening?' she asked, running a comb through her long, dank hair.

'Don't you like her?' Ella asked in surprise. 'I thought she was the sitter you always had.'

'We don't need a sitter. I don't mind staying up until you and Dad get home.'

'Actually, you have to have a sitter,' Ella said. 'It's not legal to leave children on their own.'

'Leah's only a kid herself.'

'Surely not? She's got a two-year-old-baby. She's bringing him with her tonight, by the way.'

Verity groaned. 'Stinking brat!'

They were interrupted by Harry, still in his swimming trunks.

'Why haven't you changed?' Ella demanded.

'There's only been a burglary, that's all,' he announced, bristling with importance.

'Harry! Are you sure?'

'Everything's chucked all over the place. Drawers open, clothes strewn about. And I looked out of the window and saw

30

a man legging it down the road. I say, will I have to talk to the police?'

'Quite likely. Run downstairs and tell Bernie. And then come straight back and get dressed in here. Don't touch anything in the other room.'

'Can we go and look?' Jennifer asked.

'No, the fewer people disturbing things the better. Come on, Verity, your hair doesn't need any more combing.'

They had to stand to one side on the stairs as Bernie came thundering up. Ella heard him exclaim, 'Bloody hell!' as he took in the chaos in the main bedroom, then Claudia called up, 'The lounge has been turned over as well, and your study.'

'In at the front while we were all occupied out the back,' Piers said. 'What a ghastly thing to have happened. Claudia, sweetie, I'm so sorry. And you with a state-of-the-art security system, too.'

'Which wasn't turned on,' Claudia said bitterly. 'I bet all my jewellery has gone. Pieces I was really fond of. No insurance will compensate me for that.'

'I'll ring the police,' Bernie said, coming downstairs. 'Didn't you notice anything wrong when you came in for the ice cream and coffee?'

'Not a thing. I went no further than the kitchen.'

'If Harry really did see him, he must have still been in the house.'

'What a ghastly thought! Ugh, it makes me feel quite faint.'

'I think we ought to go,' Ella said. 'Piers . . .'

'I'd like to stick around, give Bernie and Claudia bit of support. And the police will want to interview us.'

'We none of us saw anything, except possibly Harry, and if they want to talk to him they can do it in his own home.'

Piers said nothing and after waiting a moment Ella said, 'Shall I take the car, then?'

'If you must.'

'I think it will be best. And perhaps we should postpone our evening out.'

She spoke evenly, but inside she was desolate. She had looked forward to that evening with Piers. She was hungry for the time alone with him, hungry for the sort of evening they had had before their marriage, when every glance was an exchange of love and every touch a promise. It was something when he walked to the car with her and put his arm round her shoulders.

'Darling, I'm so disappointed about our evening. Must we put it off? I don't suppose I'll be all that long here.'

Ella hesitated, but only for a moment. Piers ought to know that the children were keyed up and nervous. Harry, for all his air of sturdy self-reliance, was a sensitive little boy, and only ten years old.

'I don't think this is the time to go out and leave the children,' she said. 'Especially with a babysitter they don't seem to like. Is this Leah really as young as Verity led me to believe?'

'About seventeen.'

'But she's got a two-year-old baby!'

'Under-age mother.'

'I don't think she sounds a very suitable person to leave in charge of three children. Four, if you count her own baby.'

'She managed well enough when she was staying with the kids after school every day. And I used her when I was a-courting of you, my lovely. You didn't object then.'

'I never met her. I didn't realise she was so young.'

Piers shrugged it off. 'She's not on the telephone so there's no way of cancelling tonight's arrangement. If I know Leah she'll insist on being paid.'

'I'll see to it,' Ella said.

She drove home, far from pleased that Piers had decided to stay with his friends. It was not as if they were in a state of shock. More angry than upset, it seemed to her. And it was not as if Piers could do anything, except hang around and sympathise. Quite apart from the robbery, which was extremely unpleasant, Ella was exasperated that an enjoyable day had been spoilt. She had got on really well with Bernie and Claudia, better than ever before. She had begun to see something of the attraction they held for Piers, their good humour, their careless generosity, the undeniable pleasure of their lavish lifestyle. She had not been as overwhelmed as she was when she first met them, she had held her own, joined in the conversation, contributed to the light, amusing, gossipy talk that was Claudia's speciality. She had felt that Piers was pleased with her. And it had all been going to culminate in

32

their special night out. Damn all burglars. She could have wept with disappointment.

Leah turned up punctually, pushing her large, fat baby in a pushchair. She was a short, thin girl with prominent breasts, accentuated by a tank top that barely skimmed the waistband of her mini-skirt. Her hips seemed improbably narrow for the mother of such a big baby. She wore no make-up, but her hair was a fuzzy mass of curls and enormous bright red and white spotted hoops swung from her ears.

She was not pleased to hear that she had pushed the baby all the way up the hill for no reason.

'I'm sorry, there was no way of letting you know,' Ella apologised. 'We've had rather an upsetting time. The house we were visiting this afternoon was broken into while we were all outside by the swimming pool. Harry even thinks he saw the man, but as he can only say he was thin, short, not young and wearing a dark top, the glimpse he had hasn't been much help.'

'Go on! Was that the Caldicotts' place, then?'

'Yes, it was. Do you know them?'

'Oh, sure! Me, I know everyone. Well, fancy old Bernie and Claudia being done over. Did they lose much?'

'They were still checking when we came away.'

'So why have you called off your evening out?'

'It was my decision. I thought the children shouldn't be left.'

'Bit exaggerated, if you ask me. Of course, a burglary here or there means nothing to me. My old man's been in and out of jug as long as I can remember.'

'Oh ... really,' Ella said faintly.

'What am I going to do with myself all evening now? Are you sure you don't want me to stay?'

'Quite sure.'

'You'll have to pay me. I don't see why I should be put to the trouble of coming and then be sent away with nothing.'

Her aggressive attitude faded when Ella agreed to pay her as if she had stayed until eleven o'clock. Anything, Ella thought, anything to get rid of her.

'I expect you're disappointed not to be going out for the

33

evening,' Verity remarked. 'But from our point of view it's jolly nice not to have to put up with horrible Leah.'

Ella had learnt to recognise that casual approach. Verity was leading up to something, a confidence she wanted to make if the moment was propitious.

Equally offhanded, she responded, 'What don't you like about her?'

It was Harry who blurted out, 'She brings horror videos with her, horrible ones.'

'You don't have to watch with her,' Ella pointed out.

'She follows us round the house telling us all the nasty bits. Verity was going to lend me her Walkman this evening so that I could shut her out.'

'She said people rose up out of their graves and went around doing nasty things,' Jennifer added. 'And now Harry won't walk through the churchyard because he's scared.'

'No, I'm not!' Harry said with a scowl.

'I would be, if it were true,' Ella said. 'But it's not. The dead are dead, my dears. The bit of them that was immortal goes back to God and their unimportant bodies just quietly disappear. People make up stories about them coming back because they can't face the thought that it will happen to them one day.'

'And she said Mummy would come and look at us through the window to see if we were all right.'

'Nonsense! Your mother *knows* you're all right without having to come and see.'

'Does she really?'

'I'm sure of it,' Ella said, with a certainty she was far from feeling.

There was a moment's respectful silence and then Harry said hopefully, 'So need we have Leah here any more?'

'Certainly not! Harry, dear, why didn't you tell anyone what a horrible person she was?'

The three children exchanged looks and then Verity said, 'The trouble is, people don't listen.'

They meant Piers. Ella could well imagine that Piers, desperate for help with the burden of caring for three children, would have been reluctant to dismiss even Leah for no better reason than her addiction to horror movies. But it went deeper

34

than that. She had frightened the children in her charge, and she had meant to frighten them, had even taken pleasure in it.

When Piers came home it was in a police car and the policeman who brought him took statements from all of them. Not that there was anything much they could add, except Harry, who was able to tell them only that the man he had seen was 'not young, not very tall, wore a dark jacket and was carrying a suitcase'. They handled him tactfully, although Ella did not much like the suggestion that he should go to the police station and look at some pictures to see if he could recognise the man. It had to be done, but it was distasteful and she could see that it worried Harry.

'You must go with him,' she said under her breath to Piers.

'Yes, of course.'

It ate further into the evening and it was inconclusive, since Harry could only pick out a couple of faces he said were 'something like' the man he had seen for no more than a few startled seconds.

'What a day!' Ella said when they had finally got the children off to bed. 'How were Claudia and Bernie when you left them? Have they lost much?'

'Most of Claudia's jewellery and a gold watch and a French clock from the bedroom, a couple of golf trophies, an expensive camera and a lap-top computer from Bernie's study, and a silver tea service Claudia had in the dining room. All small, portable stuff and, to add insult to injury, taken away in Claudia's Vuitton suitcase, which cost a packet. What really made them sick was the mess and confusion. And the fact that it went on while we were enjoying ourselves outside. Their insurance will cover the loss, but it's a nasty thing to happen.'

'Yes, indeed. I'll give Claudia a ring in the morning to see if there's anything I can do to help.'

'Bless you, darling. I expect she'll get her daily woman in to clear up the muddle. And talking of help, did you pay off Leah?'

'I did, and I can tell you here and now that she's never going to have charge of the children again.'

'There's no harm in Leah,' Piers said.

'She's a sadistic little monster. She's been frightening the

35

children witless with stories out of horror films. What ever made you employ her – an unmarried, under-age mother with a father who's been in and out of jail for as long as she can remember?'

'I took what I could get. She lives in a flat in a building I handle and I knew she could do with the money.'

'Leah's had a rough deal from life, I acknowledge that. I wouldn't quarrel with giving her a chance to earn what she can if it weren't for that touch of nastiness with the horror stories. I don't want her here again.'

'Then I'll leave it to you to find someone you consider suitable,' Piers said.

Leah stumped back down the hill, disgruntled at having her arrangements messed up. On the credit side, she'd been paid for doing nothing – that Ella was a soft touch – but if she had known she was going to spend an evening with no access to a video machine she wouldn't have gone to the trouble and expense of hiring 'Killers from the Black Planet'. What she really needed was a video of her own. Her mind roamed over acquaintances who might get her one cheap or, better still, give it to her as a present. For services rendered, of course. She grinned to herself as she thought of one possibility. Should she try it on? No harm in giving it a go.

She bumped the pushchair down the steps to her basement flat and was irritated when the front door opened just as she arrived at the bottom.

'You might have given me a hand,' she complained.

'Didn't hear you in time. I was in the kitchen at the back, making myself a cup of tea.'

'You've not a nerve! How did you get in? Oh, silly question! You used your professional know-how, of course.'

'Happened to have my picklocks on me,' her father said. 'How's my grandson?'

'He's all right. You can take him out of the pushchair and carry him in for me. He's a ton weight.'

'He's a lovely boy!' The baby's mouth turned down ominously. 'Don't you know your Grandad, then?'

'Why should he?' Leah demanded. 'Grandad's been inside most of his life. What do you want?'

36

'To see you, of course, girl.'

'Oh, yeah? And?' She caught sight of a big suitcase in the corner of the room. 'Oh, no! You've done a job and you want me to hide the stuff for you. No way!'

'I'll pay you.'

'How much?'

Her father took a twenty-pound note out of his pocket and put it on the table. Leah looked at it in silence. Her father sighed and added another ten pounds.

'I'll make it up to fifty when I've made a sale,' he promised.

'Why can't you fence the stuff straight away? I don't want to be mixed up in your dirty business.'

'The thing is, I think I was seen. Some kid looked out of the window as I was getting away.'

'Here! It wasn't you who did the Caldicotts' place this afternoon?'

'I'm not saying yes and I'm not saying no. How come you know about it?'

'I was going to babysit for the kid who saw you, him and his two sisters, this evening, only because of all the upset the Mum and Dad decided not to go out after all.'

'Do you happen to know how much of a look he got at me?'

'Only a glimpse – a short man, not very young, in a dark jacket.' She looked at her father, wiry and undersized, in a black anorak. 'I bet the old Bill are saying to themselves "Sounds like Reg Daley".'

'You could be right. So I can't be caught toting the swag around. Hide it for me, there's a good girl, Leah.'

'They'll be round here looking for it,' Leah said bitterly. 'Especially if they find out you've visited me. When did you ever call on your children unless you wanted to make use of them?'

'I'll raise the offer to seventy-five pounds.'

'What I really want is a video. Legit, if possible.'

'I'll ask around. In the meantime, you'll do your old Dad a favour, won't you?'

'Not down here. I'll stash it away upstairs. The people in the top flat are away on holiday and I've got their keys so I can water the plants and feed the cat.'

'Ideal. Very clever.'

'I'll have to remove it before they come back.'

'The heat should have gone off by then. The coppers will come and have a sniff round at home and it's true they might come here ...'

'They will,' Leah predicted.

'When they find nothing they'll look elsewhere.'

'You hope. Here, when you did the Caldicotts' place did you get into Bernie's dark room?'

'Where is it?'

'Off what he calls his study.'

'I tried the door, but it was locked.'

'Yeah, it would be,' Leah agreed. 'He's got a lot of expensive equipment in there.'

'Too heavy to carry. You know me, I go for the quick in and out, nothing that isn't portable.'

'I know you all right,' Leah said. 'I must want my head examined, letting you con me into being an accessory. Just don't forget my video, that's all.'

Chapter Three

Once the children had gone back to school and she had the house to herself during the day, Ella began working on her plan for making jams, pickles and chutneys on a small commercial basis. She already had some trusted recipes which could be scaled up for large batches. There would have to be less cutting up by hand and more reliance on the food processor, which would affect the texture, but that was unavoidable unless she was to be a complete slave.

She registered as a trader at a cash-and-carry outlet where she could buy large supplies of such things as dried fruit, vinegar and sugar. She located a source of cheap glass jars and she designed a label.

'"Mrs Martin's Pickles and Preserves – Made in Kits Harbour",' she said. 'What do you think? Italic script and an oval shape?'

'Looks good,' Piers admitted. 'Your maiden name?'

'Takes less space than "Armitage" and it seems to run off the tongue more easily.'

'I had no idea you were such a business woman.'

'Home economics,' Ella said. 'Fortunately, I'm not having to borrow any money to get started, but if it really takes off I may have to make a small extension to the kitchen. Would you let me do that?'

'If you use your own money, sweetheart. I can't afford to add to the mortgage.'

'Of course not.'

'Let me know if you decide to build a factory.'

'I won't go to the stock market until after I've sold the first twenty pounds of Spicy Apple Chutney,' Ella promised. 'As soon as I've got samples to show I'll do a trawl round the likely outlets. Bernie's Garden Centre is definite, but it's the only one so far.'

'Good old Bernie,' Piers said. 'He's given me his golf clubs, by the way.'

'How come? That's an expensive present, surely?'

'He listed them as missing after the burglary and then realised they were in the garage all the time. However, the insurance company paid up, he bought a new set and he's given the old ones to me.'

'But that's not honest.' Ella heard herself speaking very slowly, as if to a defective child.

'It was a genuine mistake.'

'A very short-lived one, surely? Bernie must have noticed a great big bag of golf clubs sitting in the corner of the garage as soon as he went to get his car out.'

'Funnily enough, not for a couple of days. He'd done the list by that time and he didn't feel inclined to alter it. Don't look so disapproving. It's not as if he's made any profit out of the deal. He's parted with the old clubs and got some new ones, that's all. And the money's a fleabite to the insurance company.'

'You've profited,' Ella pointed out. 'You've got a far better lot of clubs than you could have bought for yourself.'

'True. That's why I said "good old Bernie".'

'You must give them back and Bernie must return the money.'

'Darling, you can say "must" to me – though I don't like it – but you can't say it to Bernie. Besides, what's he to do with his new, even more expensive clubs?'

Ella could think of no easy answer, but she held obstinately to her belief that Piers should refuse Bernie's gift. They argued backwards and forwards. Piers' lack of understanding of her attitude filled Ella with despair.

'Surely you can see that it's not right?' she exclaimed.

'I can't, but what I do see is that it means a lot to you and I can't afford to quarrel with you, my precious. So I'll explain the situation to Bernie.'

'Will you? Bless you, Piers, that's generous.'

She would have preferred him to have recognised the morality of her stand, but at least she had persuaded him to do what she saw as the right thing and she was full of love and gratitude to him.

'Ella came over all squeamish and thought I should give you back your golf clubs so that you could repay the insurance company their measly few pounds. I don't see it that way myself, but I don't want to quarrel with her. So, can we work out an arrangement that will make her comfortable and me happy?'

'Sure. You can stow the bag in the back of the Land Rover and Ella needn't know which set you actually play with.' Bernie laughed indulgently. 'Your Ella's a sweetie, but she doesn't live in the real world.'

'It's a damn nuisance, actually, because I meant to sell off my old set. They're fairly clapped out, but I would have got a few pounds for them.'

'Money tight?'

'When is it ever anything else? Ella sets great store by this jam-making lark. It's good of you to help her out with the selling.'

'It could take off,' Bernie said thoughtfully. 'I'm impressed by the way she's set about it. You could be married to Kits Harbour's next successful entrepreneur.'

Bernie and Piers might laugh about it, but Ella was in deadly earnest over her small business venture, even to the extent of taking the three children into the local orchards to pick a glut of plums. They took a picnic and they enjoyed it, up to a point, but she soon saw that the concentration needed for sustained picking was not for them and she broke it off before they could get over-tired and bored.

The smell of simmering fruit spread through the whole house. So did the wasps.

'Sorry,' Ella apologised as Jennifer squealed and flailed out wildly. 'One of the hazards, I'm afraid. I have to make some jam to use as samples because the chutneys need to be kept for two or three months before they're ready to go on sale. I'll do three-fruit marmalade next week and after that you can have a

41

respite while I test the market.' She looked round at the rows of rich red jam with a contented sigh. 'Such a stroke of luck that I didn't part with my preserving pans.'

The stainless steel would last a lifetime and they were easy – fairly easy – to keep clean. Hygiene was one of the things that bothered her, knowing that a family kitchen was not the ideal place for manufacturing produce for sale to the public. If she ever began to expand she might have to set up a separate kitchen, to be used exclusively for her work.

When Bernie called round a week later the house was smelling of citrus fruit.

'When do I get a delivery?' he asked.

'Today, if you can take it. I can do you plum jam, apple jelly and marmalade. The marmalade still has to be labelled, but won't take more than a few minutes.' She laid a finger on the side of a jar. 'Almost cool enough for me to put on the labels.'

'I'll stick around, shall I? Where are the kids?'

'Harry and Verity are upstairs doing their homework or, in Harry's case, listening to pop music and pretending to do his homework; Jennifer's watching television.'

'I'll go and join her and leave you to finish off. I must say the jars look very smart. The labels are nice and I like the little mob-caps.'

'Red and white check for the jam, orange and white for the marmalade and I'll use green and white for the pickles and chutneys, which you'll be able to have next month – if you still think it's worthwhile. How many will you take today?'

'How about ten jars of each of the three that are ready? Just by way of a sample?'

'Great.'

Ella flashed him a radiant smile, grateful for his ready help.

'When you smile like that I can see why Piers looks so happy these days,' Bernie remarked. 'He's a lucky man.'

'Oh ... a lot of the luck's on my side,' Ella said, confused by his admiration.

She finished clearing up, labelled her marmalade and loaded the thirty jars Bernie was taking into a box, made out a neat invoice, although this first consignment was on a sale-or-return basis, and entered the delivery in a book she had bought specially for the purpose.

Harry's music was still blasting away upstairs, Verity had not surfaced and Jennifer's television programme should have been long over. Time to start dishing up the evening meal and to get rid of Bernie, even though his call was welcome since it meant she would not have to drive round to the Garden Centre herself.

Ella went through to the sitting room. The television was still on, showing a programme Ella thought unsuitable for children. Jennifer was sharing an armchair with Bernie, sitting on his knee. She was giggling in the way that her brother and sister condemned as 'Jennifer being twee'. She looked up, flushed and laughing, as Ella came into the room, then wriggled off Bernie's knee and ran out of the room.

Bernie stood up. 'She's a real little charmer,' he said fondly.

With an abruptness that betrayed her irritation, Ella turned off the television. Bernie was devoted to the children; Piers was always saying so, with the implication that he regretted having none of his own, but Ella wished he would not single out Jennifer. She was, of course, the littlest and the most immediately appealing. What Ella did not like was the way Jennifer played up to him. She was too young to understand that it was not right to exploit the affection of a childless man. Ella dealt briskly with Bernie and was not sorry to see him depart with his box of jams.

All three of the children came wandering into the kitchen as she stowed away the rest of the marmalade pots.

'What's for supper?' Harry asked.

'Fish pie and apple crumble. It'll be ready in a few minutes.'

'Shall I lay the table?' Verity offered.

'Yes, please.'

'What's that you're playing with?' Verity asked Jennifer. 'Move, so that I can put the cloth on.'

'It's a fifty pence piece,' Harry said, watching Jennifer balance the coin on its edge. 'Where did you get it?'

'Uncle Bernie gave it to me.'

'You've been smarming round him again,' Harry said in disgust. 'We *told* you ...' He broke off and cast a wary glance at Ella.

'Why did Uncle Bernie give you fifty pence?' Ella asked.

'Because he *likes* me. I'm *nice* to him.'

She sounded revoltingly smug. Ella caught the other two looking at her with acute dislike.

'You don't want to end up living with Bernie and Claudia, do you?' Harry asked. 'Especially now ...' He broke off with another look at Ella.

'There's no question of that,' Ella said.

'No, 'cause Daddy said I needn't,' Jennifer agreed. 'Can I keep my fifty pence?'

'Go and put it in your money box and, while you're upstairs, wash your hands.'

Jennifer ran out of the room and up the stairs. Ella waited until she was out of earshot. 'Right,' she said. 'Now tell me what that was all about.'

'After Mum died, Bernie and Claudia offered to adopt Jennifer,' Verity said.

'No!'

'We were terribly against it.'

'Jennifer's a pain in the ... neck,' Harry put in. 'But she's *ours*.'

'We're a family,' Verity added. 'We belong together. Mum wouldn't have liked Jennifer being given away.'

Her lips trembled and she looked down at her hands, frowning fiercely.

'Fortunately, Dad had the sense to talk it over with us,' Harry said. 'We told him what we thought in no uncertain terms.'

'And he listened,' Verity said, sounding surprised. 'The trouble was, Jennifer could see she might be on to a good thing, but when we explained what it would mean, she didn't really want to leave us.'

'And then Dad met you,' Harry said.

'And I'm certainly not in favour of splitting up the family,' Ella said. She was struggling yet again with the feeling of vital information having been held back from her. For the time being she put it out of her mind. 'I think you two will have to start being more tolerant towards Jennifer,' she said. 'It may have gone to her head a bit, being chosen for possible adoption, but I suspect it unsettled her as well. What you see as bumptiousness may be just a little girl looking for reassurance about her place in the family.'

44

'I bet you didn't expect us to be such a worry when you married Dad,' Harry said.

'I didn't know the half of it,' Ella agreed. 'That fish pie smells done. Give Jennifer a shout, Verity.'

'I think you might have explained the situation about Claudia and Bernie wanting to adopt Jennifer,' Ella said to Piers that evening. 'It only came out by chance from the children today.'

'I never took it very seriously. Bernie was keen, but I think Claudia always had reservations.'

'I dare say she did.'

'It's no easy thing, to take on responsibility for a child when you've not been a parent before,' Piers said in all seriousness.

'You don't have to tell me!'

Piers stretched out a hand to her. 'Are they getting you down?'

'It's not easy, but they're good kids. It's just ... I can't help wondering how many more skeletons are hiding in the cupboard.'

'This was hardly a skeleton, not even a mouse skeleton; just an idea that came up and faded almost as soon as it was thought of.'

'It unsettled the children, and it explains why they're so wary of Bernie and Claudia.'

'I suppose so. Silly of them, when the whole thing is over and forgotten.'

Over perhaps, but not forgotten. And she had not dealt with her real bone of contention, that Piers had not thought to tell her about it. With an inward sigh Ella decided to let it go. Piers really did not understand why his omission troubled her and even to herself she could not quite put her uneasiness into words.

Slowly, as the months went by, Ella came to terms with the reality of her marriage. Piers was as charming as ever, socially adept, sexually potent, basking in the pleasure his own good looks gave to him and everyone who came in contact with him, invariably good tempered, as long as his pleasures were not interfered with, and undependable.

At Christmas, Lucy's brother, Toby, got in touch. He wrote

45

to Piers to say he would be home from Africa for a short time and suggested that the children should be sent up to London to meet him.

'Not in the Christmas crowds,' Ella exclaimed in horror, but when Toby Greville telephoned to confirm the arrangement she took the call and found herself reluctantly agreeing that, yes, Verity was nearly fourteen, and they were, of course, responsible, well-behaved children who could be trusted to get off at the London terminus. As long as he was sure he would be there to meet them, she found herself saying weakly, and would he please ring to confirm they had arrived safely?

She was annoyed at the way he had overridden her forebodings. After the call she went to the old roll-top desk and found another of the family snapshots Piers had stowed away after Lucy's death. It showed a young man in uniform, so it must have been taken before he left the Army, with his arm round his sister, younger by several years than he must be now, she realised, but already showing an obstinate set to his mouth and a touch of arrogance in the way he held his head.

'If you want to see your nephew and nieces, why can't you come and visit them in a civilised way?' Ella asked the unresponsive picture, but she already knew the answer: because he had not come to terms with Piers' re-marriage.

The children, of course, were wild with delight at the thought of seeing their Uncle Toby. Verity was adamant that there was absolutely no reason why they should not travel to London on their own and Jennifer never gave it a thought. Harry, Ella realised, was worried, but she had to face the fact that a degree of independence would be good for him. Trying to use her imagination, she made out a list of the stations they would pass through on their journey and gave it to him so that he could check it off as they went along. Apart from that, she could only mention to the guard that there were three unaccompanied children travelling to Victoria Station in the carriage nearest to him and then go home and spend nearly two hours worrying about accidents, breakdowns and delays.

They arrived safely, they met Toby, they went to a matinee performance of *The Wind in the Willows*, had a slap-up tea and were put on an early evening train back to Kits Harbour.

Toby telephoned to say they were on their way back and again Ella took the call. It all seemed to have gone very well.

'Verity gave me to understand that *The Wind in the Willows* was a trifle unsophisticated for her taste, but I think she enjoyed it all the same,' he said.

'I'm sure she did.' Ella struggled with herself and then added, 'It was very good of you to take them.'

'I enjoyed it, too. They're a lively trio.' There was a brief pause and from the way Toby followed it up, Ella guessed that he, too, was making himself say the right thing. 'They seemed ... happy. You appear to manage them rather well.'

'The only managing I do arises out of loving them,' Ella said.

'Yes, well ... whatever the formula, it seems to work.'

'Do you want to speak to Piers?'

'Not particularly. I'll just wish you a happy Christmas and say goodbye.'

He was gone, leaving her feeling ruffled. Did he have to be so abrupt? Come to that, did he have to be so condescending? The "formula seemed to work", indeed!

'The children are on their way home,' she said to Piers. 'You'll go to the station to meet them, won't you?'

'Sure.' He held out his arms. 'We've got at least an hour and a half before I need set out. Come and have a cuddle.'

She went to him willingly enough, but as she settled herself on his lap with her head against his, Ella said, 'Do you get on with Toby?'

'Not really. He's got a very good opinion of himself. A typical young Army officer, I thought, who'd been set up in authority too young.'

'He doesn't seem to want to meet me.'

'That's his loss. What does it matter? As long as we're happy, we can manage without him.'

'Yes,' Ella agreed. 'We can, of course, but I would have liked to have been friends.'

In June Piers' mother came to visit them and Ella had to get used to hearing him called 'Perce', since she refused to use any other variation of his name.

'I don't know what came over him to change it,' Mrs

47

Armitage said. 'No, I tell a lie. I do know; keeping up with the fancy friends he made when he left home. Piers! I ask you!'

She was a small, exhausted woman, worn out with looking after a chronically sick husband.

'George would have liked to come too,' she said. 'But, of course, it was out of the question. He's gone into what they call respite care – respite for me, that is.'

'You must have a good rest while you're here,' Piers said. 'Ella will look after you.'

Mrs Armitage turned her dull gaze on Ella. 'I don't want much in the way of looking after, not like your Dad, Perce. If I can find my way down to the beach and sit in a deckchair and watch the sea, that's all the holiday I need.'

When Ella took her breakfast in bed the next day she was appalled.

'Nay, lass, that's treating me like an invalid, which I'm not.'

'The children are all over the kitchen,' Ella said. 'You've no idea what a madhouse it is, getting them off to school and Piers off to work.'

'Oh yes, I have,' Mrs Armitage said drily. 'I had the doing of it for best part of a year before George took ill and I had to choose between him and Perce.'

'Stupid of me, I was forgetting,' Ella said, flustered by her slip.

'You weren't on the scene then,' Mrs Armitage excused her.

She got up early the next day and made herself useful about the kitchen in spite of what she had said about her need for a rest.

'I'm making a delivery of pickles this morning,' Ella said. 'Do you want to come with me? We could have coffee in Ramsgate and a stroll on the sands.'

'I'll come along. You making a go of this preserves business, are you?'

'It's early days, but, yes, it's been successful so far.'

'You run it like a proper business, do you? Books kept and a separate bank account and so on?'

'Yes, indeed. I'd get into a dreadful muddle otherwise.'

'You would if Perce could dip his fingers in the kitty. You've found that out, I take it.'

'We've got a good working arrangement,' Ella said carefully.

'You're loyal, which I suppose I have to admire.'

'He's my husband and I love him.'

'He's my son and I love him, too, but that's not to say I'd trust him with my savings, if I had any.'

There was an awkward silence and then Mrs Armitage added abruptly, 'You're a good manager and it's a marvel what you've done for the children. It's a load off my mind, to know a sensible woman's looking after them.'

'I'm very fond of them.'

'Are you hoping for any of your own?'

For a moment Ella did not reply, but when she did it was with determined brightness. 'One day, perhaps. We haven't had our first anniversary yet and I've already got three on my hands.'

She was glad that her mother-in-law decided not to probe any further. Instead, she turned to a grievance which had already been aired.

'Persuade him to come back with me to see his father.'

'I'll try,' Ella said weakly.

'It's been more than a year and George feels it. You might think he's too ill to care, but he lies there brooding. A visit from Perce would cheer him up. And I could do with some help on the journey.'

Ella took it up with Piers that night. 'You ought to go,' she said.

'It's a busy time of year,' Piers said.

'You could spare a weekend.'

'I'm committed to the golf tournament on Sunday.'

Ella felt her control slipping. 'If you weigh a golf tournament against a dying father, which comes out as the more important?'

'Dad's not dying.'

'He's got Parkinson's disease and a weak heart. You know perfectly well that he can't last long.'

'Why don't you take the kids up to see him?'

'That's not what he wants. It's you he needs to see.'

'In a week or two ... I'll work something out.'

'Next weekend. Piers, you'll regret it if you leave it too long.'

'Oh, darling ... the truth is, I saw so much illness with poor Lucy I can't stand sickbeds.'

49

He looked at her with such misery in his face that Ella almost weakened. Only her own experience made her harden her heart. She had looked after both her mother and her father until they died. What made Piers think he was so special?

'I understand,' she said steadily. 'But I think – no, I know – you're strong enough and kindhearted enough to overcome your own feelings to give your father the pleasure of seeing you once more.'

A spoonful of sugar, she thought. Will it work? For a moment Piers wavered, but then he shook his head and Ella was sick with disappointment as she recognised the mulish determination on his face.

She said nothing to her mother-in-law and was glad she had kept quiet when Piers bounced in the following evening and said, 'Mum, I can't come back with you this weekend, it's out of the question, but I've got the opportunity of paying a visit to Scarborough in a fortnight's time and from there it'll be easy to pop over and see you and Dad. How's that?'

'As long as you don't let us down. Is it safe for me to mention it to your Dad? He'll be really upset if you break your word.'

'It's absolutely settled,' Piers said. He turned to Ella. 'You won't mind being left on your own for a couple of nights, will you, sweetie?'

'Of course not. Why do you have to go to Scarborough?'

She thought that Piers hesitated before he said, 'Bernie and Claudia are going for a golfing weekend and they've invited me along.'

'I see. How nice.'

'I knew you'd be pleased.'

Ella hated herself for the sarcasm in her voice as she turned to Piers' mother and said, 'You can take it that the arrangement is definite,' but she could not help it. Claudia and Bernie, damn them, had produced a solution and persuaded Piers into doing something that he should have done as a loving duty.

He came back from that weekend bronzed, fit and amorous and he spoke with such affectionate sadness of his father's deterioration that Ella opened her heart and her arms to him with all the unstinted generosity she had shown before she had begun to see through the façade that hid Piers' shortcomings

50

even from himself. He was only human, after all. Because she loved him so much she had expected too much of him. She had plenty of faults of her own, especially a distrust of Piers' friends just because they were Piers' friends. A touch of jealousy, Ella told herself ruefully. Piers and Claudia and Bernie had been a close knit trio before she joined them and it was only her prickly self-consciousness that made expanding into a quartet a difficulty.

The question of a holiday in Spain had come up again and Ella felt that she could not reasonably hold out against a free visit to the Caldicotts' villa, even though she was no great lover of heat and August in Spain was not her idea of the perfect holiday.

Of course she should have known that it would be beautiful. It was in the hills behind the coast, a sprawling, whitewashed villa in the Moorish style, with a green-tiled roof, a shady terrace and a lavish swimming pool. There was a maid, a cook and a gardener, so Ella really had nothing to do but rest and dream and enjoy herself, which she did as long as they had the place to themselves.

'Isn't it bliss?' Piers murmured one lazy afternoon as they lay on beds by the pool, shaded by big sun umbrellas, cool glasses of fruit juice clinking with ice on tables by their side. 'I always knew I was meant to be a rich man.'

'It's wonderful,' Ella admitted. 'For a holiday, that is.'

'I could stay for ever.'

'Doing what? If you dare to say "playing golf" I'll empty the ice bucket over you.'

'There are people to visit, parties to go to, restaurants to eat in ... sights to see if you want to improve your mind. A yacht would be nice.'

'Very nice,' Ella mocked him. 'It's fantasy land, Piers, you know it is. And I'm not too sold on some of those "people to visit". Are you sure that man we spoke to in the bar last night is a crook?'

'I wouldn't say so if he were within earshot but, yes, it's well known. The British police yearn to get their hands on him, but they can't establish a foolproof case for extraditing him.'

'And are those the sort of people you want to mix with?'

51

'He's an extreme case. Bernie plays an occasional round with him, by way of insurance. It doesn't do to get on the wrong side of people like that.'

Ella lay quietly, looking up at the play of light on the underside of the sunshade.

'Am I a prig?' she asked.

Piers reached out and caught her hand in his. 'A bit of a Puritan,' he said. 'Judge not that ye be not judged, that's my motto.'

Claudia and Bernie came out and joined them for the last weekend of the holiday. Claudia was pleased when Ella lavished praise on the villa.

'It is fun, isn't it?' she said. 'I spent ages getting the furnishings just right. Some people ship everything out from England, but I was determined that my house should be Spanish. And, of course, it was much cheaper.'

Bernie gave a laugh. 'What about those handmade tiles?' he asked.

'Well, yes, I admit they were an expensive item, but they're exactly right, just what I wanted.'

They had a late, and inevitably well-wined, dinner on the last evening. The children had been banished to bed, there were just a few lamps on in the house and candles, their flames barely moving, on the terrace. The sky overhead was dark blue and full of stars. There was only a sliver of a moon, gleaming faintly. Ella tilted her head back to look at it.

'Does anyone want to swim?' Claudia asked.

'Too full, too sleepy,' Ella said.

'Piers?'

Piers stood up and held out his hand to her. 'One last dip,' he said.

They wandered off, down the steps that led to the pool below, a rectangle of shimmering green from the underwater lights.

'What about you?' Ella asked Bernie.

'I don't think I'm wanted.' He sounded amused and indulgent.

Ella pushed back her chair. 'I'm going to turn in,' she said.

'Me, too.' Bernie stood up, looming over her. 'Can I have a goodnight kiss?'

He was so near that it was impossible to avoid him. Ella put up her face. 'Dear Bernie,' she murmured in an affectionate tone intended to depress passion. 'Thank you for a lovely holiday.'

She gave him a cool little kiss, but once Bernie had got hold of her it was difficult to get away.

'Are you going to struggle?' he asked.

In the light of the candles his eyes were gleaming and Ella thought that his face had a strange, puffy look. He was triumphant, believing that it was impossible for her to break his hold, and when she tried to move away he gave an excited laugh.

'Bernie,' Ella breathed.

'Yes, darling?'

'Do you know anything about judo?'

'Not a thing. Why? Are you a black belt or something?'

'Not black,' Ella said in the same deceptively gentle voice. 'I was never that good, but "something", yes, definitely "something". Now do let me go, there's a good boy, or I might be tempted to throw you.'

'I'd like to see you try,' Bernie said, really amused. 'You're a well grown young woman, but I could crush you ... ouch! Hey, Ella, stop it!'

He lost his balance, staggered wildly and then, fortunately, toppled over on to the cushioned seat that ran along the inner wall of the terrace.

'I did warn you,' Ella said. 'Are you all right?'

'I'm not hurt,' Bernie said. He no longer sounded amused, but grumpy. 'You caught me off balance.'

'That's the essence of judo,' Ella told him cheerfully. 'Now I'm going to bed. Good night.'

He muttered something, but Ella did not wait to hear what it was. She took herself off to the splendid master bedroom she had been sharing with Piers for the last fortnight. It had a balcony and before she undressed Ella stepped out on it and looked down on the swimming pool. Two bodies, closely entwined, drifted on the illuminated water, with only an occasional kick of the legs to keep them afloat. Claudia and Piers.

Ella stared down at them. She was not particularly surprised. Of course she had known what Bernie had meant

53

when he had said in his repulsively indulgent way that he would not be welcome to join his wife and friend in the swimming pool. And because they had paired up, he had felt free to make a pass at Ella.

Below her, Piers and Claudia broke apart, laughing. Ella drew back, not wanting to be seen watching them. In spite of her distaste and indignation she would not make a scene. If she confronted Piers he would either insist that she had misunderstood a moment of affection between two old friends or else, even worse, be indulgent about her lack of sophistication. She would spare herself the protestations of innocence and the amusement that would end by making her feel like the guilty one, just as she would try to forget Bernie's unwelcome attentions. Just don't let Piers try making love to her when he eventually came in, she thought rebelliously.

When Piers finally came to bed, still damp and a little chilly, Ella buried her head in the pillow and pretended to be asleep.

It could not be denied that England was a come down after their scintillating holiday in Spain. Everyone seemed to be disgruntled. The children were difficult about going back to school, revealing hitherto unmentioned holiday tasks that had to be completed at breakneck speed before the term commenced. Ella had a short, fierce argument with Verity over whether last year's raincoat could be made to do for another winter term or whether, as Verity demanded, it should be passed on to Jennifer, for whom it was far too large.

'It's Jennifer's turn for something new,' Ella said. 'It's hard sometimes, being the youngest and making do with cast-offs.'

'Yes, it is,' Jennifer agreed with what Ella had to recognise as infuriating smugness.

'Oh, Jennifer, Jennifer – everyone's favourite. I'll die if I have to wear that horrible old mac to school, I'll just die of mortification.'

'It was new last September,' Ella pointed out.

'It's old hat, it's last year's, it's ... it's Marks and Spencer's.'

'It still fits you, it's waterproof and it was your choice.'

'I was a kid last year.'

'And still are, judging by the way you're carrying on. Come

on, Verity, you know we're not made of money ...'

'What happens to all that money you earn? We have to put up with the house stinking of vinegar and horrible sticky jam all over the kitchen, but we don't seem to get much out of it.'

'You do,' Ella said evenly. 'You may not be aware of it, but you do get some benefit.'

'Like what?'

'Like five air fares to Spain, for example.'

Verity was silenced, but Ella was more hurt than she would have believed possible. Surely, of all people, Verity should have recognised that she was working her fingers to the bone to avoid the load of debt that had once burdened the household?

'Lay the table for supper,' she said.

'Let Jennifer do it. It's about time she earned some of the goodies that are showered on her.'

Verity crashed out of the kitchen and Harry said awkwardly, 'She doesn't mean it.'

'She's at a difficult age,' Jennifer said.

Ella bit back a snort of surprised laughter. Where on earth had the child picked up that?

'You're all at difficult ages,' she said. 'Okay, Jennifer, you're elected to lay the table this evening.'

Fortunately, because it looked as if they were in for a sticky evening, Piers created a diversion when he came home.

'Claudia and Bernie's burglar has been caught,' he announced.

'No! After all this time? It must be a year, surely?'

'Apparently he did a whole string of jobs and when the police finally caught up with him he admitted the lot including, as I say, the break-in at Kits View House.'

'Will they get back any of the things they lost?'

'No, they've been long gone.' Piers had one brief qualm about the golf clubs still kept for his use in the back of Bernie's Land Rover and then dismissed it.

'The other sensation is that you'll never believe who it turned out to be,' he went on.

'I'm not acquainted with many burglars,' Ella said. A quick, unwelcome recollection came back to her. 'Piers! Not Leah's father?'

'Got it in one. She said he'd been in and out of prison, didn't she? Obviously he never learned his lesson and this time he's really in trouble because he lashed out and gave a policeman a black eye.'

'I saw Leah down on the seafront this morning,' Ella said with concern. 'She didn't speak.'

'Don't worry about Leah, she'll always land on her feet,' Piers said. 'I don't think she had much time for her father so I don't imagine she'll be too upset.'

'She gave me that impression the only time she spoke about him to me,' Ella admitted. 'I can't help feeling . . .'

'Darling, there's nothing you can do. A bad man has been caught. Be pleased about it.'

'I won't have to go to court, will I?' Harry asked.

'No, because he's confessed. All the jobs he's admitted to doing will be "taken into consideration" as they say.'

The disagreement with Verity simmered down. She even made a stiff sort of apology. 'I spoke out of turn,' she said. 'I know you do the best you can for us.'

'Bringing up a family is like throwing money into a bottomless pit,' Ella said. 'And treating everyone fairly all the time is almost impossible.'

'I do know that really. And, of course, I'm not jealous of Jennifer, that would be *infantile*. She's going to be really pretty when she grows up, isn't she?'

'She's got the conventional good looks. You're the one who might turn out to be the raving beauty, in a rather unusual kind of way.'

'Me? Stringy hair, muddy skin, spots on my chin and absolutely nothing in the way of breasts, and I'm *fourteen*!'

'You've got beautiful eyes and a good bone structure – lovely cheekbones. Your spots are a passing phase, caused by eating chocolate bars in your bedroom instead of salad at the supper table. And your muddy skin is nothing of the sort, it's just your tan fading.'

'But I'm skinny.'

'Be thankful. You're just one of those people who burn off fat easily. All of a sudden you'll blossom out into something really special, but it may take a year or two yet.'

56

'In the meantime I'm stuck with me as I am,' Verity said gloomily.

'That's right, darling, we love you for your radiant personality, not your looks.'

'Oh, Mum!'

'I'll give you a new dress for Christmas – promise.'

'A *dress*, yuck!'

'All right, designer jeans.'

'I'll hold you to that,' Verity threatened.

They had seen nothing of Toby during the year, although the children had an occasional letter or postcard from him, but he managed to get parcels to them in time for Christmas, together with a letter saying that he was going on a fact-finding mission to Colombia and would not be in touch again until the New Year.

'No theatre this year,' Verity mourned. 'We're frightfully cut off, in a cultural sense, down here in Kits Harbour. Mum, I think I might join the Amateur Dramatic Club.'

Ella had never made any comment when the children had dropped the formal 'Mother' and started calling her 'Mum', but it always gave her a small glow of satisfaction.

'If you can fit it in with your school work then go for it,' she said.

'Actually, I think I may decide to be an actress.'

Help! 'Time enough to think about that in a few years' time,' Ella said.

She turned on the television news and gave it no more than half her mind until a name leapt out at her.

'... led by Captain Toby Greville. The last news of the group was three days ago, since when their radio has been silent. No ransom demand has yet been received, but it is rumoured locally that they have been kidnapped by guerillas.'

There was a short piece by a BBC reporter in Bogota, conveying an underlying disquiet that worried Ella.

'I can't believe that Uncle Toby would just disappear,' Verity said in a puzzled way.

Neither could Ella and neither, when he came home, could Piers. 'It sounds bad,' he said privately to Ella. 'If there's no satisfactory news tomorrow I shall get on to the Foreign Office.'

57

By the next day they knew that the body of one of the team accompanying Toby, a Colombian, had been recovered, and the Colombian government had reluctantly admitted that he had been killed because he had no monetary value, while the foreign nationals – Toby, a Dane and a Dutchman – were being held to ransom by a group describing themselves as Marxists.

'Uncle Toby will be all right, won't he?' Harry asked.

'I'm sure he will, with all his training,' Ella said.

'He's absolutely our most favourite person, after Dad – and you,' Harry told her.

The addition had been tactful, Ella thought ruefully. What was the attraction of this man who had made so little attempt to keep in touch? He had remembered their birthdays, which could not have been easy when he was travelling overseas, and he was good about presents, not necessarily expensive, but imaginative and unusual. The parcels stowed away and secret until Christmas Day would be a particularly poignant reminder of him this year.

'If we send Uncle Toby a Christmas card, will he get it?' Jennifer asked.

'Of course not,' Harry said scornfully, but Ella intervened. 'We've been given an address by the Foreign Office,' she said. 'Letters might be passed on. I think we ought to try.'

Inevitably, Toby's presents were the ones the children opened first when Christmas morning came. A carved wooden puppet and a red and gold painted fan for Jennifer, another puppet in leather, very grotesque, and a curious musical instrument like a xylophone for Harry, another fan and a length of blue and green shot silk for Verity.

'What shall I *do* with it?' she agonised. 'I can't sew, not well enough to make a dress or anything.'

'I see it as a jacket,' Ella said. 'Either boxy, Chinese style, or slightly fitted like an Indian jacket. I think we ought to get it made up professionally. You decide on a style and I'll find a dressmaker and pay her.'

'Oh, thank you! I do want it to be *worthy* of Uncle Toby.'

In church that morning, at the service Ella had insisted they should all attend, she prayed most earnestly for this man she did not know. She tried to picture him in the steamy heat of the South American jungle, so distant from the cold overcast

58

English winter. If he was aware of the date was he thinking of home? Come to that, what home would be in his mind, he who had never married and seemed to have no blood relations but the three children with her in the pew?

She also breathed a small guilty prayer of thankfulness that Claudia and Bernie had chosen to spend Christmas at their villa in Spain. It was relief to have a break from their all-pervading presence, especially since, beneath all Ella's dealings with the Caldicotts lay a distrust she could not overcome since she had seen Piers and Claudia together in the swimming pool in Spain. Ella had come to believe that, at least on Claudia's part, there was something more involved than a fleeting moment of holiday romance and inevitably this suspicion soured the apparent friendship between the two women. As for Piers, he accepted all admiration as no more than his due and Ella could have screamed aloud in frustration at his complacency.

The months went by and the story of the missing soldiers in the jungle faded out of the news. Obstinately, Ella went on writing to Toby and remembering him in her prayers and said so when Verity remarked wistfully, 'Everyone has forgotten about Uncle Toby.'

'I still pray for him,' Ella said.

'Do you? Do you think it does any good?'

'If I didn't think so, I wouldn't bother.'

'No, I suppose not. Can I come with you next Sunday? We could make it a special day for remembering him.'

'Of course. It'll have to be the eight o'clock service.'

'I know.' Verity sighed. 'Bang goes my weekly lie-in.'

After that she made a point of occasionally joining Ella when she left for church on Sunday mornings, something Ella had taken up when she had realised that Piers was never going to give up his Sunday morning golf. She made no fuss about it, but quietly let herself out of the house before eight o'clock, when usually everyone else was only just stirring, returning in time for a family breakfast at around nine. Harry joined Verity when she said she was doing it for Uncle Toby and since Jennifer never liked to be left out of anything she, too, came along. It was the end of a quiet time Ella had cherished, but she tried to see it as a gain rather than a loss. As for the letters, she never let a week go by without a brief note and usually one or other of the children would scrawl a message on the end. Did he get them? They had no means of knowing, but Ella had the strange feeling that as long as she kept him in her mind he would remain safe.

Chapter Four

It was a cold, wet spring. Even May was miserable. Leah's little boy had a chesty cough which made him fretful. She resented her broken nights, but she did the right thing and kept him warm indoors, her boredom occasionally lightened by a visit from one of her friends, most of whom shared her predicament of being a single parent. Many of them lived in one-roomed bed-and-breakfast accommodation and they were openly envious of Leah's luck in having a whole flat to herself. She was sometimes tempted to tell them how she'd got it, but she had been warned at the beginning that what had been given could as easily be taken away and she was sufficiently intimidated to go on holding her tongue, in spite of her desire to give the girls a good laugh.

Late one afternoon when Damien had been particularly fractious and had just gone off into a feverish doze, the doorbell rang and Leah went to answer it in the expectation of finding a girl of her own age on the doorstep.

'Oh, it's you,' she said in disappointment when she found her father outside. 'I didn't know you'd been let out.'

'I always keep my head down and earn the maximum remittance for good behaviour, you know that.'

'Good behaviour!' Leah said with a sneer. 'Pity you don't keep it up when you're free.'

'That's not much of a welcome, and your mother was no better.'

'What d'you expect? The only time she knows where you are is when you're clapped up.'

'I'm giving it up, going straight.'

61

'Oh, yeah?'

'Straight up. I'm not getting any younger and I didn't like the company I had to mix with inside this time. Cocky kids who think they know it all because they've nicked a few videos and computers.'

'You'll be telling me next you're going to get a job.'

'Why not, if I can find one? Are you going to offer me a cup of tea?'

'I s'pose so. Don't wake the kid, that's all I ask.'

'How is the little nipper?'

'He's got a cold.'

Reg Daley followed his daughter into the tiny kitchen at the back of her flat.

'Talking of work, what do you do for a living these days?'

'This and that.'

'Beats me how you manage to afford this flat. And I see you've got a new telly.'

'I get help.'

'You must do.' His eyes narrowed and he began to frown. 'Here, you're not on the game, are you?'

'No, I'm not!' Leah slammed the kettle down on the gas stove.

'If there's one thing I won't stand for, it's a girl of mine being a tart. We forgave you for Damien ...'

'Oh, thanks! I was a kid of fifteen who scarcely knew what it was to have a father and I got caught out because I had a silly lark with a boy my own age. That doesn't make me a slag!'

'All right, all right. We stood by you, didn't we? It was you who was bound and determined you were going to live on your own. And you haven't answered my question.'

'I do a bit of cleaning, a bit of childminding, I get benefit. I get by.'

When they were sitting at the kitchen table with mugs of tea in front of them, Reg asked, 'Have you still got that suitcase I left with you?'

'Gawd, that's a long time ago! Yeah, I suppose it's at the back of the cupboard where I put it after I got it back from the flat upstairs. Why? I thought you'd emptied it out.'

'There's a camera I had trouble shifting. While I was inside

I heard of someone who might take it off my hands. I can do with a bit of ready.'

'Before you start going straight,' Leah jeered.

'I've done my time for nicking the camera, I'm entitled to the profit from it.'

'That's one way of looking at it. I'll get it for you and I'll thank you to remember that I'm never, never hiding anything for you again. My heart was in my mouth when the coppers came round asking questions.'

The man Reg Daley had been told might take the stolen camera off his hands had a small photographic business in a back street on the outskirts of the town. He examined the camera thoughtfully.

'How long have you had it?' he asked.

'Oh ... eighteen months, two years, something like that. It's a good camera, as you can see, but the fact is it's too elaborate for me. I can't get the hang of it.'

'It was a present, was it?'

'Birthday present from the kids,' Reg said, improvising readily.

Donald Burtman considered. It was a fine camera, but not for one moment did he believe that it had been a birthday present, not when it was being offered for sale with an undeveloped film still inside it, which was something even the most cackhanded amateur might be expected to notice.

'Who sent you to me?' he asked.

For a moment Reg Daley hesitated, then he answered truthfully. 'Sli Voster.'

That settled it. They both knew where he had last seen Sli Voster.

'I can give you fifty pounds.'

'What? You're joking. That camera's worth nigh on three hundred pounds.'

'It must be nice to have such a generous family.'

'I won't take a penny under a hundred pounds.'

'Seventy five.'

'Eighty.'

Donald Burtman hesitated, but only for a moment. He would have to be very unlucky not to sell the camera on for a

63

hundred and fifty, even two hundred pounds. It was stolen, of course, they both knew that, but he knew the market, he could shift it with no great difficulty.

'Eighty pounds,' he agreed. 'But if you want cash you'll have to have it in two instalments, otherwise I'll have to shut up the shop to go to the bank. Fifty today and thirty tomorrow. Okay?'

'Don't try and do me down when I come in for the second bit,' Reg warned.

'I won't do that.'

After Reg had gone, Donald Burtman took another look at his purchase. It was a bargain and he was pretty sure he knew where he could unload it, but first of all he would amuse himself by developing the unfinished film.

He was a competent technician. Even though the film was out of time and must have been in the camera for something like the eighteen months Reg Daley said he had owned it, he still got good, sharp prints when he developed it. As they dried he looked at them with raised eyebrows. By anyone's standards they were hot stuff. The girl was a saucy little bit. As for the man who appeared with her in some of the poses, Donald made a guess that he had set the timing device on the camera and then joined his companion. The camera must belong to him. He must have been beside himself when it was stolen with that film in it.

Donald had to smile, picturing the gradual relief that must have come over the camera owner as the months went by and nothing of his nefarious activities came to light. And now Donald had a complete set of prints and the question was, how could he turn it to advantage?

There was nothing he could do until he knew the identity of the man in the pictures. He set to work and did a blow up of a section of one of the negatives, just a head and shoulders of the man, looking straight at the camera, a somewhat glazed expression on his face, which was not surprising, considering what was going on in the rest of the picture.

When Reg Daley came back the next afternoon, suspicious and ready to make trouble if the second instalment of his money was not forthcoming, Donald brought out the head-and-shoulders print.

'You're a local man and I've not been here long,' he said. 'Do you recognise this chap?'

It gave Reg a jolt, looking at that smirking, fleshy face. 'Why do you want to know?' he asked mechanically.

'I've got a film of his I'd like to return.'

'And, of course, you've lost the address?'

'Shall we say the man who left the film forgot to give me the address?'

Reg's temper was rising. He leaned across the counter and took hold of the photographer by his collar.

'Are you planning to shop me? Because, if you are, matey, you're trying it on the wrong chap. Was that film in the camera you had off me?'

'Yes, yes,' Don gasped. 'Let go, you're choking me.'

'I will all right if you play tricks on me. What's your game? Are you going to sell the camera back to ... to *him*? And tell him who you got it off?'

'Would I be such a fool as to ask you for his name?' Don asked, easing a finger round the inside of his collar. 'Use your brain, if you've got one.'

'What then?'

'I reckon he'll pay good money to get that film back. There are things on it that aren't for general circulation, if you get my meaning.'

'Blackmail.' Reg's nose wrinkled in something like disgust.

'Payment for my trouble in developing it. Is he a married man?'

'Oh, yes, he's married all right. A hoity-toity piece.'

'Pity for her to be upset. He'll pay up.'

'You're probably right, but it's a dirty business, blackmail.'

'But that won't stop you selling me his name and address.'

'If we can agree a price.'

'Twenty.'

'Fifty.'

Reg was surprised when the photographer agreed without further bargaining. He wished he had asked more. On the other hand, blackmail was not his game. He always said he might be a thief, but he was an honest thief; it was the way he made his living and he looked on it as a job like any other, but requiring a particular amount of skill and cunning. The shock

65

and suffering he caused by his break-ins passed him by since possessions meant little to Reg. Easy come, easy go, that was Reg's motto, and he had never in his life held on to anything for sentimental reasons, not if it could be sold for a profit. He had a fierce temper and had often lashed out at his wife and children, but he would have been shocked to have been called a cruel man and he looked on it as a positive virtue that he wouldn't touch drugs or anything to do with sex. The straightforward sale of a name and address could be squared with what passed as his conscience because it was not his responsibility what use was made of the information. He pocketed the fifty pounds and the thirty still owing on the sale of the camera and went on his way, quite cheerful apart from a niggling feeling that he had missed out on a lucrative deal.

It was the week after half term and, as might have been expected, the weather had taken an abrupt turn for the better once the children had returned to school. Ella, working in the kitchen on the preserves which had proved to be a godsend in the way of boosting the family finances, would have been just as pleased if it had continued cool and rainy. She winced as a throb of pain shot across her forehead when Verity rushed in from school, her satchel of books thumping down on the ground as she came through the door and her coat already half off.

'What time's the next news?' she demanded. 'Television, radio, anything. There was a headline on a poster about "Kidnapped men released in Colombia". I only saw a glimpse of it from the bus. It must be Uncle Toby, mustn't it? It must be.'

Ella glanced at the clock. 'There's nothing now until five o'clock,' she said.

'I should have got off the bus and bought a paper,' Verity mourned. 'But we'd passed the shops by the time I'd taken in what it said, or what I thought it said.'

'I never saw it,' Harry said.

'Neither did I,' Jennifer added.

'You were too busy making a nuisance of yourself at the back of the bus,' Harry accused her. 'Noisy lot of silly kids, that's what you juniors are.'

'We're not!'

66

'Stop squabbling,' Ella ordered. 'Come on, everyone into the car and we'll go and buy a newspaper.'

It was only a few minutes' drive to the nearest newsagents. Sure enough, the headline on the posters outside read just as Verity had reported.

'Everyone cross their fingers,' she said.

'A bit late for that,' Harry said. 'It's either him or it isn't.'

There was a photograph on the front page, the picture which had become all too familiar from the earlier reports on the television news.

'Captain Toby Greville walks out with his two companions,' Verity breathed. 'That means he's all right.'

'Did the nasty men who took him prisoner just let him go?' Jennifer asked.

'It says that their captors disappeared and left them stranded in the jungle. They spent over a week trekking back to civilisation and Uncle Toby's training and leadership were essential to their survival.'

'Brill!' Harry breathed. 'What an adventure.'

'Uncle Toby is terribly, terribly brave,' Jennifer said. 'Will he come and see us now?'

'If he does we'll make him very welcome, won't we?' Ella said.

'He'll come,' Verity said. 'I just know he'll come.'

In the perverse way of things, having made contact with Donald Burtman, Reg seemed to see him everywhere. Probably he had been around before and Reg had just not noticed him. He was, after all, not a particularly noticeable man. Now, Reg was seriously thinking of changing his drinking habits because whenever he dropped into his favourite pub, Donald Burtman seemed to be there.

Neither of them was anxious to be seen in the company of the other so they exchanged no more than casual nods and a word in passing, until the evening when the photographer came over to the table where Reg had just settled down and said in a low voice, 'Our fish has taken the bait.'

'Not so much of the "our",' Reg said, irritated by his conspiratorial air. His curiosity got the better of him and he asked, 'Have you fixed a meeting?'

'Thursday night.'

'You want to watch out. He could be wired for sound or the police could be watching you.'

'I thought of that. I'm meeting him by the side of the road that runs along the golf course.'

'Was that your idea or his?'

'Mine. Why?'

'Just that it's really appropriate. He's a great golf player.'

'So I realised once you'd identified him for me. Perhaps that put the idea into my head. There are a few trees, but you can see for miles from there. No hope of a police car being hidden.'

'Maybe not. It still seems chancy to me.'

'For a couple of grand I'll take the risk.'

'A couple ... here, if I'd thought there was that much in it I'd have charged you a bit more for the info. I reckon you owe me.'

'Not on your life! And you boasted you didn't touch blackmail?'

'Keep your voice down. I don't like it and I don't say it's right, but all the same, a measly fifty out of two thousand, that's a poor return for my help.'

'You took it quick enough when I offered it. Sorry, old pal, that's all you're getting.'

He went off laughing in a way that nettled Reg. He drank up his beer and ordered another and sat brooding over it until an acquaintance came and joined him.

'D'you know that chap I was talking to a minute ago?' Reg asked.

'Photographer, isn't he? Yeah, I know him, sort of. Got a bit of an iffy reputation. He was had up for sending filthy pictures through the post or something of the sort. I thought you were more particular who you drank with, Reg.'

'I am. I did a bit of business with him and I reckon he did me down. Not that I want to get mixed up in his kind of filth,' he added virtuously. 'But I do hate to be done.'

'Write it off to experience,' his friend advised.

'That's not my way. Dogged, that's me, especially when it's a question of money. I'll have to have another word with Mr Photographer Burtman.'

68

Chapter Five

Kits Harbour looked much the same as Toby Greville remembered it. The station was perhaps a little shabbier. Unintelligible graffiti had been scrawled across one of the posters, but the platforms had been swept and the bright red slatted seats were new.

There was a taxi standing outside. Toby hesitated and then moved towards it. Lucy's house (he still thought of it as Lucy's house) was within walking distance of the station, even for a man not yet fit after an ordeal that would have brought the strongest to his knees, but Toby thought that he would fix himself up with somewhere to stay and get rid of his bag before visiting his sister's family. His late sister's family.

'Do you know somewhere quiet and reasonable where I can stay for a few days?' he asked the taxi driver.

He was a middle-aged man, solid and red-faced. He pretended to think, but Toby guessed that the answer was a foregone conclusion.

'If you don't mind me recommending something in the family, my sister runs a decent little private hotel,' he said. 'It isn't on the sea front, but if it's quietness you want that's not a consideration. The season hasn't properly got started so she's more or less bound to have a room. Tell you what, I'll give her a call on my mobile as we go along. If she's full up, which I doubt, she'll be able to recommend somewhere else.'

The telephone call was short and satisfactory. Before they had reached the top of the High Street Toby was fixed up with bed and breakfast, with an optional evening meal, if notice was given in the morning, at Belview Private Hotel.

There was more traffic than he remembered in the High Street.

'Busy,' he commented to the driver.

'Beginning to pick up. We get a lot of day trippers these days. You know Kits Harbour?'

'I used to come here a lot.'

Before Lucy had died. Before he had left the Army and joined the Red Cross. Before he had been held captive.

He looked out at the middle-aged women with shopping trolleys, the young mothers with pushchairs, the elderly men taking their daily walk. They were so preoccupied, so unknowing. As the taxi paused at a pedestrian crossing, Toby caught sight of a board outside a newsagents, the same newsagents where his niece had first seen news of his release, if he had but known it. 'Kits Harbour – Battered Body on Golf Course', it read. So, he was wrong; even here, the jungle was not far away.

They drew up in front of a tall red brick Edwardian house in a street of similar houses. Most of them displayed bed and breakfast or private hotel signs. Belview looked as good as any of them. There were neat beds of French marigolds in the small front garden, the red-tiled path looked as if it had been not merely swept, but washed, and the curtains were clean.

Toby felt in his pocket for some loose change to pay the taxi driver and then changed his mind.

'Could you hang on while I dump my bag and then take me to Jemima Road?' he asked.

'Sure. Have to charge you waiting time.'

'That's all right. I won't be more than a few minutes.'

Provided the room was satisfactory, and as soon as he set eyes on the landlady Toby knew it would be. She was a duplicate of her brother, dark-haired, with a high-coloured face, a sturdy figure and a shrewd way of sizing up a prospective customer.

'I can give you my best double,' she said. 'Or there's a smaller single at the back, but the double's got a shower and toilet *en suite*, which you might like if you're staying a day or two.'

Toby chose the double room, as she had known he would as soon as she set eyes on his good new clothes, his highly

70

polished shoes and his close haircut. He was tanned so dark he might have been a foreign gentleman, she thought idly, as she led him up the stairs, which he wasn't, not with the way that he talked. There was something familiar about him, but she couldn't quite put her finger on it.

She showed him his room and the facilities and went downstairs to consult her brother. When Toby came down again they turned to him, their faces alight with the curiosity he had begun to dread.

'Excuse me asking,' the landlady said. 'But aren't you the man that got taken hostage? The British army officer?'

'And hacked your way out with your friends?' her brother added.

Most of his friends. Everyone seemed to have forgotten about the Colombian who had been left in his blood in the roadside. Better not to think about that.

'That's me,' he said, trying to look cheerful about it. 'Toby Greville, but not 'Captain', if you don't mind. It's only the papers who've revived that. I've had it up to here with reporters.'

'Reporters!' the landlady snorted. 'I wouldn't give them the time of day.'

Her brother made no such commitment, Toby noticed.

'What brings you to Kits Harbour?' the taxi driver asked.

'I've got family connections here. I thought I'd look them up and have a seaside holiday. Shall we go?'

Two nieces and a nephew. A brother-in-law. And a new ... what? He could hardly call her a sister-in-law. A new woman who had taken his dead sister's place. A stepmother for the children. A woman who did not know him and yet had written with obstinate persistence, week after week, in an effort to make contact with him, and some of the letters had even been passed on to him.

It was a visit he should have made long since. He had promised Lucy that he would keep an eye on the kids and all he had done since her death was send them presents and take them on one visit to the theatre. They had seemed happy enough; he had salved his conscience with that. How was he to know that he would disappear from sight for so long? Nine months; battered, weary, sick, dragged from place to place,

71

able to communicate with his captors in only the most basic terms, fighting to keep up morale, and then, when the gang had inexplicably decided to abandon them, the difficult decision to walk out, the terrible doubts about whether they had made the right choice, the desperate clinging to the map in his head, the fears and doubts as to whether the landmarks he believed in were not hideously similar but misleading mountains and valleys.

'How did you do it?' the taxi driver asked.

'The sun always rises in the east,' Toby replied briefly. 'And the stars are fixed.'

Clear nights, but days too often obscured by mist and drenching rain. The dense, claustrophobic jungle, the sounds and smells. Insects, slithering things, the feeling of being stalked, by humans or by animals. Feet that were spongy and raw, stumbling over inhospitable terrain. He wanted to forget. Why did people keep reminding him about it?

'You were a proper hero,' the driver persisted. 'They ought to give you a medal.'

'God forbid,' Toby said.

He finally managed to shut the driver up by being uncommunicative and they got away. He remembered the house in Jemima Avenue. A decent-sized, modern house with four bedrooms. They could probably have made room for him if he had wanted to stay there, but Toby preferred to be on his own. He wanted a chance to stand back and size up the situation. He had to get to know the children all over again.

The front door was opened, after a delay, by a woman in her late twenties or early thirties. She wore a serviceable apron, a garment which might have been chosen to show off her admirable figure. The cream calico, tightly tied round the waist, revealed the round outline of her breasts, the curve of her hips and the slight, pleasing swell of her stomach. Quite a tall girl, not exactly a beauty, but pleasant enough; grey eyes, fair complexion, flushed at that moment as if by heat. There was something about the way her light brown hair was tied back under a scarf knotted behind at the nape of her neck and the pure oval of her face that reminded him of a painting he had seen somewhere. Vermeer! She had the look of a Dutch housewife.

72

He started to speak, but she forestalled him.

'You don't need to tell me! You're Uncle Toby.'

She smiled and he wondered why he had thought her plain.

'The children haven't stopped talking about you ever since we heard the news of your survival and, of course, we've seen you on television. Do come in.'

'I ought to have been in touch,' Toby said. 'But they shoved me into hospital and then there was the debriefing.'

Hours of careful questioning, the effort to remember, the things he had not wanted to say. Hopefully he could put all that behind him now.

'Don't you have any luggage? Haven't you come to stay?'

'I found digs in the town.'

'Harry will be disappointed, he was planning to share his room with you. Would you mind coming through to the kitchen? I'm in the middle of making chutney and I need to keep giving it a stir.'

There was a smell of vinegar and spices in the kitchen and an array of jars that made Toby stare.

'Making it on a large scale, I see,' he commented.

'I'm in business – "Mrs Martin's Pickles and Preserves". Doing quite well, actually. I'd dearly like to have a little van with the name on the side, but it wouldn't be very practical for ferrying the children around.'

She paused in her stirring to look at him, taking in his thinness, the lines on his face, the fatigue he was holding at bay.

'Do sit down,' she said. 'Give me a minute or two and I'll make you a cup of tea. The children will be home in about half an hour and I want to be finished before they arrive.'

He pulled out a kitchen chair and sat down, watching as she turned out the gas under her enormous preserving pan, admiring the deftness with which she ladled the dark brown chutney into the waiting jars.

'You don't go and fetch the kids from school?' he asked.

'No, they come on the bus, all together. It means Jennifer has to wait for the others to finish, but the Junior school makes provision for that. Jennifer, I may say, takes exception to staying on at school for an extra half hour. It will help when she moves up into the senior school next year.

'Little Jennifer ...'

73

'She's ten.'

'Yes, of course. I'll find a difference in them. I haven't seen them since we met in London that time.'

'Eighteen months ago.'

'I couldn't help being posted abroad.' Toby was annoyed to hear himself speaking defensively.

'Or being taken prisoner,' Ella agreed, but they both knew that he had had leave before he went to Colombia. He could have visited Kits Harbour, just as, earlier, he could have attended the wedding of Piers to this quiet, pleasant girl.

'You wrote to me,' he said abruptly.

'Did the letters really get through?'

'Some of them. Enough to make me feel I wasn't forgotten.'

She was filling the kettle, glancing at the clock on the wall as she ran the tap.

'I'll be glad when the children are home,' she said. 'It's silly, because they're only coming a short distance and in the company of other children, but we've had a nasty local murder and it makes one jumpy.'

'I saw the headline. Was it the golf course where Piers plays? I presume he still plays?'

'Oh, yes, every Sunday and any other time he can manage,' Ella said, and there was something in her voice that made Toby think that Piers hadn't changed.

'I don't know any details,' Ella went on. 'Just the bare fact that a man's battered body was found, not actually on the links, but in the belt of trees that runs along the side of the road.'

The water began to boil and she made the tea, fetched a tin from the cupboard and put half a dozen biscuits on a plate.

'Shortbread,' she said absentmindedly. 'Home made.'

When the tea was poured she sat down at last, bone weary if the truth were told. She was pleased to see Toby Greville, more for the children's sake than for her own, but presumably it meant one extra for supper and with half her mind she was debating what she could take out of the freezer that would be adequate for six and celebratory enough for this reunion.

Moussaka, there was a big dish of that and she could put it in the microwave, with salad and a glass of red wine – she would ring Piers and get him to buy a bottle on the way home

– and an icecream dessert, shop bought, but he would have to put up with that.

She looked up and found Toby watching her.

'Sorry,' she said. 'Not day dreaming, just thinking about a meal for this evening. You will stay, of course?'

'If it's not too much trouble?'

'No, I've got it sorted out. You aren't on any special diet, are you?'

'Just food and plenty of it. We were very restricted at first, but I'm over that phase now.'

'You had a bad time,' Ella said.

'Worse than you can imagine.' Something about her quiet sympathy made him add: 'I couldn't have shared a room with Harry; I still get bad dreams.'

'And wake up screaming?'

'In a cold sweat, at any rate.' He grimaced. 'I'm trying to put it behind me.'

'Yes, of course. I'm afraid the children will expect to hear about your amazing adventures.'

'I can handle that. Some of it was amusing, interesting, real boys' adventure stuff. I'll tell them the good bits.'

He helped her with the washing up, not very handily. He might be great at jungle survival, but domesticated he was not. Probably he rarely had to do these chores for himself. She wondered idly whether now that he had come through a remarkable ordeal he might settle down and marry. He was an attractive man, about her own age, or perhaps a year or two older, very tall, too thin at the moment, but she doubted whether he ever carried much spare flesh, very straightbacked and upright, with a competent air about him, in spite of his unhandiness with a tea towel.

The big preserving pan had been cleaned and wiped and put away and the jars of chutney were cool enough to be labelled when the front door crashed open and Harry's voice called, 'Mum, we're home!'

'As if I couldn't hear,' Ella murmured. 'I forgot to warn you that they called me "Mum". We started more formally, but gradually they came round to it. I hope it doesn't upset you.'

'No ... of course,' Toby said, confused by the question.

'In the kitchen,' Ella called. 'And we've got a surprise visitor.'

They crowded in: Verity, who must be fifteen, taller than he remembered, almost a woman; Harry, a dark haired boy with a loosened tie that had slipped round under his ear and his shirt half out of his trousers; and Jennifer, the baby, no longer a baby but a pretty, wide-eyed little girl.

'Uncle Toby!' They surged towards him and then stopped, brought up short by shyness, by a difference they sensed in him, and uncertainty how to greet him. It was Jennifer, the least inhibited, who flung her arms round him and hugged him. Toby reached out and put one hand on Harry's shoulder. Over Jennifer's head he met Verity's eyes and his heart turned over. She was so like Lucy, her dead mother, the sister who had been his companion all through their exiled childhood. He had failed her by not keeping watch over them and it was no thanks to him that they seemed to have survived, even to have been remarkably lucky when Piers married Ella Martin.

Ella slipped out of the room while they were still absorbed in one another and went to telephone Piers. Piers was enthusiastic, as she had known he would be. Piers was always ready to welcome a visitor and the fact that Toby was, in his way, a celebrity was an added pleasure.

'Sure I'll bring home a bottle of wine,' he said. 'And I think I can get away early. I was going to have a quick round with Bernie, but he's not feeling too bright and, in any case, the police are crawling all over the greens. What do you think, shall I ask Bernie and Claudia to come over?'

'Let's keep it a family evening,' Ella said quickly. 'I think that's what the children would prefer. Toby is planning to stay a few days ...'

'With us?'

'No, he'd found himself a room before he came here.'

'Tactful.'

'I suppose ... yes. We'll ask Bernie and Claudia another evening, if you think they'd like to see him. No big parties, though; he's still not a hundred per cent fit.'

'Right, message received. See you later.'

Ella leaned against the wall, wishing that she felt less tired. It would be a good evening, she was sure. Piers could be relied on to be charming in front of a visitor. And at other times, Ella added quickly. She was being unfair to him. Piers was always

76

ready to please; it was not his fault that she found his unrelenting bonhomie so wearing.

After three days at the Belview Private Hotel, Toby said to Piers, 'I think I might stick around in Kits Harbour for the rest of my leave. You're in the business, do you know of a holiday flat I might rent for a month?'

'I'll have a look at the books. It shouldn't be too difficult to find you something.'

'One bedroom will do, but I'd like a decent bathroom and something in the way of cooking facilities.'

'And clean,' Ella put in. 'Some so-called holiday flatlets I've seen left a lot to be desired.'

'We've got some well-managed places on our books,' Piers said. 'Call in the office tomorrow morning, Toby, and I'll tell you what's available.'

By mid-day the following day Toby had the keys to a flat which was highly recommended by his brother-in-law, but before going to view it he called on Ella.

'You're the domestic expert,' he said, tossing the keys in his hand. 'Come and give me your opinion.'

Ella hesitated. 'I've got to go to Dover ...'

'Fine. Come and give the flat the once over and I'll buy you lunch, either here or in Dover, whichever suits you best.'

'If you'll help me load up the car,' Ella bargained.

'Consider it done.'

The flat was everything Piers had promised; light, airy, and being on the top floor it even had a distant view of the sea.

'According to Piers, the owner of this desirable residence is abroad until the New Year, which is why it's available for short lets,' Toby explained. 'What do you think?'

'It's certainly a cut above most of the places that are purely meant for holiday tenants. You can see that this belongs to someone who's lived in it himself ... or herself.'

'Himself. A young engineer working on a project in Saudi Arabia.'

'If the rent is within your limit I would certainly advise you to take it.' Ella went into the kitchen and opened a few doors. 'The cooker needs cleaning and the fridge hasn't been

77

de-frosted since it was installed by the look of it. Personally, I would wipe out the insides of the cupboards before I put any food in them, the windows may have been cleaned on the outside but no one has done the inside, and a good going over with a duster would improve all the rooms. Apart from that, I've got nothing against the place.'

'Apparently there's a girl in the basement who is prepared to do cleaning if required. Piers said she'd be glad of the money. I could have a word with her as we go out.'

'If you've made up your mind to take the flat.'

'Yes, I've decided.'

'Toby ... why? I mean, there are more exciting places than Kits Harbour where you could spend your leave.'

'I've had all the excitement I need, thank you. Besides, now that I've made contact with my family I want to see something of them.'

'Leaving aside the past year, which you couldn't help, you managed pretty well without seeing them over the last few years.'

'Yes ... well, I was abroad a great deal, and I had a girl who took up a lot of my time. She dropped me while I was lost in the jungle, not being the faithful type like you, noble Ella.'

'There's nothing noble about me,' Ella said, startled.

'It takes a fair degree of commitment to be loyal to Piers.' He reached out one long finger and touched her lightly in the middle of her forehead. 'The Piers pleat,' he said. 'Lucy had it, too. A perpetual frown mark, caused by being married to an uncertain provider.'

'There are compensations,' Ella said, moving away. 'I love Piers.'

'Lucy said the same, but it didn't stop her living in a state of constant anxiety.'

'I don't want to talk about this,' Ella said. 'I can assure you that we are managing very well.'

'Because you're a natural business woman. These preserves of yours, I've seen them all over the place in the last few days.'

'I'll give you a jar of marmalade for your first breakfast in the flat,' Ella said, moving towards the door. 'Come on, let's interview the cleaning lady and then I really must get on.'

The basement steps led down to an area with whitewashed

walls. Not badly looked after, Ella thought, looking round critically. A gay windowbox and a tub of petunias by the door looked pretty. Pity about the overflowing dustbin in the corner.

Toby rang the bell and after a wait long enough for them to wonder if there was any one in, the door was opened by a girl with a lively toddler trying to push past her to see the visitors.

'Leah ...' Ella said in dismay.

'Hello, what do you want?' Leah looked past Ella to Toby and she gave a selfconscious toss of her wildly curling hair.

She was holding a hand up to the side of her face, concealing one eye, and then, deliberately, she took her hand away and displayed an atrociously bruised face.

'Leah! What on earth happened?'

'Fell against something, didn't I? Don't expect me to smile 'cause I split my lip, too.'

Before Ella could say any more, Toby intervened. 'I'm coming to live in the top flat for a few weeks,' he said. 'I was told you wouldn't mind doing a bit of cleaning for me?'

'Sure. Will you let me in or will you give me a key?'

'The keys aren't mine yet. I'll finish making the arrangements and call round tomorrow – about ten o'clock? – to open up the flat for you and discuss what needs to be done. Do you feel up to cleaning windows?'

'Why not? A black eye won't stop me climbing steps. I'll charge you by the hour and I'll want paying in cash.'

She named a figure which Ella thought too high, but Toby closed with it and she told herself that it was not her business how he spent his money. She was dismayed by Leah's re-entry into their lives, without being very sure why. Toby, after all, was not likely to be worried by Leah's penchant for horror movies.

As soon as they were back in the car, Ella said, 'What do you really think happened to her face?'

'She's been beaten up.'

'That's what I thought.'

'How do you come to know her?'

'She used to babysit for Piers, until I put a stop to it. She filled the children up with stories of vampires and zombies until they were afraid to go to bed.'

'She won't frighten me.'

'No, I suppose not. I wish I could be sure she's an adequate cleaner. Don't pay her unless she does a decent job.'

'Right, ma'am. Do you want lunch now or after you've dropped off your delivery?'

'After, if you don't mind, then I can forget about it and enjoy myself.'

'I'd like you to do that,' Toby said.

They drove to Dover and he waited in the car while Ella dropped off small deliveries to two shops. Looming above him he could see the massive walls and towers of Dover Castle and then, if he turned his head, the sweep of the white chalk cliffs along the coast. Lines of cars and lorries inched towards the docks. Above the throb of the engines he could hear the harsh cries of the seagulls which dipped and soared over the shore.

'My next port of call is in Sandwich,' Ella said when she rejoined him. 'I've left it until last because it's on the way home and I thought it might be a good place to get lunch.'

'Suits me,' Toby said idly.

'I hope you haven't been bored, sitting around while I do my deliveries.'

'Not at all. What I've been wondering is, where do you go from here? In the way of business, I mean.'

'That's something that's been bothering me,' Ella admitted. 'I could trundle on as I am, but that could lead to stagnation and decreasing sales. Anything else, either thinking up new lines or trying new outlets, means expansion and I'm not at all sure how to set about it.'

'At the moment it's very much a cottage industry,' Toby suggested.

'Yes, I'm a one-woman conveyor belt. When I started I got Piers to agree that, if necessary, I could expand the kitchen. Now, I'm not sure that's the best way to go about it.'

'If you had no ties what would you do?'

'I'd probably still be teaching,' Ella retorted. 'I'm not of a size to get tied in with a supermarket, even on a small scale. One idea I have considered is mail order.'

'Would there be sufficient demand?'

'I don't know. Jars of preserves are heavy so delivery costs would be high. I really need some specialist advice, but that would cost money and my profit margin hardly justifies it.'

'Put up your prices.'

'And kill my present market? What I really dream of is having something like a small unit in an industrial estate and employing staff, but that would mean the end of my actual hands-on cooking role, and I'd regret that.'

'If you want a sleeping partner I might be prepared to put up a bit of capital.'

'Goodness!' Ella gulped. 'You almost made me drive the car off the road. I hadn't thought ... it never occurred to me ... you hardly know me.'

'I know you very well indeed. You must feel it too, that sense of instant rapport?'

'I suppose because of all those letters I wrote to you.'

'Perhaps. And the resemblance to one of my favourite paintings. Two seconds after I met you I thought "Yes, that's her; I'm home."'

'I do have some money of my own,' Ella said, with a feeling that the subject needed changing.

'How on earth have you managed to keep it out of Piers' hands?'

'If he really needed it, Piers would be welcome to every penny I've got,' Ella said stiffly, knowing in her heart that it was not quite true. 'I just happen to have part of the proceeds of the sale of my parents' house which I've kept in a separate account ...'

'In your sole name. Wise girl.'

'Piers is careless about money, as everyone seems to know, but I won't be disloyal to him behind his back. He's a good father ...'

'He certainly did right by the children when he married you. How did you come to meet?'

'Through the school. I taught Verity; Piers came to parents' evenings.'

'Never say! I wouldn't have thought that was his scene.'

'You don't do him justice.'

It was only two years. Two years since she had met Piers, less than two years since she had married him. Then she had loved him beyond all reason; now, when she was wiser and less bedazzled, it was a question whether she did not love the children rather more than she loved Piers.

In duty bound, to please Piers rather than Toby, who gave the impression that he could live without it, she invited Claudia and Bernie round for a meal.

'Kids aren't wanted,' Verity said bitterly. 'I do think it's the most utterly nethermost humiliation to be made to have an early supper and sent off to our rooms. I'm *fifteen*!'

'Sorry, pet,' Ella said equably. 'I just can't cope with five adults and three children. It's not a kitchen meal, it's a polished dining room table, lace mats and candles in silver candlesticks event.'

'To impress Claudia.'

She was right, but Ella said, 'In honour of Toby.'

'He's *our* uncle!'

'And you've seen a lot of him in the last few days. This is an evening for the adults. Come on, Verity, you don't often get banished and I don't often have the chance to show what I can do. Claudia may have the glamorous surroundings, but I'm a damn sight better cook.'

'The only time you get a decent meal at their place is when Bernie does a barbecue,' Verity agreed. 'What are you giving them?'

'Grilled goats cheese with baby salad leaves, baked tuna steaks with garlic and sundried tomatoes, and cream-filled profiteroles with chocolate sauce, which I'm not sure Bernie should eat, so I've also provided a fruit salad; cheese and biscuits, for anyone who's got room, and coffee.'

'Cor! I don't suppose there'll be any left-overs?'

'I might manage to save a profiterole or two.'

'And what are we having?'

'Quiche and salad,' Ella admitted.

'I knew it! *Deprived*, that's what we are.'

All the same, she co-operated to the extent of clearing the table and stacking the dirty dishes in the dishwasher when the children's meal was finished, while Ella dashed upstairs and did a hurried change into a dress which hardly ever saw the outside of the wardrobe these days.

She had not spoken very seriously about Bernie's dietary

needs because most of the time he ignored his heart condition and did exactly what he wanted to do, including eating too much of entirely the wrong sort of food, but that evening Ella was shocked to see that he looked really unwell.

'Don't say anything, but Bernie was taken ill the other evening,' Claudia murmured. 'He felt so rough that he drove himself straight to the doctor's and the doctor wouldn't let him drive home. I had to get a taxi and go and pick him up.'

'Where was he taken ill?'

'Up on the golf course, would you believe? All that fresh air and exercise and his poor old ticker still plays him up.'

'I'm sorry.'

'He may hold back on the food this evening. Don't say anything if he does, will you? I'm sure it'll all be absolutely wonderful, but his appetite is a bit fickle.'

As far as Ella could see, Bernie did not stint himself on the first two courses, but he did make an heroic effort and refrain from the profiteroles.

'And I'll leave out the cheese,' he said. 'But I must have a spoonful of your good fruit salad.'

'It was a splendid meal, Ella,' Toby said.

She smiled at him, glad that he had enjoyed it, considering the effort she had put into it. He had Claudia on his other side. Rather too tarted up for the occasion, Ella thought, and very definitely out to impress Toby. He seemed to be able to cope. Had plenty of practice, probably. He must be sought after where ever there were women around. Not so obviously good-looking as Piers, but definitely attractive. Younger than Piers, too. It came as a shock to realise that Piers was over forty. It was only when one put him next to someone like Toby that one thought of Piers ageing.

She was just about to suggest leaving the table when the doorbell rang. Ella glanced at Piers. 'You go,' she said. 'Why don't you all go into the lounge while I put the coffee on?'

She took the opportunity to stack some of the dirty dishes and carry them through into the kitchen. Chaos, she thought, glancing round with a grimace, but it would help if she started loading the dishwasher while she waited for the kettle to boil. She could hear Piers talking to someone at the front door and a murmur of voices from the sitting room and then, to her surprise, Piers apparently asked their fresh visitors in. Ella looked again at the muddle in her kitchen and decided that unless Piers called her she would keep out of the way and deal with the mess. The diversion, whatever it was, would give her a few extra minutes to get cleared up.

By the time she went through to the sitting room with the coffee Bernie was emerging, accompanied by two large policemen. Ella stopped short, balancing the heavy tray. Bernie went out of the front door without looking at her.

'What's happened?' Ella asked.

It was Piers who answered her. 'The police think Bernie may be able to help them with the enquiries they're making about that killing on the golf course. He was up there that evening, you see.'

'Can't they talk to him here?'

'Exactly what I said,' Claudia said, crowding into the doorway behind Piers. She looked flushed and angry, and there was a shrill note in her voice. 'It's too ridiculous, insisting on him going to the police station. And I don't see why I can't go with him.'

'You can follow us in your own car if you like, madam,' one of the policemen said patiently. 'But if you do come you may have a long wait. Much better to stay with your friends or else in your own home. Of course, if you want to make a statement ...'

'A statement about what? I know nothing about that man who was killed and neither does my husband. And I warn you, he's a sick man. He had to go to the doctor only the other evening ... damn it, it was that night!'

The two policemen glanced at one another. 'No doubt we'll hear about that from Mr Caldicott,' one of them said.

'I must go with him,' Claudia said in a distracted way. 'Piers ...'

Bernie, waiting all this time in and half out of the front door, spoke to her over his shoulder. 'Go home, Claudia. You can be much better employed there. You'd better have my keys.'

'But what can I do?' Claudia asked in a confused way, taking the sizeable bunch of keys he held out to her.

'Use your head, for God's sake! Get on to Dr Denman. And call my solicitor. I'm not saying a word unless he's with me.'

He left, accompanied by the policemen, giving the inescapable impression of being under escort.

'I must put this tray down before I drop it,' Ella said. 'Claudia, do come and sit down.'

'I must go home.'

'Have a cup of coffee first. Come to that, why not stay here and wait for Bernie to telephone you when he's through?'

'No, I must go home.'

'I'll go with you, of course,' Piers said.

'No ... no, I'll be all right. I must make those telephone calls.'

'I'll do that for you. Have you got the numbers?'

'Yes, I think ... where's my bag?'

She found her address book and handed it to Piers.

'There's an emergency number for Dr Denman,' she said. 'You'd call this an emergency, wouldn't you?'

There was an hysterical note in her voice, but she sat quietly and was persuaded to drink a cup of coffee while Piers telephoned. The solicitor, it was obvious, was surprised, and none too pleased, to be contacted at home, but Bernie was a friend as well as a client and he agreed to go straight to the police station.

In spite of Claudia's protests, Piers insisted on driving her home in his car, leaving Bernie's BMW outside their house.

'And I thought Kits Harbour was such a peaceful backwater,' Toby remarked as the front door closed behind them.

'I don't know what to make of it,' Ella said, frowning. 'Surely they're making rather heavy weather of someone having been on a golf course where he's a regular player at around the time violence was being done?'

'That was my thought, too. There must be something more. It's a curiously late hour to be asking for a mere talk. I suspect they mean to keep him overnight.'

'There's nothing we can do,' Ella said uncertainly.

'No. Shall I help you get straight?'

They worked methodically and almost in silence until Ella switched on the dishwasher and said, 'There's nothing more I can do tonight. You've been a great help. I can see you're getting more domesticated by the day. Has Leah cleaned the flat satisfactorily?'

'Her work's okay, but I do feel the need of a chaperone.'

Ella laughed. 'I can well believe it.'

'Would you like me to stay until Piers comes back?'

'Who can tell what time that may be? Claudia may want him to stay with her.'

'I see,' and Ella thought that he did, indeed, see rather more of the situation with Claudia than she would like to put into words.

It was nearly midnight before she let Toby out of the house and an hour later before Piers came home. Ella had got ready for bed, but she was still downstairs, curled up on the sofa, with the radio playing very softly, when she heard his key in the lock. She jumped up and went into the hallway.

'What's happened?' she asked.

'I left Claudia, because that was what she wanted, but I went on to the police station. It seemed the least I could do. Everything was held up because Bernie wouldn't make a statement until his solicitor arrived, quite rightly in my opinion. His doctor came, too, and he insisted that Bernie couldn't be kept in a cell overnight.'

'Were they going to do that?' Ella asked, appalled. 'But why are they being so hard on him?'

'Because of the golf club.'

For one moment Ella thought wildly of the comfortable redbrick club house, then she realised what Piers meant.

'It was the murder weapon?'

'Yes, and the thing that makes me feel awful is that it wasn't even Bernie's club. It belongs to me. It just happened to be in the back of his Land Rover and Bernie took it out and used it more or less at random.'

'I don't understand.'

'His story is perfectly logical, if you aren't prejudiced, as the police obviously are. He'd been to a Rotary Club dinner and was driving home. He felt a bit off colour and he thought a bit of fresh air would do him good. His road home took him along the side of the golf course, so he parked his car, got out and did a bit of putting, up on the fifteenth hole. It was late, so there was no one about, but at this time of the year, up there in the open, it stays light until nearly eleven o'clock, light enough for him to play a few strokes anyway. Then he realised it was doing him no good, he hadn't got his heart pills with him, and he felt alarmed enough to get back in the Land Rover and drive straight to his doctor's house.'

'Leaving the golf club behind?'

'Of course.'

'But how did they trace it to Bernie? Come to that, how can it possibly be yours? Your clubs are where they always are, cluttering up the hall.'

'I don't play with those even though I take them with me each time because of your qualms,' Piers said impatiently. 'I'm talking about the set Bernie gave me. He always keeps them in the back of the Land Rover.'

'The ones that were supposed to have been stolen a couple of years ago,' Ella said evenly.

'That's right. Oh, I know you thought they'd been given up to the insurance company, but that was an entirely illogical thing to do.'

'You lied to me. You went out of your way to deceive me by carting the old clubs around.'

'Don't make a song and dance about it. This isn't the time to be splitting hairs about ethics, not when Bernie is in such trouble.'

Ella let it go. She had fought that battle and obviously she had lost it. What did puzzle her was Piers' continuing concern about Bernie.

'You still haven't told me how they made the connection to Bernie,' she said. 'The police haven't got his fingerprints on record, surely?'

She had spoken carelessly, almost flippantly, but she caught her breath when she realised that Piers was looking at her with distaste, even anger.

'There was something more,' he said reluctantly. 'Earlier today they found the dead man's wallet in the undergrowth some way away from his body. There was no money in it ...'

'So surely the motive was theft?'

'You would think so. But there was also a photograph. They showed it around at the club house – Bernie's livid about that – and, of course, it was identified immediately.'

'Bernie?'

'Yes. His golf club identified as the weapon that killed the

87

man, his photograph in the wallet; I suppose the police were justified in asking questions.

'But *here* ... how did they know he was here?'

'Claudia played a ladies' foursome this morning and she happened to mention that she'd be dining with us.'

'And, of course, that well-known hero, Captain Toby Greville.'

'Do you have to be so shrewish?'

Ella was silenced, knowing she had been unnecessarily acid.

'Bernie's perfectly innocent, of course. It's coming to something when a man can't get a breath of fresh air without being suspected of murder. It's up to his friends to stand by him. I've told Claudia that if he's up to playing our usual game of golf in the morning then I'm prepared to go round with him.'

'It's morning already,' Ella said wearily. 'We'd better get some sleep.'

Chapter Six

It was nearly three o'clock in the morning before Bernie got home and, because he had given his keys to Claudia, he had to ring the bell for her to let him in. She was still dressed, not in the slinky green dress she had worn for an evening out, but in a track suit that had seen better days.

'You look all in,' she exclaimed, taking in Bernie's exhausted air and grey face.

'I feel it. I could do with a drink.'

As she handed him a whisky and soda Claudia asked, 'What's the situation?'

'We got the police to admit there were no fingerprints on the golf club, it had been wiped clean. So there's nothing to connect me with the killing except that the club was mine.'

'Piers' really.'

'Out of my car and I've admitted using it that evening. They're trying to make something of the fact that I didn't come forward straight away to say I'd been there, but it was pointed out to them that they'd been cagey about what was used to hit the man and I played up my bad turn. They've got nothing on me, not really.'

'Except the photograph.'

'That, yes.'

'There's something you're not telling me,' Claudia said. 'Damn you, Bernie, you can't keep secrets from me, not after what I've done for you tonight.'

He gave her one quick, shamefaced look. 'You understood what I was trying to tell you?'

'Considering I had a perfectly good set of keys of my own

89

and that clumsy hint about being better employed at home, yes, I got the message: you thought the police might come nosing around and there were things you didn't want them to see.'

'What did you do?'

'I opened up the dark room, the only room I couldn't have got into without your own set of keys, and had a look round. Quite apart from anything else, there were pictures of me I didn't want pawed over by coppers.'

'There's nothing wrong with a man taking a few nude pictures of his wife. They were perfectly tasteful; beautiful, in fact.'

'All the same, I turfed them out. And the yellow folder in the bottom drawer of the filing cabinet.'

'Did you look at it?'

'I didn't need to. I've never been under any illusions about your secret photographic sessions, Bernie.'

'I did no harm,' he muttered. When Claudia made no comment, he asked, 'What did you do with the pictures?'

'There's a lot to be said for living in an isolated house if you want to do work in the garden late at night. I shredded them in the garden shredder, negatives and all, and one or two magazines I thought looked a bit iffy. Then I put the shreds of paper on the compost heap and worked them well in.'

'Clever.'

'Yes, I'm clever. And loyal. Not many wives would do as much for their husbands. And in return you can tell me the truth about the man who got his head bashed in.'

'I didn't kill him.'

'All right, so you didn't kill him, but you had some reason for being on the links besides wanting fresh air.'

'Practice ...'

'On the *fifteenth*? I can't remember when you took a stroke over par for that hole. You'll have to be more convincing than that.'

Claudia waited and eventually Bernie spoke, as she had known he would.

'I did go to meet him. He had some photographs of mine.'

'The same sort as I've destroyed this evening? How did he get hold of them?'

'The film was in that camera that was stolen. When it first

90

went missing I was worried, but nothing happened and I assumed the film had just been taken out and chucked away. I thought I was safe. Not that the pictures were actually *illegal* . . .'

'No under-age kids?'

'Certainly not!'

Claudia's mouth moved in a way that was both cynical and contemptuous. 'But not the sort of thing you'd put in the family photograph album?'

'Not exactly.'

'You're a bloody fool, but we've been through all that before. So he was blackmailing you?'

'I paid him two thousand pounds.'

'You should have gone to the police.'

'I thought I could clear it up on my own. Damn it, I did clear it up. He gave me the negatives and the set of prints he'd made and I drove off . . .'

'Leaving the golf club you'd been toying with behind?'

'Yes, that part of the story's completely true. He was a bit late for our meet and I was restless, so I fooled around on the green for a few minutes, then I dropped the club and forgot all about it. I stopped the car about a quarter of a mile down the road and burnt the photographs. That's when I began to feel queer. The smoke got on to my chest and I couldn't stop coughing. I thought I was going to pass out. I hadn't got my pills with me.'

'You never have unless I remind you.'

'I can't understand that film surfacing such a long time after the camera was stolen.'

'Perhaps it's only just been sold? Would the beastly little man have bought it?'

'Like a shot, I should imagine.'

'So the motive for the murder must have been theft. Two thousand pounds – in cash, I presume? Yes, of course, it would have to be. And no one has said he had money like that on him when he was found.'

'You're going to suggest I come clean to the police. Not likely! At the moment there's absolutely nothing to connect me to him except a blown up head and shoulders photograph of me, which I know, but haven't said, was taken from one of the

91

snaps in the camera. If I keep quiet it'll all blow over.'

'If the case isn't solved it'll always be hanging over your head. People will never be *sure*.'

'No one who knows me will ever believe I would bludgeon a man to death.'

Few people who knew him would believe that he had kinky sexual tastes. She had connived, she had turned a blind eye, had even participated in some of his games. There had been an excitement in it, something to tickle a jaded appetite, but even that had faded. The truth was, she was sick to death of Bernie, and now it looked as if he was getting them into real trouble, but she needed his money and nothing would persuade her to give up the lifestyle he provided.

'Let's get some sleep,' she said. 'Piers suggested you should golf with him as usual in the morning.'

'I intend to do just that.'

'Brazening it out? I suppose it's the only way. Oh, for God's sake let's leave it for tonight.'

When Piers arrived the next morning, driving Bernie's car, they were up, but only just. Claudia went to the front door, retying the sash of her satin kimono as she went, and was not pleased to see that Piers had brought Ella with him.

'I came to see if you were all right, if there was anything I could do?' Ella said. In the face of Claudia's hard self-sufficiency her generous impulse began to seem foolish. 'If not, I'll walk home along Kits Bay. Toby has taken the children out for the day.'

'I'm just going to have a shower,' Claudia said, with the clear indication that Ella would be in the way.

'Come in,' Bernie called out. 'I'm in the kitchen. Have some coffee with me.'

Piers accepted the coffee, but Ella refused. Claudia was standing in the doorway, looking unwelcoming, and she felt like an interloper. Bernie spread a slice of toast with butter and marmalade and bit into it. With his mouth full he said, 'Did I take that damn pill?'

There was an infinitesimal pause and then Claudia said, 'Of course you did.'

Bernie stood up, ready to go. 'What's the weather like? It looks great.'

'The wind's keen, better take a jacket,' Piers said.

It was Claudia who opened the hall cupboard and took out a blue anorak. Ella, standing a little way apart, saw her slip her hand into a pocket and caught a flash of bright colour as Claudia took something out and dropped it into her own kimono pocket. She held the anorak out to Bernie. 'I'll come up and join you later, same as usual,' she said.

There was nothing to stop Ella suggesting that, since the children were not at home, there was no reason why she, too, should not drive up and join them at the club house for a pre-lunch drink, especially since Piers was without his car and dependent on Bernie for a lift home. None of the others seemed to think of it and suddenly she knew that she could not face the crowd in the club house, the curious glances, the whispers. Let Bernie and Claudia and, come to that, Piers play the game of pretending there was nothing wrong. If they didn't want her support, and they showed no sign of wanting it, then she was just as pleased to take the coward's way out and walk away.

She stood with Claudia and watched the car drive away. Claudia turned back towards the house and, as she did so, something slipped out of the shallow pocket of her kimono, a little box, brightly enamelled. It hit the front door step and burst open and small white pills scattered on the gravel driveway.

Instinctively, Ella bent down to retrieve the box and as many of the pills as she could see.

'Don't bother,' Claudia said impatiently. 'Just my sweeteners, that's all. Have a nice walk, Ella.'

The tide was out. Ella went down the steps and on to the sand. It was rippled where the waves had passed over it and she had to skirt some slippery rocks, black and white hard flint, splashed with bright green seaweed. Apart from a man and a dog further along the beach she was alone. Kits Bay was not as popular as Harbour Bay, hidden from sight at this point by the curving arm of chalk cliff which separated the two beaches. She could, if she was prepared to scramble, and if the tide was low enough, get over the rocks at the edge of the water and into a tiny, secret bay otherwise reachable only by a dark flight of steps cut down the inside of the cliff. From there the walk home would be far quicker than if she retraced her steps and went back up the stairs at Kits Bay.

She took off her sandals and paddled bare foot through the pool of water at the edge of the rocks. A curl of foam tickled her ankles, a strand of seaweed wrapped itself round her calf, and she had to stoop to pull it away. Then she was in the bay and completely alone.

As she stood in the curve of the solitary beach Ella had a moment of intense happiness, but by the time she had walked across the dry sand, pulled her sandals on to her gritty feet and negotiated the dark, slippery stairs in the passage through the cliff, it had faded and she had remembered the horror of sudden death and the involvement of the man Piers, at least, considered to be his closest friend.

Bernie was easily annoyed, might even be said to have a quick temper, but Ella could not believe that he would so far forget himself as to strike a man down and kill him. And yet she sensed there was something wrong, just as she had always felt there was something suspect about Bernie. Piers would be loyal to him and there seemed to be nothing she could do but follow his lead.

Piers had lied to her about those golf clubs. An old lie, kept up for a couple of years. She was hurt, but not as hurt as she would once have been. Unconsciously, Ella straightened her shoulders and lifted her head as she emerged into the sunlight and the chilly wind. She would not dwell on it. The truth was, she was no longer sure whether it was her perhaps exaggerated moral stand over cheating the insurers or the fact that Piers' apparent acquiescence had represented a small victory over Bernie and Claudia that weighed most with her.

She was home in good time to prepare the salad lunch she and Piers were going to share; they had agreed to eat properly later when Toby brought the children home. Ella smiled as she thought of Toby. He had proved to be a real asset and she had the pleasant feeling that his stay in Kits Harbour had done him good. He had lost the look of strain he had had when he first arrived and she was sure he had put on some weight.

By half past two Ella was feeling aggrieved. True, she had not agreed an actual time with Piers, but there was an unspoken agreement between them that he would leave the golf club on Sundays no later than two o'clock. Of course, he had not taken his car, but had driven Bernie's, which meant that he was dependent on Bernie for a lift home.

As the minutes ticked by Ella began to wonder if there was anything wrong. At three o'clock she rang the Caldicotts' number, but there was no reply, only the answering machine. She put the telephone down without leaving a message, reluctant to let Claudia know that she was checking up on Piers. She could ring the club house, but if they were having a convivial time, celebrating some extraordinary feat on the greens, or even Bernie's release from police custody, Piers would not thank her for having him called to the telephone.

Twenty minutes later the telephone rang at last.

'Ella ...'

'Piers! I was getting worried. Is everything all right?'

'No ... no, something terrible has happened. Bernie ... he had a heart attack. Ella, Bernie's dead.'

For a moment Ella could do nothing but whisper, 'No, no.'

'We were right out on the tenth hole when he had a seizure. I yelled for help to the nearest people and then I left him and ran for the club house to call an ambulance. There was a doctor going round and they fetched him and he gave heart massage, but it was no good. By the time the ambulance reached us he was gone.'

'Piers, how dreadful. Claudia, where is Claudia?'

'She's here with me. I'm at their house. There was nothing we could do. She's distraught, completely laid out. I'll have to stay with her.'

'Of course. Is there anything I can do? Shall I come round?'

'No, I don't think so. The doctor's given her a sedative, a very strong one, because she was quite hysterical. I'll give you a call later, but I'll probably stay all night.'

When Ella put the telephone down she found that she was trembling. It had been a shock, even though she had not liked Bernie. How horrible to have to admit that when the man had only just died. Poor Bernie, he had never done her any harm, but he had monopolised far too much of Piers' attention and he had not been a good influence on him. Piers' 'easy come, easy go' attitude to money had owed a lot to his association with people who were far better off then he would ever be and, Ella suspected, not over-scrupulous about the way they gained their wealth. The trouble with Jennifer was over and forgotten, leaving nothing but a slight unease in Ella's relations with Bernie. Let him rest in peace, poor man. And poor Claudia. How would she cope without her husband?

'We don't have to go to Bernie's funeral, do we?' Harry asked.

'No, I don't see any need for that,' Ella said. 'I must go, of course, and Dad. Toby?'

'I hardly knew the man.' And liked him less, but he refrained from saying that. 'The kids and I will go off somewhere together.'

'That'll be fab,' Harry said. 'After the funeral will Dad come home?'

'If Claudia is all right.' Ella tried to keep her voice neutral, but the truth was she had hardly seen Piers since Bernie's death and she was beginning to be slightly irritated by the way he dropped in for a clean shirt and a quick word and then went back to Claudia again. Poor Claudia, she thought conscientiously. One really shouldn't grudge her the company of an old friend, if only the old friend had not been one's own husband and the father of three very demanding children who would have benefited from his presence in the house.

They were a little out of hand, unsettled by an atmosphere of unanswered questions and strange suspicions they did not quite understand. Jennifer, in particular, was inclined to be tearful. She had, she insisted, been Uncle Bernie's favourite and she was 'upset' by his death. There was a touch of self-importance about her tears, which the others were quick to jump on, and she was swiftly diverted when Verity said spitefully, 'If you're going into mourning, you can't very well parade up and down the High Street in a pink crinoline, can you?'

'Mum!' The look Jennifer turned on Ella was truly stricken. 'I can still wear my costume, can't I?'

'Of course, Uncle Bernie would have wanted you to do something that's for the good of the town,' Ella said, improvising rapidly.

In response to Toby's enquiring look, she added, 'Dickens Week. You know about our link with him, of course.'

'I'd forgotten,' he admitted. 'Are the children taking part?'

'Jennifer's been recruited to play the part of Little Em'ly as a child, from "David Copperfield", you know. People from the town take part in tableaux along the front and walk around in costume. She's very much looking forward to it.'

'And I'm helping back stage with the play. We're doing scenes from "Bleak House". And next year we're doing "Great Expectations" and I'm going to try for the part of Estella,' Verity said.

'As long as it doesn't interfere with your GCSE exams,' Ella agreed.

Their minds were momentarily diverted as they explained all about Dickens Week to Toby, for which she was thankful. It was difficult to know how much to tell them and she would have been glad of Piers' support. They knew, as everyone locally seemed to know, that Bernie had been questioned about the murder on the golf links. What was not common knowledge was that the police had turned up at his house with a search warrant and had been in the process of going through his possessions, particularly his photographic equipment, at the same time as Bernie had been having his fatal heart attack on the golf course. Presumably they had found nothing to link him with the murdered man since the case was still open.

Claudia had gone to pieces completely. She alternated between sitting around staring into space, as still and silent as a woman carved out of stone, and bouts of hysterical weeping. The one thing that seemed to give her any relief was Piers' continued presence and he would be staying with her until after the funeral.

For the funeral, at least, Claudia pulled herself together. She wore unrelieved black and rather too much make up, but she behaved with dignity and managed to speak a word of thanks to Bernie's many business associates who pressed about her with condolences. Piers was by her side, one hand under her elbow, protective and watchful.

Ella had an idea that he was not entirely pleased with her for not going into the same deep mourning as Claudia, but Ella had consulted her wardrobe, her bank balance and her personal preference and had decided that her navy blue winter coat over an admittedly old, but perfectly acceptable, navy skirt and jumper, was as sombre as she was prepared to go. She never wore a hat in the normal way, but she had made the concession of buying a velvet beret which disconcerted her by sliding gently upwards on her hair and had to be tugged down whenever she thought no one was looking at her.

The Caldicott family tomb had been opened up to receive Bernie's coffin, which was a surprise to Ella, who had expected a cremation, until Piers pointed out that the Caldicotts were a very old local family with a fine Victorian monument in the local churchyard.

As the congregation of mourners made their way out of the church after the Vicar and the coffin, Ella caught sight of someone at the back of the church whose presence really surprised her. What was Leah doing at Bernie's funeral service? She was wearing a duffle coat and a black chiffon scarf tied over her hair and her face was a picture of misery, streaked with tears and, Ella noticed, still showing nasty signs of bruising. For half a breath Ella hesitated, but Leah shrank back in the pew and turned her head away. Ella looked round for her in the churchyard, but Leah did not go to the graveside.

Chapter Seven

Toby's leave was coming to an end. Soon he would have to leave Kits Harbour, report back and see what the Red Cross had lined up for him after his long absence. Toby grimaced to himself; a spell as an administrator, that was what he foresaw, and it was by no means a welcome idea.

He had accomplished what he had come to Kits Harbour to do, made contact with Lucy's children, seen that they were all right; rather more than all right, damned lucky. Ella ... a dream of a girl. The kids could hardly have done better by way of a stepmother. If only Piers didn't blow it. He was as unsatisfactory as he had ever been, all charm and bonhomie, and as trustworthy as a snake. What was it with him and Claudia? True, she was his best friend's widow, and she had suffered a sudden bereavement which had shaken her to the core, but she clung to Piers in a way Toby thought exaggerated and he could see Ella was not happy about it.

Restlessly, Toby stood up. It was mid-afternoon and not the sort of day he wanted to spend indoors. There was a wind, but he was in the mood to welcome a stiff breeze blowing through him.

He ran down the stairs and out of the front door. Leah was in the basement, just letting herself in to her own flat, struggling to get her child's pushchair over the step.

'Give us a hand,' she demanded.

Toby could hardly refuse, but he would have been just as pleased to have avoided her. Leah was becoming a nuisance. He regretted having given her a key so that she could let herself into his flat to clean it. Now he could never be sure that he would not find her there when he returned home, ostensibly 'tidying up' or putting away in the kitchen some cleaning materials she claimed she had had to buy for him. He had taken to locking up his correspondence, not that there was anything particularly private about it, but he was reasonably sure Leah would read anything she found lying about.

Worst of all, she had given him strong hints that her sexual favours were available, and he was annoyed to find himself disturbed and unsettled, even though he was not in the least attracted to her and would not, he told himself, touch her with a bargepole.

He lifted the pushchair inside her flat, refraining from pointing out that this would have been unnecessary if she had unloaded her fat little boy. Toby felt sorry for the child, who never seemed to walk anywhere or play with any other children.

'I'm going to make a cup of tea. Come in and have one with me,' Leah suggested.

'Sorry, I'm in a hurry,' Toby said.

'You're always running away. Anyone'd think you were afraid of me.'

She laughed up at him, impudent and insinuating, but he was suddenly seized by the realisation that there was something pathetic about Leah. Surely she was thinner than she had been a week or two ago? The bruises on her face had faded, but she looked pale and drawn, with dark shadows beneath her eyes. The hand she laid on his arm was like a claw.

I don't want to get involved, Toby thought. Damn it, Leah is a girl who can look after herself.

Regretting every syllable, he said, 'Leah, are you all right? Is there anything wrong?'

'Nothing I won't snap out of. If you must know, I've put in for help with the rent and they're taking for ever to get it sorted out. I'm a bit short of the ready. How about giving me a bit on account? Or a nice little present? I'll make it worth your while.'

Toby felt in his wallet. 'I can give you ten pounds,' he said. 'It's not on account and I don't want anything for it.'

'Well, thanks! You couldn't make it twenty, I suppose?'

'No, I couldn't! I've left myself short as it is.'

He turned away, but his annoyance made him add, 'How is it that you need help with the rent now when you haven't before?'

'I had an arrangement that fell through,' Leah said sulkily. 'Don't rub it in. I could kick myself every time I think about it. How was I to know I'd be left high and dry if the silly pig died?'

'Your baby's father?'

'Nah. Not him! I'm not saying who it was, but you can take it from me I've been dropped right in it.'

Toby let it go. She had got ten pounds out of him and that, he decided, was all the cash and sympathy he was going to waste on Leah. What had she been hinting at? That someone who had died had been paying her rent? Piers might know, since it was his firm which managed the building. Not that Toby had any intention of questioning Piers about the unsatisfactory Leah. He could ask Ella.

Toby came to an abrupt halt in the middle of the High Street. He had meant to go for a blow along the front and here he was, his feet instinctively taking him up the hill. Towards Ella.

He turned and strode off in the opposite direction, down the hill and along the front, with the harbour below him on the left. If the tide was out he could walk all the way along the sand to Ramsgate and then come back along the top of the cliff or get a bus, as the mood took him.

He went down the steps and on to the sand. It was a bit wet, but it looked as if his walk would be feasible. He was well on his way, enjoying the tumbling waves crashing on the shore, tasting salt on his lips from the spray caught up by the wind, feeling the damp sand giving beneath his feet, when he saw another solitary walker coming towards him from the opposite direction.

He knew her even when she was some way off. There was no mistaking that long-legged stride, the way she dug her hands into the pockets of her jacket, the lift of her chin as she savoured the fresh cold air blown off the sea. She saw him, too, and took her hand out of her pocket to wave.

'I was on my way home, but I couldn't resist a few minutes by the sea,' she said. 'I'm feeling rather pleased with myself.

I've just landed a big new order. Come back with me and I'll give you a cup of tea to celebrate.'

'Well ...' Toby hesitated.

'Not if you're doing anything else, of course,' Ella said.

What else could he pretend to be doing? Did he want to pretend? Did he want to avoid the meeting? No, of course, he did not.

'How are things? Apart from the new order?' he asked.

'Oh, so-so. Piers has come back home, which is a bit of a relief. I know Claudia is an old friend, but I do think she's taken advantage of him lately. She doesn't seem to be able to make a decision without consulting Piers, and he's not even an executor of Bernie's Will.'

'Good for Bernie. He probably knew about Piers' lightfingered way with other people's money.'

Ella came to a halt. 'Toby, you mustn't talk about Piers like that to me.'

Toby stood looking out to sea. 'I don't like him. I never have. He ran Lucy ragged. And now you.'

'I'm managing. This isn't something I'm going to discuss with you. It's entirely between me and Piers.'

'Do you still love him?'

'We've been married two years. We're no longer starry-eyed, but, yes, of course I still love him.'

He turned to face her and she looked at him with her chin raised, her mouth set in an obstinate line. As their eyes met she said, 'It wasn't a question you had any right to ask.'

'No. Very well, a change of subject. Who, do you think, has been paying Leah's rent?'

'Goodness, how should I know? Her baby's father was supposed to have been a schoolboy even younger than she was, so I don't imagine she's ever had any support from him. What makes you ask?'

'She touched me for ten quid and she said she'd had an arrangement about her rent which had come to an end because the man died. At least, she described him as "the silly pig", but I presumed she meant a man.'

'The building belongs ... belonged ... to Bernie.'

'Lord! I never thought of him.'

'I wish I hadn't.'

102

'Was there ever anything between them? I mean, if he was letting her live there rent free ...'

'I don't want to know. Are you coming home for that cup of tea?'

'Yes, please. I want to see the kids. It won't be long before I have to leave.'

'You're not looking forward to it, are you?' Ella asked as they began to walk towards the cliff steps from which he had just come.

'I still feel the same as I did when I left the Army: I want to do something to help. I'm a bit doubtful about what kind of job I may be offered.'

'Surely the Red Cross will be pleased to have you back?'

'There's a slight feeling my team shouldn't have got itself captured, a hint that my Army background might have made me take risks, which actually is something no good soldier would do unnecessarily. I'm standing out for another mission in the field, but I may be offered a more deskbound job.'

'Which you wouldn't want.'

'Not unless I was offered an inducement to settle down.'

Ella tucked a companionable hand through his arm. 'A proper home of your own. What you need is a wife to boost your morale. Don't you know any nice girls, Toby?'

'Not many. Not nice ones.' He had meant to hold his tongue, but now he went on recklessly. 'The girl I want is married to someone else.'

Ella took her hand away and began to climb the steps. 'I'm sorry about that,' she said.

'Don't pretend you don't know what I mean.'

She turned her head to look over her shoulder at him. 'No, I don't know,' she said. 'I haven't the faintest idea what you're talking about. It's time you left Kits Harbour, Toby.'

'I want to go, but I'm tied hand and foot. I'm helpless. I can't leave.'

'The children will be home from school.' Ella left him standing and ran up the rest of the steps.

'I can't leave *you*,' Toby said to the empty air.

He was afraid she would drive away without him, in spite of her invitation, but she was waiting in the car when he reached the cliff top. She looked completely composed, almost as if she had really not understood what he had been trying to say down on the seashore, but that was because Ella had already made up her mind that the only way she could deal with Toby's attraction to her was to pretend it did not exist.

It was a reaction to his long ordeal, she told herself. It had been a mistake to encourage him to spend his leave in Kits Harbour. It was too quiet, too restricted in its social contacts; he had had little opportunity to meet girls who might have been a pleasant distraction for him. Instead, with her mind on the benefit to the children of having an uncle who took an interest in them, she had taken him into the family circle and filled him with a romanticised view of domestic life. He seemed to look on her as some sort of saint, long-suffering and noble – that was what he had called her once – noble, whereas Ella knew all too well that inside she was a seething mass of impatience and resentment.

She totally distrusted Claudia's influence on Piers. Every day she dreaded to hear that he had been persuaded to throw up his job and take over the management of Bernie's business which, in Ella's opinion, would be a disaster. Piers coped very well with an established routine, a business which depended to a certain extent on his ability to get on with people, and an experienced staff to back him up. He was not the man to head up a complicated business empire of property and garden centres.

Bernie's death had been deeply upsetting and one of its worst aspects, in Ella's opinion, was that it left open the question of his possible involvement in the murder of the man on the golf links. They still knew so little. The dead man had lived locally, had had a business which brought him in contact with people, developing films, selling cameras, attending weddings, taking studio portraits, and yet there was little information about his life outside the shop. Ella had even been into the shop, closed now, to buy the occasional film. She remembered him as a middle-aged man with sparse hair, combed across his head to hide his baldness, and an over-obliging manner; a bit of a creep, in fact. She knew no harm of him; neither did anyone else, it seemed. Piers had said, without any particular interest, 'Pity the shop's closed; it was a good place to pick up a cheap camera and I've been thinking of getting a

104

camcorder', which made Ella thankful that the shutters had been closed on that particular project.

As they drove towards Jemima Road, Toby asked, 'Am I being given the silent treatment as a punishment for stepping over the mark or are you really lost in thought?'

'My mind is wandering,' Ella said. 'Do you think I should let Verity take her boyfriend up to her bedroom so that they can do their homework together?'

'Provided they keep the door open.'

'Verity says I have a prurient mind.'

'I presume you've given her all the usual warnings?'

'And then some! Verity's always been the quiet conformable one. I never bargained on her turning into a teenage rebel.'

'I haven't seen any signs of it.'

'She has a deep well of silent obstinacy, very trying and very difficult to cope with.'

'What's the boy like?'

'A wimp, but I suspect he might be the sort of wimp who makes an unexpected pounce to prove that he's not a wimp.'

'Shall I offer a few lessons in self defence?'

'I could provide those,' Ella retorted. 'I used to be quite a judo expert. I used it on Bernie once ... oh, God, Bernie! My mind keeps going back to him and that damned murder. We're not really involved and yet it hangs over us. The golf club that killed the photographer man was one that Piers used every week and that's a horrible thought.'

'Piers' fingerprints weren't on it, I take it?'

'It was wiped completely clean and that's one thing that almost entirely convinces me that Bernie wasn't guilty. I can imagine him snatching up the nearest weapon and lashing out and killing someone by accident, but then I think he'd have been overcome by remorse and would have rushed off to get help for the poor victim. I just don't see him being cool enough to wipe away his fingerprints and drive off.'

They had arrived at the house in Jemima Road. He had ten minutes, perhaps a quarter of an hour, of her undivided attention before the children descended on them. Not that he ever had her undivided attention. Part of her mind was always occupied by family problems; the next meal, an order for preserves, what time Piers was likely to be home.

105

'Do you ever think about yourself?' Toby asked as he followed her into the house.

'All the time. Right now I'm thinking that instead of wasting time walking on the beach I ought to have gone and got my hair cut.'

'It looks fine to me.'

Ella shook her head so that the strands of hair flew out round her head. 'No shape, no style.'

She went very still as Toby's hand touched the side of her head, his fingers combing through her hair and coming to rest at the nape of her neck. As he drew her towards him with an inexorable pressure, Ella doubled up her fists against his chest in a vain attempt to hold him at bay.

'No, Toby,' she said, but it came out in a breathless whisper, not at all the forceful refusal she had intended.

Toby took no notice. He found her lips, but it was a botched, unsatisfactory kiss because Ella wrenched her head to one side.

'Let me go,' she said.

'Don't try your judo tricks on me. I might break your neck.'

'The brutal and licentious soldiery,' Ella said. For a moment she let her hand sink down on his shoulder with her forehead pushed against his chin and they stood very still.

'I wouldn't hurt a hair on your unshorn head,' Toby said unsteadily. 'I love you.'

'No.'

'Yes. Look up, Ella, sweet Ella, my own dear, darling Ella.'

She tilted back her head to look up into his face with an expression of such anguish that Toby caught his breath.

'Don't look like that! Ella, please ...'

He closed his eyes and sought her lips blindly and this time she did not resist him, but clung to him, responding unreservedly to the pressure of his lips and the delicate touch of his tongue. It was not until Toby shifted to bring his body still closer to hers that Ella tried to disengage herself.

Reluctantly, Toby let her go and Ella moved away, her head swimming, until she came to rest with her hand on the wooden table.

'Can you wonder I worry about my teenage stepdaughter when a grown woman can't be trusted in her own kitchen?' she said unsteadily.

106

'Tell me you love me.'

'No. No, I won't do that.' Ella took a deep breath, steadying herself. 'Just for a moment I allowed myself the luxury of leaning on someone instead of being the perpetual propper-up. You're an attractive man, Toby Greville, and, as you've found out, I'm as susceptible as the next woman. There's nothing more to it than that.'

'You lie in your teeth, my darling.'

'That's what you want to believe. I'll stick to my version. Think, Toby, think! There's no future for us, neither as a temporary arrangement nor as anything more permanent. I can't have an affair with my husband's brother-in-law.'

There was a crash as the front door burst open.

'I can't face them. I'm going into the garden,' Ella said desperately.

She ran out of the back door, making for the herb garden she had established in a sunny patch on the far side, and began plucking leaves, mint and rosemary, marjoram and sage, none of which she needed for the meal that evening. She held her posy up to her nose and breathed in the clean, medicinal aroma. Slowly, the world began to right itself. What she had said to Toby was no more than the truth. There could be nothing between them. There was nothing between them. A moment's madness. Damn it, she was thinking like a maudlin soap opera. Come on, Ella, pull yourself together. Be noble! Go and get the children's tea ready.

She had no sooner set foot in the kitchen than Harry announced, 'I've decided to be a vegetarian.'

'Oh, great! That's all I needed. I'm sorry, twenty-four hours notice is required for a radical change in diet. Tonight you eat the same as the rest of us.'

'I can't put off my principles. I've made up my mind and I want to start *now*.'

'I knew this would happen as soon as I heard Sally Slocombe was teaching you. Mathematics! I ask you, what has diet to do with mathematics? But she drags her propaganda into everything.'

'It's not propaganda,' Harry protested. 'We had an interesting discussion and it all makes sense to me. We ought not to exploit the animal kingdom ...'

'The king of the animals is reckoned to be the lion, and you can't get more carnivorous than that,' Verity remarked.

'Oh, very funny! I might have known no one would understand.'

'Cool it, Harry,' Ella said. 'Make me a list of what you feel you can eat and I'll do my best to accommodate you.'

'I've got a leaflet.'

'I should have known. As long as it includes fish, cheese, eggs and dairy products, I won't quarrel with it, but for a growing boy, especially one who sees himself as a star of the football field, protein is essential, in my opinion.'

'I can have beans and things,' Harry said vaguely.

'I've said I'll do what I can. Now, out from under my feet all of you. Go and do your homework or take Uncle Toby down the garden or something.' She looked at Toby with a wry smile. 'The real world,' she said. 'It insists on breaking in.'

She was still feeling ruffled when Piers came home later. Toby had refused her offer of an evening meal and taken himself off with no more than one long look at her which Ella had done her best to ignore.

Piers bent over and brushed her cheek with his lips, a meaningless gesture conveying no more than a mild affection. Where had it all gone, the sweetness and the passion? Dissipated, not in one big wave of disillusionment, but in the endless tiny disappointments that accumulated day by day.

'I'm tired,' she said.

'Had a hard day?'

'A hard day, a hard week, a hard month, a hard year. I need a holiday, Piers.'

'Bernie's death ...'

'Yes, I know. It disrupted all our plans.'

'Incidentally, I wondered if you'd like this, as a memento of him.' He felt in his pocket and brought out a small gold box, a modern piece, enamelled in bands of brilliant colour. 'Bernie kept his heart pills in it, the ones he didn't have with him when he had his attack. Claudia can't bear to have it around; understandably, I suppose. She asked me to get rid of it.'

'She didn't suggest you gave it to me?' Ella asked, her eyes fixed on the bright little box. An unwelcome recollection came back to her and with it a horrible suspicion. Claudia taking something out of Bernie's anorak pocket, Claudia dropping a box, this box, and pills spilling out of it. But Claudia wouldn't ... would she?

'I'd rather not have it,' she said. She sought for a reasonable excuse for her refusal. 'Too personal.'

'I know what you mean,' Piers agreed.

'Has Claudia reached any decision about the future yet?' Ella asked, her mind still on the implications of that small box.

Piers turned away and when he spoke it was with just sufficient carelessness to alert Ella to the fact that he was hiding something.

'She intends selling the garden business, but she'll keep the various properties for the sake of the income, and they'll be managed for her as they were for Bernie.'

'You're not involved?'

'No more than I have been in the past, through my firm.'

That was a relief, but Ella was still uneasy. 'Is she staying in the house?' she asked.

'As to that, I don't know, I'm not sure. She has some idea of going to Spain.'

'You don't mean permanently?'

From Ella's point of view that sounded like a remarkably good idea. With Claudia and Bernie – poor Bernie, she added conscientiously – out of the way there might be a chance of having Piers to herself, something she had never experienced in the whole of her married life. Perhaps even yet they could resurrect their marriage and make it into what she had always wanted, a partnership of equals irradiated by passionate love.

'She might decide to settle there,' Piers admitted. 'She wants to go out for a short visit to help her make up her mind, but she's finding it difficult to nerve herself to go on her own. I might take a few days off and go with her.'

In a reasonable way, totally at variance with the surge of anger inside her, Ella said, 'Perhaps Claudia would like a woman's company for a change. Why don't I go to Spain and you stay home and look after the family?'

'My job ...' Piers said automatically.

'If you can take time off for a holiday abroad, you can surely be spared for a few hours a day for domestic reasons.'

'Claudia needs a man to help her.'

'Her and me both! Damn it, Piers, I've been endlessly patient. I know Claudia's had a rough time, I've made allowances for your long friendship, but the idea of her not being capable of getting herself to Spain and making up her own mind whether she wants to stay there is ludicrous.'

'You've never lost a husband – or a wife. You don't know what it's like.'

There was sufficient truth in this to leave Ella hesitating for a reply. Besides, what was the use of fighting? If Piers had made up his mind to go to Spain then Piers would go to Spain.

'Is she paying your fare?' she asked nastily.

'We haven't discussed it, but I dare say she will, as a business arrangement. I shall be advising her.'

'On what? On how to spend her money?'

'On whether to invest in property in Spain. Fortunately, the villa has always been in her name.'

'Lucky old Claudia. I'll just make myself quite clear and then we'll drop it: I do not want you to go to Spain with Claudia. Understood?'

'I hear what you say, but I can't pretend to understand your attitude,' Piers said stiffly. 'Surely you can spare a little sympathy for a woman who's been so cruelly bereaved?'

'I've said I don't want to talk about it any more, not now, but I do suggest you let Claudia know how I feel. Oh, I almost forgot, there's a letter for you from your mother. Take it away and read it while I grind some glass for your evening meal.'

She wished she had not made that exasperated remark when Piers came back into the kitchen ten minutes later with his mother's letter in his hand and a shocked look on his face.

'Mum says Dad's really bad,' he said. 'Sinking fast, according to her. She wants me to go up there.' He gave the sheet of paper an irritated shake. 'Why on earth didn't she telephone?'

'Ring her now and arrange a visit,' Ella suggested.

'I suppose I must.'

It was a grudging response, but Ella was relieved that Piers was prepared to do his duty, particularly after she had spoken to her mother-in-law and realised how near death was to the father-in-law she had never met.

'Do you want me to come with you?' she asked Piers.

'What about the children?'

'Nora Becker will come and stay with them, I'm sure.'

With her network of local friends, Ella had had no difficulty in establishing a group of suitable babysitters; she only wished that she had had more occasion to use them.

'Leave it until I've seen the situation for myself,' Piers decided. 'If anything happens ...'

'I think it's more a case of "when".'

'I'm afraid you're right. I'll go into the office tomorrow morning and leave straight from there around lunchtime. I'll give you a ring in the evening.' Piers sighed. 'This is going to eat into the time I was hoping to spend in Spain.'

With a supreme effort Ella stopped herself from retorting 'Good!' Instead, she went to check that Piers had sufficient clean shirts and underclothes to carry him over a few days away, and then she dished up the evening meal and spent an heroic evening discussing nothing more controversial than the route Piers would take to the north and whether, if she joined him, she should take her car or travel by train.

Piers' father died thirty-six hours after his son had arrived at the family home.

'Mum's bearing up well,' Piers reported to Ella over the telephone. 'In many ways it's a relief that it's all over.'

'One says that, but it doesn't really lessen the grief, not at first,' Ella said, out of her own experience. 'You won't be coming home between now and the funeral?'

'I think I'd better stay. And you?'

'I can leave tomorrow. I've got the arrangements all set up.'

'Mum will be pleased. She seems to want you.'

Someone else wanted Ella, too. Toby was blankly astonished that she would not be around for the last few days of his visit to Kits Harbour.

'Have I got to say goodbye to you *now*?' he asked when she telephoned him.

'There won't be time in the morning. I'm catching an early train to London.'

'But, not to see you. Ella, we can't part like that.'

'It's for the best. And it's not for ever. You'll be back, preferably with a nice girlfriend, or even a wife.'

'That's not likely.'

'Keep an eye on the children for the time that remains.'

'I'll do that, but it's you I want to see.'

'Goodbye, Toby.'

She put down the telephone and stood for a moment with her forehead against the wall. Goodbye, Toby, she thought. If I had met you at another time I might have loved you, and what a different life that would have been. I mustn't let myself regret the choice I made, that will only lead to bitterness. There's still time to pick up the pieces and make a good marriage out of what Piers and I have. I'm going to fight, I'm determined to keep him. I can't afford to indulge in romantic dreams about what might have been. Goodbye, Toby.

It helped that Mrs Armitage received her like the daughter she needed to see her through the difficult passage between the death and the funeral. She asked Ella to pack up her late husband's clothes, to write letters to people who might want to come to the church, and together they set up the plates of cold meat and salad Mrs Armitage thought it appropriate to offer to those who came back to the house afterwards.

They stayed until the day after the funeral. Ella offered to take Mrs Armitage back to Kits Harbour, but she was adamant that she wanted to be in her own house.

At Ella's suggestion they left quite late in the day and stayed a night at a hotel. It was only a small break, but mercifully they could now afford the occasional indulgence and she felt that time alone together would be valuable.

Piers was a silent companion, which was not like him, but their dinner *à deux*, with a good bottle of wine, and the warm comfort of their room, seemed to help him to relax.

As they undressed he suddenly said, 'Poor old Dad. I wish you'd known him as he was a few years ago. He was the life and soul of any party and he and Mum were champion dancers.'

It was not the image Ella had formed of his parents and she was interested.

'Oh, yes, they were very social, in a quiet, local way,' Piers said. 'Dad was a great one for joining things – Rotary, Masons, British Legion. Once I was grown up I thought it was pretty grotty, but they enjoyed themselves. It came hard on both of them when all that was curtailed.'

He turned away and in an unexpected gesture drew the back of his hand across his eyes.

'Don't be afraid to grieve,' Ella said gently. 'It's only natural. Come here, my dear, and let me comfort you.'

She lifted the bedclothes and he lay down beside her. She held him quietly in her arms, kissing him softly, until Piers gave a convulsive shudder and clutched her to him.

'You're so good to me,' he muttered, with his lips against her ear. 'Don't be so *good*, Ella.'

'We may have our differences – who doesn't? – but I'll always be here for you when it matters,' Ella promised.

He shut her mouth with a fierce kiss and his hands began to move over her body. They made love with an intensity and a completeness that had been lacking for longer than Ella cared to remember.

Afterwards, as they lay quietly together, Ella found herself smiling into the darkness. This was what they had needed, time together, an opportunity to renew the love they had first brought to their marriage. It had been so sweet; it was not possible for this piercing pleasure to be mislaid under the trivial misunderstandings of everyday life.

'Darling, are you awake?' she whispered.

Piers stirred lazily by her side. 'Mm, just.'

'Listen, there's something I've been thinking about, no, more than that, longing for. We've been married two years, things are on an even keel, the children have accepted me, and we've just shown how much we still love one another. You know, I told you before we married, how much I want a child of my own. Don't you think now is the time? I'm thirty-one, I don't want to leave it much longer.'

She felt his slight recoil and she was disappointed when all he said was, 'What about your business?'

'I can do some stockpiling. Getting pregnant won't happen overnight, not even after such a night as this. My system will have to sort itself out after I come off the pill, but some time during the coming year, I do want to feel I've got that hope in front of me.'

'It'll be a big upheaval.'

'No more than we can cope with.' Disturbed by his lack of enthusiasm, Ella raised herself up on one elbow and leaned over him, wishing she could see his expression. 'I know it's a bit hard on you, having to go through the baby years all over again, but think how rewarding it will be – and how happy it'll make me.'

'Yes.'

'Does that mean "Yes, darling Ella, I'll do my best to make you a mother?"'

'It means come off the pill and we'll see what happens.'

'That's all I ask.' She snuggled down beside him, serenely sure that once the longed-for baby was on the way she could coax him into being as thrilled as she would be herself.

Chapter Eight

Leah was worried. She sat hunched up over the kitchen table, twisting an end of her wiry hair round her fingers and scowling at a sheet of paper scrawled with figures in front of her. She was getting benefit to help with paying her rent, but while she had been waiting for the money to come through she had run up debts she could not now afford to repay. Never get into the hands of the loan sharks, she'd heard it said often enough, and now here she was, up to her ears, just because she'd listened to that bloody fool, Jo, who lived the sort of hand-to-mouth existence Leah despised, and been talked into taking a loan that sounded like a good deal until you started paying the interest.

Toby had gone and with him the small, but regular, income Leah had enjoyed for cleaning his flat, not to mention the convenience of being able to pop in when she knew he was out for half a jug of milk, a bit of tea or coffee, a few biscuits and an occasional egg. Toby had never commented; Leah doubted whether he had noticed the swiftness with which his marmalade disappeared or the frequency with which she had replaced cleaning materials. She despised him, as she despised everyone she was able to trick, but she did miss him and his useful mini-market on the top floor.

Nothing would make her approach her parents. Leah shuddered at the memory of the last time she had seen her father, his face contorted with rage, his hand raised against her.

There was that suitcase he had left with her after he'd done the Caldicotts' house. She had taken it for granted that he had removed everything from it, and the suitcase had remained

115

undisturbed in the cupboard where he had first hidden it.

Leah hauled it out, sneezing at the cloud of dust that came with it. Damien, now a sturdy four-year-old – she'd be able to get him into school next year, thank goodness – came stomping out from the kitchen to see what was going on.

'Get out of my way,' she snapped at him.

'I help.'

'No, you won't. Keep away, it's dirty.'

The case itself was a good one, she might be able to get a pound or two for that. The thought cheered her, although a pound or two would go nowhere towards reducing her load of debt. When she got it open it appeared to be empty. Trust Dad for that, she thought sourly; she ought to have known he wouldn't leave anything behind.

In spite of what she had said, Damien crept nearer and began to play with the open suitcase. He climbed inside it and began to rock, pretending it was a boat.

'Don't ruin it,' Leah said. 'I'm going to sell it.'

Interestedly, Damien began exploring the elasticated pockets. 'Pretty thing,' he said approvingly, holding up something that caught the light and sparkled.

'Here, give me that.'

Leah snatched it from him. It was a diamond ring, a good one, three big stones set in gold. How had her father come to overlook that? She guessed how it had been, a handful of jewellery hurriedly snatched, stuffed into a convenient suitcase, stowed away for years on end while he was waiting for the theft to be forgotten, then another period while he was in prison: he might not even have known he'd got it.

Damien was pulling at her hand, trying to get his pretty thing back from her.

'Stop that,' Leah ordered. 'You can't have it. It's mine. And I'm going to sell it for lots and lots of money.'

The question was, where? Nowhere too local where there was a risk of her being recognised as Reg Daley's daughter. They might alert the police. Even worse, a local purchaser might get in touch with her father, where ever he was, and then she really would be in trouble.

Leah sat back on her heels and considered the problem. She had to look as if she might have a diamond ring for sale, that meant taking a bit of trouble with her appearance, and parking Damien with one of her girlfriends: it was no use going into a respectable jeweller's with a grubby brat in tow. She would sell the suitcase first. Then, with that money, she would buy something suitable to wear from the Hospice Shop. Something dull and respectable, Leah thought scornfully, and she would resist the temptation to cut six inches off the hemline, at least until after she had completed her mission.

She got twelve pounds for the suitcase, and saw it on sale in the junk shop a few days later for twenty. Twisting lot, she thought. It made her anxious about the amount she could expect to get for the windfall ring.

In a wine-coloured dress that covered her knees, a tweed jacket with a red fleck in it which was a little shabby but obviously good of its kind, and, the most telling touch, her springy hair bundled away in a loose plush beret, Leah looked so different she might almost have been in disguise.

'Where the heck you off to?' her friend Jo asked when Leah left Damien with her.

'Canterbury.'

'What, going to the cathedral, or something?'

'I might, I just might, have come into a small legacy,' Leah said grandly. At that moment she almost convinced herself that it was true.

'G'on! You'll be all right for a small sub when you come back, then?'

'I need every penny of it to get me out of the mess you helped me into,' Leah retorted. 'I might bring back a cake for your tea, but that's all.'

She caught a bus into Canterbury, which was slow but the cheapest way she could go. She had a plan of which she was secretly proud. She found a jeweller's shop and went in. The young man behind the counter sized her up as a customer wanting a silver chain or a watch strap and was surprised when she produced the ring.

'It's been left to me and I want to know how much it's worth so that I can insure it properly,' Leah said.

'How much was it valued at for probate?' the assistant asked.

That shook Leah, who knew nothing about the process of

117

administering a dead person's estate, but with only the briefest pause she invented an answer. 'Eight hundred pounds,' she said.

'We don't really do valuations, not across the counter.'

'But it's only one ring and there's no one else in the shop.'

'Well . . . all right.' He screwed a glass into his eye. 'They're good diamonds. I'd say it was undervalued at eight hundred, but that's not unusual for probate purposes. I think you ought to insure it for two thousand.'

'Wow!' Leah managed to suppress some of her elation, but not all of it.

'Of course, that's for insurance. You'd get a lot less if you sold it,' the young man added hastily.

'I'm not going to sell it,' Leah lied. 'What I'd really like is a proper box to keep it in. Do you sell those?'

'We've got some nice red leather ones at fourteen pounds.'

He must be joking! 'No, they're much too big,' Leah said.

She was determined to present the ring properly when she really tried to sell it and eventually tracked down a minute snap-top purse in a toy shop which set her back less than a pound. She spent a little time roughing it up, rubbed it with dust and dulled the clasp by sucking it so that it did not look so brassy. Clasping and unclasping it in her hand so that it took on a creased and shabby look, Leah was pleased with the finished effect.

This time she went to a better class jeweller's shop and said immediately that she wanted to sell her ring.

'It was left to me by my father,' she said, fixing the salesman, an older man this time, with a candid gaze. She made use of the lesson she had learned at the first shop. 'It was valued for probate at twelve hundred pounds, although I was told I ought to insure it for more than that.'

It was a fine ring. Twelve hundred pounds was not an unreasonable valuation for it. All the same, he hesitated, not anxious to buy over the counter from someone he did not know, and not as impressed by Leah's new image as she would have liked. He cast his mind over the most recent list of stolen property he had seen. There was nothing on it he could recollect that reminded him of this ring, nor were there any identifying marks on the inner surface.

118

He decided to take a chance. 'I could offer you nine hundred pounds,' he said.

Leah shook her head. 'I couldn't possibly let it go for less than the probate valuation,' she said, trying to sound as if she knew what she was talking about. What the hell *was* a probate valuation when it was at home and in bed?

'Twelve hundred pounds? It depends on how you want to be paid. If you can take a cheque I might go up to one thousand.'

He had expected her to hesitate, but Leah had her answer ready.

'I would drop to eleven hundred if you'd make the cheque out to the Helping Hand Finance Company,' she said.

So that was why she needed the money. The jeweller felt a twinge of sympathy for her.

'A thousand and fifty, and I'd want a receipt from you explaining the transaction. I don't want to be associated with that lot.'

On that basis they struck a bargain. The jeweller knew he had paid rather less than their true value for some stones that might be worth taking out of their setting and selling on separately, and Leah was elated because she had never really expected to get into four figures.

The important thing was to get the loan paid off as quickly as possible. When her bus came she took a ticket right through to Ramsgate, found the battered door which concealed her 'finance company' and climbed the stairs. It was a wrench to part with her new riches. She watched resentfully as the cheque disappeared, forgetting that she had no right to the money it represented.

She felt in her purse when she got out into the street once more. If she was going to take the promised cake back to Jo, she would have to walk home, all the way along those dreary cliffs. She hesitated, but pride made her dive into the nearest bakery and select a squishy cake for their tea. She hadn't even had any lunch, and her a rich woman dealing in diamonds.

She was walking towards the seafront when she saw Ella in front of her. Leah eyed her back speculatively. She had never been on really good terms with Ella, not since the prissy bitch had given her the push for frightening the kids, but she might be good for a lift if handled right.

119

Leah lengthened her stride, resenting the way her skirt flapped against her legs. 'Hello, Mrs Armitage,' she said.

Ella, her thoughts miles away, turned her head and blinked, almost not recognising Leah in her unusual clothes.

'Leah! How are you? You look very smart.'

She would think so, Leah thought scornfully. Smart was the last thing she felt, tarted up like a dog's dinner in a frumpish outfit that would have suited her mother.

'I had to go and do some business in Canterbury.'

Ella tried to imagine what business Leah could have in the cathedral town, and failed. 'Where's Damien?' she asked.

'I parked him with my friend Jo.' Her face darkened. 'It's all Jo's fault that I got myself in a mess with a loan shark and I've had to sell something to pay off the loan. Not that it is paid off, not all of it. Do you know that they charge you interest and then, if you don't keep up, they charge you interest on the interest?'

'I've heard about it,' Ella admitted.

'Any chance of a lift home? I haven't even got enough left to pay my bus fare.'

Ella could hardly refuse. She was tempted to remark on the cake box Leah was carrying, but she held her tongue and was glad she had said nothing when Leah went on, 'I promised Jo a cake for tea if she looked after Damien for me, which was a daft thing to do when I'm so skint. I could walk, but my feet hurt.'

The pathetic quality Toby had noticed suddenly struck Ella, too. Suppose this were Verity? Not that Verity would ever end up in such a mess, Ella thought hurriedly, but suppose ...? 'Of course I'll give you a lift,' she said. 'I've left my car in the supermarket car park.'

'Have you still got shopping to do?'

'No, I did it and then went to the Dash shop to see if they'd got anything cheap and cheerful in my size.'

'I got these things at the Hospice Shop,' Leah said, putting Ella's sortie into the reduced-price clothes shop into perspective.

'Good for you!' Ella said cheerfully, refusing to get the point. 'You really do look very nice.'

'Glad you think so,' Leah said.

She subsided thankfully into Ella's car and slipped her feet out of the shoes she was wearing instead of her usual trainers.

'Toby's gone then,' she remarked.

It grated, hearing Leah refer to him so casually by his Christian name. Ella suppressed her irritation and agreed quietly that Toby had indeed gone.

'I miss him,' Leah said with a sigh. She rather hoped that Ella would assume that there had been more between her and Toby than the cleaner-and-employer relationship, but Ella knew better than that. 'Where's he going next?' Leah asked.

'He's reported back to his headquarters for orders,' Ella said.

Talking grand, the silly cow. Reported back to headquarters for orders, Leah repeated inside her head. She sounded just like what she used to be, a schoolteacher.

At the back of her mind, Ella had been thinking about Leah's debt situation. 'This loan you had, did you know there was an organisation which will help you get out of difficulties?'

'I don't want anyone interfering in my business.'

'But if you've paid off the principal ...'

'What's that?'

'The actual loan.'

'Oh, yeah, I've done that.'

'And they're still charging you interest?'

'On what they say I didn't keep up with. It doesn't sound right to me.'

'Nor to me. If the rate of interest was exorbitant – too high – they might be able to get it wiped out. Otherwise, from what you say, it'll just mount up and up and you'll soon be no better off again.'

And no more diamond rings. What she said was all too true. 'Where is this place then?' Leah asked.

'I'll find the address and put it through your door.'

In a few minutes they reached Jo's bed-and-breakfast place. Leah scrambled out. 'If I let you have the address of the Debt Management people, you will make use of it, won't you?' Ella asked.

'Yeah, prob'ly,' Leah said. 'Can't do no harm.'

No words of thanks for the lift, Ella noted, as she prepared to drive away.

121

'Money doesn't go far these days – now that my rent isn't being paid,' Leah said.

She slammed the car door and turned away. As Ella glanced over her shoulder to check that it was safe to pull out from the curb she caught a glimpse of a smirk on Leah's face. She had made that last remark deliberately, intending Ella to understand something from it. Ella remembered that she and Toby had spoken about Leah's mysterious benefactor. Bernie? Could it have been? And did it matter? Not to Ella, she decided.

She wished that Leah had not started her thinking about Toby. Not that she hankered after him, not now that she had patched things up so satisfactorily with Piers. There was no real reason for the little ache of regret she felt when ever his name was mentioned. She was not going to let him turn into one of life's 'if onlys', she decided, even if she did have to work at it a bit.

Claudia had not yet gone to Spain. Ella would be just as pleased when she had left although she refrained from saying so to Piers. She took it for granted that his absence from the office during his father's last days had meant that it would be impossible for him to go with Claudia. She was wrong.

'I just don't see how you can take any more leave,' she protested when Piers broke it to her that he would still be going to Spain.

'I got compassionate leave for Dad's death, so my annual holiday is intact.'

'And Claudia can't manage on her own?'

'I explained before, she wants to look round for a use for her money when the house and garden centre are sold.'

'Do you really think you can help her?'

'Of course.'

'Be careful; you know next to nothing about property law in Spain.'

'Naturally we'll take local advice.'

Ella was far from happy. Piers was being too cagey. She felt he was keeping something from her and so she persisted, 'You aren't seeing this as any sort of a permanent move, are you? Because, if so, I'll warn you now that nothing – and I really mean *nothing* – will make me go and live there.'

122

Still Piers avoided looking at her. 'There's no idea of that,' he said.

'Not now, Piers, not now, when we've reached such a good understanding and I'm hoping to become pregnant.'

She wished he looked happier at the idea. Not that there were any prospects, not yet, but she had her mind so firmly fixed on the hope of a baby of her own that she could not believe that it would not happen.

To Leah's surprise she got a sympathetic hearing from the Debt Management organisation and some very practical advice. More than that, after a couple of interviews they made a suggestion to her that was very much to her taste.

'A television programme is being made about these high-interest loans and the way people are trapped into a spiral of debt,' she was said. 'Would you agree to take part?'

Leah's eyes glistened. 'Sure!'

'It could be done without your face being shown if you preferred to be anonymous.'

'No, I don't mind appearing.'

The producer of the television programme latched on to Leah straight away. Just like Toby and Ella, he saw that she could be projected as an object of compassion. The little boy, too, was an appealing child. Leah made the most of the difficulties of finding work when there was a child. She suppressed the existence of her mother living nearby, and the fact that until recently she had lived rent free. In any case, most of the interview centred around her forlorn attempt to provide for herself and her little boy by taking what had turned out to be a crippling loan.

There was only one sticky moment and that was when the interviewer asked, 'You paid off the loan?'

'Yes, I did.'

'How did you do that?'

Leah opened her eyes very wide, her face the picture of truthfulness. 'I had a stroke of luck. I was left a diamond ring.'

'By someone in the family?'

'By an old lady my Dad had done a kindness to,' Leah improvised. 'I sold it and I used every penny to pay back the money I'd borrowed.'

'But it wasn't enough.'

'No, they said I still owed interest and then they started charging for that as if it was another loan.'

The rest of the programme concentrated on the ethics of lending money to impecunious young people and the way they could get ever deeper into debt and Leah did not appear again. She was disappointed to learn that it would be some weeks before the programme was shown, but at least it gave her time to alert all her friends, most of whom were openly envious of her chance to appear before a camera.

Ella bore in tight-lipped silence Piers' absence for two weeks in Spain. Verity tried to find out what she thought about it, but Ella refused to be drawn.

'Just so long as Claudia's not persuading Dad to go into business over there,' Verity said.

Since this was exactly Ella's own fear she was at a loss to know what to say.

'Dad knows I'm not prepared to move to Spain,' was all she replied.

It was a relief when Piers came back, looking remarkably fit, and, Ella realised after the first few minutes, exceedingly reticent about Claudia's plans.

'We'll talk about it tonight,' was all he would say, which Ella interpreted as meaning that he had something to tell her he would not reveal in front of the children.

Her heart sank and she went through the rest of the day with a constant nagging worry at the back of her mind.

She unpacked Piers' suitcase and threw his dirty clothes into the washing machine. It would not have hurt Claudia to have attended to that little chore before they left her well-appointed villa, but Ella doubted whether the idea had occurred to her.

'Okay, let's have it,' she said at last, when even Verity, who had hung around in a way that to Ella suggested that she knew that there was news to be heard, had taken herself off to bed.

'There are big decisions to be made,' Piers said in a portentous way that made Ella want to shake him.

'One decision's already been taken,' she said. 'I'm not going to Spain.'

'I've accepted that. But I am.'

124

It took a moment for that to sink in, then Ella said in a disbelieving whisper, 'Without me?'

'If you won't go where my work is, then I have no choice.'

'Your work ... what about your job in Kits Harbour? What have you done, Piers? What has Claudia done?'

'She's negotiating to buy a small apartment block, just eight flats, all with balconies, a nice garden and a swimming pool.'

'You sound like an estate agent's brochure. So, Claudia has found somewhere to put her money. What's that to do with you?'

'She wants me to manage it for her. She intends them to be holiday flats, of course, so there'll be a lot of coming and going. We may make a deal with a tour agency, but that's something for the future.'

'You don't speak the language, you don't know the people, you don't know anything about Spanish regulations. It sounds like a recipe for disaster.'

'I knew you wouldn't offer me anything but discouragement. That's why I didn't put you in the picture before we went.'

'Strange, the way it's all turning out to be my fault. I can't believe this is happening. You can't leave me on my own in England with the children and this house to run, and all the worries and anxieties, while you swan off to a job in the sun, working for a woman I seriously distrust. It won't be a proper job, Piers, especially if you sell time in the flats to a tour operator.'

'I'm sorry, but it's all decided.'

'Just like that, without talking it over, without any thought about how it's going to affect all our lives. No! I won't accept it. Have you given notice at the office?'

'I'll do it on Monday.'

'Wait a few days. Give me time to talk to Claudia. Surely she can find someone else, preferably a local man, who can run her apartment block at least as capably as you, and quite possibly better.'

'Thank you! That shows what you think of me, doesn't it? Don't talk to Claudia. You'll only get hurt. Claudia thinks more highly of me than you do. It's me she wants, not just any old manager.'

'How true,' Ella said bitterly. 'It's you she wants, and at any

125

price it seems. Surely you can see? She's taking you away from your home and children – and your wife. The job is a sweetener, something to keep you amused, while she takes over your life.'

'You still don't understand, do you? I've tried to put it as delicately as I can, but if you want it in brutal terms, I'm leaving you, Ella.'

'For *Claudia*?'

Piers shrugged and turned away. 'Claudia and I go back a long way.'

'Are you still being delicate? Do you mean you've been lovers in the past?'

'Yes, of course.'

'But . . . Bernie? He was your friend!'

'The best. Bernie was . . . very understanding.'

'He knew,' Ella said. 'I think that's disgusting. You committed adultery with his wife and he connived at it. What a set up!'

'Look, all I'm saying is that Bernie knew the strain I was under. If he suspected that Claudia was good to me, he was civilised enough to turn a blind eye.'

'It's not my idea of civilisation.'

'No, you'd tuck your skirts round your ankles and keep your legs tight shut.'

'If that's your definition of fidelity then there's nothing more to say. You mean to go to Spain and live with Claudia, on her money. Am I expected to divorce you? Piers, this isn't true, it can't be true.'

'Certainly I want a divorce. If you don't get it, then I will, sooner or later.'

The bewildered feeling that this was not really happening, that some trick was being played on her, that she was ill, delirious, hallucinating, almost overwhelmed Ella.

'I thought we'd begun to understand one another in quite a new way,' she said. 'You made love to me . . .'

'You seemed to expect it.'

Ella shuddered from head to foot, in disgust at him, and herself. 'We talked about having a baby.'

'You talked about it.'

'I might be pregnant. Have you thought of that?'

There was a prolonged pause. Piers looked sulky, nothing more than that. He's not really sorry, Ella thought in despair. He doesn't like having a scene and he's annoyed because I'm not giving him what he wants without making trouble, but he's made up his mind to do what he thinks is best for himself and I can't shake him.

'I suppose I'll have to come clean,' Piers said at last.

'That'll be a change.'

'Oh, shut up, can't you? When Lucy was first ill the doctor thought it would be a good idea for her to come off the Pill. So I had a vasectomy.'

If Ella had been standing up she thought she would have collapsed. As it was, the room seemed to spin round her and she had to close her eyes.

From somewhere in the dizzying darkness she heard her voice say, 'But I would have known.'

'It makes no difference to ... performance. It's just that no sperm can get out.'

'Before we were married,' Ella whispered. 'We talked about a family. I told you I wanted a child of my own.'

'And I said we'd think about it later, or words to that effect. To tell you the truth, I thought when you found what a handful my three were you'd change your mind.'

'You let me take the Pill for two years, knowing it wasn't necessary.'

Piers shifted uncomfortably on his seat, but made no reply.

'Even when we spoke about it again, just recently, you said nothing. You knew what I was hoping. And all the time you were just humouring me. Tell me, was I ever anything to you except a housekeeper, a means of getting your finances straight, a nanny for your children?'

'Of course you were! I loved you, Ella. But it's time for me to move on. I've evolved and left you standing.'

'In two years?'

'That's the way it seems to me. I can see new opportunities opening up in front of me; you just want to stay put. With Claudia I can have the life I've always wanted, the life I was meant for.'

'A kept man, living off a wealthy woman.'

'That's wicked, and cruel! I'll earn my keep.'

'I'm sure you will; Claudia will see to that. As for cruelty ... I need a new definition of the word. I never thought anyone could be so thoughtlessly cruel and then try to justify himself. What about the children?'

'I'm not going to land you with them. Claudia has offered to pay the fees for boarding schools. We thought you should stay in this house and they could come to you for short holidays and out to Spain for longer ones.'

'You *have* done a lot of thinking in the past fortnight,' Ella said, in a falsely admiring way. 'I love them. Have you taken that into consideration?'

'That's why I'm giving you reasonable access.'

For one hysterical moment Ella thought she was going to burst out laughing. Reasonable access. The three children she had watched over, for whom she had worked every moment of the day, the children who relied on her and believed in her; she was to be allowed reasonable access to them by the man who had betrayed their mother's memory, run them into debt and now proposed to give them as a fresh stepmother a woman who couldn't wait to push them off to boarding schools.

'You take my breath away,' she said, with the same sarcastic intonation she had used before.

Piers seemed to be at a loss. Perhaps he had not expected her to take his defection so quietly. If I weren't so numb, I'd be angry, Ella thought. I can't take it in, I just can't believe this is happening.

Her silence goaded Piers into saying, 'Don't just sit there. Say something. Give me a reaction.'

'I can't think ... I can't feel anything. Piers, we married one another for *life*, not just until something better turned up. What have I done wrong? Haven't I been a good wife to you, a good mother to the children?'

'Yes, I suppose so. These things happen, sometimes you can't help yourself.'

'Oh, can't you! These things happen if you put yourself in the way of letting them happen. If you found that Claudia was a temptation to you, then you should have stayed away from her.'

'We were thrown together. We couldn't help our feelings.'

'Your feelings! Lust, greed and a liking for the easy life.

128

Think what you're throwing away, Piers, think! The respect of your children ...'

'Not if it's explained to them in the right way.'

'There is no right way. What you are doing is wrong. There's no cosmetic way you can dress it up as anything but the most wicked betrayal.'

'If you look at it like that I can hardly go on living with you, can I?'

That made Ella pause. Did she want Piers in her life? No, at that moment she did not.

'If you come to me in the next couple of days,' she said carefully, 'And say that you've made a mistake and ask me to forgive you, then I'll take you back.'

'To me, it doesn't seem like a mistake. I believe I'm doing what I was always meant to do.'

'Shrugging off your responsibilities. You're good at that.'

Piers got to his feet and began walking about the room. He still had his unconscious elegance of movement, his fine, well-proportioned body, but Ella saw, as if for the first time, the gleam of silver in the hair at his temples, a hint of scragginess in the cords of his neck, veins standing out on the backs of his hands. An ageing man – not old, far from that – but no longer young; a dissatisfied man, who valued the easy things of life above honour and responsibility; a man who had everything except integrity.

'What you have to understand,' he said over his shoulder, 'Is that this is settled. I can't be talked out of it.'

'I'm still offering you time to think it over,' Ella said steadily, against all her instincts.

'Don't try to hold on to me ...'

'I'm not! Right at this moment I can't wait to see the back of you. You think I'm being possessive, I think I'm being generous.'

After a long pause Piers muttered, 'Some time we're going to have a talk about the practical side.'

'Let's start now. Where are you going to sleep tonight?'

It was obvious that Piers had not thought about that.

'Claudia's not expecting you?' Ella asked.

'No, she didn't know I meant to talk to you tonight. It's a bit late ...'

'You're turning my entire life upside down and yet you jib at getting your mistress out of bed. Are you afraid of annoying her?'

'Of course not.'

'You should be, she's done away with one husband.'

Piers was so shocked that it was a struggle for him to speak. 'That's a wicked, wicked thing to say,' he managed at last.

'She took Bernie's heart pills out of his anorak pocket and sent him out without them. I saw her do it. That enamelled box, remember? You told me yourself he kept the pills in it. No wonder Claudia didn't want to have it around. She may even have had a conscience about it, though given her present performance, I doubt it.'

'I didn't think you had it in you to be so nastily vindictive!'

'Ask her.' Ella watched him for a moment. 'You don't dare. You're afraid it might be true. No, worse than that; you think that if it is true, the fact that you know may upset your pleasant arrangement with your new, rich wife. She wouldn't be rich, let alone free, if Bernie hadn't died. Just think about that.'

She had driven him away. Piers, his face rigid with disgust, slammed out of the house, the front door crashing to behind him. Ella heard the sound of his car starting up and then he was gone.

Chapter Nine

Ella woke feeling as if she had flu. A couple of hours heavy sleep had taken the edge off her fatigue without refreshing her. Her head ached and her eyes were sticky. Her limbs were leaden; it was an effort to turn over to look at the clock. The empty space beside her in the bed, where Piers should have been, brought recollection rushing back. She sat up with her head bowed over her bent knees. What was she going to do?

She heaved her legs over the side of the bed and felt with her feet for her slippers. Shrugging on her dressing gown she shuffled to the bathroom. She collided with the door jamb and put out a hand to steady herself.

She was reluctant to face her reflection. When she looked into the glass she saw a woman who looked like someone with a hangover, bleary-eyed, hair on end from all the tossing and turning she had done, colourless cheeks. A wash and a comb through her hair improved her appearance marginally, but it was an effort to force herself to leave the bathroom where at least she could lock the door against the horror of the day ahead.

She still had to tell the children. Of course, Piers might take advantage of the offer she had made and reconsider. What would she do if he did? Could she live with a man who revolted her? Straightening her shoulders and tying her belt with a vicious yank, Ella decided she would battle it through, if she had to. For the sake of the children. But in her heart she knew that Piers would not come back.

It was Sunday. She had no doubt where Piers and Claudia would be so she might as well take the children to church, if they wanted to go. As for herself, there would be some vague comfort in following a familiar routine, but what was the use of praying when she didn't know what to pray for? It would be hypocrisy to pray for Piers to come to his senses and return to his wife and family when she was none too sure that she could bear to give him house room, in spite of her brave words the night before.

He had said that he did love her – once. But it was not love that had made him conceal his inability to give her the child she had told him she wanted; it was expediency. He had needed her, but once he saw a newer, better prospect in front of him Ella became expendable. Used and discarded, she thought, as she began to dress. Like a plastic bag from a supermarket.

She should have foreseen that the children would want to know where their father was.

'You'd think he could have given up his game of golf for one Sunday morning,' Verity said, taking it for granted that Piers was sticking to his accustomed habit. 'He hardly saw us yesterday.'

'He's got things to talk about with Claudia,' Ella said. 'She's buying an apartment block in Spain.'

'They've had a fortnight to sort that out,' Harry pointed out.

'It's complicated,' Ella said. 'Are we all going to church this morning?'

'I would have gone if you'd got me up in time for eight o'clock,' Verity said. 'But I've got a project to write up and I'll have to stay at home and get it done. At least the house will be nice and quiet.'

'You might peel the potatoes for lunch,' Ella said.

Verity wrinkled her nose, but made no other objection, and they left her to her project. It was a fine morning, so they walked to the church. Ella said good morning to all the regulars, vaguely surprised that they treated her as if she were the same woman they saw every Sunday morning. Can't they see that I'm a used plastic bag? she thought. She heard perhaps one word in ten of the service. During the sermon she thought about Claudia's proposal to send the children to boarding school. If she could look at it dispassionately, which was almost impossible, was there anything to be said for the idea? Not for Verity, making such good progress towards taking her GCSEs and establishing a healthy social life which Ella had bent over backwards to encourage; she would be devastated at leaving her beloved drama group. What about Harry? He needed a man in his life and perhaps he might do better in a boarding school than in a house full of women. On the other hand, in spite of his sporting prowess, he was a sensitive boy, terribly prone to worrying, in need of constant reassurance. Given that support he got on happily with his life, but if it were withdrawn, Ella thought that he would suffer. Jennifer might adapt better than the other two, but she, too, would hate being taken away from her friends and the environment that was familiar to her. What was the alternative? Could Ella fight against the boarding school idea if the children's father wanted it for them? They were not her children. Everything came back to that. But neither were they Claudia's and the boarding school idea was undoubtedly hers. Bloody Claudia.

The only thing she brought back from church was a bleak but steady determination to keep the children if she possibly could. Ella had no illusions about what she was proposing to take on. Three children, who were not her own, no man to help her, and not likely to be one, not for the foreseeable future, since she could think of few men who would be prepared to take on such a burden. It was no use thinking that the load would be light, even if she got adequate finance from Piers. It was not the money, it was the parental responsibility that might be more than she could cope with. Toby ... better not to think about him. She had sent him away and she could hardly call him back in order to take on a duty she shrank from herself.

Verity flung open the front door as soon as they were inside the gate.

'Dad's been here,' she said. 'He's packed up all his clothes. He's left us!'

So it was on her, sooner than Ella had expected and before she had prepared what she was going to say.

'Come inside and sit down and I'll explain,' she said.

They waited, looking at her in a way she felt was almost accusing, so that she wanted to cry out that it wasn't her fault.

'Dad told me last night that he was going to live and work in Spain with Claudia,' she said. 'I offered him a chance to think it over, but obviously he's made up his mind. Did he say anything to you this morning, Verity?'

'He said he loved us and was going to work something out that would make us all happy,' Verity said in a way that betrayed her opinion of that.

'I won't live in Spain,' Harry said quickly.

'When you say "live with Claudia", do you mean *live* with?' Verity asked.

'He wants to marry her.'

'What about you?'

'He's asked me to divorce him.'

It had been too sudden. They were looking as stunned as she had been last night.

'I ought to have softened it for you,' Ella said. 'But once you knew he'd gone ...'

'What's going to happen to us?' Jennifer asked.

'There are two possibilities. Claudia has offered to send you all to boarding schools. Don't turn that down without thinking about it, you might enjoy it.'

'No, we wouldn't,' Harry said with certainty.

Jennifer suddenly ran to Ella and clambered on her lap, a thing she had not done for a long time. 'I want to stay with you,' she said.

Ella put an arm round her and was appalled to feel her small body trembling.

'That's what I'd prefer,' she said steadily. 'I thought I'd offer to give Dad a divorce on condition that we keep this house and you live with me.'

'Is that what you really want?' Verity asked. 'I mean, it's not as if we're your kids.'

'I've put too much into getting you sorted out to give you up easily. I'll put up a fight to keep you if you're really sure it's what you want.'

There was a swift exchange of glances and then Verity said with certainty, 'It's what we want.'

'Then I'll put it to Dad and Claudia.' Ella stood up and a wry smile twisted her lips. 'It'll be a darn sight cheaper for Claudia than paying fees to boarding schools. Did you remember to do the potatoes, Verity?'

'I couldn't think about *potatoes* with this on my mind,' Verity said, shocked.

134

'Think now. I'm going to go and change out of my church clothes and you and Harry can do the same, Jennifer.'

As they climbed the stairs Jennifer said, 'Perhaps Uncle Toby could come and live with us. It was nice when he was here.'

Ella put her foot down carefully on the next stair, afraid she might stumble. 'Uncle Toby's work will take him abroad again any time now,' she said.

She remembered that a couple of days later when she had a letter from Toby, not a long letter, just a stiff little note saying that he had been asked to go on a mission to Afghanistan and would be away for several months at least. Letters from home, he said, would be welcome 'though I don't expect you to write with the devotion you showed when I was a captive in Colombia. My captivity is of a different kind now, as you well know.'

Afghanistan! Thinking about it, Ella told herself that Toby had a mistress, too, and her name was danger. He was hooked on adventure. She gave him credit for wanting to help his fellow man, but would his 'mission' have had the same allure if he had been asked to go to Brixton or Liverpool? What would he do if she wrote posthaste and told him she would shortly be free? Would he abandon his assignment? Ella thought not. He would stand by his contract and she supposed she had to admit that he would be right. 'Duty! "Stern Daughter of the Voice of God"', she murmured out loud. 'Damn Toby, why does his timing have to be so lousy?'

The weeks between the making of what Leah thought of as 'her' television programme and its showing on the screen seemed endless. She had boasted about her interview so often that her friends told her they were sick of hearing about it. All the same, she rallied everyone she knew to watch it when the programme finally went out.

In some circles, particularly at the local police station, it caused amusement and discussion the next day.

'Did you see Reg Daley's girl, Leah, on the box last night, talking about getting out of debt by selling some diamond ring Reg got from an old lady he did a kindness to?'

'He relieved her of the worry of looking after her jewellery, I expect,' a colleague suggested. 'Is it worth following up?'

135

'I doubt it. The ring's gone, we know that, and Reg put up his hand to all his outstanding jobs before he did his last stretch. The "old lady" will have had her insurance money and might not thank us for getting her property back, even if we could trace it. Let it go.'

'Reg has been lying low lately, hasn't he?'

'Perhaps he's reformed. If Leah's story had any truth in it, it's the first time I've known him to bail one of his kids out of trouble.'

Leah was still preening herself on her television appearance and scanning the papers for a mention of the programme when her father called on her.

He wasted no time on preliminaries. 'What diamond ring?' he demanded, pushing his way into the flat as soon as she opened the front door.

'Oh, Dad ...' Leah eyed him warily, recognising the signs of temper his wife and family knew all too well. 'I found it.'

'Where?'

'In that leather suitcase you left with me ages ago.'

'So you knew it belonged to me.'

'It belonged to whoever you stole if from,' Leah retorted.

Almost casually, Reg Daley brought up his hand and dealt her a blow that sent her staggering to the other side of the room.

'You knew it was mine, and you sold it,' he said.

'I needed the money!'

'You've got ways of making money, as we both know.'

'Not now, I haven't.'

'How much did you get and where's my cut?'

'I used every penny to pay back a loan. If you saw the telly you know that.'

The second blow caught her under the chin and she collapsed on the sofa. Damien, disturbed by the loud voices, came stumbling in, bleary with sleep and ready to cry.

'You! Go back to bed!' Reg ordered. 'Otherwise I'll give you the same pasting I'm giving your mum.'

'Touch one hair of his head and I'll stick a knife in you,' Leah threatened.

Reg gave a jeering laugh, but he contented himself with dealing her one last slap across the cheek with the flat of his hand. 'Shut your mouth! And next time, if you've got property of mine, remember that it *is* mine, not yours to be sold off when the fancy takes you.'

He started to go, with Leah screaming after him, 'There'll never be a next time. That's the end! I never want to set eyes on you again!'

She was shaking all over, her jaw was bruised, her lip was bleeding, and Damien was bawling his head off. 'Oh, shut up,' Leah said, but she picked him up and cuddled him, holding him tightly. 'That's the end,' she repeated in a whisper. 'He's never going to do that to me again. Don't cry, ducky, don't cry. Mummy's going to put nasty Granddad away for good and all.'

She was down the police station early the next morning, 'I want to see Detective Inspector Crooms,' she said. 'No, I won't talk to anyone else. I know him, and he knows me. Tell him it's Leah Daley.'

She had to wait, but eventually the Inspector came out to see her.

'My word, someone had it in for you, Leah,' he said, looking at her half-closed eye, her swollen mouth and the livid bruise on her cheek.

'My Dad. I've had enough, Mr Crooms.'

'You want to make a complaint against him?'

'More than that. I want you to put him away for so long he won't even remember he had a daughter. I'm turning him in for that murder up on the golf links.'

The excitement was almost as satisfying as the television interview. Once she was started on her story there was no stopping Leah.

'Shall we get the diamond ring out of the way first, Leah?' Inspector Crooms suggested.

'What diamond ring?'

'The one you said you sold, on that television programme.'

'There wasn't no diamond ring.'

'But you did pay off a sizeable debt? Where did you get the money?'

'I earned it. There was this man living in the top flat. I did for him, if you see what I mean.'

'I never heard you went in for prostitution, Leah.'

137

'No more I do, except for one man I'll tell you about, and that was more a case of special services,' Leah opened her eyes as wide as her injuries would permit. 'Don't put words into my mouth, Mr Crooms. All I meant was that I did my upstairs neighbour's cleaning, and he was very grateful.'

'So your loving Dad didn't make you a present of a diamond ring?'

'Not him! I made that up because I couldn't say I'd earned the money or I might have lost my benefit.'

'All right, I'll buy it, Leah. You didn't have a diamond ring, and the diamond ring wasn't stolen and Reg didn't bash you up for selling something you didn't have.'

'You've got it. And you can't charge me with handling stolen property or anything like that. Now can we get on with what I really came to see you about?'

'The murder. You reckon it was down to your dad?'

'Too right I do! There was this camera, see. Now that *was* stolen, from Bernie Caldicott, the Garden Centre man.'

'He died.'

'Yeah. You suspected him of topping that photographer man, but you were wrong. Dad had the camera for ages before he sold it. In fact, not until after he came out of nick. What he didn't realise was that there was a film still in it, which the photographer developed, and the pictures were, well, shall we say a bit hot? The photographer – what was his name?'

'Burtman – Donald Burtman.'

'Well, this Burtman decided Bernie would pay to get his pictures back.'

'Blackmail.'

'Right. He made the mistake of telling Dad about it, which made Dad steam because he reckoned if there was money to be made he was entitled to his share. That's the way he thinks, he's always after his cut.'

'And if he doesn't get it he turns nasty?'

Leah caressed her swollen jaw. 'You can say that again. So when Burtman went to his meet with Bernie, up on the golf links, Dad was there too, hidden in the trees. He waited till they'd done their business and then went and asked for what he thought was owed him. It might have passed off all right, only Burtman was feeling cocky because he reckoned he'd been

138

clever. He'd handed over the film and the prints he'd made, but what he told Dad was that he'd made a second set of prints and he was planning to sell them one by one. He said he'd threaten to photocopy them and enlarge them and put them up on the wall of the Golf Club if Bernie didn't pay up.' Leah paused. 'That would have given the old cats a thrill,' she said thoughtfully.

'Come to the point, Leah. Was it a fight? A straightforward quarrel over money?'

'Burtman made the mistake of showing Dad the photos. And the girl with Bernie was me.'

'You posed with Bernie Caldicott for pornographic photographs?'

'Don't call them that, Mr Crooms,' Leah protested. 'They were a bit ripe, I admit, and we neither of us had any clothes on, but they were for his eyes only and I just looked on it as a bit of a joke. Say one thing for Bernie, he was always good for a laugh. He paid my rent, too, and gave me plants for my window box. I miss him.'

'Are you saying Reg Daley lost his temper and attacked Donald Burtman with a golf club and killed him?'

'He never admitted it, not in so many words, but he spilled out the story about the camera and the blackmail an' that. He was beside himself when he came to see me. He's got a thing about his women keeping off the streets and he thought I'd been really vile. I reckon he lashed out at Burtman like he did at me. He beat me up worse than he did last night, only last night I decided enough was enough.'

There was a long silence. 'Well,' Leah said. 'Are you going to put him away?'

'It's a bit thin. But it's a convincing story, it certainly convinces me, but I wish we'd got some more concrete evidence.'

'There weren't any fingerprints, or you'd have pulled him in straight away,' Leah guessed. 'His prints are so well known you'd probably recognise them at a glance. Cunning old devil! I wouldn't have thought he was calm enough to clear up after himself. Well, I've got one more thing I can give you. The photographs. He brought them down and threw them at me and when he went he left them behind. Plenty of fingerprints on them.'

'Both Daley's and Burtman's,' the Inspector said. 'It provides a link between them, if nothing else. All right, Leah, we'll pull him in. You do realise you'll have to give evidence, don't you?'

For a moment Leah hesitated, then she nodded. 'I'll go through with it. I owe him nothing. If it hadn't been for him, dragging me down, I might have made something of myself, been a model, or an actress, anything!'

'"Golf Links Murder – Man Held by Police".' Harry read out the headline in the local paper. 'It doesn't say who, though, just that "a man is helping the police with their enquiries". Why do they always say that?'

'In case he turns out to be innocent,' Ella said absently. 'Harry, are your dirty football clothes in the bag you've left by the front door?'

'Yes, do you want them?'

'You know the drill; put the filthy things straight into the washing machine . . .'

'Add soap powder and turn on,' Harry chanted. 'Most boys I know don't have to wash their own clothes.'

'You're a male chauvinist piglet and chucking a few things into a machine doesn't count as washing them.'

Harry grinned and went to fetch his muddy football strip. They had settled down, Ella thought optimistically; they had adjusted to Piers' defection. The only thing that was worrying her, and she had not shared it with the children, was the attitude Claudia had taken towards the idea of Ella having custody of them. Ella wanted it to be a formal arrangement, something that could not be upset without legal intervention. But Claudia, out of what Ella regarded as nothing but idle mischief, was inciting Piers to insist on keeping his parental rights; and Ella's solicitor was doubtful how the decision would go if it came to a fight. She was not, as everyone kept pointing out to her, the children's actual mother.

Piers and Claudia had taken off for Spain. Claudia seemed, to Ella, to be in haste to depart, leaving the sale of Bernie's garden business and the Kits Bay house to be completed by agents. Piers had left his job without notice, which had not endeared him to the company who employed him. Was Claudia afraid he might have second thoughts if she did not whisk him out of the country? Surely not; she must know that a moneyed life in the sun was just what Piers had been looking for. It was to be hoped that she would not load too much responsibility on to him, otherwise he might let her down and where would their idyll be then?

It still hurt. The realisation of being a deserted wife would suddenly come to the surface of her mind without warning and Ella would feel the pain like something that threatened to tear her apart. Her mind would go blank, words would freeze on her lips and it was only when she had absorbed the pain that she would be able to wrench her mind back to whatever she was supposed to be doing.

She had written to Piers' mother and that had not been easy, especially when she got a letter back saying that it was no more than Mrs Armitage had expected, but Ella thought it right that her mother-in-law should have her son's address in Spain. With a touch of hardness, she thought that if there was an emergency Piers could come back and deal with it.

Money was a problem since Piers, in spite of his future prospects, had removed half of their joint account and converted it into Spanish pesetas. She ought to have thought of that and struck first, Ella told herself, knowing that she lacked the ruthlessness to close an account containing Piers' salary cheque. Let him have it, she thought wearily, she could earn enough to keep them until a proper settlement had been worked out, and that, it seemed, awaited Claudia's whim over custody of the children.

She learnt of Reg Daley's arrest from Leah herself. They met at the check-out in the local supermarket and Leah immediately accosted Ella.

'Here, is it true Piers and Claudia have eloped to Spain?' she demanded.

There seemed little point in denying it. 'You could put it like that,' Ella said.

'She didn't waste much time, did she? Poor old Bernie scarcely in the ground and she's away with someone else's husband. She always was a nasty piece, though Bernie wouldn't hear a word against her. Seems to me if she'd been all she should have been to him he wouldn't have got up to his funny tricks.'

141

Ella, acutely aware of an interested audience in the queue behind her, merely smiled, a stiff movement of the lips, but Leah, equally aware of listening ears, and relishing every moment, went on 'You know my old man's been banged up for that murder?'

Ella was packing her bags, anxious to get away. Leah waited for her and, since there was no help for it, Ella walked to the exit with her.

'That was all down to Bernie, too,' Leah said, ignoring instructions from the police to discuss the case with no one. 'He was being blackmailed over some photographs of him and me together and my Dad saw the pics and went berserk. At least, that's what we reckon happened, only at the moment he's denying it. What I say is, if he was mad enough to come and knock me about then he must have done the same to the photographer bloke.'

'You and Bernie,' Ella said, her mind reeling.

'Yeah, we'd been going together ever since I had a Saturday job at the Garden Centre while I was still at school.'

'But that's appalling,' Ella said, standing stock still in the middle of the car park.

Leah laughed. 'Don't look so shocked. I'd been at it since I was thirteen. Bernie wasn't the first by a long chalk.'

'Your baby ...'

'No, not Bernie's, more's the pity; he'd have seen me right. I couldn't pin it on him because I fell for Damien while Bernie was away convalescing after his first heart attack. He was gone two months and I was well away when he got back. He wasn't so keen on me after that; I wasn't his little girl any more; but he didn't mind using me to pose for his pictures, and he found my flat – at least Piers did – and Bernie paid the rent.'

'I'm surprised your father didn't murder Bernie rather than the photographer,' Ella said faintly.

'He didn't know nothing about it till he saw the photos. Just as well, 'cause like you say he would have kicked up merry hell.'

They had reached Ella's car. Leah paused hopefully. 'Aren't you going to offer me a lift? I've got extra shopping 'cause my boyfriend's staying with me.'

'Damien's father?'

142

'Yeah. He's been away, but he's moved back to Kits Harbour and he came and looked me up. He's ever so taken with Damien and I always say a boy needs a father. If he could get a job we might get married.'

'That would be nice,' Ella said automatically. She opened the boot of the car and watched with resignation as Leah stowed her shopping away. 'I expect you can do with some support at this difficult time.'

'I s'pose so,' Leah agreed, looking surprised. 'Actually, Craig and all my friends think I'm ever so brave, giving evidence against my own father. Mum won't speak to me, but she'll come round if he goes down for a good long stretch.'

'But you say he denies it?'

'Well, he's got to, hasn't he? Do you mind if we stop at the newsagents? I promised I'd get a paper for Craig for his racing this afternoon.'

Reg Daley's steadfast denial of the killing of Donald Burtman was a puzzle to the police, too. In accordance with his usual practice, he readily admitted what he could not really deny: that he had met Burtman and quarrelled with him over the blackmail money and the additional pictures, but the story he stuck to was that he had knocked the photographer down, taken his wallet and the pictures and left him lying on the ground, groaning and angry, but still alive.

'As I live and breath, Mr Crooms,' Reg said. 'We had a bit of a fight, or would have done if he'd been half of a man, and I knocked him down. I think he hit his head against a tree, but as for that golf club you've been waving about, I never set eyes on it. On the head of my grandson, I didn't know there was a golf club there, let alone picked it up and used it.'

'You were sufficiently fired up to go and beat up your daughter.'

'I went and had words with her, as any father would have done after seeing those pictures. I ask you, would you have liked it, if it'd been your daughter?'

Detective Inspector Crooms looked at the photographs in their plastic cases. 'Not much,' he admitted.

'So I gave her a talking to.'

'You hit her.'

143

'A *severe* talking to. Did she come and complain to you then? Did she say "My Dad's been and topped the man who had these pictures"? No, she did not. She's made that part of the story up since because I didn't like her saying, on TV, mind you, that I'd given her a diamond ring, which I never did.'

'You beat her up again.'

'I've got a temper. I don't deny it. But I know how far to go. I might lash out if my old woman or one of the kids gives me cause, but beating a man to death, no! That's not my style, Mr Crooms, and well you know it.'

'The trouble is,' Inspector Crooms said after the interview, 'there's something in what Reg says. His wife's complained more than once about him assaulting her, though she's never pressed charges, but he's an undersized little runt and women and children are his kind of target.'

'If he was beside himself with anger, he might lash out and do more damage than he realised until it was too late.'

'He might. I wish we'd got something more than Reg's admission that he was at the scene of the crime and those fingerprints on the photographs. There was a graze on the back of the victim's head, wasn't there?'

'A bad graze and some fragments of tree bark in the wound. We found blood on the trunk of one of the trees.'

'Consistent with Reg's story of knocking him down.'

'And then while he was lying on the ground Reg snatched up the golf club and finished him off.'

'That must have been the way of it.'

'He's the only suspect we've got.'

'Bernie Caldicott?'

'He's dead.'

'And if he wasn't I'd be asking him some pretty straight questions about the way he lied to us about his movements that night,' Inspector Crooms said. 'I've half a mind to talk to his widow again.'

'She's gone to live in Spain, taking someone else's husband with her.'

'Oh, God! It'd take a bit of swinging to get expenses for a trip to the Costa Brava.'

'You don't really think Reg Daley's innocent?'

'I don't know, I don't know. I can see two scenarios, both of the nightmare kind. One, he did it, but we don't get a conviction; two, he didn't do it and gets life and in a few years' time the verdict's quashed.'

'In the meantime, he's charged and we keep our fingers crossed?'

'And try to come up with something that will settle my doubts.'

It was October before Reg Daley appeared before a Magistrates Court and was sent for trial, charged with the murder of Donald Burtman on the fourteenth of June. The details revealed at that hearing made juicy reading even though the man who had been blackmailed by the dead photographer was not named.

'Mum, was it Bernie?' Verity asked.

'What makes you ask that?' Ella asked, giving herself time to think.

'The police came and took him away from here that night, didn't they? And it says in the report that the man is dead. It has to be Bernie.'

'You're right, of course. Oh, Verity, I don't want to talk about it.'

'Did they think he'd done it?'

'He was under suspicion. I don't know what he told the police, but this story of blackmail didn't come out until recently. It's horrible!'

'We always knew Bernie was a bit kinky,' Verity pointed out reasonably. 'I say, no wonder Claudia left the country. Do you think she knew?'

'Just as well he died, in a way,' Harry put in.

'Don't say that!' Ella said sharply, in her mind a picture she wanted to suppress of a little enamelled box falling to the ground and spilling out pills. If Claudia had known about the pornographic pictures, about the blackmail ... it certainly supplied a motive for wanting Bernie out of the way. It wasn't murder, Ella thought, not exactly; she couldn't have been sure that Bernie would succumb; but she must have known the stress he was under, it must have been in her mind that it was a way of getting rid of him.

145

And taking my husband, Ella thought. She had put the divorce proceedings in hand. There would be no difficulty in providing Piers with the freedom he wanted; the only delay would be over the terms of the settlement she wanted. For herself, Ella would have been prepared to walk away with nothing but the hard won experience of the last two years, but the children's future must be safeguarded and for that she must have sufficient income to continue living in the family house and it must be independent of her earnings since no business was infallibly profitable.

'Mrs Martin's Pickles and Preserves' were doing well, but she had sold nothing to Bernie's Garden Centre since it had been put on the market and there was no guarantee that the purchaser would continue the arrangement she had had with Bernie.

What she needed was some capital so that she could expand. Ella remembered ruefully that Toby had offered to back her. Had his offer been disinterested? It had come before he had started to think he was falling in love with her, at least she thought it had. She had stamped down hard when he had declared his love. The truth was, she did not believe in it. Toby had been ripe for love and there was an intimacy between them because of the letters she had written while he was a captive. Ella wished now that she had a better recollection of what she had put into those letters. At the time it had seemed no more than trivial day-to-day chit-chat, but she suspected they had been more revealing than she had intended and had left Toby with the feeling of knowing her a great deal better than was really the case.

It was over. She had sent him away. It was not the time to write and suggest he should lend her twenty thousand pounds, neither did she want him to know about the divorce. An appeal might give him the impression that she wanted something more than money and Ella shrank from that with a sensitivity that was almost morbid. She didn't want pity from anyone, but least of all from Toby.

As for her own feelings, she was too battered to think about taking on another man. If she could just live quietly with the children, that would be enough, she told herself, but somewhere at the back of her mind a voice protested, 'I'm only thirty-one; is this all life has to offer me?'

146

She put the thought away from her and tried to turn her mind towards Christmas. She was thinking of making up some special little boxes of homemade sweets and there was no time to be lost in sounding out the market. The people to whom she showed her samples were enthusiastic and Ella felt sufficiently encouraged to go ahead in a modest way.

She was in the middle of a batch of marzipan apples, giving them an enticing flush of ripeness with food colouring, when the telephone rang. She wiped her fingers, annoyed with herself for forgetting to switch over to the answerphone when she had such a fiddly job in hand, and froze as she realised the caller was Piers.

'I want to talk about arrangements for Christmas,' he said.

'Christmas?'

'You do understand I'm expecting the children to come out to me here?'

It was Piers' voice, but it was Claudia talking. She was annoyed that Ella was being obdurate over the divorce settlement and this was her way of jerking the noose.

'I'm not sure they'll want to come,' Ella said.

'They're my children and I expect them here with me,' Piers said. 'I want to book the flights soon, to get the advantage of cheaper fares. I need to know the date they break up from school.'

Ella gave him the information, only half of her mind on the conversation, while the other half was full of desolation at the idea of Christmas without Verity, Harry and Jennifer. On her own. Had Piers thought of that?

She told the children as soon as they came home from school and met with an instant rejection of Piers' proposal which ought to have cheered her, but in reality forced her to face the repercussions if they thwarted him. On the face of it, it was a very reasonable request. A father wanted his children with him for Christmas. Who could quibble with that? If she fought against it, she would be going against the terms of the agreement they had almost succeeded in hammering out.

She put it in that way to the children, but only Verity understood her dilemma.

'If we go for Christmas, could we come home to you for New Year?' she suggested.

'We could have two Christmases,' Jennifer said.

'I'll put it to Dad,' Ella said. She reached for the telephone. 'Do you want to speak to him?'

Reluctantly, with a bit of coaxing, they all agreed to say a brief word to their father. Did Piers realise how difficult it was for them? They did not know what to say, the problem was as simple as that. Ella's heart ached as she listened to their stilted little phrases. After Harry had said that he was quite well, that he had scored two goals in his last football match and that he 'wouldn't mind' coming to Spain for Christmas, provided he could come home for the New Year, he thrust the telephone over to Ella.

'As you will have gathered, the enthusiasm is not great,' she said evenly. 'Can we settle that they will come to you on Saturday, twenty-first December and return on the following Saturday?'

'I suppose so. Actually, there are bigger celebrations for New Year than Christmas over here and if we're not lumbered with the kids we can go to the Golf Club New Year's Eve Ball.'

'How nice for you.'

'Don't be sarcastic, Ella. You can't expect Claudia to give up everything for the sake of children who aren't her own.'

'No, I wouldn't expect that of Claudia,' Ella said gently, and left it to him to make the obvious comparison.

'I want them here,' Piers said. 'I didn't realise how much I'd miss them.'

'It was your choice. I gave you your chance to draw back and you blew it.'

'I'm not having regrets, don't think that. Everything's going marvellously· well. We're having quite a heat wave at the moment. Swimming every day, meals on the terrace, blue skies ...'

'And the company of the woman you love. What could be better?'

'Nothing, except having my children with me. Don't rile me, Ella, I could still change my mind about the boarding schools.'

'I'll fight if you do. Oh, drop it, Piers. We're on the point of reaching what the lawyers call an amicable settlement. Let's not squabble over the telephone.'

'About that settlement, I think we can probably give you everything you've asked for, but there's one condition that'll have to be written into it – and don't think it's me being petty minded, it was my lawyer who thought of it – the whole thing will have to be reconsidered if you re-marry.'

'Tell him to put it in writing and send it to my solicitor,' Ella said wearily. 'I suppose I'll have to agree.'

So that was the answer to the question she had asked herself: was there anything more in life for her? No, there was not. If, as a result of a new marriage, the children were sent to live with Claudia and Piers, could she ever be happy?

'What I have to do is make myself independent,' Ella said out loud.

'How?' Verity asked.

'I forgot you were there,' Ella said. 'Expand the business, I suppose.' And that, although of course she would not say so, would also have been easier if the children had gone to boarding school.

Her hopes were given a boost the next day when she drove past Bernie's Garden Centre and saw signs of new activity. Ella drove in and parked. 'Has the sale gone through?' she asked one of the staff.

'Good morning, Mrs Armitage. Yes, we've got a new boss. He's out the back, if you want to see him.'

Ella took the box of samples of her sweets out of the car and went in search of the new man. Was it ever going to be possible to think of the place as anything but Bernie's garden centre?

It would if the purchaser of the centre had anything to do with it. He was more than ten years younger than Bernie, full of ideas and bursting with enthusiasm.

'So you're "Mrs Martin",' he said.

'Mrs Armitage, really; Ella Armitage. Martin was my maiden name. What I want to know, of course, is whether you will be continuing the arrangement I had to supply pots of jam and chutney for sale in the Garden Centre?'

'Yes, I like the look of your stuff and my wife tells me it tastes great. Coming up to Christmas we ought to get good sales.'

'What about sweets? I've done these and they're proving quite popular with the shops I've approached.'

That was a white lie because so far she had only sold a few boxes to a cafe in Canterbury.

'They're handmade, so a little bit expensive,' she went on cautiously.

'Very attractive, but I don't like the box.'

'Neither do I and I've got something better on order, gold foil on the outside and frilly white paper as lining. Have a taste.'

'You've discovered my weakness; I've got a sweet tooth. What's this?'

'Coconut ice. The others are vanilla fudge, marzipan apples and pears, chocolate truffles and peppermint creams. It's a completely new line and I'm calling it "Mrs Martin's Confectionery".'

'Keeping the old-fashioned feel. I like it, but you're going to have to shave your prices for me. I've looked at the margin Mr Caldicott was allowing you and in my opinion it was way over the top.'

'We might be able to come to an arrangement,' Ella said. 'Depending on the quantities you are prepared to take.'

By the time she left the garden centre she had secured an order for double the quantities of preserves she had been supplying to Bernie, admittedly at a price that made no allowances for friendship, but it was still good business, and her new line was well on the way to being launched, with the new owner prepared to push it aggressively for the Christmas season because, as he said frankly, he was in dire need of a novelty or two to spice up his seasonal trade.

It was still no more than a cottage industry. If she was to achieve real expansion then she would have to employ someone to help her, and that was a step Ella had difficulty in contemplating.

Still riding high on her feeling of success, she was in no mood for a visit from one of her teaching friends who had come to deliver an off-the-record warning.

'You're going to have trouble with young Jennifer unless you take steps to pull her up,' she said. 'She's been skiving off afternoon school.'

'Playing truant? Oh, no!'

'You'll remember the way it works. She goes out at lunchtime and doesn't come back, then puts in an appearance just in time to get on the school bus to come home. I doubt whether her brother and sister realise what's happening.'

'I'll have a word with her. Thanks for letting me know.'

'There's more. She's got friendly with a girl who's really bad news. Her mother's had several convictions for shoplifting and I'm afraid there's a suspicion that the daughter is going the same way.'

Feeling slightly sick, Ella waited until her friend had left and then went to Jennifer's bedroom. With a nasty feeling of spying on the child she went through the drawers and shelves. At the bottom of a drawer, pushed under a pile of underclothes she found two new T-shirts, still in their transparent envelopes.

Jennifer came home, bouncy and assertive, as she had begun to be recently. She had apparently no suspicion of having been found out when Ella said, 'Jenni, I'd like a word with you; upstairs in my room, I think.' It was only when Ella sat down on the edge of her bed and said, 'Were you in school this afternoon?' that she began to look wary.

'Yes, of course,' she said.

'But you have skipped afternoon school several times recently, haven't you? Did you imagine I wouldn't be told? That wasn't very clever of you, Jennifer.'

Flushed and sulky, Jennifer muttered, 'Everyone does it.'

'Really? I wonder they bother to open the school in that case. When you say "everyone" I take it you mean one or two of your particular friends? Not very nice friends if they encourage you to do something wrong.'

'It's not *wrong*, not really,' Jennifer said.

'Then why do you feel it necessary to be underhanded about it? Why don't you say, "By the way, Mum, I'm not planning to be in school this afternoon"?'

'Of course, *you* wouldn't like it.'

'You're right about that. Where do you go?'

'Oh, round the shops and that. The Amusement Arcade in Margate and that sort of thing. It's only a bit of fun.'

'Where did you get these, Jenni?' Ella reached over and picked up the two T-shirts from her bedside table. She was secretly relieved when Jennifer turned red and then white and looked frightened. 'If you bought them, where did you get the money?'

'Won it on a slot machine,' Jennifer said, improvising wildly.

'Have you got a receipt? And why aren't they in a shop bag?'

It took a bit more probing, but finally Ella got Jennifer to admit that she had taken the T-shirts from a shop in Kits Harbour High Street 'for a laugh'.

'I don't find it at all funny to know that my stepdaughter is a thief,' Ella said. 'We don't go in for those kind of "laughs" in this family.'

'Well, pay for them then! Dad would, I'm sure,' Jennifer said.

'You will pay for them, out of your pocket money, and you'll come with me to apologise to the shopkeeper.'

'No!'

'Yes, Jennifer. First thing tomorrow morning. Then I'll take you on to school. I shall ask to be told immediately if you don't show up for any part of the school day and if you do this silly thing of playing truant any more then I'll have to come and collect you every lunchtime and keep you with me until it's time to return you for your classes.'

Jennifer began crying in a resentful, defeated kind of way. Ella's heart ached for her, poor, silly little girl. She tried to put an arm round her, but Jennifer shrugged it off. Ella got up and found a good big handkerchief, one of Piers' handkerchiefs, she thought wryly, and handed it to Jennifer so that she could blow her nose and wipe her eyes.

'I love you very much,' she said. 'That's why I can't bear to see you spoiling your life. What effect will it have on your future, do you think, to have a criminal record as a shoplifter?'

'They don't do anything to you, not if you're just a kid,' Jennifer said.

'If the Social Services get to know of your activities they may think I'm not taking proper care of you and decide that your father is a better person to be responsible for you.'

'Boarding school might have been fun.'

'If you really mean that there's still a chance I could take up Claudia's offer,' Ella said steadily, not sure whether the child meant it or whether it was a last attempt at defiance.

'No! Don't send me away! Please don't send me away!'

152

Suddenly Jennifer was crying wildly, all pretence forgotten. She collapsed in a defeated heap against Ella and Ella put her arms round her and hugged her tight.

'It's all right, darling, it's all right. I don't want to lose you. Just try to behave, that's all. You don't know how important it is to get a good education and spoiling your chances by silly escapades like this just isn't worth it. Are you very fond of this new friend of yours? The one who talked you into playing truant?'

'She doesn't ask questions. About Dad and Claudia and the divorce and that. She just thinks it's normal. And she's fun and she thinks all the teachers are morons and she's ever so much more grown up than the other kids.'

'Shall we have her round to tea?'

She almost held her breath, but it was no real surprise when Jennifer said, 'No ... no, I don't think she'd fit in.'

'Why not?' Ella asked, smoothing the hair back from Jennifer's hot forehead.

'She laughs at things. I mean, it seems all right when we're down the town, but this is *home*.'

The next morning Ella took Jennifer to the shop where she had acquired the T-shirts.

'My daughter has made a mistake and she would like to apologise,' she said pleasantly. 'She picked up these T-shirts and now realises that she didn't pay for them.'

'Just a mistake, was it?' the shopkeeper said, none too pleasantly.

'That's right,' Ella said firmly. 'Say you're sorry, Jennifer.'

Jennifer stared at her shoes. 'Sorry,' she muttered.

'We lose too much stock that way,' the shopkeeper complained.

'But this time you're being paid in full,' Ella said. 'I'd like a receipt, please.'

When they left the shop Jennifer said sullenly, 'I don't want the beastly T-shirts.'

'That's all right, you're giving them to the charity shop.'

'But I'm paying for them!'

'You deserve some punishment. You've got off lightly, Jennifer. Be thankful.'

'Have you told Harry and Verity?'

'They know you've been playing truant and they've promised to keep an eye on you in future. The other business is just between you and me.'

She felt she had scored a small triumph when Jennifer said, reluctantly but with feeling, 'Thanks.'

So that had passed off all right, Ella thought optimistically. She tried to be particularly attentive to Jennifer in the next few weeks and it was a relief to learn from the school that both her work and behaviour had improved.

Having weathered that shock it was all the more unwelcome to learn from Harry's end-of-term report that he had been reprimanded twice for insolence.

'Why, Harry?' she asked.

'They're just a lot of old women,' was all the defence Harry could offer.

'Thanks! So am I an old woman, or you make me feel like one. Being rude to your teachers is not good tactics. They've got the upper hand, no matter what you say to them.'

'You're on their side because you were a teacher yourself.'

'True,' Ella admitted. 'I do feel for the poor souls. If you've got a real complaint, Harry, then tell me about it. Otherwise, try to keep a civil tongue in your head.'

'Nothing's the same,' Harry burst out. 'Stupid old Burlington asked me why Dad hadn't come to watch the football match against Dartford and I told him to mind his own bloody business. Dad always used to come and watch the important matches, and I scored two goals and he wasn't there.'

'I don't know what to say,' Ella admitted.

'Why couldn't you make him stay with us? You'd only been married a couple of years and when you came we thought everything would be all right and now he's gone off with rotten old Claudia and we're all lopsided.'

Should she have put up more of a fight? Swallowed her pride, kicked up hell? Would it have had any effect?

'If a man has really made up his mind to do something there's not a lot you can do to dissuade him,' she said, but it sounded feeble.

'Why do you have to divorce him? If you don't, he might come back.'

Did she want Piers back, with his sterile, facile lovemaking, his charming ways when he was getting his own way, his improvidence, his lack of moral fibre? No, she did not, not even for the sake of the children. Not even to get her own back on Claudia.

'It's a question of integrity,' she said. 'I can't live with Dad again, not after the way he's let us down. It would be a pretence and that's no basis for marriage.'

Harry looked baffled. 'Couldn't you let him live here and not be like a husband and wife?' he asked.

'Dad wouldn't accept that. He's happy with Claudia, you see. It'd be a poor substitute to live like a monk with a reproachful wife lurking in the background all the time. Besides, he's thrown up his job and I'm damned if I'm going to keep him.'

'You never think about anything but money.'

'Harry! I do! I think about you and Jennifer and Verity all the time. I love you. So, come to that, does Dad. He really, really wants you for Christmas. He told me how much he misses you.'

'I bet he would come back, if you asked him.'

'No, he wouldn't,' Ella said wearily. 'If I don't divorce him then Dad will just wait the necessary time and divorce me. There's no happy ending for this story, Harry.'

Ella was more devastated by this conversation than by Jennifer's wrong-doing. She had thought the children had accepted the situation and she had been wrong. Because they had kept quiet she had thought they were all right, and beneath the surface they were full of doubts and uncertainties. What could she do to put things right? Nothing, except go on, day after day, loving them and demonstrating that love, trying to build up the confidence that had been shaken, trying to remember that their father's defection was as painful for them as it was for her.

'I hope you haven't got any shocks stored up for me,' she said to Verity.

'I don't think so, though inside I *boil* with resentment at the way Dad's treated you. I've given Barry the push because I'm definitely off men, probably for ever.'

'Oh, darling, I do hope not! One broken-down relationship doesn't mean you have to condemn half the human race.'

155

'Well, maybe not. Actually, I haven't got time for boyfriends at the moment. I do find they take up a lot of room in your life.'

'True,' Ella agreed, trying not to smile.

'My big news is that the Drama Group are doing a boiled-down version of "Great Expectations" for Dickens Week next year and, guess what?'

'You've been offered a part?'

'The young Estella.'

'Congratulations! All those lovely snooty speeches to Pip. I couldn't be more pleased for you.'

'I'm over the moon. Mum, are we going to have to take a present for Claudia when we go to Spain for Christmas?'

'I hadn't thought about it but, yes, of course you must, as a matter of politeness, if nothing else.'

'A box of your sweets laced with arsenic?'

'Don't tempt me! No, something smelly and pretentious for the dressing table or the bathroom, I think. We'll make it a joint present and I'll put you in charge of it. Harry might hit her over the head with it. Verity, do make them behave, won't you?'

'I'll try, but it's going to be difficult. Jennifer and Harry take the view that if we play up we might not have to go again.'

'But then you won't see Dad. And you do want to see him, don't you?'

'Not really. It's so embarrassing. I mean, him living with Claudia. How could he possibly prefer her to you?'

'Don't imagine I haven't asked myself the same question!'

The days flew by: end of term events, a carol service, last minute shopping, a rush of orders for the sweets of which Ella was heartily sick, packing; and then, on the Saturday before Christmas, the long drive to the airport. Ella put the children into the charge of a stewardess, even though Verity said with some force that she was entirely capable of seeing that none of them fell out of an aeroplane, for goodness sake. They would be met at the other end, nothing could possibly go wrong, but Ella made them promise to let her know that they had arrived safely.

The drive home was dreary and when she arrived there were boxes and boxes of sweets to be packed and labelled. She would deliver them on Monday, ready for the last minute shoppers, and after that she would be free for the rest of the week, except that she really ought to use the space provided by the children's absence to replenish her stock.

It was lonely in the house on her own and yet, in a way, Ella was glad of the respite. Without any interruptions she could use the time to clear her mind and try to make decisions about the future.

The sight of the small fir tree in the living room, carefully decorated but without much point when there was no one to see it, made her gulp. Tears, she thought scornfully; what was the point in shedding tears? She switched on the fairy lights and poured herself a glass of sherry. There was, of course, nothing on television she wanted to see. She would get herself some supper shortly, have a bath and an early night. Tomorrow she would go to church and join in the cheerful singing; she still had her proper Christmas to come when the children came home for the New Year.

The telephone rang and Ella reached out a hand for it, anticipating that it would be a call from Spain to report their safe arrival. The line was poor, very crackly, with the sound coming and going spasmodically. It was a man's voice, that much she could make out, and then it became clearer and she heard, 'Ella, that is you, isn't it? I'm glad I got you. It's Toby. Can you hear me?'

'I can hear you,' Ella said faintly. 'What a surprise! Where are you? In Kabul?'

'No, I'm in Pakistan for a few days and I thought I'd seize the opportunity to wish you all a merry Christmas. It's not celebrated here, of course, except by a few beleaguered Christians. What are you doing?'

'Just having a quiet drink by the fire. How are you, Toby? Are you well? And happy?'

'I'd be better and happier if you were with me, but I suppose I'm not allowed to say that. Don't ask me what I'd like for Christmas because I might tell you. One thing I will mention, though, is that I'd be glad of an occasional letter. Has anyone written to me, because nothing seems to be getting through, not even via the Red Cross.'

'We have written,' Ella said.

'Damn, I was afraid things had been going astray. Not that one can wonder at it with the chaos in Afghanistan. Look, I might get cut off at any moment. Can I have a quick word with the kids?'

'They're not here.'

'That's disappointing. I doubt whether I'll be able to make another call. I must start back tomorrow. Where are they?'

'They flew off to Spain this afternoon.'

'Spain? Without you? I don't understand.'

'Toby, I didn't realise you were so out of touch. Stand by for a shock. Piers has left me and gone to live in Spain with Claudia. The children are visiting them for Christmas.'

Ella heard her voice thickening and hoped Toby would put it down to the bad line.

'I can't believe I'm hearing this,' she heard him say, but he sounded very faint and far away. 'Ella, what's happening? Are you divorcing him? Ella, can you hear me?'

'Yes,' Ella said, answering both questions, but there was no further response, just a click and a whirring noise. She thought she heard her name repeated over and over again, but it might have been imagination and, in any case, Toby could quite obviously not hear anything she said.

The telephone rang again as soon as she put it down. Ella snatched it up, but it was only Verity, loud and clear, reporting that they had had a good flight and Dad had been at the airport to meet them and it was surprisingly warm even though night had fallen.

'Uncle Toby just rang,' Ella forced herself to say. 'It was a terrible line, but he sends his love and best wishes.'

'Oh, how *miserable* that we missed him,' Verity mourned. 'Had he had our Christmas cards?'

'No, but they may be waiting for him when he goes back to Kabul. He was somewhere in Pakistan. He was surprised to hear that you were in Spain.'

'Anyone would be,' Verity said. 'I'll have to go. Claudia's got a meal waiting for us. See you soon, Mum. Have a happy Christmas.'

'You too, dear. Give my love to Jennifer and Harry.'

The tears were running down Ella's cheeks as she put the telephone down. Damn Toby, she thought, searching for a

158

handkerchief. I would have been all right if he hadn't rung. Just like him to chuck me a couple of words of what might be love and then disappear into the void. I am not in love with him; I won't be in love with him; I can't afford any more complications. It's just like Verity said, men take up too much space in a woman's life. I shall go and make myself a cheese omelette and have it with a glass of wine and some fruit and coffee. A proper little orgy. Oh, Toby, Toby; I could do with you *here*, not thousands of miles away making pretty speeches about what you'd like for Christmas.

In Canterbury jail Reg Daley requested a Christmas visit from his wife, guessing that the influence of the season would work on her sufficiently to make her come.

'A damned awful Christmas this is going to be,' Mrs Daley complained as soon as she was sitting opposite him.

'Worse for me,' Reg said.

'Serves you right,' but it was said automatically, his physical presence working on her as it always did so that she forgave him all his peccadilloes and even his occasional violence.

'Now, you look here, Angie; I never did it. True, I had a bit of an argument with Burtman, and I pinched his wallet ...'

'And how much did I see of that?'

'I've got it laid by for a rainy day. I can put my hands on it when I want it.'

'You went and beat up our Leah.'

'So would you have done if you'd seen those pictures. I was really disgusted. The thing is, Burtman was alive when I left him. A bit uncomfortable, I admit, but alive.'

'But he croaked afterwards.'

'Not from anything I did to him. Leah can clear me, if she goes about it in the way I'll tell you.'

'But will she do it after the way you treated her?'

'I reckon she will, if it's put to her the right way. I was going straight until this charge cropped up, you know I was, Angie. I'm too old for prison. I can't take it like I used to, and the new kids coming in are a nasty lot, not like my old mob. Tell Leah that if she sees me right there'll be no hard words about her turning me in and I'll make her a tasty little present.'

'Out of what you've laid by for a rainy day?'

'That's right. They don't come much wetter than this. I want out and Leah can do the trick.'

'Of course you'll go to the party,' Claudia said. 'Girls of your age love parties.'

'I won't know anyone,' Verity said.

'They're all prepared to be friendly – if you'll let them.'

'I haven't got anything to wear.'

'I'll give you your Christmas present in advance. Come and try it on.'

The dress had a black velvet sleeveless top and a very short scarlet satin skirt of overlapping panels which shifted as Verity moved. She looked in despair at her thin, milk-white arms emerging from the black velvet. Everyone else would be tanned all over.

'What about shoes?' she asked.

'I made the shop send three pairs of sandals for you to try on. And I can give you some black tights.'

On the night of the party Verity got ready in a mood of sullen resignation. There was no getting out of it, but that was not to say that she had to pretend to enjoy it.

'You look weird,' Harry told her.

'It's a nice dress,' Jennifer said.

'But it's not *me*.'

'No, it's not. I think it's mean, sending you to a party and leaving us at home. And on Christmas Eve, too.'

'Exactly! Who wants to go to a party on Christmas Eve?'

Piers drove his daughter to the house where the party was to be held. It was one of the larger villas, belonging to an ex-patriate Englishman with a great deal of money to throw around. He owned a helicopter, a yacht, a powerful speedboat and two large cars. He was currently on his third wife – as Piers would be soon, he reminded himself uneasily – and he had two children, a boy of seventeen and a girl of Verity's age. They would, Claudia said optimistically, be nice friends for Verity.

The party started at ten o'clock. 'But that's bedtime!' Harry had said incredulously.

'Not in Spain,' Jennifer pointed out. 'You know that's the time most people have dinner.'

160

'Grown up people, not kids.'

'Verity isn't a kid,' Claudia said. 'It's time she grew up. She's very young for her age.'

The villa was blazing with light and shuddering to the sound of disco music when Piers drew up outside.

'How will I get home?' Verity asked, panic-stricken.

'There'll be plenty of people to give you a lift,' Piers said. 'Or, if you're really stuck, ring me and I'll come and pick you up.'

She had to go in alone. Calling up all her reserves of courage, Verity went up the steps, through the pillared entrance and in through the open front door. The music crashed over her and she stood in the hall, looking round for a clue what to do next. She saw Lolinda, the daughter of the house, and thankfully made her way over to her.

'Hi! You're Verity, aren't you?' the girl asked. 'Nice to see you 'n all that. Grab yourself some floor space and dance.'

It was not that Verity couldn't dance. Indeed, she was rather good at it. But to walk on to the floor cold and start dancing on her own, that was more than she could do.

'Come, we will dance together,' a voice behind her said.

Verity turned. He was the most beautiful thing she had ever seen, tall, dark, with eyes like ... like brown velvet; slim, athletic, and a fabulous dancer. It did not need Lolinda's wail of, 'Oh, Miguel! I wanted to dance with you!' to tell Verity that she had captured a prize. Perhaps, just possibly, there was something in this party business after all.

Even the disco hired by the richest man took an occasional break. In the comparative silence that fell, broken only by shouts and laughter, Verity turned her delighted face up to Miguel. 'Oh, *thank* you!'

'But it is I who should thank you. You dance very well. Have some champagne.'

Verity took a tentative sip from the glass he handed her and wrinkled her nose. People actually *liked* this stuff? She would have to drink it as Miguel had given it to her. Resolutely she swallowed it, but by that time her partner had wandered away and left her.

She tried to join in, helped a little by her first glass of champagne, but the rest of the crowd all knew one another and she

161

was definitely an outsider, especially since Lolinda had taken exception to having her favourite man snaffled.

She was not much of a hostess, in Verity's opinion, since she took no trouble to see that her guests were having a good time, but concentrated on her own enjoyment. The parents were nowhere to be seen and Verity guessed they had been sent out for the evening.

She danced with Lolinda's brother and with another youngster whose name she never caught, but the highlight of the evening had been that first dance with Miguel and after that it was downhill all the way as far as Verity was concerned.

The food was good, if one happened to be feeling hungry at midnight. She nibbled a couple of lobster patties, a chicken vol-au-vent and some meat balls on a cocktail stick and then, attracted by sounds of applause, wandered back into the room which had been cleared for dancing.

The boy called Miguel had leapt on to a table and was performing a flamenco dance. Verity winced at the damage his heels were doing to the polished wooden surface, but he did look marvellous, his head arrogantly tilted, his hands clapping in a staccato rhythm that echoed the drumming of his feet. Lolinda was circling the table, swishing her skirts in imitation of a gypsy dancer, but when Miguel took no notice of her she tried to clamber up on the table to join him. Miguel kicked out with one of his flashing feet, caught her under the chin and sent her sprawling, to cheers and laughter from his audience.

Miguel concluded his dance and jumped, knees bent, heels almost touching his buttocks, and landed perfectly on the floor, just opposite Verity. He was flushed, out of breath, laughing and triumphant, and he seemed to have no idea that Lolinda was crying bitterly and bleeding from a gash on her chin.

'You hurt her,' Verity said.

'Who?' Miguel glanced over his shoulder. 'Oh, her! Silly cow. Come, I need a drink.'

He had taken hold of her arm, just above the wrist, and Verity could not free herself. She let him drag her to the buffet, but when Miguel took more champagne, Verity helped herself to the orange juice she had already been thankful to find available.

162

'What is your name?'

Looking up into his smiling, clouded eyes Verity saw that he had no recollection of her, no memory of having danced with her earlier this evening. She had thought he might be drunk, but now she began to suspect that he had taken something else.

'Are you on drugs?' she asked, with the bluntness that Claudia deplored.

'Nothing serious,' Miguel said, amused. 'Just Ecstacy. You would like?'

He felt in the pocket of his tight fitting trousers and then, frowning, in the inside pocket of his jacket, until he found a small white envelope and tipped two tablets out on to his hand.

'No, thanks,' Verity said, backing away.

'It will loosen you up, give you better enjoyment.'

'I'm fine, thanks all the same.'

Miguel replaced one of the tablets and put the other into his mouth. 'Get me a glass of water, *querida*,' he ordered.

'Spit it out,' Verity said. 'It's not good for you, especially if you've had some already.'

'You are such a prude. Don't I speak marvellous English? I have been at school in America, you know. Get me some water.'

'Get it yourself.'

Miguel frowned, looking puzzled. 'Don't you like me? Wouldn't you like to have sex with me? You are very skinny, but you have beautiful eyes. Get me my water and I will take you upstairs.'

Oh, no, you won't, Verity thought grimly. She marched to the buffet, seized a pitcher of iced water and flung the contents full into Miguel's face. There was a shout of delight from the onlookers, but Verity did not wait to see the result of her gesture. She walked out, right out of the house, until the darkness and the cooler air outside brought her to a halt.

She would have to go back inside and ring her father to come and collect her. She turned and was brought up by a sudden horrified realisation that she did not know the telephone number of Claudia's villa. There must be a telephone directory somewhere in the house, but Verity quailed at searching for it. She could hardly ask Lolinda, who would undoubtedly be furious with her. Perhaps she could find one of the servants, although they seemed to have wisely made themselves scarce.

Cautiously, she crept back to the hall and then down the stairs to the kitchen quarters. She heard voices and opened a door. Four men in their shirt sleeves sat playing cards round the table. They looked up in surprise as Verity came in and one of them got up.

'Do you speak English?' Verity asked.

'Certainly, señorita. What is it you wish?'

'I want to go home, but I don't know the telephone number of the villa where I'm staying.' In spite of a resolute effort, her lower lip quivered ominously. 'If I could ring my father he would come and fetch me.'

'What is the name of the villa?'

'The Villa Medina. It belongs to Mrs Caldicott.'

The oldest man in the group, gnarled and weather-beaten, said something in Spanish and a laugh went round the table.

'Pedro says that it is no distance if you go down the hill by the old path.'

Verity looked doubtfully at the strappy sandals that were already making her feet hurt.

'He is offering to take you on his donkey.'

To the man's surprise, Verity's face lit up. 'Oh, that would be *fun!*'

'You think so? Very well, when we have finished this hand he will take you.'

The card game resumed, with a lot of vigorous slapping down of cards on the table and exclamations. At last, amidst laughter and groans, the man who spoke English laid down his cards triumphantly and scooped up the small pile of money in the middle.

'Did you not enjoy the party?' he asked Verity.

'No, not very much. They all started to behave in a very silly way so I thought I would go home. Dad – my father – thought someone would take me, but there was no one there I would trust to drive a car tonight.'

'You have reason,' he said drily. 'Which is not to say that they will not try. Pedro speaks no English, but he is a good man, very trusty. You will be safe with him.'

'Does the donkey have a name?'

164

He looked surprised, but he put the question to Pedro.

'Modestina,' he said. 'And I never knew that before.'

Modestina had a saddle, hard but serviceable, and Verity in her short skirt had no difficulty in mounting the little donkey. Pedro took the bridle in one hand and a long stick in the other and they set out. The night was dark except for the stars overhead, but neither Pedro nor Modestina seemed to have any doubt of the way. They clattered through the garden of the villa and out the far end into a grove of orange trees, following a narrow, stony track. There was a faint, sweet scent in the air.

When they emerged into the open Verity could just make out the sea below them. It was Christmas Day, she realised, and here she was, riding on a donkey with an old man leading her, just like the Virgin Mary. She couldn't have been much older than me, she thought. Gosh, there's a thought. It was almost worth going to that horrible party to be going home like this. The air was cold on her bare arms, but against her legs she could feel the donkey's warm, rough pelt.

She began to recognise the houses they were passing. In a few minutes they had reached the Villa Medina and she was sliding off the donkey's back. She sought in her mind for her scanty words of Spanish.

'*Muchas gracias*,' she ventured.

'*De nada*,' Pedro replied. He took off his battered old hat in a gesture that was positively courtly.

'Happy Christmas,' Verity said. 'Er ... *Buon natale!*'

Pedro nodded and then he led Modestina away and Verity let herself into the house. She tried to be quiet, but her father appeared at the top of the stairs, shrugging on his dressing gown and yawning.

'You got home all right then,' he said. 'Did you enjoy it?'

'No, it was *horrible*. I say, do you think we could make a cup of tea?'

'I don't see why not. Come into the kitchen and tell me all about it.'

He filled the kettle while Verity settled herself at the table.

'There were no adults there,' she said. 'And the kids were unbelievably stupid. The one's who didn't get drunk were on drugs.'

'No! I didn't know it would be like that.'

'Honestly, Dad, you might have guessed. Bernie and Claudia always mixed with a pretty funny crowd out here.'

'Why didn't you ring me?'

'I hadn't got the number. Would you believe it? Absolutely elementary.'

'I should have thought of that.' Piers made the tea and for once he looked really bothered.

'Dad, I came home on a donkey! It was great. We came down the hill by an old mule track and it was all quiet and still and smelling of orange blossom.'

'Who on earth was at the party with a donkey?'

'His name was Pedro and he was about ninety. I think he was a gardener or a farmer or something. He didn't speak any English.'

'You make my blood run cold. You could have been kidnapped or attacked or anything.'

'There was a nice servant at the house who said he could be trusted. Besides, you could *see* he was a nice man by the way he treated his donkey.'

'It's not an infallible rule,' Piers said drily. 'Still, I'm glad it turned out all right.' There was a short silence and then he said, 'Claudia meant it for the best. She was worried about you finding it dull here.'

'It's not dull exactly, but of course it's not like being at home.' Verity waited a moment and then asked carefully, 'I suppose it's permanent? You're not likely to come back?'

'Of course it's permanent.' He spoke too sharply, something Verity was shrewd enough to notice and wonder about.

'You really like it here?' she probed.

'Naturally I do. Think what I had before. A dull job, with little hope of advancement. Now I'm at the beginning of an exciting new venture.'

'The apartment block, you mean? You call that exciting?'

'Claudia means to expand if it's a success, and I see no reason why it should fail. We could be laying the foundations of a new business empire, and look at the surroundings – sun, sea, beautiful scenery. I mean to get a boat. Next time you come we'll do some sailing.'

'That'll be nice,' Verity said, but somewhere inside her there was a tremendous sadness.

'Everything's working out at home?' Piers ventured to ask. 'Ella's okay?'

'Oh, yes. She works very hard, of course.'

'But she's not too unhappy?'

'Do you care?'

'I do, as it happens. It wasn't an easy decision, to give up what I had, including you kids, to come to a new country and start a new life. I agonised over it for ...'

'Several days,' Verity interrupted him. 'Look, Dad, I accept that your mind's made up and the divorce is inevitable. Just don't expect me to pretend I like it, that's all. We've lost out, Harry and Jennifer and me, and it matters to us, terribly. If you're happy I'll try to be glad for you, though I really think you need your mind examined, but we're *not* happy and not all the treats and parties in the world will put that right.'

She had thought he would be angry, but all he said in a defeated way was, 'I'm sorry.'

Verity stood up. 'I do still love you, in a sort of way,' she said. 'I'm too tired to say it properly tonight. I'm going to bed.'

She was late coming down to breakfast, which made Harry and Jennifer look at her reproachfully.

'You might say Happy Christmas,' Harry said.

'Oh, sorry. Happy Christmas, Harry. Happy Christmas, Jennifer.'

'There are loads of presents for us under the tree in the sitting room,' Jennifer said. 'We wouldn't open any of them until you came. Did you enjoy the party?'

'Not much, but guess what? I came home on a donkey!'

'You are lucky. No one ever offered me a ride on a donkey.'

They opened their presents, too lavish, too extravagant, and said polite thank yous.

'We haven't brought our presents from home because Mum said we could have a second Christmas at the New Year,' Harry explained. He fixed his eyes on Claudia. 'Do you like that glass bowl with talcum powder? We chose it ourselves and it cost an awful lot of money.'

'It's beautiful,' Claudia said hastily. 'And the powder is from the range I use.'

'I was the one who remembered that,' Jennifer told her.

167

'Thank you, darling. I gather the party was a bit of a fiasco, Verity?'

'Not quite my scene,' Verity said, feeling against her will that she ought to apologise for her lack of enjoyment.

'They're a sophisticated lot. I suppose you're a bit young for them.'

The telephone rang and Claudia went out to the hall to answer it. They could hear her exclaiming and then she came back looking so shaken that Piers instinctively got to his feet.

'Get me a drink,' she said. 'The most awful thing has happened. A terrible accident . . .'

'Not Mum?' Verity exclaimed. 'It wasn't a call from home?'

'No, of course not. Some of the young people who were at the party with you last night. Lolinda, and a boy called Miguel Da Costa – his father's a millionaire and his mother's a film star . . .'

'I danced with him.'

'Did you? I thought you said you didn't enjoy yourself? Miguel won't be doing any more dancing, poor little sod.'

'He's not dead?'

'He might as well be. He was driving his sports car, with Lolinda beside him and two more girls sitting on the back of the seat behind them. He ran off the road and crashed. Lolinda isn't badly hurt, but the other two were flung out and have broken bones and head injuries.'

'And Miguel?'

'They had to amputate his left leg.'

'Oh, no! No! I can't bear it.'

'Don't have hysterics, you hardly knew him.'

'You don't understand. If you'd seen him last night, dancing on a table . . . he was . . . he was so . . .'

It was no use, there were no words she could find to describe Miguel's vitality and animal grace. 'He was taking Ecstacy,' she said flatly. 'I expect that's why he crashed. That, and the drink. I told you it was a horrible party.'

'His poor parents,' Claudia said. 'What a Christmas.'

It subdued them all. Harry tugged at Verity's arm and whispered, 'Are we going to church? There's an English service at eleven o'clock.'

'Will it make us feel any better? All right, let's get ready. It might be a good idea to get out of the house.'

168

They were surprised when Piers came with them. Claudia was too busy on the telephone, ringing all her friends to tell them the terrible story. 'Spoiling everyone else's Christmas,' Harry commented, but not in Piers' hearing.

They did feel better when they came back from the familiar service and well-known carols and the walk had got rid of the last of Verity's lingering headache. She still found her eyes filling with tears during the day whenever she thought of Miguel, but she said nothing to the others and they had a happier day than she had expected, except that Jennifer over-indulged in food and drink and woke Verity up in the night with the pathetic wail, 'Verity, I've been sick!'

Verity roused herself. 'Where?' she asked.

'All over my bed. It's horrible, horrible. I feel awful.'

'Go and call Claudia,' Verity said, with an evil smile in the darkness. 'She wants to be mother, let her cope with it.'

She was sorry for Jennifer, though it wouldn't have happened if she hadn't been such a little pig, but she relished the sound of Claudia's disbelieving voice as she was brought out of her bed to deal with soiled sheets and a tearful little girl who insisted that she needed to have a bath *now*, not in the morning, and to have her hair washed and dried as well.

By lunchtime on Boxing Day, for which she had arranged a barbecue round the swimming pool, Claudia had recovered. She was in her element entertaining the rich and, in some cases, glamorous expatriates who lived in the adjoining villas.

The children were studiously polite and all her friends approved of them and thought she was tremendously brave to be a stepmother to them.

'Is she really our stepmother?' Jennifer asked Harry.

'Not yet,' Harry said. 'Perhaps not ever if you help out like you did last night.'

'I was sick!'

'Yeah, it was great.'

They were quizzed about what they meant to do with their lives.

'I'm going to be an actress,' Verity said with serene certainty.

'You'll have to like partying rather better than you do at the moment, sweetie,' Claudia commented.

'A serious actress.'

'And Harry?' one of the men asked.

'Harry's a champion footballer,' Piers said with pride.

'A short-lived career. What do you really mean to be, Harry boy? A property wheelerdealer, like your Dad?'

There was a ripple of laughter which Piers did not appear to appreciate.

'Actually, I'll probably be a clergyman,' Harry said.

There was a startled silence. 'Of all possible professions, that's the last one I would have expected,' their questioner said. 'How about that, Piers? Did you know you'd got a budding padre in the family?'

'It's news to me,' Piers said.

'I spoke to the Vicar,' Harry explained. 'And he said if I felt the same in three or four years' time I could talk to him about it again.'

'You'll probably want to be something quite different by then,' Piers said.

'No, I don't think so.'

'I'm going to be a vet,' Jennifer said importantly. 'Do you know Verity came home on a donkey on Christmas Eve? I do think she has the most tremendous luck.'

'My stepchildren are all a little eccentric,' Claudia said.

'Better a donkey than a sports car,' somebody put in and for a moment a shadow fell over the party.

'Let's not get morbid,' someone else said. 'That Da Costa boy was riding for a fall.'

There was a murmur of agreement, while Verity thought savagely, then why didn't someone pull him up? They put it away from them, unwilling to spoil a day's enjoyment, and no one noticed that Piers' older daughter had to go indoors and wipe her eyes.

On the day the children were due home Ella made up her mind to set out good and early, just in case she ran into any delays. As soon as she set foot outside she knew it was going to be a difficult journey. There was a thin rain falling, which had led her to believe that the weather had turned warmer, but that was far from being the case. As the rain hit the ground it froze. Two steps from the front door Ella came to a halt, unable to keep her feet. Seriously alarmed, she stepped on to the bare, rough earth of a flower bed and managed to shuffle as far as the garage door.

Inside the garage there was a bag of sand which she had used to mix with compost for some of her plants. She got a trowel and scattered it liberally over the drive. With that to give her a foothold she was able to walk to the front gate and treat the path outside as well as a section of the road. The road, she thought optimistically, did not look as dangerous as the path, perhaps because the passing cars were keeping it from icing over. It was not a day when she would have chosen to set out on a long drive, but she could see no help for it.

It was a relief to find the main road and the motorway relatively clear. She made good time to the airport, parked, checked that the flight was still expected to arrive on time and treated herself to a coffee, which she felt she needed.

She was waiting in the arrivals area, scanning the faces of the people coming through, long before she could reasonably expect Verity, Harry and Jennifer to have claimed their luggage. When she caught sight of them, looking round warily as if they were afraid she might not be there, she felt a lump in her throat. What a fool she was to have let them get so dear to her, and yet how rewarding it was to see the way their faces lit up with delighted smiles as they caught sight of her.

'You all look brown,' was all she could think of to say.

'We had lots of sun, but it wasn't always very warm,' Verity said.

'Did you have a good time?'

'Some of it was good, some of it was *awful*. How about you? Did you miss us?'

'Of course I did. For me, Christmas starts now. It's a horrible day back home, freezing rain, black ice. I thought at one time I wasn't going to be able to get the car on the road.'

'Will we be able to get home?' Jennifer asked.

'I'm sure we will. I had no trouble once I was on the main road.'

They had only been away a week and yet in some subtle way they had changed. They were tired, that was obvious. Too many late nights, Ella diagnosed.

'Any messages?' she asked casually.

171

'Dad sent a letter. I'll give it to you when we arrive,' Verity said, and with that Ella had to be content for the time being.

Jennifer and Harry both fell asleep in the back of the car as they sped down the motorway. Verity sat beside Ella, silent and tense. Once, when Ella had to brake more quickly than she liked, she heard Verity draw in her breath sharply.

'We're all right,' Ella said. 'The road's not slippery, not here.'

'Could we slow down a bit?'

'I'm well within the speed limit.'

'I just feel ... I didn't know it would affect me like this.'

'Tell me. I can see something happened while you were away.'

'A boy I met crashed his car and had to have a leg cut off.'

'Verity, how terrible. Did you know him well?'

'We'd only met that evening. I danced with him. He was ...' Again she tried to convey Miguel's quality and failed. 'He was a great dancer,' she said lamely.

'I'm truly sorry.'

'It was all his own fault,' Verity said. 'That makes it worse. He shouldn't have been driving, not in the state he was in. I threw a jug of water over him, but obviously it didn't bring him to his senses.'

'It seems not,' Ella agreed. 'Look, darling, we can't talk properly now. Tell me all about it when we get home.'

'Yes, I will.'

'Do you want to stop on the way?'

'No, I'd rather keep going.' She glanced over her shoulder. 'And the other two are asleep. Did you know Harry was thinking of going into the church?'

'Good grief! No, I certainly didn't.'

'He came out with it at the Boxing Day barbecue round the pool. Consternation all round.'

'I can imagine. Well, what can I say? If it's what he really wants ...'

'I suspect that's what Dad has written about as much as anything.'

They lapsed into silence and the rest of the journey went well except, as Ella had feared, for the last half mile. There was an icy slush on the road which was beginning to freeze in the growing dusk. She could sense a worrying lack of grip of the tyres on the surface and slowed down to a very sedate speed. She negotiated the turn into Jemima Road with a real feeling of thankfulness. If she could just get them up the first slope of the road and make the sharp turn in at the front gate without slithering into the edge of the curb or a gatepost, she would be profoundly thankful. It had been an exceedingly fatiguing day.

As she approached the house Ella could see flashing lights. An ambulance. A police car.

Harry roused himself from the back of the car. 'Has there been an accident?'

'Goodness only knows. Stay where you are while I go and find out.'

Ella parked on the far side of the road and made her way gingerly through the treacherous slush to her front gate. The ambulance men were lifting an inert figure on to a stretcher on wheels, watched by two policemen.

'I live here,' Ella said. 'What's happened?'

'Are you Mrs Ella Armitage?' one of the policemen asked.

'Yes, I am.'

'Can you identify this man?'

The man on the stretcher struggled to raise himself on one arm while the ambulance men tried to stop him from moving. The light from the security light on the porch fell on his face.

'Toby!' Ella exclaimed.

'Slipped on the ice. Broke my leg. Couldn't raise anyone to help me. Nobody going by ...'

'Can you wonder at it on a night like this?'

'Knew you had a burglar alarm so I levered myself up and broke a window. Thought that would bring someone.'

'We were alerted because there was no reply from your keyholder,' the policeman said.

'My neighbours are away and I've only been out for the day,' Ella said. 'This is Captain Toby Greville, my ... my brother-in-law. I wasn't expecting him, but certainly he meant no harm. Where are you taking him?'

'To Margate,' the ambulanceman said. 'As well as the broken leg he's had a nasty blow on the head. We suspect there may be a bit of concussion, so they'll certainly keep him in overnight.'

Ella stooped over the stretcher. 'I can't come with you,' she said. 'I've got three exhausted children in the car and I'm pretty worn out myself. I'll see you tomorrow.'

Chapter Ten

'I survived seven years in the Army, kidnapping in Colombia, bullets and bombs in Afghanistan, only to be felled by a patch of ice in Kits Harbour,' Toby said.

'I do think it was a clever idea to set off the burglar alarm,' Harry said.

'I don't think Ella admires my initiative.'

'If the insurance company won't pay up for the new window, then you will,' Ella said. 'If you knew the trouble I'd had to get someone to come out on a Sunday, and the Sunday before New Year at that, to put in a new pane of glass!'

'I'm sorry, but it was better than dying of hypothermia. For all I knew, you might have gone away for days on end.'

'True. I suppose I'll have to forgive you.'

She had taken Harry with her to the hospital, leaving the two girls behind, so that there would be room in the back of the car to transport Toby in some comfort.

'I don't want to be a nuisance,' he said. 'I could get a room or something, like I did before.'

'Don't be silly. You need looking after. We've got it all arranged. You can have the sofa bed in the lounge. It's not the most comfortable bed in the world, but you're used to roughing it, and it means you won't have to struggle up and down stairs. Thank goodness we've got a downstairs cloakroom.'

She was avoiding looking at him, dismayed by her desire to put her arms round him and comfort him. He looked so forlorn in his pyjama jacket, with his hair on end, and a big red graze on his forehead.

The hospital, overwhelmed by the number of casualties the

175

icy conditions had brought in, was only too anxious to get rid of him. He was handed painkillers and an appointment card, wheeled out of the ward, into a lift and manoeuvred into Ella's car almost before she had had time to draw breath.

'Six weeks in plaster,' Toby complained. 'I'll go mad.'

'What about your work?' Ella asked as they left the hospital car park.

'What indeed! I swapped my leave period with a colleague because ... well, you know why. I was only supposed to be in England a week, but I doubt whether they'll want me back as one of the walking wounded. We've got more than enough of them as it is. I've been told I can have a lighter plaster put on after a couple of weeks and I might be able to travel then.'

'You can stay with us as long as you like,' Harry assured him. 'It'll be brilliant. We're all staying up to see the New Year in to make up for having to go to Spain for Christmas.'

'You'll have to tell me all about that,' Toby said. 'I'm exceedingly interested in your visit to Spain.'

'That can wait until later,' Ella said firmly.

The weather had not improved. Snow was falling and looked as if it had set in for a heavy fall.

'We were swimming outdoors last week,' Harry commented. 'But it does seem much more natural to see the snow.'

'Natural it may be, but I could live without it,' Ella said with a sigh.

'Does it snow in Afghanistan?'

'I'll say it does!' Toby said with feeling. 'And it's cold enough to freeze your ... toes off.'

They arrived at the house and Ella turned in the drive with as much thankfulness as she had felt the evening before.

'I'm not taking the car out again until after the New Year,' she said. 'If anyone wants to go anywhere, they can walk.'

'Jolly difficult for Uncle Toby on crutches,' Harry pointed out.

'He'll just have to make up his mind to stay indoors; provided, that is, that we can manage to get him indoors.'

With the aid of the children and a determined effort from Toby they managed to lever him out of the car and into the house.

'Mum, I never gave you Dad's letter,' Verity said as soon as they had settled Toby by the fire.

176

'Help, I forgot all about it. I'll read it while I'm taking my shoes and coat off upstairs. Be an angel and make Uncle Toby a cup of coffee.'

She ran up the stairs, unbuttoning her coat with one hand. In her bedroom she sat on the bed and tore open Piers' letter. He had obviously found it difficult to write, it was very stiffly worded, but it did contain an apology for sending Verity to a party that had been totally unsuitable. Claudia, he said, had meant it for the best.

There was one passage that made Ella pause. 'This business of sending the kids to Spain for holidays may have to be re-thought,' Piers wrote. 'I was pleased to have them with me, but they didn't enjoy themselves as much as I hoped they would. We must have a talk about it before Easter. Perhaps I'll come over to England and take them somewhere. You might let me know if anywhere suitable occurs to you.'

Ella was folding the letter up when Verity put her head round the door.

'I made you some coffee, too,' she said. 'I brought it up in case you hadn't finished reading Dad's letter.'

'Finished reading it, but not finished thinking about it,' Ella said. 'I gather the holiday was not an entire success?'

'How could it be?' Verity asked unanswerably. 'Mum, I asked Dad if he was dead set on going on living with Claudia. At least, that isn't how I put it, but it was what I meant. He said it was absolutely permanent, but the way he said it made me wonder if it was.' She paused and swallowed and then went on in a rush, 'If he wanted to come back, would you have him?'

Ella was at a loss. She had made up her mind, she thought she had made up her mind, that there could be no possibility of living with Piers again. But, for the sake of the children? She sat for a moment in thought and then she said, 'No, I can't take him back.'

'I was afraid you wouldn't.'

Ella looked at her stepdaughter helplessly. So young, and yet so nearly a woman. How much could she understand of the trials and betrayals of a failed marriage? Should she tell Verity about the vasectomy? Would she ever understand unless she knew? And yet, it seemed unfair to burden the girl with the knowledge of her father's long deception.

'There are some things so personal that it's difficult to talk about them,' Ella said carefully. 'But there's one thing I must point out: apart from your vague suspicion, Piers has shown no sign that he wants to come back. He might leave Claudia, I can foresee a possibility of them splitting up, but I don't think he'd want to return to me.'

They sat in silence for a moment and then Verity added, 'He's not really a bad man.'

'He has many good points,' Ella said steadily, though she would have been hard put to name any of them. 'He loves you children,' she said conscientiously. 'He's suggesting he might come to England at Easter and take you somewhere more congenial than Marbella.'

'Just him, not Claudia?'

'Do you think she'd want to come?'

'I doubt it!'

'If you can think of anywhere you'd like to go, let me know and I'll suggest it to Dad.'

'Stratford-on-Avon!'

'What about the others? Not much fun for them. Unless … if you had a long boat on the canal and tied up at Stratford for a day or two?'

'Great idea! Even Harry would enjoy that. Shall I talk to them about it?'

'Better wait until I've put it to Dad. Come on, we've been up here ages. Uncle Toby will think we've deserted him.'

'You don't mind having him here, do you?' Verity asked as they went down the stairs.

'I could have done without it,' Ella said, but she was thinking more of her own ambivalent attitude towards Toby than about the nuisance of having an incapacitated adult to look after.

The children were delighted to have him, of course, and he was patient with them, even letting them entice him out into the back garden to make a snowman the next day when the snow was deep but the sky had cleared and there was a glitter of cold winter sunshine.

'Anyone who falls down and breaks a second leg will lie out on the ground until the robins cover him up with leaves,' Ella said caustically. 'Which leads me into telling you that you'll be alone this evening because we're going to the pantomime.'

178

'Couldn't we get an extra ticket for Uncle Toby?' Verity asked.

'I've tried and it's full.'

'I don't actually mind whether I go or not. He could have my seat.'

'Meaning you're too grown up for pantomime, and I'm not?' Toby asked. 'Thanks for the thought, but I really don't think I can get myself into a theatre seat and sit in one place for hours on end.'

'Does your leg hurt an awful lot?' Jennifer asked sympathetically.

'It's not too bad, but I'll not be running a marathon this year.'

'Silly! This year ends tomorrow!'

'So it does,' Toby agreed solemnly.

They enjoyed the pantomime, although Verity was adamant that she could have played either of the leading roles better than the actors who took them. When the children had all trailed off to bed, Toby caught Ella's hand as she tried to pass him.

'I have to admire the way you've managed to avoid talking to me for the last two days,' he said. 'How about giving me ten minutes now?'

'There's not a lot to say. You will have gathered that Piers and I have split up and he's living in Marbella.'

'With Claudia.'

'With Claudia,' Ella agreed. 'So, there's going to be a divorce. If our letters hadn't gone astray, you would have known weeks ago.'

'When you say "our" letters, do you mean you wrote?'

Ella did not reply, and Toby answered himself. 'No, you didn't. Why not, Ella?'

'Lots of reasons. I didn't want to seem to be inviting you to go back to that foolishness in the summer.'

'Is that what it was to you? Just foolishness? It went deep with me.'

'I just couldn't bring myself to write as if I were saying "What do you know, I'm free after all; how about it, Toby?"'

'Over-scrupulous, that's what you are. Now that I know, what are my chances?'

'At the moment, very slight,' Ella said slowly. 'My divorce won't even be heard until February. I won't be truly free until round about Easter. In the meantime, I'm in limbo, and I don't just mean in a legal sense. I can only take one step at a time. I can't see as far ahead as April or May, let alone considering another lifetime's commitment.'

'Yes, I see. I wish you'd tell me the whole story so that I can understand what happened.'

'I don't like being disloyal, but everything started going wrong from the moment I married Piers. I was so desperately in love! I would have walked barefoot over broken glass to get to the altar with him.' She paused as Toby shifted in his chair and looked at him shrewdly. 'You don't like hearing that, but it's something that you have to accept.'

Haltingly at first, and then more fluently she ran over the catalogue of debts and extravagances, of responsibilities shirked and small dishonesties condoned.

'Of course, I didn't know Claudia had been Piers' mistress in the past.'

'In Lucy's lifetime?'

'I believe so.' She touched his hand briefly. 'I'm sorry, Toby.'

'I suspected it. And so, I think, did Lucy.'

'Talking to you like this is an indulgence I'm not sure I should allow myself.'

'Get it off your chest. Have you told anyone else?'

'Not everything, just the bare bones.'

Unburdening herself to another adult mind, having the sympathy of someone who was unequivocally on her side, was a luxury Ella had not experienced for a long time. Never experienced, she realised with a shock. To whom had she ever spoken with such frankness? No one, not with any friend, not even – regrettably – with Piers.

She even spoke about the vasectomy, the final betrayal.

'I suppose I can understand why he had it done,' Toby said dubiously.

'I honour him for the original decision,' Ella said quickly. 'Don't think I blame him for that. But he should have told me. He married me, knowing I hoped one day to have a child of my own, and knowing that it wasn't possible. I put it off, for

180

obvious reasons, and then after we'd been through a difficult patch and been reconciled, I talked to him about it again. And still he didn't tell me. It was only after he'd made up his mind to leave me that it came out. That finished Piers for me. I can't live with him again.'

'There's surely no suggestion that you should?'

'Not on my side, and not on his I'm sure, in spite of Verity suspecting he might be having second thoughts, not as long as Claudia keeps putting up the money to keep him in the style Piers thinks has always been his due.'

'I can't help asking again where I come in? When you're free and beginning to recover.'

Would she ever recover? The hurt had gone so deep that there were times when Ella doubted whether she would ever get over it. If she did make a fresh start it would be easier with Toby than with anyone else. But would that be fair on him?

'The trouble is, you're one of the few men I *could* marry,' she said. 'Because you know the background, because of your good relationship with the kids, because with you as their sort of stepfather they'd probably be settled and happy. I'm afraid of letting it influence me too much.'

'You couldn't love me for myself alone?' Toby suggested with a wry grin.

'I might have been able to, if I didn't have so much on my plate. If I re-marry the whole of the agreement I've hammered out with Piers will have to be negotiated all over again. I can't face it, not just yet. Suppose he has a change of heart and insists on the children going to him? I would have to fight, even if it cost every penny I had. Look at what might have happened to Verity because of Claudia's careless indifference. Oh, you haven't heard that story.'

Quickly she put him in the picture and was pleased and reassured by the blackness of his frown, but she concluded, 'Always I come back to the realisation that they are not my children and Piers is their natural father. He wouldn't like me marrying you, he might turn vindictive and take it out on them.'

'My guess is that Piers and Claudia would be just as pleased to leave the kids in our hands.'

'You're probably right, but I don't feel I can gamble on it.'

181

'So I go away with nothing?'

'You're my dear, dear friend. I find you physically attractive ...'

'Don't think I wouldn't capitalise on that if I wasn't burdened by a load of plaster!'

'I know you would,' Ella said with a reluctant smile. 'Which is why I'm asking you to go away and leave me alone, not just for weeks but for several months. You don't, in fact, have much choice, do you? You ought not to be in England now and you'll have to go back to your warring factions as soon as you're mobile, won't you?'

'Too right I will. Can I stay until I'm fit to travel?'

'And how long will that be?'

'I expect I'll be in England for the full six weeks that I'm in plaster. I may be asked to do some administrative work in London, but I'd like to be able to come to Kits Harbour at weekends. I can hold your hand while the divorce goes through.'

'Figuratively speaking?'

'Not on your life! Holding your hand is just one of the liberties I shall take.'

'It still leaves the future uncertain,' Ella said. 'If we were to get together, I wouldn't want a husband who was constantly on the other side of the world.'

'We'll have to think about that. What about your own business? Still doing well?'

'Too well! Never mind your other promises, just tell me I'll never have to roll another truffle ball in cocoa and I'm yours.'

'That's an offer too good to waste! I'm no business expert, but I might be able to make some suggestions about organisation.'

'Any ideas would be welcome. I'd better let you get to bed. You must be worn out. Do you want a painkiller?'

'I'll live with the discomfort tonight. I'll have a goodnight kiss, though.'

Ella bent over him and deposited a chaste kiss on his forehead. She laughed as Toby tried to catch hold of her. 'No more, not tonight,' she said. 'You've wormed half a promise out of me, be content with that.'

On New Year's Eve Toby got the kiss he was determined to press on Ella. Warm and firm and full of promise, his lips engaged hers until she broke away, shaken and confused, and desperately aware of the presence of the children. Toby grinned at her and said with deliberate emphasis, 'A *very* happy New Year, Ella darling.'

She would have scolded him the next day, but she guessed that was just what Toby wanted, a chance yet again to put his case for an eventual match between them. Instead, she was very cool and businesslike and Toby, after one shrewd look at her, followed her lead and plunged into a study of her business activities.

By the end of the week, Toby was satisfied that everything Ella had told him was true. She was doing remarkably well and if she were to go further she would need assistance, a working kitchen, a delivery van and some sort of partner to give her back up and additional capital.

'I think I ought to introduce you to an ex-Army colleague of mine,' he said. 'Andy Portland, a first class chap, with an extraordinary flair for helping small business ventures. He set himself up as a consultant and last time I saw him he was wiping the floor with the opposition.'

'Andy, this is Ella Armitage, stepmother to Lucy's three youngsters. You've seen the details I sent you so you know what's needed. Can you help her?'

'I'm sure I can.' Andy Portland stood up, smiling warmly, and shook hands with Ella. He was very much the same type as Toby, tall and straight-backed and well groomed, with a decisive look about him. He looked at Toby with interest. 'What have you been doing to yourself? Ski-ing accident?'

'I should be so lucky! I slipped on the ice at Ella's doorstep. Now, I'm going to leave you together because I've got a tricky interview with my headquarters, who are not pleased with me.'

Ella had not bargained on that. She was intimidated by the smartness of Andy Portland's London office and not at all sure how to conduct herself in this vital interview. Just in time she stopped herself from looking appealingly at Toby. Andy was leaning back in his chair, watching her. She was the one he wanted to talk to, of course. He already had all the financial details; what he was doing today was assessing her personally, to see whether she was capable of handling the expansion of business she said she wanted. She set her jaw. Of course she was capable; she could do anything she set her mind to, including convincing this smooth young man of her worth.

Two hours later, Ella met Toby for lunch, and in response to his enquiring look, gave him a brilliant smile.

'So it went well? I knew you'd get on with old Andy.'

'He was really encouraging. In fact, he thinks he already has some clients who would welcome a chance to come in with me. Toby, I'm so thrilled! And frightened, too, I have to admit.'

'No need to be. You can handle it. You know, of course, that my own offer of extra capital still holds?'

'I can't take your money. No, Toby, I won't even discuss it. Besides, I need a more personal involvement than that and you, I take it, will be going back to Afghanistan?'

'I've been given an austere rebuke, though I did nothing actually wrong, just swapped leave with an obliging colleague. I've been dragooned into helping out with fundraising – not my favourite occupation – until my plaster comes off. Reluctantly, I think I'll have to base myself in London. Provided the bone knits as it should, I'll be going back into the field in the middle of February.'

About the time her divorce would be heard. Did Toby realise that? If he did, he preferred not to comment on it.

'Can I come down for weekends?' he asked.

'I suppose so.'

'Try to sound more welcoming,' Toby urged. His smile was difficult to resist.

'I'll always be pleased to see you,' Ella said sedately.

At the end of January Reg Daley came to trial for the murder of Donald Burtman.

His daughter, keenly anticipating her moment of notoriety, decided to play it demure and wear the outfit she had purchased from the Hospice Shop. She was conscious of making a good impression when she took the witness stand. She kept her voice low as she took the oath and had to be asked if she would try to speak up.

184

She was taken through her evidence, faltering artistically when she spoke of her father's violence. Reg gritted his teeth and ignored her when she looked at him with big, soft eyes. They were approaching the critical point and he hoped Leah would not be so carried away by her performance that she would forget her lines.

'Did your father tell you that he struck Donald Burtman?' counsel for the prosecution prompted her.

'Yes. He said he'd pushed him and he'd fallen against a tree.'

'Did he say what happened next?'

'Dad took the photographs, the duplicate ones, and he came on down to me and beat me up.' Leah touched her chin artistically. 'He said it would be a lesson to me not to do anything like it in the future and he'd warned the photographer that if he ever caught him dealing in photos of me again he'd make him sorry he ever lived.'

Counsel looked down at his brief. There went the case for the prosecution. Smoothly, he went on to elicit details of Leah's injuries, trying to establish the picture of Reg Daley as a man unable to control his temper, but he knew that his colleague for the defence would not let that naive speech pass him by.

Sure enough defending counsel rose to his feet in a leisurely way and took Leah over her evidence again.

'Your father said he'd told Mr Burtman that "if he ever caught him dealing in pictures of you again, he'd make him sorry he'd ever lived". Is that correct?'

'That's right,' Leah agreed. Her eyes widened. You had to hand it to the kid, she really had got it in her to act, Reg Daley thought. But it was going to cost him, it was definitely going to cost him.

'I never thought ... it makes it sound ... Mr Burtman must have been still alive, mustn't he?' Leah asked.

'The jury may believe they are entitled to think so,' her father's counsel agreed.

It was not conclusive, but it weakened the case against Reg Daley beyond the point of reasonable doubt. After a lengthy withdrawal the jury found him 'Not guilty'.

'It was never a strong case,' Inspector Crooms said gloomily. 'If we could have found just one of Reg's prints on the murder weapon, we could have nailed him.'

'Funny the daughter never remembered him saying that about the dead man until today.'

'Funny! You can call it that if you like. I wonder how much it cost Reg to buy Leah? I should have remembered that in the last resort the Daleys stick together.'

'If Reg didn't do it, and I know you always did have doubts, then who did?'

'Good question. The next best suspect is dead. This is one crime we're never going to solve.'

Claudia stood on the balcony outside her bedroom and looked down on the swimming pool, two levels below, just as Ella had once stood and watched Claudia and Piers swimming amorously together. There were half a dozen of her friends in and around the pool. Miguel's father was there, still trying to come to terms with the mutilation of his handsome son. His wife was off somewhere making a film and Miguel was at the best clinic in Spain, being fitted with an artificial leg.

Piers was down there, a spare and elegant figure; less weighty than the other men, and not only in terms of flesh. They were all go-getters, wealthy by means of their own efforts, not particularly scrupulous, but successful, very successful. Piers was not in their class, and they knew it, just as Claudia was beginning to know it.

The truth was, she missed Bernie. It was not that she regretted her annexation of Piers: she had wanted him and she had taken him; only now, she was not quite sure what to do with him. It was nearly March, the divorce would be made absolute soon, and Piers was talking of a wedding. Claudia had reservations about that. They were doing all right as they were. Perhaps they should go on living together for a time before taking that important step.

There was something missing in their relationship, it had become almost staid. With all his faults, Bernie had been an exciting man. There was an edge of danger in their life together and Claudia, without realising it, had become addicted to the thrill of secrets kept hidden, even secrets she found repulsive.

She knew about Reg Daley's acquittal: her friends back

home had seen to that. She supposed she ought to be glad of it since she was satisfied in her own mind that he was innocent, but on the whole she was indifferent. Clear in her mind was an image of what had happened that night. Bernie, she thought, had told her the truth up to the point when he had burnt the film and the photographs, but then, she believed, he had been struck by the recollection of the putter he had left behind. As if she had been there she saw him walking back through the trees by the side of the road – he would not have bothered to turn the car in that narrow lane to go back such a short distance – to where he had parted with the blackmailing photographer. He might have witnessed the end of Burtman's interview with Reg Daley, but on the whole Claudia believed that had been over and Daley had left before Bernie arrived.

What would Bernie's reaction have been, coming upon the man who had shamed him and jeered at him and taken his money, helpless on the ground in front of him? Claudia had no doubt about it. He had seized the golf club and struck out wildly again and again, brutal blows that had released his anger, left him gasping for breath, and killed his victim.

He had not panicked. Once he had recovered from his paroxysm of rage and realised what he had done, Bernie's mind would have been cool. He was too used to risk not to pause and weigh up the consequences. She saw him bending over Donald Burtman to confirm that he was dead and that was when he had got the blood on his shirt cuff which she had noticed when he undressed that night. She had wondered about it, and wondered still more when she had seen the shirt the next morning in the dirty linen basket with the cuff still damp and faintly stained where Bertie had rinsed away the blood. She had put it into the washing machine and, just to be on the safe side, she had sent the suit he had been wearing to the cleaners, because, with Bernie, you never knew what he might have been up to.

She had not connected him to the murder until she had heard about the golf club. On the whole, Claudia thought it had been a clever move to leave that behind. If Bernie had put the club into his car there would have been traces of blood and hair in the boot which the forensic experts would certainly have found if he had ever been suspected of the crime. He could have taken it somewhere and thrown it away, but by that time his violent emotion was beginning to take its toll and he might not have felt capable of driving any distance to a safe spot. Better by far to clean up the shaft and handle, and Bernie would have done a thorough job on that, and throw it down on the grass. He would have been prepared to admit – had admitted – his presence on the fifteenth hole that evening. His story had been plausible, and might have been believed, if it had not been for the photograph Burtman carried in his wallet. As it was, Claudia knew the police were not satisfied, would never be satisfied now. Bernie's death had been ... fortuitous.

Had Ella told Piers about Claudia's manipulation of the heart pills? Claudia thought that she had, but Piers was not the man to probe into anything so distasteful, not when she might tell him the truth and he would have to face up to the fact that he was enjoying the fruits of something that was not a killing, Claudia told herself that it was definitely not a killing, she had not *known* that Bernie would die, and she had been horrified when it had happened, but it might be called an assisted death, and one of the things that clouded her relationship with Piers was the realisation that he knew what she had done. He ought to have spoken out and then she could have told him that she was sure, absolutely sure, that Bernie would have preferred death to an appearance in court to give evidence about his unfortunate involvement with the blackmailing photographer. It was the way she had come to justify her action to herself. That, and her conviction of Bernie's guilt, but she would never speak to Piers, or anyone, about that.

She missed Bernie's business acumen. Piers had neither his cunning nor his skill in striking a bargain. He was nice to have around, a delicious lover, an escort who did her credit, but if he was to become her husband she wanted more than that.

The children were a damned nuisance, too. Claudia believed that she could charm them, buy them, in fact, into accepting her. She had not bargained on the hard graft in being a parent. One thing was certain, Piers would have to accept that there would be fewer holidays in Marbella than he had expected.

Her gaze followed him as he swam the length of the pool

and hauled himself out of the water. She still fancied him and didn't want to part with him, but he was not as young as he had been. She watched as a younger man, unmarried, still in his twenties, tanned golden brown all over, barely decent in his scanty swimming trunks, dived into the blue water of the pool. What a dish! And available, if what she had heard was true. Piers would be going to England for Easter. There would be no harm in giving herself a little treat while he was away.

She leaned over the balcony and the young man looked up and waved. Claudia waved back and called, 'I'm coming down!' The young man turned away, smiling to himself. Hooked! All that lovely money and no competition but dear old Piers, who was not a force to be reckoned with and, unless he was mistaken, yesterday's man.

Ella inspected herself carefully in the long looking glass. Her one good suit had been getting more airings in the last few weeks than it had in the previous year. She was about to leave for yet another business meeting. So far, she was committed to nothing, but she had a feeling that this was it, and she knew that Andy Portland was very hopeful of a good outcome from the introduction he was effecting.

She had been to see him twice since Toby had brought them together and had come to like and trust him. The visits to London had been good for her. She had begun to know her way around the tricky streets of the City and she walked into Andy's office with an assurance that had been lacking the first time they had met.

For all that, her prospective business partners were a surprise.

'Mr and Mrs Patel,' Andy Portland said.

The man was dressed in a conventional business suit, but his wife wore a sari of grey figured silk, with a discreet hint of gold thread in the border.

'So you are Mrs Armitage, not Mrs Martin?' she asked.

'Martin was my name before I married and I preferred to use it as my business name,' Ella explained.

She could see that the sheets of figures Toby had helped her to prepare were laid out on the desk. Presumably the Patels were satisfied with what they had seen or they would not have asked for this meeting.

'Our situation is that we wish to set up a small chain of delicatessen shops,' Mr Patel said.

'How small is a small chain?' Ella asked, disguising the fact that this was rather more than she had expected.

'We have options on three premises, all on excellent sites, one in Canterbury, one in Dover and one in Sandwich. We are also negotiating for premises on an industrial estate where we would manufacture our products.'

'We do not propose to cure our own hams, you understand,' Mrs Patel put in. 'But we expect to make our own sandwiches daily and such things as samosas, koftas – you know that they are little meat balls which are eaten with various sauces?'

'I don't know much about Indian food,' Ella admitted. 'Forgive me, but where do my products come in?'

'We would, of course, sell your excellent pickles and chutneys and other preserves in the shop, and use them, too, in our sandwiches. We would also, if we were able to come to an agreement, like to call the shops by your name. "Mrs Martin's Fine Foods", perhaps. Something of that nature.'

'And what would my role be?'

'We want your name, your recipes and your supervisory ability.'

'There's nothing out of the ordinary about my recipes,' Ella said honestly. 'You could get the equivalent out of any cookery book. I've made one or two adjustments ...'

'And it's those adjustments which make your products unique,' Mrs Patel said with a dazzling smile.

'What makes my stuff special is using good quality ingredients,' Ella said. 'If you were to cut corners, go for the cheap and easy alternatives, then "Mrs Martin" would be no different from what you can buy in any supermarket.'

'Precisely!' Mr Patel seized on the point with an eagerness that surprised Ella. 'We are aiming for a high class operation. The sandwiches will cost a little more than the ordinary "cheese and tomato", because we will use special breads, unusual combinations of ingredients and, as I have said, your excellent pickles and chutneys. We have suppliers lined up for the ham Mrs Patel has mentioned, for smoked salmon, for excellent cheeses, and so on and so forth.'

'Do you already have experience in this business?'

190

'We do, indeed. My father has a well-established shop in Bradford, specialising in Indian foodstuffs and I, of course, have been concerned in it ever since I left school.'

'My family owns two Indian restaurants,' Mrs Patel put in. 'I am a chartered accountant and well accustomed to looking after business interests.'

Ella blinked at the idea of this elegant lady in grey silk as an accountant, but there was no denying the intelligence in those dark eyes. Mrs Patel had her head screwed on.

'You're both a great deal better qualified than I am,' she said. 'I fell into my little business almost by accident.'

She thought that Andy Portland looked pained, but she saw no point in being anything but honest.

'You're built it up from scratch,' Mr Patel said. 'I was impressed by the way it had grown.'

'It's got to the point where I have to ask myself what comes next,' Ella said. 'Either I go on in my slightly amateur way, which involves me in a lot of actual cooking and leaves me little time to exploit the advantages I've already gained; or else I just sell out, which would disappoint me and leave me without the work I've come to enjoy; or else I go in with you or someone like you, and I must admit that seems the most attractive option.'

'Good! We, too, have come to a parting of the ways. I have two younger brothers who can follow me into our father's business. I want to strike out on my own. We have spent many hours discussing the possibilities. You understand that as well as your expertise we would want you to provide some of the capital?'

'I've discussed that with Mr Portland.'

'If we confined ourselves to one shop, then we could set up entirely on our own,' Mrs Patel said. 'But that would not justify the expense of the industrial estate premises. We would have to prepare goods in the shop, and that would mean that, for instance, the Canterbury site would not be large enough. It seems to me that we need one another.'

'Would the appearance of the shops be uniform?'

'Ah, that is something dear to my heart! I have done a design, which you will have to approve. The lettering for the shop front is based on your labels and the colouring is mainly a sharp green and white, very fresh and pleasant looking.'

191

'Staff . .. We'll have to employ quite a lot of people.'

'Of course. At first we will get by with no more than two in each shop and, I think, just three in the preparation premises, plus one van and a driver. We see the preparatory work as being your particular responsibility.'

'It's a big undertaking.'

'You need time to think?'

'I do, indeed!' Ella pulled herself together. 'I'd like to see the three shops and the proposed preparation site; I'd like to have a list of the suppliers you're thinking of using; and, of course, Mr Portland will have to satisfy me that the operation is ...' she sought in her mind for the correct phrase, '... financially feasible,' she brought out triumphantly.

'On a personal side, I think it is fair to say that we are likely to be compatible,' Mrs Patel said. 'I believe we could work with you, my husband and I. And you?'

'Yes,' Ella smiled at her warmly. 'I'm immensely excited and stirred up about it. There may be snags to be overcome, but I really hope that we will be able to join forces.'

She made arrangements for the visits she thought necessary and the Patels left.

'Wow!' Ella said, sinking back in her chair as Andy Portland returned from showing the Patels out. 'Andy, can I do it? I mean, can I provide enough money to interest them in taking me in?'

'It'll take most of your capital, including what you've stashed away from the sale of your parents' house. However, they're serious when they say that what they're after is your name, your image and your expertise.'

'What expertise? I'm just a family cook who's done a bit of marketing.'

'You're more than that, Ella. You've operated very shrewdly so far. When you started, did you expect to reach the sales you're achieving at the moment?'

'No, and I've got the callouses to prove it,' Ella said, looking ruefully at her roughened hands.

'Could you teach other people to make your preserves?'

'Yes, of course. There's nothing difficult about it.' She stopped. 'I see what you're getting at. I should stop the hands-on work and become a supervisor.'

'A manager. You're good with people, Ella. Look at the way you won over your three stepchildren.'

Look at the way I lost my husband. For a moment Ella felt a spasm of pain. Another week and her divorce would be finalised. A new life seemed to be opening in front of her, but that didn't mean she was without regrets for the dream that had ended in disillusionment and heartache.

Toby had gone back to Afghanistan, with nothing settled between them except his obstinate assertion that he loved her and would win her over one day. She was missing him with a dull relentless ache that she tried to keep out of her mind. He had been immensely helpful in sharpening up her thoughts about her business venture and she certainly owed him a lot for his introduction to Andy Portland, or she would if the partnership with the Patels materialised.

'I must go,' she said. 'I'm not making any decisions, not yet, but I'm certainly interested. Dazed, but interested! I'll be in touch after I've viewed the premises.'

'There's still some bargaining to be done,' Andy said. 'Such as how much you're going to get out of the business, which you didn't touch on. Leave it to me. I'll drive as hard a bargain as I can.'

'Not too hard,' Ella said. 'I want this partnership. I think it might be the beginning of something really good for me.'

She travelled home in a dream. Three shops! She had got no further than thinking of employing a couple of people to help her out with the cooking and perhaps investing in a van rather than stacking boxes in the back of the car. 'Mrs Martin's Fine Foods'. That didn't sound quite right. She would have to work on it. Her original set up had had a faintly Victorian air about it. 'Mrs Martin's Excellent Provisions' – that might be better.

'I'm about to become an entrepreneur!' she informed the children.

'Does it mean you'll have to work in London?' Jennifer asked.

'No, it's a local venture. I'll have to put in fixed hours every day, I suppose, but it'll all be in one place.' She reached for a notepad. 'I must remember to stipulate that my existing customers mustn't suffer.'

'Is it all settled?' Verity asked.

193

'By no means. There are lots of points to be worked out, including whether I can afford it. I may be a bit busy for the next few weeks.'

'I had a letter from Dad this morning.'

'Yes, I saw. Any messages?'

'He's keen on that idea of a long boat for the Easter holiday and he says will you go ahead and book it.'

For a moment Ella was conscious of a spasm of irritation. Why couldn't Piers do his own booking? She had done her part when she had sent him the brochures.

'Oh, all right,' she said resignedly. 'I'll see to it tomorrow. Did he give you the dates?'

'Any time during our holidays, but not for more than a week. Mum, could you get the programme for the theatre at Stratford as well?'

'The main programme may not have started by Easter,' Ella warned her.

'As long as I get to the theatre,' Verity said. 'I've got a rehearsal tonight, by the way.'

'Is the play going well?'

'Some of the people are a bit stiff. In my opinion, that is. I'm doing all right, I think.'

'Enjoying it?'

'It's bliss!'

Ella glanced at the calendar to see the date before she wrote a cheque and got a shock that drove all the breath out of her body. She was within two days of having her divorce made absolute and she had forgotten all about it.

She sat back in her chair in front of the roll-top desk which had once concealed Piers' disastrous muddle of unpaid bills and after a moment's reflection a pleased smile came to her face. It was good that she had forgotten it. After all the agonising and heartbreak she had come through to the other side. She was on the brink of achieving a new life, with such exciting possibilities that everything else had been consigned to the back of her mind. She no longer worried about the children: they had proved to be more resilient than had seemed possible at one point, and Ella had a feeling that her own new assurance, her more relaxed attitude, had been of more benefit to them than her sleepless nights had ever been.

The telephone rang and she stretched out her hand towards it, the new mobile telephone and answering machine she now found essential.

'Ella? It's Piers.'

That was unexpected. Had he, too, been struck by the realisation that the tie between them was almost severed?

She responded coolly and Piers went on in a rush, 'Would it be all right if I stayed in the house for the night before I take the children away?'

'Why not?' Ella said, not bothering to take time to think about it. 'Our divorce will be final by then.'

'Will it?'

'The day after tomorrow.' She regretted being so specific when Piers asked, 'Have you been counting the days?'

'No, I'd forgotten all about it until five minutes ago. All I meant was that we'll be free agents by Easter and there'll be no risk of jeopardising the divorce procedure.'

'Oh, I see. I'll come straight from the airport, then, and be with you by late afternoon.'

'Don't make it too early. I'm desperately busy and if you come before four o'clock you may find no one at home.'

'What's keeping you so occupied?'

It was a lovely moment, and made all the more so by his patronising tone of voice.

'I'm expanding my business. I'm about to join forces with a couple of partners and we're opening three delicatessen shops and a small manufacturing unit.'

Ella would have taken bets on Piers' instinctive reaction: 'Where did you get the money?'

'Is that any of your business?'

'Not so long as you haven't mortgaged the house.'

'Don't be stupid, you know it's not in my power to do that. Nothing I do will ever harm the children's rights, you can be sure of that.'

'Yes ... of course I'm sure or I wouldn't have left them with you.'

To Ella's ears he sounded repulsively self-righteous, but she swallowed her impulse to give him a set down and said, 'I'll see you on the third, then?'

'That's right. I'll look forward to hearing about your plans.'

How much would she tell him? Not a lot, Ella thought. The last thing she wanted was Piers getting involved in her bright new venture. It would take away the gloss to have him throwing doubts on the scheme.

The person to whom she longed to talk was Toby. He had encouraged her, argued with her, insisted that she had something to offer a prospective partner, but even Toby had not foreseen the outcome of her introduction to the Patels.

Because talking to Piers had unsettled her, Ella took a sheet of paper and began writing a letter to Toby, a long personal letter, not the scrappy additions to the children's notes that she had been sending him since he went back to Afghanistan. Their letters had been getting through and Toby had let them know that all their earlier missing letters had come to light in a mailbag jettisoned from a stolen jeep.

The situation in Afghanistan was as volatile as ever. Toby passed it off lightly, but Ella guessed that he was frequently in danger, from rockets and mortar bombs and bullets. He was battling with hunger, disease and mutilation, with orphaned children and widowed women, and men suddenly left powerless to support their families because of the loss of a limb or their sight. What would he think of her obsession with sandwiches and samosas? He would be amused, Ella decided; and pleased. For a brief space of time he might be lifted out of the harsh world he was forced to inhabit.

She wrote on, telling him everything, even about the design for the shops and the reckless way she had thrown everything she had in the world into the new venture.

'I may be mad,' she wrote. 'But at least the house is secured to the children and I have the right to live in it for as long as I want, and provided Piers doesn't stop paying his life insurance, which was one of the things I insisted on in the settlement, then they will have some money to come in the future. Of course, I may end up a millionaire. How about that?'

She was exaggerating, but Ella did think there was a serious possibility of making a real success, and possibly a lot of money, from 'Mrs Martin's Excellent Provisions'.

She told him about Piers' telephone call and proposed visit

196

and mentioned the imminent end to their marriage. And she told him that she was missing him and looked forward to seeing him again. She did not say that she loved him, because Ella was by no means sure that it would be true, nor did she say that she would have been glad to have him with her to help her with the business, because rather to her surprise Ella was relishing doing it all herself. Toby had given her the initial push and provided the introduction to Andy Portland which had proved so fruitful, but all the decisions had been Ella's own and she wanted to keep it that way.

In the normal way she would have kept her letter open so that the children could add their messages, but this was something personal between them, something she wanted to be from her alone. She sealed it up and put it in her handbag to post.

Chapter Eleven

'Do you really need to clean the cupboard under the sink, just because Dad's spending a night in the house?' Verity asked.

Ella sat back on her heels and looked up at her stepdaughter. She was hot, tired and incredibly dirty and, of course, Verity was quite right, she was only having this blitz on the housework for Piers' benefit, even though she knew that he would be oblivious to her hard labour.

'You know me too well,' she said, clambering to her feet. 'I didn't realise I was so obvious.'

'I expect you've been doing some *cordon bleu* cooking, too?'

'I have laid on something special for tomorrow night,' Ella admitted.

'Does it still matter to you what Dad thinks?'

'I'm afraid of laying myself open to criticism, I suppose. The house has been a bit neglected while I've been so busy with the business.'

'What you need is a daily woman.'

'You may be right. Supervising the cookery unit is going to take up a lot of my time.'

'It really is going to go ahead?'

'Yes, we've reached a final agreement. My next chore is to buy the equipment I need. Fortunately, I know where to go for it and exactly what I want. Then I have to engage my staff. Mr Patel is seeing to the van and the van driver and Mrs Patel is engaging the shop assistants. Honestly, Verity, I don't know whether I'm on my head or my heels!'

'When's the Grand Opening?'

'The Canterbury shop will open the first week in May; Dover the week after that, and Sandwich the following week. I have access to the cookery unit immediately after Easter. A week today, in fact. Can you wonder I'm in a flat spin?'

'Well, the house certainly won't need cleaning for a week or two, will it?'

'It won't get it! Do you think this holiday with Dad is going to work?'

'I believe so,' Verity said slowly. 'Not having to go abroad, and having him on his own, will both help. And there'll be something to do on the boat, if it's only opening and closing locks. I'm *praying* for fine weather.'

'It would certainly help,' Ella agreed absently. 'I'm just going to wipe the kitchen floor over and then I'm finished.'

'Are you sure? Have you cleaned behind the bath taps with an old toothbrush?'

'Horrid girl, stop laughing at me. The next thing I'm going to clean is myself. While I'm having a bath you can put our supper casserole in the oven, do the vegetables and lay the table.'

Ella finished her housework and went up the stairs smiling to herself. Verity was maturing into a remarkably nice young girl. True, she had her mood swings and unreasonable moments, but she did not seem to suffer from any of the more serious teenage problems. Ella suspected that the shock she had had in the summer from her transient involvement in the drugs-and-drink scene and the horror of Miguel's accident had had a chastening effect which, with any luck, would last until Verity was adult enough to make decisions with her head and not her tumultuous young emotions.

'Where's Dad going to sleep?' Harry demanded, meeting her at the top of the stairs.

'I did wonder whether to put him in with you.'

'That's what I want to know.'

'But on the whole I think it'll be better if he has the sofa bed downstairs like Uncle Toby did.'

'That's all right then, because if you were going to put the camp bed up in my room then I'd have to move my frog spawn. You will keep an eye on it while I'm away, won't you?'

'A close eye,' Ella promised. 'Where's Jennifer?'

'I'm washing my hair,' Jennifer called from the bathroom. 'Because you're too busy to do it for me.'

'How thoughtful,' Ella said faintly. 'Don't use too much shampoo, will you, darling?'

'I've got lots and lots of bubbles,' Jennifer said with satisfaction.

'I thought you probably would have.'

A quarter of an hour later, with Jennifer's hair combed free of tangles and the hair dryer droning busily in her bedroom, Ella ran cold water into the bath to clear the inches of shampoo lather, undressed, locked the door, ran her bath and at last subsided into delicious, relaxing hot water.

She hoped the children would never realise how much she was looking forward to being free of them for a whole week. It would not even be possible for her to work, not properly, between Friday and Tuesday. She could have a rest, and goodness knows she needed it.

A companion would not have been unwelcome, provided that companion could have been Toby, she thought wryly. It was annoying the way the thought of him kept running in her mind. What would she do if he turned up unannounced, as he had at the New Year? Welcome him with open arms. Ella slowly soaped one thigh. Literally with open arms, she admitted to herself. Good job he didn't know that, or he might take steps to get himself on the next flight home. She smiled to herself, liking the idea of his eagerness.

'Mum, how many potatoes shall I do?' Verity called through the door.

'They're quite big; do one each and two over, six altogether. And use up all the brussels sprouts.'

'I've brought you up a glass of sherry.'

'Are you growing wings, or something? Put it on my dressing table, I'm just getting out.'

Ella heaved herself out of the bath. She had had all of twenty minutes peace and quiet, and she had a whole week to look forward to. The annoying thing was, once they had gone, she would miss them.

Facing Piers was more difficult than Ella had anticipated. It was the first time they had met since he had walked out, all the

200

negotiations about their divorce having been done through lawyers.

'You're earlier than I expected,' she said, which she realised did not sound particularly welcoming, but then why should she welcome him?

'I hired a car at the airport and had an easy run through.'

There was an awkward silence. 'The children are looking forward to this holiday,' Ella contributed.

'It could be fun, if the weather holds up.'

'They've packed wet weather gear, just in case.'

'Good. What are you doing with yourself while we're away?'

'A million and one things. I told you I was expanding my business, in partnership with a couple of other people, and I've only got until the end of the month to install equipment in our new premises and train staff to use it.'

'Sounds interesting.'

'It's hair-raising! We're having a snack lunch and then I'll have to leave you with the children while I dash off to see whether the sinks have been put in and connected and the water heater is up and working. Two cookers, a freezer and a refrigerator are due for delivery tomorrow, followed by the work tables, food processors and so on. It's taken some planning, I can tell you.'

'Actually, I thought I might go up to the golf club this afternoon, see if any of the old crowd are around.

'Just as you like.'

'You weren't counting on me to stay with the kids?'

'No, Verity will be in and she's old enough to be responsible for them now. I'll only be gone a couple of hours, unless anything dire has gone wrong.'

'Straight after your snack lunch, then.'

'Soup, cheese and biscuits and fruit. I'll do something a bit more special for tonight.'

She drove away after lunch feeling irritated. Surely Piers could have made this visit without feeling it necessary to go back to his home-from-home to see his golfing cronies. She wondered what the atmosphere would be like in the club house. Was Piers prepared for the gossip that had spread like wildfire as a result of Reg Daley's trial?

* * *

201

He was not. She found that out in the interval before she dished up the dinner that evening when Piers absentmindedly helped himself to a drink and then looked round in confusion and said, 'You don't mind?'

'Help yourself. Old habits die hard, don't they?'

'What do you want?' Piers asked, ignoring her question.

'Just a meagre sherry. I've opened a bottle of wine to go with the meal.'

'Oh, good.'

Piers handed her the drink and sat down in the armchair he had always used. He was looking moody and did not seem inclined for conversation.

'Did you see anyone you knew at the golf club?' Ella asked, with a touch of malice.

'Several people.'

'You didn't play?'

'No. I could have done, I'm still technically a member.' He took a long swallow of his drink and then burst out, 'I didn't realise what a lot of talk there'd been about Bernie and that damned photographer. People seem to be taking it for granted that Bernie did it. It's unbelievable!'

'Is it?'

'Damn it, Bernie had his faults ...'

'Such as a liking for dirty pictures and young girls.'

Piers downed his drink and got up to help himself to another. 'I didn't know,' he said. 'And yet ... he was the best and warmest friend a man could have.'

'You mean he condoned your adultery with his wife?'

'If you're going to talk like that we'd better drop the subject. It wasn't ... you've never realised how devastated I was over Lucy's illness. I would have fallen to pieces if Claudia hadn't held me together. That sort of closeness ... well, you just wouldn't understand.'

'So when Bernie died you felt you had to return the favour?'

'God, you can be a bitch!'

'I can,' Ella agreed, getting to her feet. 'As you said, this conversation is better discontinued. I'm off to the kitchen. You might give the kids a shout and tell them dinner will be ready in ten minutes.'

She had to pause when she got to the kitchen to control her

202

shaking. It was ridiculous, it was really stupid, to get in a state about Piers and Claudia at this stage of the game. She was rid of him, she was glad to be rid of him, and raking up past betrayal was no way to send him off in a good frame of mind to deal with three critical children. The truth was, she was tired. She had done too much in the run up to this holiday. Verity had put her finger on it when she said what Ella needed was someone to help her in the house. One more thing to do, find a cleaning woman.

Zooming into the supermarket to stock up on food for the weekend before going on to her new cookery unit, Ella stopped at the noticeboard she had never bothered to read until now, on the off chance that someone might be advertising their services as a cleaner. A card caught her eye, not for an individual, but for a company. She remembered that a similar card had been put through the door and she had thrown it away with the rest of the junk mail. It looked quite hopeful. She made a note of the telephone number and turned back to her trolley.

'Hello, Mrs Armitage.'

It was Leah, pushing her little boy in a buggy, a bulging bag of groceries stuffed underneath.

'Looking for a cleaner?' she asked.

'I think I've found one,' Ella said hastily. Anyone but Leah!

'I might have obliged at one time,' Leah said. 'Not now, though. Me 'n Craig are getting married next Saturday. He's already moved in with me and I've really got my hands full.'

'Congratulations,' Ella said.

'Yeah, I'm really chuffed. I've got ever such a nice gown, off the shoulder, ivory satin, but I'm not wearing a veil, just a wreath of silk roses.'

'A white wedding,' Ella said faintly.

'Yeah. Damien's going to be page boy. And we're having a slap-up wedding breakfast in Margate. My Uncle Tom's got a greengrocer's shop there, but he's been ill so Dad's been running it for him. Truth is, I don't think Uncle Tom will be coming back.'

'You've, er, patched things up with your father, then?'

'Oh, sure! Dad's paying for the wedding and everything and he's given Craig a job, driving the delivery van. Craig loves it.

Him and Dad go up to Covent Garden a couple of times a week ever so early in the morning and Craig can belt up the motorway 'cause there's no one about. He's done a ton more than once.'

'Over a hundred miles an hour?' Ella guessed. 'Aren't you worried he'll have an accident?'

'Not him. Dad says he'd have made a super get-away driver if Dad still had the contacts he had in the old days, which he hasn't. He's a reformed character, honest he is. He didn't do that murder, you know, Mrs Armitage.'

'So the court decided.'

'Which means we both know who did do it, don't we?'

'It's better not talked about,' Ella said firmly. 'Well, Leah, what can I say? Good luck and best wishes.'

She finished her shopping, feeling bemused, but when she finally reached her car and had stowed her shopping away, Ella sat with her hands on the steering wheel and gave way to helpless laughter. It really wasn't funny at all, she told herself sternly, but there was something irresistible about Leah and her complete unawareness of anything out of the ordinary about the full panoply of a white wedding with the child of the union as a page boy and the bride given away by the father against whom she had recently given evidence in a murder trial. What a family! What a Leah!

'It was an absolutely super holiday,' Harry said. 'We didn't want to leave the boat. It was great!'

They were untidy, crumpled and in need of a good wash. Even Piers was less sleek than usual, but he looked pleased with himself, as well he might in the face of the children's enthusiasm.

'Dad let me steer the boat,' Harry went on.

'Mum, we got to Stratford,' Verity put in urgently. 'To the theatre!'

'Was it good?'

'It was out of this world! It was stratospheric!'

'It was Shakespeare,' Harry said.

'That was why it was so wonderful.'

'And Jennifer? Did you enjoy it, too?'

'Yes, I fed the ducks and I helped us go through the locks.'

Piers groaned. 'Don't remind me about the locks!'

'Hard work?'

'You can say that again! I've lost pounds. Still, it was worth it. Of course, we were lucky with the weather.'

He looked with pride and fondness at the wind-reddened faces and tousled hair of his three children, while Ella watched him curiously. Oh, Piers, it could always have been like this. Why couldn't you see it before it was too late?

She chased the children off to unpack. 'And bring all your dirty washing down straight away, so that I can load the washing machine.'

'Does that include mine?' Piers asked.

'No, I'll have more than one load with the children's things. You must take your washing back with you. You'll be leaving in the morning?'

'Yes, and I could do with a clean shirt to travel in.'

'Buy one.'

'No need to snap at me. Are you jealous because the children enjoyed themselves with me?'

'Of course I'm not,' Ella said, although there was just a trace of truth in what he said. 'What gets me, just a bit, is that you've given them such a good time, really put yourself out for them, obviously enjoyed doing it, and yet tomorrow you'll walk away without a backward glance.'

'It's the way you wanted it.'

'How can you say that?'

'Do you want to put the clock back?'

'If you mean would I want to be married to you again, no, thank you. I'm doing very nicely on my own, but while you've been having a happy time I've been working twelve hours a day setting up this new business, and it's annoying to have you standing around looking pleased with yourself just because a holiday with your children – which I suggested, and I booked – has turned out well. You've got it easy, Piers. If they all wake up tomorrow morning with chickenpox, you're not the one who'll have to cope.'

'They haven't been in contact with chickenpox, not as far as I know,' Piers said, looking bewildered.

'It was just an example of what might happen. I've got the chores and you've got the amusement. Would you mind giving

205

your mind fairly soon to what's going to happen in the summer? I'd quite like to book myself a holiday and I need to know when I can expect the children to be away again.'

'Marbella is hotter than we really like in August. Claudia and I may go away for the whole of that month.'

'Taking the children with you? No, of course not.'

'I'll come up with a plan for July. Or September.'

'Do that. And let me have the dates.'

'Darling, you're fabulous.' Sebastian raised himself on one elbow and looked down at Claudia. She must be, what – forty-two or -three? They had all known she was several years younger than Bernie, but all the same she was certainly well into her forties. Not that one could tell, not for certain. Her body, oiled, exercised, massaged and pampered, was as firm as a girl's, but with a maturity that he found exciting.

Claudia moved lazily, her breasts rising as she stretched her arms above her head. 'You, too, darling,' she said. 'Wonderful.'

He had not been bad. What he lacked in subtlety he made up for in vigour. Nice to know that she could attract and satisfy a younger man.

'We must do it again,' Sebastian murmured.

'Piers will be back in a couple of days.'

'Does that matter?'

'It would to Piers.'

'Yes, but I mean, to you? Is it permanent, this thing with Piers?'

'He left his wife for me.'

'Tough luck on her, just as it'd be tough luck on Piers if you decided to give him the push.'

Claudia swung her legs off the bed and stood up, shrugging on a cotton wrapper. 'I couldn't do that, not at this stage of the development of my apartment block.'

'I could manage that as well as Piers. Better, in fact, because I speak the language.'

Claudia turned to look at him, still sprawled on the disordered bed, his brown limbs splendid against the white sheets.

'You're twenty-seven, aren't you, Seb? Have you ever had a job?'

'Way back in boring old England, when I first left college.'

When he had been kicked out of his university, but Seb did not intend mentioning that.

'Did you take a degree?' Claudia asked with interest.

Sebastian hesitated, but these things could be checked and he didn't want to be caught out in a lie. 'Actually, no,' he said. 'I neglected my studies. I was too interested in living.'

'In easy living,' Claudia said. 'So you came to Spain. And what have you done since you've been here?'

'A bit of chauffeuring, helped in a gift shop, ran an art gallery. This and that. People have been kind.'

'And you lived with Gilda Tavistock, didn't you? Did that pay well?'

'Darling, I was *devoted* to Gilda. She housed me and fed me for a time, and we slept together it's true, but she was a difficult woman and it couldn't last. I'm an independent person, I don't like being tied down, and I resented the way everyone thought – just as you seem to – that I was being kept.'

'You weren't?'

'I made a contribution. Gilda had no complaints until she started getting jealous, quite unnecessarily, I may say, because I was totally faithful.'

Claudia picked up the heavy gold wristwatch she had made him discard because it dug into her back.

'"To my heart's delight – Gilda",' she read. 'Quite a nice souvenir.'

'She liked giving me presents.' Sebastian sounded sulky. He tried to retrieve his position. 'It wasn't the reason I stayed with her. While it lasted I loved her.'

'Good for you. I wouldn't have called her a particularly lovable woman.'

'It's over and done with. One of the mistakes of my youth. Let's get back to you and me. Do you really want to get up so soon? Come back to bed.'

'I don't think so.' Claudia touched him lightly and regretfully on the cheek. He was madly attractive and she fancied him like hell, but he was a luxury she had decided she couldn't afford.

'You're a sponger,' she said. 'A delightful one, I admit, and you certainly give full value in bed, but what I need at this stage in my life is a touch of respectability and a man who will help run my business interests or, at least, can be trusted to do what I tell him, and I think Piers fits the bill as well as anyone.'

'Don't you love me even a tiny little bit?'

'Enough to hope this won't be our last encounter.'

'I don't perform on demand,' Sebastian said haughtily.

'Don't you? I thought that was your speciality.'

He made one last try to get something out of her.

'Let's go and have a shower,' he suggested.

As the water cascaded over them, he said, 'If it's business you're interested in, I've got an option on a beach café that might make you a good profit if you come in with me. All I need is a bit of capital to get it started.'

'Give the details to Piers,' Claudia said, reaching through the shower curtain for a towel. 'I wouldn't dream of making an investment unless it had his approval.'

Sebastian contained his annoyance, but he was quieter than usual as they shared a drink on the terrace. He had thought that Piers was a cipher, tolerated by Claudia because he was her lover. Apparently he had got that wrong, which put out all his calculations. A night wasted, not to mention the time and effort he had put into wooing her. They would, as Claudia had said, no doubt go on seeing one another, but if she thought she was getting him for nothing she could think again.

'So it was a success?' Claudia was looking particularly well, sparkling with life and rather more blonde than she had been when Piers went away.

'You've done something to your hair,' he said. 'You look marvellous.'

He bent over her, but all he got was a cheek to kiss.

'Thank you, darling.'

'Done anything special while I've been away?'

'Lazed around. I went dining and dancing with young Sebastian one night.'

'Enjoyable?'

'Very. I was highly flattered when he made a pass at me.'

'The boy's got taste.'

Claudia smiled to herself. 'He has his points.'

208

'Have there been any developments on the building front?'

'Not as much as I'd like, considering we've got bookings for the first week in May. You'll have to get after them, darling.'

'First thing tomorrow. Right now I've got other things on my mind.' He bent over her again. 'Show me how much you've missed me.'

Claudia went with him willingly enough. The fling with the young Sebastian had been all she had hoped it would be, but Seb had been mistaken in thinking he could disguise his mercenary streak. Claudia knew all about young men like Seb. Take 'em, use 'em and chuck 'em out, was her motto, and Seb's clumsy attempt to get money out of her for his fictional beach café had finished him as far as she was concerned.

In the cool dimness of their bedroom Claudia reflected that Piers was, after all, quite delightful, if one put aside a hankering for novelty. She could build a new life with him, which she certainly couldn't with the likes of young Seb. She was well able to keep an eye on his financial shortcomings and she did Piers the credit to believe that he would never intentionally cheat her, though he would probably fall short of pursuing the ultimate dollar as ardently as Bernie.

In the aftermath of their lovemaking she said lazily, 'When are you going to make an honest woman of me?'

'Darling! It's what I want more than anything,' Piers replied. 'Next week, if you like.'

'How shall we do it?'

'Do you want to make a splash? Have a large party?'

'I don't think so, not here. Let's do something out of the ordinary.'

'Elope to Las Vegas?'

'Now there's an idea! Shall we?'

'Why not? I'll make enquiries as to how we go about it, whether there are any special conditions for two Brits tying the knot over there.'

'Not in Las Vegas, surely? They'll marry anyone.'

'Better make sure. Claudia, I'm thrilled about this. I thought you might just want to go on as we are.'

'I've decided it's safer to be conventional. Piers, was there much talk about Bernie back home?'

'I went to the golf club and wished I hadn't. People were

pretty sticky. Poor old Bernie, he's not here to defend himself and now that Daley character has got off they seem to be making Bernie the scapegoat.'

'Poor old Bernie,' Claudia echoed automatically.

'Claud, I have to ask you. Did you hold back his heart pills? I mean, on purpose?'

'Ella told you that story. You might take into account the way she feels about me. I'm a bit hurt that you have to ask.'

'Sorry. It's been on my mind since I discovered the way people were thinking about Bernie. If he did it ... you might have felt he was better not facing trial.'

Claudia had given herself a moment or two to think. Now, she improvised freely. 'When Bernie had his bad turn the night of the murder the doctor gave him some different pills,' she said. 'I thought he had those with him. I took the old pills out of his pocket to stop him confusing the two lots. You know how vague he was about taking his medicine.'

'Such a simple explanation,' Piers said. 'You may be sorry I asked, but I'm glad because of the way it's cleared the air.'

Such a simple explanation. Pity it wasn't true. But Piers would never know and she had got back the love and trust that was due from him, considering she was condescending to marry him and endow him with all the worldly goods that had come to her as a result of Bernie's death.

'There's a letter from Dad,' Verity said, handing it over the breakfast table to Ella.

'Good, I was hoping to hear from him soon about summer holiday arrangements.'

'Will we have a holiday with you as well as with him?'

Ella hesitated. 'I'm not sure. I'm hoping he'll take you away for a fortnight so that I can have one week away on my own and one week here catching up on everything I need to do. If that works out then, yes, we might be able to go away somewhere, but not for more than a week and it'll have to be a last minute arrangement.'

'You work terribly hard over your shops. Is it worth it?'

'They're doing very well, making us lots of money, and although it's hard work, I am enjoying it.'

'You've lost quite a lot of weight, you know.'

210

'I'm having to wear a belt round my skirts,' Ella agreed. She looked at Verity's shadowed face and added gently, 'I'm perfectly well, darling; just a bit overworked.'

'I know it's daft to worry,' Verity muttered. 'But what would we do if we lost you?' She looked blindly out of the window. 'Mum started by just getting thin.'

'I know. Truly, I'm okay, and in the summer I'll concentrate on putting up my feet and let the pounds pile up. Now, let's see what Dad's got to say.'

She read the letter through and then turned back to the beginning again.

'Everything all right?' Verity asked, still watching her.

'Dad and Claudia are getting married at the end of June. In Las Vegas.'

Verity wrinkled her nose. 'Tacky!' she said.

'Not necessarily.'

'Going all that way. At their age! Does that mean he's backing out of a holiday with us?'

'No, he's got some ideas about that. Oh, Jerusalem, look at the time! Give Harry and Jennifer a shout. If you don't leave in five minutes you'll miss the bus.'

'I've got a rehearsal tonight,' Verity said, struggling into her coat.

'I haven't forgotten. Get those two downstairs while I clear the table. I'm due in Canterbury at nine o'clock.'

Ella wanted time to think about Piers' proposal for the children's summer holiday. What he was suggesting was that he and Claudia should stay on in the United States after their wedding and the children should fly out to join them.

'After that, I'm not sure,' he wrote. 'Could you find out what they'd like to do. Disneyland? A dude ranch? Touring around and staying in motels? A river trip on a paddle steamer?'

Ella thought it over as she drove into Canterbury, where it was her week to inspect the shop. Not Disneyland, Verity would despise that, although Jennifer and possibly Harry would enjoy it. Certainly not riding around in a car and looking at scenery. A river trip? Too immobile for three lively youngsters and too similar to what they had done at Easter. The ranch sounded like the best idea. They would love the idea of riding.

211

She checked the stock in the Canterbury shop, looked the staff over and took unobtrusive note of their way with customers, had a look out the back to make sure rubbish was not accumulating, cast an eye over the standards of cleanliness and by the end of the morning was well satisfied that everything was running smoothly.

'Any suggestions?' she asked.

'We could do with more soft drinks, especially now the weather is getting warmer. People who buy sandwiches want something to drink with them.'

'I'll look into it,' Ella promised.

She took a packet of her own sandwiches and ate them in the car as she drove to the unit on the trading estate. Verity was right, she reflected; this was not the way to live and it certainly did nothing for her digestion. She would make a resolution to sit down and eat properly in future, even if it were no more than a cheese roll.

She was not expected at the unit until later. As she walked in one of the staff gave her a startled look and then flushed deeply and looked away. Ella said nothing, but she went into her small office, put a sheet of headed paper into the typewriter and typed a short letter.

'Melanie, come in and see me, would you?' she said, looking into the busy work room.

When Melanie came into the office her hair was bundled up into the cap she was required to wear, which it had not been when Ella arrived.

'That's an improvement in your appearance,' Ella said. 'But your hair was hanging loose when I arrived and I presume it had been that way all the morning?'

Melanie shrugged. She had long fair hair, very beautiful hair, hanging way down below her shoulders and, as Ella well knew, she hated not having it on display.

'I've told you before,' Ella said evenly. 'You can plait your hair and wear your cap, you can tie it back and wear your cap, or you can do what you've done now and put the whole lot up inside your cap. What you can't do is leave it hanging loose.'

'Plaiting makes it go crinkly.'

'Then take one of the alternatives. I've already warned you twice.' She leaned forward and handed the girl the letter she had written. 'This is a third warning, and in writing. One more infringement of our rules and you're out, is that understood?'

'I suppose so.'

Ella tried for a little understanding. 'Melanie, we can't risk a customer finding hair in our products. You'd find it unpleasant yourself, wouldn't you?'

No response except another shrug. Ella persisted. 'Besides, it's dangerous. I know you think you couldn't possibly do yourself any harm with such things as food processors, but believe me, it is possible. I don't want to see you scalped, so please, in future, keep your hair tied up and out of the way.'

She had a word with her senior operative. 'Did you tell Melanie to put her cap on?'

'I did, but she won't listen to me.'

Ella suppressed a sigh. 'You'll have to be a bit more forceful if I'm to leave you in charge. Melanie's not a bad kid, and a good worker, if only she weren't so vain of her hair. By the way, there was a cigarette end on the floor. Who's been smoking?'

'Brian came in with a fag on when he brought the van round to load up. I told him to put it out and he chucked it on the floor and stamped on it.'

'All right. If it happens again tell him to get rid of it outside. Now, let's get down to the orders.'

'Mrs Patel rang to say the new chutney had been selling well in Dover. I wrote down what she said. And the apple and cheese in walnut bread is going a bomb in Sandwich.'

'Great! I'll let you know shortly whether there'll be any changes in production for the rest of the week.'

She worked until five o'clock and then drove home. Not a bad day. No big problems, plenty of good news about sales. Melanie was a nuisance, but with any luck she would fall into line and if she didn't then she would have to be replaced, which would not be difficult with the high rate of unemployment on the coast.

As Ella had anticipated, the children seized eagerly on the idea of spending a holiday on a ranch.

'In America!' Jennifer said, deeply impressed.

'That's where they have ranches,' Harry informed her crushingly. 'Will it be a real ranch, with cattle and everything?'

'I don't actually know,' Ella said. 'Dad's making the

arrangements for this one. I suppose Verity has told you that he and Claudia are getting married?'

'We knew it was coming,' Harry said. 'I think he's nuts. Have we got to have her along on our holiday?'

'Only for a few days at the beginning I think Dad said in his letter. Yes, here it is. She'll leave you after a day or two to go and visit some friends in New York and she'll fly back to Spain separately from you and Dad. Dad will bring you home, but you'll have to fly out on your own.'

'With a planeful of other passengers,' Harry pointed out. 'No problem. We're quite used to travelling, you know.'

'Yes, of course,' Ella agreed meekly. 'So, the decision's made? You'll go to the United States and come back with bow legs and wearing stetsons?'

'And chewing tobacco,' Jennifer said unexpectedly.

'You dare! I'll write to Dad tomorrow.'

'As long as it doesn't clash with Dickens Week and the play,' Verity said.

'Of course not; that would be before the end of your school term. You're not expected to join them until mid-July.'

Jennifer had outgrown the costume she had worn for Dickens Week the previous year, but Ella added a flounce of curtain lace to the skirt and she was able to appear once more along the front and in the High Street.

'You'll have to be a different character next year,' Ella said. 'You're getting too old for Little Em'ly.'

'Perhaps I'll be in the play, like Verity.'

They all went to see Verity in *Great Expectations*. It was an amateur production, but well done, and Verity performed the part of Estella with an aplomb that startled Ella.

'She was quite good, wasn't she?' Harry asked afterwards. 'But I liked the convict best.'

'Verity wants to go to an acting school,' Jennifer said. 'Will she be able to?'

It gave Ella a little shock to realise that this was not a decision she could make, not without Piers' consent.

'We'll have to consult Dad,' she said diplomatically.

'I don't see why he should decide when he doesn't live with us,' Harry said.

'That's the way it is,' Ella said, squashing further discussion. 'Let's see if Verity is ready to come home with us.'

Verity, very flushed and shining-eyed, was clearly reluctant to abandon the rest of the cast.

'There's a party,' she explained. 'I can stay, can't I?'

The man who had played Magwitch, his pleasant expression curiously at variance with his villainous make-up, said, 'My wife and I will see her home, Mrs Armitage. We won't be staying late; we're both worn out.'

All the same, Ella waited up, even though she, too, was on the edge of exhaustion. Verity was sixteen and had a front door key, but Ella could not feel easy until she heard the car draw up outside and Verity's quick footsteps coming down the path. She grimaced to herself; this was something she was going to have to get used to; Verity was growing up and although she still accepted Ella's authority it would not be long now before she started wanting more independence.

'Did you have a good time?' she asked.

'Yes, it was great. It wasn't a big party, you know. Just a few bottles of wine and soft drinks and some snacks, but we had music and we danced on the stage. Everyone was pleased with the way the play had gone so there was a good atmosphere. You did enjoy it, didn't you?'

'Very much and I thought you were really good.'

'I want to take it seriously, you know; go to acting school and all that.'

'Take your "A" levels and we'll think about it then.'

'As long as it's understood that my mind's made up,' Verity said suspiciously. 'Shall I talk to Dad about it while we're in America?'

'Do that, but don't bang on about it too much, will you, darling? Tell him what you want and then leave him to think it over.'

'Talk it over with Claudia, you mean. After all, it'll be her money that pays for it. And don't think that doesn't rankle, because it does!'

'Your father has a perfectly good job and earns a salary.'

'Supervising the painters changing the colour of the walls because Claudia doesn't like pink.'

'And arranging the lettings of the flats and keeping the bookings sorted out.'

'Honestly, the way you defend him!'

'I loved him once,' Ella said, and something in the way she spoke silenced Verity.

Chapter Twelve

'It's more of a holiday place than a real working ranch,' Harry said.

'It'd have to have all mod cons and a bit of luxury with Claudia coming along,' Verity said.

'I didn't think she was going to be here.'

'Only for the first three days,' Verity consoled him. 'She's trying to be nice to us.'

'I like it better when she's not. It's only pretence any way.'

'There's lots and lots of space, and lots and lots of horses, and it's fun having a cabin,' Jennifer put in. 'And we're the first English visitors they've had staying here and they think the way we speak is real cute.'

'If I catch you being cute I'll scrag you,' Harry threatened.

They were at the Two Dollar Ranch in Colorado, a wide spread of rolling grassland, baking under the summer sun, with the old original ranch house serving as a cookhouse and dining room and surrounded by log cabins which were more spacious than any old time cowboy had ever dreamed of. They had three bedrooms, a sitting room with cooking facilities at one end, and a shower room with plenty of hot water. Claudia, who had resigned herself to roughing it for three nights for the sake of good relations with her new husband, was pleased with the comfort of the place, and still better pleased to find some congenial companions amongst the other holidaymakers. Of course, she should have known it would be all right, it had been recommended by one of her Marbella friends and God knows it was costing enough.

'Can we go and see the horses?' Harry demanded as Piers

217

unloaded the last of the luggage from the car.

'Why not? You'll find most of them are out for the day, but there are a few in the far paddock.'

'Corral,' Harry corrected him.

'Right! We'll walk down and join you shortly and then go and see what the programme is for the next few days.'

'There are leaflets and things in the bedrooms,' Verity said.

They walked down to the place where they could see the horses. 'Just look round,' Harry said. 'Miles and miles of nothing.'

'Poor old Claudia, she'll hate it,' Verity said. 'I bet she wears jewellery with her jeans.'

'Gold chains,' Jennifer agreed. 'They're beautiful, but she doesn't have any idea, does she?'

Feeling cheerfully superior, they climbed up the fence and hung over the top, chirruping hopefully to the horses. They snorted and tossed their heads, but one mare began to pick her way towards them.

'Hi, there,' a voice behind them said. 'If you're making up to old Lila there, you'd better have something to give her. She'll take it real hard if she comes all the way over for nothing.'

He was a battered-looking man in his fifties, with very short grizzled hair, a weather beaten face, and the wiry, stocky build of a lifelong horse rider. He had a saddle and saddle bags slung over one shoulder, his serviceable denims were tucked into worn boots and his shirt was a faded version of the colourful check to which Piers had treated himself in preparation for his stay on the ranch.

'Name's Phil Blackburn,' he said. 'Might have an old apple or two tucked into these bags, you can give her ladyship.'

'Does Lila like apples?' Jennifer asked.

'Sure does. Here y'are.'

'They're a bit shrivelled.'

'Lila don't care. Hold one out on the flat of your hand and she'll pick it off real careful.'

The other horses, seeing that one of their number was enjoying a treat, came over and jostled for attention. Harry and Verity took their turn to feed the ones who could reach them.

'They're very wet feeders,' Verity said, wondering what to do with her slimy hand.

218

'They slobber a bit,' Phil Blackburn agreed. 'You must be the three British kids I heard were coming?'

'Yes, we're Verity, Harry and Jennifer Armitage.'

'Well, I hope you have a real good time. My grandparents came from England. From Somersetshire.'

'Just "Somerset", no "shire",' Verity corrected him.

'Is that so? I've always meant to go over and look up the place they were born, but I never got around to it. Are you coming to the hoe-down this evening?'

Verity looked doubtful and Harry asked, 'Is it something to do with hay?'

'Not so's I ever noticed. It's just another name for a dance.' With a touch of cynicism he added, 'We use these expressions so's the customers feel they're having the real Western experience. You ever done square dancing?'

'Yes!' Jennifer said eagerly. 'I have, and it was fun!'

'Right, see you in the barn after supper.' He looked them over with experienced eyes and asked, 'What about riding?'

'We've never done any,' Harry admitted.

'Except the donkeys on the beach,' Jennifer added.

'You'll be coming out with me tomorrow, then. If you're planning on riding, that is.'

'We are,' Harry said. 'What else is there to do?'

'There's a swimming pool out back of the ranch house and you can go white water rafting. River's a bit high, but she'll have settled down by Wednesday, when the next trip's planned. You can go gold-panning ...'

'Gold!'

'Sure. Used to be a lot of mining in these parts. You can visit an old mining town, a real ghost town, spooky old place, gives me the shivers. Anything else you want to know?'

'Why is it called Two Dollar Ranch?'

'Because the man who first settled here was down to his last two dollars when he arrived. It's all in that fancy brochure they've had printed about the place, you can read it up.' He paused and added thoughtfully, 'And some of it's true, too.'

'We're going to like it here,' Jennifer assured him.

'Hope you do. Now, I've got some chores to do.' He put two fingers in his mouth and whistled piercingly and the one horse which had held aloof wheeled round from the far end of the corral and galloped towards them.

'He's nice,' Harry said.

'Best of the bunch. No one rides Ranger but me.'

They watched respectfully as Phil Blackburn saddled up and swung himself up on the black horse.

'I'd be obliged if you'd undo the gate for me,' he said, and Harry rushed to obey his new friend. Phil pulled on the wide-brimmed hat which had been hanging on his back from a cord round his neck and touched it courteously as he passed the two girls.

'He's not for show. He's *real*,' Verity said.

'He didn't have any guns,' Jennifer said.

'Well, of course not, there aren't any bandits now. But you can see he does proper work, not just riding out with tourists.'

'Like us,' Harry said.

'Yes, but at least we know we're tourists.'

When Piers and Claudia strolled down to join them they were full of information. Piers held up his hand to stem the torrent.

'One at a time! You're deafening me. You want to go to the barn dance tonight, riding tomorrow and what else was it?'

'White water rafting,' Harry said. 'It'll be brilliant. Wham, bam! Shooting the rapids!'

'Don't get too excited,' Piers warned. 'Are you hungry?'

'The evening meal is repulsively early,' Claudia complained. 'Do we really have to dine at six-thirty?'

It was not quite as bad as she had feared since she was able to indulge in a prolonged cocktail hour before actually sitting down to eat, while the children, who were both hungry and tired, had an earlier meal. By that time the idea of square dancing was not as welcome as it had seemed when they had first heard about it, but they put up a valiant fight against their travel fatigue and joined in several energetic dances before Jennifer began to droop and Verity said, 'I think she'll have to go to bed.'

She tried to suppress a yawn herself, but Claudia said, 'I suppose you're all tired. Can you find your own way back to the cabin? Dad and I will be in later.'

It was quiet outside the barn. Stars were coming out overhead, a small breeze sprang up and ruffled the dry grass, somewhere a horse snickered. They dragged their weary feet up the hill towards their cabin and struggled with the unfamiliar lock.

'We never unpacked,' Verity said.

'Perhaps Claudia will have done it,' Harry suggested.

'Some hope!'

She opened Jennifer's case and found her nightdress and toilet bag.

'Mum's packed the things we'll need first on top,' she said.

'Sensible Mum.' Harry yawned earsplittingly. 'She'd like it here, wouldn't she?'

'Yes, she would, and so would real Mummy,' Jennifer said. 'I'm going to wash.'

'Sometimes when she says things like that I don't know whether to hit her or burst into tears,' Verity said.

Harry looked puzzled. 'I suppose I know what you mean,' he said. 'Do you ever think about her now? Our proper mother, I mean?'

'Not often. Such a lot has happened.'

'Now that Mum – Ella – has got this business of hers, do you think she regrets having us to look after?'

'She says not,' Verity said. 'She didn't *have* to have us. She could have made Dad take us.'

'I'm glad she didn't. I mean, Dad's all right and on a holiday like this he can be super, or he will be when we've got rid of Claudia, but that's what he's for, isn't it? Holidays.'

'He's not strong on every day life,' Verity agreed. 'Don't say anything to him about me wanting to go on the stage, will you? I'm going to edge into it gently.'

'Right. And we'd better keep off my idea of going into the church, because he certainly doesn't like that.'

'Do you still think you'll do it?' Verity asked curiously.

'I feel sort of settled inside myself about it.'

'But you're not really very good.'

'You have to have practice,' Harry explained.

They had a half day's ride the next day under Phil Blackburn's watchful eye and went gold-panning in the afternoon. Harry and Jennifer were ecstatic when they detected flecks of gold in their pans. Verity, who suspected that the stream had been

221

salted with gold for the benefit of the visitors, was not so lucky.

'Whole day ride tomorrow,' Phil told them. 'I reckon you're up to it.'

They glowed with pride and swaggered as they made their way back to the cabin.

'I'm not sure I'm up to a full day out, no matter what our guide may say,' Claudia murmured. 'I'll spend some time by the pool.'

'If it's okay by you, Dad, Phil says we could sleep out later in the week,' Harry said. 'A real camp with a fire and sleeping on the ground.'

'My poor old bones!'

'We could go without you.'

'No, I'd like to do it.'

'Thank God I'll have departed by then,' Claudia said, only half seriously. She had, against all the odds, rather enjoyed this unusual break, but enough was enough and she was looking forward to shopping in New York.

'What about tomorrow? White water rafting isn't quite your thing, is it?'

'I think I'll come along. I was a bit bored by the pool today because most people had gone off somewhere. It's not dangerous, is it?'

'Only mildly. You have to wear a hard hat.'

'Death to the hairstyle!'

'Phil says the river is tetchy,' Harry said. 'It could be *quite* dangerous.'

Since he obviously wanted to regard the expedition as an adventure Piers did not contradict him, but he had no real misgivings about making the descent down the Colorado River even though the following morning their guide, a young man called Pete, said that the water was higher than usual for the time of year and running fast.

Claudia rather liked the look of Pete. He was very dark and brawny. She felt a thrill as he handed her into the boat and showed her how to handle the paddle.

'I'll be with you all the way, of course,' he said. 'And I'll be navigating and using my oar to keep us on course.'

'Are we going to get wet?' Claudia asked.

'I wouldn't be surprised, with the river running the way she is. Jennifer's more than eight, isn't she? I'm not taking kids below that age on this trip.'

'I'm eleven, almost,' Jennifer said, deeply offended.

'Sorry, ma'am, I'm not good at guessing ladies' ages. Everyone got their life jackets properly tied?' He glanced round the remaining people waiting to embark. 'I need one more to balance this raft. How about you, Gary?'

Gary, a heavy, fifteen-year old, clumsy but likeable, who had been showing a tendency to hang around Verity, moved forward with alacrity. His mother, apparently, would have preferred the family not to be separated, but in response to her agitated murmur her husband said, 'Quit mollycoddling the boy' and she allowed herself to be persuaded into the second of the three rafts which would be doing the run.

The water at the point where they embarked was running swiftly but calmly. They paddled as they had been shown, but it was hardly necessary because the current carried them along and they had leisure to watch the banks on either side.

'I like this, it's easy going,' Claudia said.

'The hard bit's to come,' Pete said. 'But don't you worry, I'll look after you.'

She glanced back over her shoulder at him, coquettishly pleased by his concern for her. Pete, who could fend off middle-aged women with the same ease he displayed in pushing the raft away from hidden rocks, smiled with conscious charm and made a mental note to keep away from her.

The river narrowed and the banks grew steeper. The water was noticeably choppier.

'We're entering the canyon,' Pete called. 'Remember what I told you. All dip together and listen out for my word of command to veer right or left. Gary, keep time.'

It was mostly an illusion, since he could, if necessary, correct their mistakes with his own big oar, but they liked to think they were in control, and this was a nice bunch of kids. They called the woman Claudia, so she was probably their stepmother. Not difficult to imagine her being involved in a divorce. A recognisable type, and not one he liked. He rather wished he had not co-opted Gary into his raft; the youngster's movements were unco-ordinated, even jerky.

223

Pete roused himself to start paying serious attention to their passage. They were being tossed on real waves now and the canyon walls rose sheer on either side. Avoid the boulders on the left, he thought automatically. Steer right and then for the middle to shoot the first rapid, no more than a foot or two's drop, but it made the passengers squeal.

They plunged through the foaming water, spray dashing in their faces, half-deafened by the roar as the river forced its way through the narrow gorge and then, abruptly, everything went wrong at the same time.

There was an eddy in the wrong place. Pete registered it immediately; his knowledge of the river ran through his mind like an often repeated film. Something had changed, a rock had shifted on the river bed or fallen from above. Not serious, he had seen it in time, he could manoeuvre them round it. He raised his hand in a gesture he hoped the guide in the following raft would see, although he, too, was too experienced not to be alert for the tricks the river could play.

At precisely the same moment, just when Pete's attention was distracted from his passengers, Gary gave a curious hoarse cry. He fell backwards, his legs shot out in a totally involuntary movement, kicking Harry, immediately in front of him, so hard that Harry fell forward against Claudia. She squealed, lost her paddle and leaned over the side to try to retrieve it. Piers, half blinded by water, lunged towards her to stop her overbalancing. Gary, in the throes of a violent epileptic fit, heaved and struggled in the bottom of the raft.

'Sit still, sit still!' Pete yelled, desperate to stop them foundering on the rocks through which they were plunging.

The raft, buoyant but out of control, swung round rear side on to the next set of rapids, with Pete trying to correct its passage and all his passengers in such disarray that he hardly knew whether or not they were still on board. The raft struck an enormous boulder and spun round again, tipping as it did so. Claudia was flung out and Harry after her. Again Piers made a despairing attempt to clutch at one or the other of them. He managed to get a hand on Harry and struggled to hold him, but they were tossing too wildly. He felt the boy slipping away from him, over-reached himself and followed Harry and Claudia into the water.

224

They could see Claudia, her blue helmet visible above the waves, her arms flailing in an impossible attempt to swim in that tumultuous water. Piers and Harry, too, were momentarily in sight and then they disappeared. The raft, too light and lopsided, bobbed on. Gary moaned and jerked and then lay quiet.

There were no choices, no way of stopping; they had to go on until they reached quieter waters. Pete, white-faced and sick, steered the raft to the landing place.

The guide in the raft behind him knew what had happened, the passengers seemed bewildered, not sure that they had seen what they thought they had seen.

'Gary?' his mother asked as soon as she was on dry land. 'Is Gary all right?'

'He's recovering,' Pete said. He tried to restrain himself, but it burst out of him. 'To the end of my days I'll never forgive you for letting that boy come on this trip.'

'We didn't know he'd have a seizure,' Gary's father protested.

'No, no, all right, let's not get into an argument now,' Pete's companion intervened. 'Pete, I'll take a kayak downstream, see if I can locate anyone. You alert the ranch, get them to send someone down in case any ...' ... any bodies, he wanted to say, but not in front of Jennifer and Verity ... 'in case they've landed up on a strip of land in the canyon.' He glanced round. 'Can someone look after the girls?'

Verity was standing with her arm round Jennifer. She could not take in what had happened.

'Are they dead?' she asked.

'There's a chance,' Pete said. 'They were all wearing helmets and life jackets. You'd be surprised how buoyant the human body can be.'

The search went on for hours. They found Claudia first, her helmet intact but her life jacket ripped, her body battered where she had been swept round and round in a whirlpool where the boats never ventured, until she was flung up to hang lifeless, wedged between two rocks.

Piers and Harry were located by the fleet of kayaks that set out from the ranch. As Pete had suspected, they had been thrown further off-course than Claudia and had not been

225

carried along by the main stream of water. They were found on a narrow strip of pulverised pebbles in the heart of the canyon, Piers' arm still flung protectively over his son.

'Alive,' the leader of the rescue team reported. He bent over Piers, 'but only just.'

Harry stirred and coughed and a stream of river water and vomit poured out of his mouth.

'The boy's got nasty gashes on his thigh and chest and he's lost a lot of blood by the look of it, but he'll be O.K. The man ... he's breathing, but I won't say more than that.'

Harry began to cry, weakly and heartrendingly. 'All right, son, you'll be all right.'

'Dad!'

'He's here, hurt but okay.'

'Not dead?'

'No, not dead.'

They took Harry as fast as they could to the nearest hospital. His wounds were stitched, he had a blood transfusion and the verdict was that he would make a good recovery. They took Piers, too, but he died on the way.

Chapter Thirteen

Ella snapped her suitcase shut and locked it. She had half an hour before the taxi arrived to take her to the station; just time before she left to look round the house and make sure that everything was in order. She had had a good three days at home on her own, no worries, no distractions. Verity had telephoned to say that they had arrived safely in the United States and the Two Dollar Ranch looked as if it would be fun; now Ella was off for a week on the Isles of Scilly, to stay at a comfortable hotel and have a well-earned rest. She would have another three days at home before the children returned and that would give her time to re-stock the freezer and make plans for the rest of the summer holidays.

The telephone rang. Ella hesitated, but of course she had to answer it.

'Mrs Ella Armitage? This is Lois Pressinger from Two Dollar Ranch, Colorado.'

Something was wrong. Ella had a hideous feeling that her stomach had turned over.

'Mrs Armitage, are you on your own?'

'Yes, I am.'

'Is there a neighbour or someone who could come to you because I've got some real bad news for you.'

'Please tell me. I'll call in a friend if I need to. Is it ... is it the children? An accident?'

'An accident, yes, but the children are okay. Harry's had a nasty gash and needed a transfusion, but he's recovering fast.'

'Piers? Something's happened to Piers?'

'Both Mr and Mrs Armitage have died following a boating accident.'

'And the children were with them?'

'They were all in the same raft. Mrs Armitage, we're looking after them as best we can, but they need someone of their own with them at this time.'

'Yes, yes ... of course. I'll come, just as soon as I can get a flight. Tell them ... tell them I'm on my way. Give them my love, all my love.'

As she put the telephone down the front door bell rang. Ella went to open the door, too dazed to know what she was doing, and looked with blank, shocked eyes at the man on the doorstep.

'Your taxi,' he said.

Her taxi. She had been just about to go away on holiday, leaving her address with no one because it was for such a short time and it had not seemed necessary. Thank goodness the telephone had rung in time. Her bag was packed, she could write from the airport to explain her non-arrival at St Mary's.

'Can you take me to Heathrow instead of the station?' she asked. I've just had some bad news and I've got to go to America straight away.'

'Don't see why not. I'll ring the office and clear it with them.'

'I'll get my case.'

'Don't forget your passport.'

Her passport. Yes, of course, thank goodness he had mentioned it. Money ... she had enough to pay the sizeable taxi fare and she could get some dollars at Heathrow. Thank God for a bank balance that showed a healthy credit. She found the details of the children's holiday, too, with the directions for getting to Two Dollar Ranch. Her driving licence, she would need that if she hired a car. As to the flight, surely she would find someone at Heathrow who would put her in the way of getting the first available place.

'Sorry to hear you've had bad news,' the taxi driver said, obviously hoping for further details.

'The people with whom my ... children are on holiday have died in a boating accident.'

'Shocking! Related to you?'

Piers ... oh, Piers. 'No,' Ella said. 'Not related to me at all.'

* * *

228

She felt as if she had been travelling for ever when she finally stumbled out of her hired car into the hot Colorado sunshine. Through a haze of fatigue she explained who she was and found herself enveloped in the immense American solicitude she had already discovered on her journey. She had spoken all the time of her children, not her stepchildren; it saved tedious explanations. The fact that they had been on holiday with their father and his new wife had been accepted without comment, but it might have been more difficult to get across the fact the Claudia was, in fact, his third wife and the children's second stepmother. Claudia was dead. How was it possible that Piers and Claudia could be dead?

'The kids have gone out with Phil Blackburn,' she was told. 'Phil's driving Harry in the pony and trap and the girls are riding. Phil said it was better for them to have some distraction rather than just sit around. He's been staying with them in the cabin. We offered for a woman to be with them, but they seemed to want Phil.'

'Can I stay in the cabin, too?'

'Sure can. It's booked till the end of next week. After that, I have to say that with the best will in the world we'll be hard put to it to find room for you. Of course, we'll do everything in our power to find you other accommodation if you're staying on.'

'I hardly think that'll be necessary.'

'There has to be an enquiry and the children being the only people who saw what happened, apart from our own employee, will be called on to give their account.'

'I see. I hope it will be possible to get that over as soon as possible.'

'So do we. Mrs Armitage, I'm not supposed to say I'm sorry, in case it prejudices our chances in a court of law, but it isn't humanly possible not to tell you how sad we all are about what's happened.'

'You're very kind.' Ella smiled, a difficult, weary smile. 'I won't quote you.'

The cabin was more like a small bungalow. Easy to see which rooms the children had taken and the unknown Phil Blackburn was apparently sharing with Harry, so she could take the room

229

with the double bed. The room Piers and Claudia had shared. No point in having qualms about that. The sheets and towels had been changed, and probably were every day; it would have been as impersonal as any other hotel room if it had not been for the clothes still hanging in the closet, the toilet articles scattered around, Claudia's cosmetics on top of the dressing table.

With a feeling that she could not bear to look at these personal reminders, Ella found their suitcases and began packing everything away. She had just finished when she heard the sound of horses' hooves and wheels on gravel. By the time she got to the front door Verity and Jennifer had dismounted and Harry was being helped down from the trap.

It was Jennifer who saw Ella first. 'Mum!' she said. Her lower lip trembled and her eyes filled with tears. Ella held out her arms and Jennifer fell on her with a sound like a primaeval howl of anguish. Holding her with one arm, Ella stretched out her other to Harry and Verity. As they stood in one awkward, grief-stricken huddle, she looked over their heads to the grizzled man by the pony trap.

'I'll take the horses down and come back later to see if you need me,' he said.

'Let's go inside,' Ella said.

They all bore the marks of the shock they had suffered. They moved slowly, as if their limbs hurt; their eyes were dull and they looked down at the ground, not around them with their usual alertness. The recent exercise in the open air had given them a spurious colour in their cheeks, but when it faded their faces had a strange, pallid waxiness.

Harry was the only one who was obviously wounded. He showed Ella his stitches and she shuddered at the thought of what might have been if he had lost any more blood. She sensed that they were reluctant to talk about the accident, but to say nothing about it would have created a barrier they might never break down so she asked a few careful questions and it began to come out, slowly at first and then in a flood.

'We were having such a nice time,' Verity said pitifully.

'I'm glad your last memory of Dad is such a good one,' Ella said.

'He saved my life,' Harry said. 'He held me tight and

stopped me getting banged against the rocks. Only, of course, he ...' He stopped, swallowed and looked down.

'He was unconscious when they found him,' Verity said quickly. 'He wasn't suffering any pain.'

'Do you think he knew Harry was all right?' Jennifer asked.

'I'm sure he did,' Ella said. 'Now, tell me about Mr Blackburn.'

'He's our friend,' Harry said. 'They wanted to move us out of here and put us in the house and treat us like invalids.'

'And with hordes of other people,' Verity said.

'Looking at us,' Jennifer added.

'We said we'd rather be here and Phil – he told us to call him Phil – he just moved in and stayed with us.'

'Everyone's been very kind,' Verity said. 'They've been sending meals up to us because we didn't feel like going into the dining room, but we haven't wanted much.'

'Can we go home soon?' Jennifer asked.

'As soon as I can fix it,' Ella promised. 'There are arrangements to be made.'

Speaking in a high, hurried voice, Harry said, 'What I want to know is, where's Dad going to be buried?'

'Do you have any thoughts about that?'

'He ought to be with Mummy.'

'And Claudia with Bernie,' Jennifer said.

'I'll see what I can do,' Ella promised.

By the time Phil Blackburn returned, bringing with him a hot meal for all of them, Ella was almost blind with fatigue. The long journey, the emotional turmoil, the strain of the children's grief, the way they depended on her so completely, all took their toll. She swallowed a mouthful or two of the chicken and sweetcorn, but all she wanted to do was to lay her head on a pillow and close her eyes.

'I guess your Mum's too tired for anything more tonight,' Phil said. 'Ma'am, do you want me to go or stay?'

'Please stay,' Harry said.

'Harry's been restless at night,' Phil said, looking steadily at Ella to convey a message. 'He's been glad to find me in the room when he wakes up.'

'I'll be grateful if you'll stay,' Ella said. 'Tomorrow ... I don't know. You're right, I'm too tired to make sense tonight.

Darlings, I'm sorry, but I've got past remembering when it was I set out and I must have some sleep.'

'You're here,' Verity said. 'That's all we need.'

There were endless loose ends to be sorted out. The children had to endure being questioned about the accident. The boy who had the fit, Ella was told, was too traumatised to say anything.

'At least that's what his parents say,' Phil told Ella. 'They've put him in a clinic for counselling.'

'I doubt if he remembers anything about it.'

'Probably not. They say they had no reason to think he might be due for an epileptic episode. Apparently there's a theory that watching the movement of the water might have brought it on.'

'I've heard of such things. So, where do we stand now, Mr Blackburn?'

'Phil, if you don't mind.'

'If you'll stop calling me "ma'am",' Ella said with a smile.

'It just comes out. The verdict is "Accidental death" and no one person is held responsible, which is a relief to the people who run this dude ranch and especially to young Pete, who blames himself, though I've told him not to.'

'I haven't spoken to Pete. I must see him and reassure him.'

'Ma'am ... Ella, there's something else I ought to tell you; there's been an ambulance chaser nosing round.'

'A what?'

'Don't you have them in Europe? A lawyer who specialises in claims for damages after an accident.'

'Oh, yes, I suppose we do. But we don't have a claim if it was an accident with no one to blame.'

'I guess he'd call that pretty naive,' Phil said drily.

Phil was right, the smart young lawyer who called on Ella later that day almost laughed out loud at her simplistic view of what had happened.

'You could get damages,' he said. 'I put it to you, Mrs Armitage, that you owe it to the children to seek damages. You could sue the Two Dollar Ranch, the guide in charge of the raft and the parents of the sick boy.'

'But I don't want to.'

'We're talking here about a million, two million dollars. The death of a father of three children ... without him, they need all the support they can get.'

You don't know the half of it. They're no worse off without Piers than they were with him. Any support they need will come from me, the same as it always has.

'I'm sorry, but I really can't undertake a long expensive law suit in a foreign country,' Ella said.

The lawyer blinked. Ella had the distinct impression that he had never before thought of the United States as being foreign.

'No result, no fee,' he said. 'That's the basis on which I work. Are you their legal guardian? Because, if so, you have a duty to do your best for them.'

Was she the children's legal guardian? When they had parted she had insisted on Piers making a Will and appointing her to that position if he died first.

'Does marriage invalidate an existing Will?' she asked.

'Sure does. Have you got problems there? Because, if so, I'd be happy to sort them out for you.'

'It's much too complicated and nothing can be done until we return to England. I appreciate your concern and your wish to be of service, but we will not be taking proceedings against anyone, there will be no claims for damages and I'd be grateful if you'd go away and leave us in peace.'

As soon as the lawyer had gone, still protesting that she was making a mistake, Ella turned to the suitcases she had packed. In a zipped compartment inside the lid of Claudia's case she found a large manila envelope containing Bernie's death certificate, confirmation of Piers' divorce, the new marriage certificate and two Wills, prepared in England, as a letter from Claudia's solicitors made clear, but signed and witnessed in Las Vegas immediately after the wedding ceremony. Well organised Claudia, Ella thought, sitting back on her heels.

Claudia's Will was straightforward. She left a sum of money to the Kits Harbour Golf Club for the purchase of a trophy to be known as the Caldicott Cup 'in memory of my late husband, Bernard Caldicott'; Ella wondered how the club would like that in view of the suspicion that Bernie had been responsible for a murder on their own golf links; she directed

233

that various pieces of jewellery should be given to friends and left five hundred pounds to a cousin living in Cornwall. Apart from that everything went unconditionally to Piers, who was also her executor.

Piers' Will was rather more complicated because he had to make provision for the children. Ella's right to remain in the family home was re-stated, which was something of a relief, and she was named as the children's guardian, but the executor of Piers' Will and the trustee to act for the children was not Ella, but Toby.

This was something that needed thought. If Claudia had died first, as seemed to be the case, then everything she owned would have gone to Piers, how ever little time he survived her. And Piers' estate was to go to the children. All Claudia's money. Even allowing for inheritance tax, Verity, Harry and Jennifer had suddenly become very rich indeed.

Crouching there on the floor, with the papers Piers and Claudia had signed spread out in front of her, it came to Ella that there would be an enormous amount of work involved in dealing with this complicated inheritance. And only Toby could deal with it. Toby, who was on the far side of the world and almost impossible to reach. He did not even know that Piers was dead. She would have to write to him.

She wrote the letter and hoped she had made it clear that she thought his presence in England was essential, at least until they could get some working arrangement set up. Would he come? Surely he could not refuse.

'I'm sorry about that awful scrappy note I sent you from the airport while I was waiting for a flight to America,' Ella said to her mother-in-law. 'I was afraid to come to the telephone in case my name was called and I didn't hear it.'

'It was a shock, but there was no way you could dress it up so that it wouldn't have been a shock,' Mrs Armitage said.

She had come to Kits Harbour for the funeral. Ella, feeling her way for the right thing to do, had arranged a cremation in Colorado and for the ashes to be sent to England to a local funeral director who had found a suitable date for an interment ceremony. Claudia's urn would be placed in Bernie's family tomb and Piers, as the children wished, would join their mother.

The children were still very subdued and the worst of it was that Ella felt bound to take some interest in the business she had neglected for the last few weeks. The Patels had been wonderful, but she had committed herself to the venture and she could not totally dissociate herself from it. She was shamed by the realisation that work was a distraction and relief, and tried to deny it when Mrs Armitage spoke about it.

'Nothing like one worry for driving out another,' her mother-in-law said. 'I can see that this business of yours needs your attention. Are Verity, Harry and Jennifer still coming to me for a week or two?'

That had been the plan before Piers' death. Their grand-mother had said she would be pleased to have them for at least one week during their summer holidays and at that time they had been keen on the idea. Now, Ella was hesitant about sending them anywhere.

'The change might do them good,' she said. 'On the other hand, they seem to cling to the idea of staying at home.'

'I've noticed that, but you've got too much on your hands to be with them all day and every day. I was wondering whether you'd like me to stay on here until they go back to school?'

'It would be the most tremendous help. To know that there's always someone here. It's what they need more than anything.'

'If they want to go to the beach I can take my knitting and sit in a deckchair. They might like to show me Dover. Believe it or not, I've never been there.'

She did far more than that. The first time that Ella felt she could spend a full day at work she returned to a dinner of roast chicken, roast potatoes and fresh green beans with a summer pudding to follow.

'You're spoiling me,' Ella protested.

'I sliced the beans,' Harry said.

'And I cut the crusts off the bread and lined the pudding basin,' Jennifer said. 'And Verity whipped the cream, so we all did something. Are you pleased?'

'I'm overwhelmed! And am I dreaming, or has someone done the ironing?

'It passed the afternoon away,' Mrs Armitage said. 'I'm not one to sit doing nothing.'

Having her there was a real comfort, not just for the work

she did, but for the company. She had nothing out of the ordinary to say, her comments on most events were predictable, she might even have been called dull, but her presence was soothing. She did not often speak of her dead son, but when she did it was in a forgiving spirit. Ella thought her too charitable, but she admired the way she talked about Piers to his children, telling them of things he had done in his own childhood which they did not appear to have heard before. She saw their memories of him beginning to take on a rosier gloss, which might be false, but was kinder than the harshness of reality.

In the absence of any reaction from Toby, Ella took it on herself to visit Claudia's solicitor, who had drawn up the two Wills.

'It's a complicated business,' he said, which was no more than she knew already. 'In the absence of the executor it's difficult to settle the estate.'

'I must surely hear from Toby soon. I'm beginning to wonder if he received my letter, although I sent it to the usual address and they're usually good about passing letters on to their people in the field. I wonder, since I'm the children's guardian, can you give me some idea of what they've inherited?'

'The house and the garden centre were sold,' the solicitor said cautiously. 'And a considerable capital sum was sent to Spain to pay for the new apartment block, which of course is part of the estate. Then there's the Spanish villa and, in this country, two small blocks of flats in Kits Harbour, three former boarding houses now let to bed-and-breakfast tenants in Cliftonville, part ownership of an office block in Ramsgate and an interest in a freight business trading with the Continent.'

'It's unbelievable.'

'The late Mr Caldicott had varied business interests. There are also some stocks and shares, but most of his money went into the property. Some of the property, I may say, is giving us cause for concern.'

'Why is that?'

'It's not in a good state of repair, and new government regulations made it imperative that some work is done on it soon.'

'Could I go and see for myself? I know I can't do anything,

but at least I could report to Toby if he got in touch with me.'

The solicitor hesitated. 'Don't go on your own,' he said.

'Why not?'

'You might be lynched.' He looked at her thoughtfully and said, 'The Social Services are getting militant about the bed-and-breakfast places, not without cause. If you asked to be shown round at least it would demonstrate an awareness of responsibility.'

'But I'm *not* responsible,' Ella protested.

It was something she had to repeat when the young woman from Social Services met her two days later.

'Until the two Wills are proved there's no money available,' she said. 'And I can't do anything at all about it because I'm not an executor. All I can do is report to the man who's meant to be acting.'

'You speak as if he's on the far side of the moon.'

'He might as well be. He's in Afghanistan, working for the International Red Cross.'

'Oh. I suppose he's doing good work, but tell him he's needed here.'

Ella had heard that some of the bed-and-breakfast accommodation was sordid, but nothing had prepared her for the three houses she was taken to visit that morning. She thought of Bernie and his opulent, self-indulgent life, of Claudia with her clanking gold jewellery and her villa in Spain and she was sickened.

'The children mustn't know about this,' she said.

The social worker looked at her curiously. 'I'm sorry?'

'My three stepchildren. They own these houses. I don't think they've yet taken in how rich they've become as a result of the deaths of their father and his new wife, but if they knew the source of the money they would be revolted.'

'I'm glad to hear it.'

'Why don't the tenants withhold their rent?'

'It's paid by DHSS direct to the managing company, and if it wasn't paid they'd be out on the street. Any roof is better than no roof, especially if you have two or three young children.'

Four rooms on each floor, most of them occupied by one or two adults and at least two children. Because the houses had once been boarding houses for holidaymakers the rooms had washbasins, which now also had to do duty as sinks. One big bed and a couple of mattresses on the floor was normal. There was little other furniture. One bathroom and one lavatory to each floor. Leaking roofs, broken windows, dirt-encrusted hallways and stairs, sagging walls which looked as if they were held up by the layers of bulging wallpaper. A smell of urine and stale cooking. A feeling of hopelessness. Children crying, women snapping at them, a man's voice raised in futile anger. Grinding poverty, fecklessness, drink and drugs and despair.

'Something will be done, I can promise you that,' Ella said. 'Oh, God, why doesn't Toby get in touch with me? I feel so helpless!'

She put in a few hours' work at the industrial unit, her mind distracted by the sights and sounds and, still more, the smells she had encountered, and drove home feeling totally exhausted.

'There's a letter for you,' her mother-in-law said. 'Got "International Red Cross" on the envelope, so perhaps it's what you've been waiting for.'

The message was brief. 'I'm getting a colleague going to a more civilised part of the world to fax this through to the London office for onward transmission to you.'

That meant nothing too personal in the wording, Ella realised.

'Desperately sorry to hear of the tragic accident. Quite impossible to act as executor at this distance. Suggest I give you power of attorney to take over from me. Fondest love to all – Toby.'

'Fondest love!' Ella said. 'If he comes back to this country, I'll kill him!'

Chapter Fourteen

When Ella sat down to write to Toby she was so incandescent with rage she thought her words might scorch the paper.

'I will, of course, ask for a power of attorney to be drawn up,' she wrote. 'What else can I do? But don't imagine, dear Toby, that I believe you have any right to unload this duty on me. You can hardly have taken time to consider the difficulties involved in administering the complex estate of a very rich woman which has now passed to three orphaned children. Who, for instance, is to go to Spain to close up the villa and put it on the market? Who is to check up on the lettings of the Spanish apartments? Don't tell me I can employ people to do these things, I know I can, but who is to choose the agents in the first place?

'You are, no doubt, doing work of great humanitarian importance, but would you mind admitting that there are people in this country who need your help at least as much as your Afghans do? No, I am not talking about Verity, Harry and Jennifer, glad though they would be to see you, but about the people living in properties which Bernie should have been ashamed to own. If you could see the degradation, the sheer horror of the lives being lived in houses from which your nieces and nephew are now entitled to make a considerable profit, you would have some idea of my indignation. I've promised that "something will be done" – a vain promise until money is available, which it won't be until the Wills are proved and the estates wound up. Come to that, since you are the children's trustee, I still won't have the right to spend any of their money unless you authorise it. Am I to wait weeks on end for replies to my letters when action should have been taken yesterday, if not before? And who is actually to *do* what is necessary? The solicitors and agents say, "It's up to you, Mrs Armitage" and, "What ever you think, Mrs Armitage", which is of no practical help at all. I'm at my wits' end to know how to cope so please don't send me any more sympathy and fond love, they don't even begin to solve my problems.'

She posted the letter without giving herself time to consider and felt considerably better for having got it off her chest. By the next morning she was feeling guilty about complaining to a man who was doing good work in trying circumstances. Probably it was impossible for him to come home and he would be upset by her rantings. The trouble was, when she had sent him word of the two deaths she had allowed her mind to dwell on a lovely daydream of Toby rushing home to be with her, sharing her worries, comforting the children. A loving companion and helper, that was what she wanted, and she should have known better than to expect it from a man dedicated to giving his compassion to the poorest of the poor.

The rich have their problems, too, Ella thought, sorting through Claudia's jewel case to find the pieces intended for her friends. Not that she could part with the diamond rings and emerald pendant until they had been valued for probate, she remembered, and no doubt some of the jewels were at the villa in Spain, so she was really wasting her time. It was typical of the futility she felt because there was so little she could do.

She had written to the housekeeper at the villa and had the letter translated into Spanish. When the reply came it, too, had to be put into English before she could read it. Everything took so long!

'I ought to go out to Marbella,' she said out loud.

Harry's head jerked up. 'We don't have to come, do we?'

'No, and I'm not going yet. Until Uncle Toby's power of attorney comes through I have no authority and the Spanish are such sticklers for legal formalities.'

'You don't want to take a few days over there before I go?' her mother-in-law asked.

'I'll tell them to put everything on hold – or the Spanish equivalent – until I'm able to take decisions.' She leaned back in her chair to look at the older woman. 'Must you leave us?'

'As soon as we've got the children back to school. I've been glad to be here and I'll come again any time you need me, but this isn't my part of the world and I'll be glad to get home. I've got things arranged for the autumn that I'd be sorry to miss.'

'Yes, of course; you've got your own life to lead.'

Ella spoke mechanically, her heart falling at the thought of being without her mother-in-law's help. She would manage, she would have to manage, but she could not help wishing that she did not carry always at the back of her mind the nagging worry of what she was to do about the bed-and-breakfast tenants.

'I don't want to go back to school.'

Ella put down the pen with which she was making a list of essential jobs to be done before the beginning of term and looked at Harry. His expression was mutinous and he was kicking the leg of the kitchen table in a way that set her teeth on edge.

'Because of the accident?' she asked.

'Everyone will look at us and they'll ask questions and I don't want to talk about it.'

'I've written to the headmistress to tell her what happened.'

'It's not her, it's the other kids.'

'I could arrange for you to go in late the first morning and that would give your class teachers time to tell them about it and ask them not to talk about it.'

'We'd be ever so late,' Jennifer pointed out. 'If we miss our usual bus there's not another for ages.'

'I could drive you, just that one morning. And pick you up in the afternoon as well.'

'It would be nice if you always took us by car.'

'Don't push your luck! How about it, Harry? Would that help?'

'S'pose so.'

'That's settled then.'

'I don't know how I'm going to play football,' he burst out. 'My leg's ever so weak.'

'You were badly cut and the tissues are taking time to heal. It will get better, I promise you.'

'I expect I'll be dropped from the team.'

'For a week or two perhaps. You'll be as good as ever before Christmas.'

'Christmas! That's *months* away!'

'Not that many months. I'm up to my ears in plans for Christmas hampers.'

'Do you think Uncle Toby will come and see us for Christmas this year?' Jennifer asked.

'I don't know. I haven't heard from him.'

Verity looked up from the book she was reading, sitting with it propped up on the table in a way that could not have been comfortable. It was something Ella had noticed, the way the children all tended to congregate round her in the kitchen, whereas in the past they would have dispersed to their own rooms or the living room. She said nothing, although it hampered her, realising that they needed to be in touch with her, especially now that Mrs Armitage had gone back to Yorkshire and she was the only adult available to them.

'If the Taliban take Kabul, the international organisations might get pushed out,' Verity said.

'What's the Taliban?' Jennifer asked.

'You watch the news, you ought to know. They're a militant religious group who think Western ways are wrong.'

'They won't hurt Uncle Toby, will they?'

'He'll keep out of trouble,' Ella said. 'Or so I hope. Having him far away and out of touch is bad enough. It'd be even worse if anything happened to him.'

'Yes, it would,' Harry said. 'Never mind about silly old Wills and things, we want Uncle Toby to be safe because we love him.'

He sounded overwrought almost to the point of tears and Ella could have kicked herself for her careless words.

'Of course we do,' she said quickly. 'I wasn't thinking of anything serious happening to him, but I bet if he finds a patch of ice he'll fall over again and what will he do without us to pick him up?'

'Break another window,' Harry said with a watery smile.

'There aren't any windows in Kabul,' Verity said. 'Mum, did you ever read *Wuthering Heights*?'

'Is that what's keeping you so quiet? Yes, I've read it.'

'Don't you think it's rather a lot of twaddle?'

'Verity! It's supposed to be one of the great love stories of all time.'

'Huh! Not an ounce of commonsense amongst the lot of them. I've got to write an essay about it before the beginning of term and I simply don't know what to say.'

'Say what you think. At least it'll be original.'

The return to school went off better than Ella had hoped. They were all very quiet and seemed not to want to join in any out-of-school activities, which relieved her of chauffeuring duties, but left them on her hands, very dependent and wanting her attention all the time. She recognised a quiet, obstinate under-swell of determination that she should make them her first priority. If she had given up her work they would have been delighted and relieved, but she was determined not to do that. The Patels had been wonderful, taking over all her duties for far longer than had been intended, but she could not let that situation continue, she had a duty to them as well as to her poor, wounded children.

She felt perpetually tired. The lack of any holiday, coupled with a profound emotional shock and the need to prop up the children, drained her of energy just when she needed to do twice as much as usual.

The news from Afghanistan was not good. Ella paid more attention to it than she ever had before. Just as Verity had fore-told, the international agencies were finding their work so difficult that there were strong hints that they would discon-tinue their efforts, if only temporarily.

The Power of Attorney to which she had been obliged to agree took longer to draw up than Ella thought reasonable and she was reluctant to despatch it into the uncertain maelstrom of war-torn Afghanistan, but she sent it off to the usual forward-ing address and waited for it to come back.

'I suppose it's got through,' she said as September turned into October.

The social worker who had taken her to view the bed-and-breakfast houses was impatient for the action Ella had promised to begin.

'I can't do anything without authority,' Ella pointed out for the umpteenth time. 'If it were my money, I would start laying it out immediately, but until the estate is settled the funds just aren't available.'

'Couldn't you pay for repairs yourself and claim the money back later?'

'I don't have that kind of capital,' Ella retorted.

She had the annoying feeling that the other woman did not believe her, but it was true that her resources were spread very thinly indeed, which was another reason for keeping up her efforts to foster the delicatessen business.

By the middle of October it was definite that the international agencies had withdrawn from Kabul and still there was no word from Toby. Ella scanned the newspapers, trying to glean a word or two which might give her some clue as to his whereabouts. Until the day in the middle of October when she let herself into the house after a gruelling day of dashing from the cookery unit to the shops and her suppliers, to be greeted by Harry and Jennifer falling over themselves to be first with the news.

'Uncle Toby's here!'

As Ella went through the kitchen, Toby got slowly to his feet.

'I suppose I should have known you'd just turn up without warning,' she said.

'I rang you from Heathrow, but all I got was the answering machine. How are you, Ella?'

'As you see – worn out. And you?'

'Frustrated. I've come home because there was nothing I could do in Afghanistan at present and it seemed I might be more useful here.'

'That's true enough. Did you get the Power of Attorney?'

'Yes, and your previous letter.'

Ella looked at him warily. 'I was at the end of my tether when I wrote that.'

'So I gathered.' He spoke gravely, but there was a hint of amusement in the way he regarded her which Ella resented.

'I'll be around for a week or two at least,' Toby went on. 'You must put me in the picture.'

'Are you staying here?'

'If you'll have me.'

'You'll have to sleep on the sofa bed.'

244

'No problem.'

A welcome idea presented itself to Ella. 'I'll ring my contact in Social Services,' she said. 'And get her to take you round the property I wrote about.'

'Why don't you take me?'

'I'm too busy.'

'Mum works terribly hard,' Jennifer said. 'She's hardly ever at home when we get in.'

'I'm always here,' Verity put in quickly. She reached for the teapot. 'I made tea for Uncle Toby. Do you want a cup, Mum?'

'I do indeed. I'm dead on my feet. Toby, I was planning to have cauliflower cheese and bread-and-butter pudding this evening. Not exactly *haute-cuisine*, I'm afraid.'

'It's good,' Jennifer assured her uncle. 'Mum puts bits of crispy bacon in the cheese sauce and we have it with grilled tomatoes.'

'Sounds delicious. My diet has been much more limited than that in recent weeks.'

'Will you be going back?' Verity asked.

'That's a good question and the only answer I can give is "it all depends".'

Not a satisfactory reply, Ella thought, as she began her preparations for supper. Depends on what?

She got her answer when they had eaten and the children had dispersed to do their homework.

'I'll help with the washing up,' Toby said.

'It all goes in the dishwasher,' Ella said.

'Then I'll load the dishwasher. Sit down.'

She sat and watched. She wanted to be pleased to see him, but she was too weary to feel anything very much. Besides, she had not got over her disgruntlement over his unsatisfactory response to Piers' and Claudia's deaths, and she was wary about his reaction to her infuriated letter.

Toby came and joined her at the kitchen table. 'That's that,' he said as he sat down.

'It would be if you'd turned the machine on,' Ella said, getting to her feet.

In spite of herself she had to smile in response to Toby's groan. 'You're still not very domesticated,' she said.

'Dishwashers are few and far between in Afghanistan.'

'I suppose so. Is the situation very bad?'

'Like I said before – frustrating. A degree of law and order has been restored, but at such a price! The women are forbidden to work which means few doctors and even fewer nurses. There are young widows with children who now have no way of earning money to feed them. You've probably seen pictures of cassettes and films being burned and television sets destroyed. Some attempt will have to be made to come to terms with the new rulers – if they survive – but for the time being everything is at a standstill.'

'So you've come home. What I want to know, of course, is what Verity asked.'

'For how long? The situation is a little difficult. My contract is due for renewal, assuming my services are still wanted, but until I've assessed the situation here I don't know whether or not I'll accept if I'm given the chance of continuing with the Red Cross. If I opt out, then I'll be unemployed.'

'Well, while you're thinking it over, could you also give your mind to the problem of sorting out Claudia's estate?'

'That's what I'm here for. Ella, I'm truly sorry I didn't realise what a load of trouble had landed on your shoulders. Was Claudia really so rich?'

'The children won't be millionaires, not individually, but it's not far off that level. It's the source of the money, or some of it at least, that worries me. You'll see what I mean when you've visited the three bed-and-breakfast houses. There's a sort of caretaker or warden who's supposed to be in charge, but he seems to do very little, possibly because he despairs of making any difference.'

'I'll go and see the solicitors tomorrow to find out exactly what my duties and responsibilities are.'

'If you can get an appointment.'

'They'll see me fast enough if I threaten to return to Afghanistan with nothing settled.'

'You wouldn't really do that, would you?' Ella asked appalled.

'Not after moving heaven and earth to get back to England,' Toby admitted. 'I can't make any decisions until I've investigated the situation here; including, my darling, our situation.'

246

'I don't think we've got a situation,' Ella said carefully. 'It's the children who need you.'

'I thought they seemed admirably normal, which I put down to your courage and loving care.'

'You only saw the surface. These are damaged children, Toby; deeply, deeply hurt. There's been too much tragedy in their lives: the loss of their mother, their father's desertion and then his death, just as they were beginning to make friends with him; even Bernie's sudden death affected them. They cling, like limpets. Even Verity, who was beginning to turn into an adult, has gone back to childhood again. It's very worrying.'

'And you bear the brunt of it.'

'Of course. That was what I took on when I married Piers.'

'Do you grieve for him?'

Ella was reluctant to answer that, but she thought Toby deserved to understand her frame of mind, at least as far as she understood it herself.

'When he left me I was terribly hurt, but I was also furiously angry, and that carried me over the worst of it. Death has a way of wiping out the bad memories. I find myself mourning for Piers the way he used to be, the way I thought he was when I married him. Yes, I grieve, and I waste a lot of time wondering where I went wrong, whether there was something I ought to have done which would have kept us together.'

'That would have taken a superhuman effort, given Piers' character.'

'I ought to have been able to influence him ... If I had made more of a fight to detach him from Bernie and Claudia ... I don't know.'

'They were a long standing habit, it would have meant endless quarrels. You have no cause to blame yourself.'

'I know that really, but still the fact of his death gives me a lot of pain.'

'I could help you get over it.'

'Not yet,' Ella said. 'Not yet.'

She ought to have been prepared for the energy with which Toby threw himself into getting the complex details of Claudia's estate sorted out. He was a man accustomed to getting things done. In no time at all he set up a remarkable rapport with the social worker who had been decidedly aggressive when it was Ella she had to deal with. He saw the solicitors who were acting in connection with both Claudia's and Piers' affairs and galvanised them into action that seemed positively frenzied by comparison with the stalemate that had prevailed until he came home. Above all, he visited the properties which had so troubled Ella and came home looking grim.

He was still staying with the family and taking some of the burden of caring for the children off Ella's shoulders.

'Unless I've arranged anything different with you beforehand, I'll always be here when they get home from school,' he said. 'Then you can work a longer day, which you seem to need.'

The extra hour or two tacked on to the end of her working day meant that Ella was no longer passing from one job to another at a fast gallop. She could take time to think about solutions to problems instead of making snap decisions which sometimes turned out to be wrong, she could listen to her staff and have more leisurely discussions with the Patels. She still felt tired, and she carried within her a heavy weight of grief and distress and old memories which never entirely left her, but some of the burden had been lifted because Toby was there to share it with her.

'I've got the bed-and-breakfast houses sorted out, at least as a temporary solution,' he said. 'I'm told that now that the summer season is at an end some of the people on benefit who are not really local residents will be leaving.'

'That's true,' Ella agreed. 'Quite a few move to the coast in the summer months, presumably in the hope of picking up temporary jobs.'

'While enjoying sea air and days on the beach, weather permitting,' Toby said drily. 'There are vacancies now in those three revolting houses so we're planning to move everyone out of one house while it's being done up and a few more amenities installed.'

'The difficulty will be to keep it decent once the work is done,' Ella said with a sigh.

'The present caretaker – the so-called – is well past retirement age so I've given him the push, though I put it more tactfully than that.'

'But where will he live? I didn't think very highly of him, but you can't turn him out on the street.'

'I've done a deal with the Council. They've found a place for him in sheltered accommodation and in return I've agreed to move in and take over management of the houses.'

It took a moment for that to sink in, but when it did Ella exclaimed. 'You can't do that! The condition of his flat was appalling!'

'There's not much I don't know about living in squalor,' Toby said.

'I suppose not,' Ella admitted reluctantly. 'But I bet you aid workers had reasonable living quarters and kept yourselves clean.'

'And ate better than most of the people surrounding us,' Toby agreed. 'We had to keep fit if we were to be of any use. I don't propose to move until the place has been fumigated and given a coat of fresh paint.'

'But your job! Your work!'

'I've resigned. I am the new caretaker of the three houses, for which I shall draw a small wage and have free living quarters.'

'I can't believe it!'

'Sandra the Social is doubtful, too. She thinks I'll be too authoritarian, but I've promised to remember that I'm not in charge of an Army barracks.'

'I suppose it will satisfy your need to be uncomfortable while you're doing good,' Ella said.

'That's not a very pleasant thing to say. I'm no masochist. I enjoy the good things of life as much as the next man. But there's one thing I do know: if you want to establish order you need to be on the spot. Once I've got the three houses running properly, and believe me, it's going to take time, then I'll turn my mind to some other task.'

'Abroad?'

'That depends. And don't say "depends on what" or I'll think you a real simpleton.' He did not wait for her response to that, but went straight on: 'Tell me, do the kids realise how rich they've become?'

'I don't know ... I suppose not, we've never talked about it.'

'They ought to be told. Shall I do it or will you? Or shall we talk to them together?'

'Together.'

'Good, that's a word I like to hear on your lips.'

Ella was forced to smile. 'You never give up, do you?'

'I'm a man who knows what he wants.'

They were helped in the task of telling the children about their inheritance by a chance question from Harry.

'Mum, did I understand that these horrible houses Uncle Toby is doing up belong to *us*?'

'I'm afraid so.'

Jennifer and Verity looked up, as if this were something they, too, had wondered about.

'How could they?' Jennifer asked.

'From Uncle Bernie to Claudia and from Claudia to Dad,' Verity said slowly.

'And from Dad to you,' Ella agreed.

'But that's horrible,' Harry exclaimed. 'We hated Claudia, and Uncle Bernie was a crook.'

'A perverted crook,' Verity added. 'We don't want his money.'

'Are we very rich?' Jennifer asked.

'There's a lot of property,' Toby said cautiously.

'Bernie owned that block of flats where you lodged last time you were here,' Verity said. 'And there's the villa in Spain.'

'And the new apartments Dad was managing,' Harry added.

'And other interests,' Toby said. 'Added to which, both Claudia and Piers were extremely well insured.'

'I expect that was Claudia's idea,' Verity said gloomily. 'Do we have to take it? Can't we renounce it or something?'

'Not until you come of age. In the meantime, as you will realise, I have the task of sorting it all out and administering the money on your behalf.'

'Why you, not Mum?'

'Dad appointed me executor of his Will and made me your Trustee.'

'Doesn't Mum get any of the money?' Harry asked.

'She gets an allowance for looking after you and the right to live in this house for life.'

'It doesn't seem much.'

'I bet that was Claudia's doing, too,' Verity said.

'I prefer to earn my own money,' Ella said quickly.

'So would we. At least – I suppose there's no reason now why I shouldn't go to RADA, if I can get a place?'

'We can afford the fees.'

'But I don't see how I can be a rich clergyman,' Harry said. 'It doesn't seem right.'

'You can give it all away when you're of age,' Toby pointed out. 'Or, on the other hand, you could use it to do a lot of good, as I suppose you could say we were doing by improving the lodging houses.'

'Will we be rich enough to do absolutely anything we like?' Jennifer asked.

'It's a lot of money, but not that much. Do any of you have anything to say in favour of keeping the Spanish villa, or shall I sell it as Ella wants?'

'I never want to go there again,' Verity said.

'The trouble is, in the summer months, when we could make best use of it, the weather is really too hot,' Harry said. 'And it seems daft to have a house you only visit a couple of times a year.'

'Jennifer?'

'I don't specially like it, except for the swimming pool.'

'Right, that's settled. I'll go over next week and sort it out.'

Ella made an involuntary movement and Toby looked towards her with a smile. 'Come with me?' he suggested.

'You don't need me.'

'Oh, I do, I do.'

Verity shot them a glance of sudden enlightenment, but it was Jennifer who planted her elbows on the table and said, 'I tell you what, Mum, you and Uncle Toby ought to get married.'

'That's what I keep telling her,' Toby agreed, wickedly amused by Ella's confusion.

'Jennifer, you really are the absolute pits,' Harry said in disgust. 'I know we talked about it, but I told you not to say anything.'

'As well as earning my own money, I prefer to settle my own future,' Ella said. 'Hasn't anyone got homework to do? Get out of my kitchen, all of you.'

The children went, but not Toby. Ella seized an onion and chopped it in half, not so much beginning the evening meal as providing an excuse for the angry tears that had sprung into her eyes.

Toby moved round the table and put his arms round her, turning her to face him. 'I don't particularly want to talk to you with a lethal-looking knife pressed to my chest,' he said. 'Could you put it down? That's better. Now, would you please tell me why you're so dead set against marrying me? There's always been something between us, certainly on my side, and I think on yours too. The last time we talked about it you were trying to be a faithful wife to an unsatisfactory husband and I had to accept that, but you found me attractive, you kissed me very sweetly; I might even have pushed you to go further if I hadn't had a faint spark of old fashioned honour in me. And yet now, when you're free and I still love you, you won't let me get near you, although it seems so obvious . . .'

'Too obvious,' Ella burst out. 'Too damned convenient. Can't you see? You're one of the few men in the world I could marry. You accept the children, you're related to them, you're involved with them, you even love them.'

'Which is why it seems an ideal arrangement,' Toby said, but he spoke slowly, beginning to see the thinking behind her hesitation.

'Too ideal,' Ella insisted. 'I just can't be sure and I don't think I'd ever be sure that in marrying you I wasn't doing the expedient thing. I don't know my own feelings because there's such a confusion between what I want to do and what everyone can see is a damned good idea.'

'If we were in a closer relationship,' Toby began, but Ella interrupted him.

'Sex would only complicate the situation still further. It was because the sex was so marvellous that I fell into marriage with Piers. I'm not getting trapped like that a second time.'

'Heaven forbid that I should make you feel trapped,' Toby said, letting his arms drop away from her.

'I've upset you.'

'I don't like being compared with Piers,' he admitted.

'You'll go away again,' Ella said. 'You can't be an underpaid caretaker for the rest of your life.'

'Why not? It's a job that needs doing.'

She wished he didn't look so despondent. Tentatively, she touched his hand. 'I'm sorry,' she said.

'I've half a mind to throw you over my shoulder and carry you off to my lair and ravish you,' Toby said.

'What I really need is a holiday,' Ella said, glad to see the smile back in his eyes. 'Two or three months lying on a sunlit beach with palm trees and blue sea, and nothing to do but sort myself out.'

'You'd be experimenting with coconut jam by the end of the first week,' Toby said. 'Sure you won't come with me to Spain?'

'Quite sure.'

'I'll take Sandra the Social,' he threatened.

'Don't call her that, the children have started to take it up. You could do worse.'

'I could do a great deal better. And so could you, much better than this half-life you're leading. Think about it while I'm away.'

The difficulty was to think about anything else. In the days while Toby was in Marbella her thoughts turned constantly towards him. She liked him, she trusted him, the children adored him, and whatever decision she came to he was going to be involved in all their lives for years to come. He would not remain unmarried. Ella faced that squarely and realised that it would be extremely painful to see Toby in love with another woman. Why then, did she find it so difficult to turn to him herself? Because it felt like taking advantage of him. Pride, that was what it was. She just couldn't face the idea of being under an obligation to a man who was prepared to share her burdens. If she were free, as she had been when she married Piers, then she would have succumbed to the attraction she certainly felt for Toby. As it was, every time he approached her she stepped away, conscious of the enormity of the commitment that marriage to her would mean and unwilling to exploit the feeling he said he had for her.

She felt obliged to leave work early while Toby was not around to be at home when the children returned from school, even though Verity assured her it was not necessary.

'You're turning into a martyr,' she said, a trifle put out that Ella apparently did not consider her competent to take charge of her younger brother and sister for an hour or two.

'I'm not, am I?' Ella said, appalled.

'Definitely signs of a halo. It's jolly hard being on the receiving end of your sacrifices. I mean, how are we supposed to live up to it?'

'You could start by picking up the clothes from your bedroom floor.'

'That's more like it! The occasional snappy answer and one selfish act a week and we'll feel much more comfortable.'

'All right! That was the front door bell. Go and see who it is.'

It was the girl Toby called Sandra the Social and she was decidedly put out to hear he was in Spain.

'He might have told me,' she complained.

She was an attractive girl in a downbeat kind of way. No make-up and straight fair hair which hung untidily round her face, but she had a good figure, accentuated by the way she cinched in the belt of her raincoat. What did Toby make of her? He poked fun at her earnestness, but they had been working closely together for weeks now.

'The thing is, I promised to keep him in touch with developments about a job that would suit him down to the ground,' Sandra said. 'I expect he's told you about it?'

'Only vaguely,' Ella said, refusing to admit ignorance.

'You've probably heard about the Care Village we want to establish? For long-term and respite care for the disadvantaged? I think Toby would be the perfect Administrator to get the scheme off the ground.'

'But has he got the necessary qualifications?' Ella asked, startled.

'More than most. Toby,' Sandra said reverently, 'is a problem solver. Look at the work he's done for the Red Cross.'

'Yes,' Ella agreed. It occurred to her that she had, in fact, very little idea of what Toby had been doing in Afghanistan. He had no medical qualifications so presumably he had been involved in administration. Planning, Ella thought vaguely. Like Sandra said, a problem solver. And a good one. She felt at the same time annoyed with herself for not knowing more and a vague sense of pride because he was well regarded.

'He promised to come to a Council meeting tonight, not to take part, but just as an onlooker,' Sandra complained. 'When he gets back you can tell him from me that he's let me down.'

'I'll tell him,' Ella said. 'Unless I hear anything to the contrary, he should be back on Tuesday.'

'Ask him to get in touch.'

She went, leaving Ella slightly ruffled. Of course, it was entirely Toby's business, but he might have told her that there was another job on the horizon. After all, she had protested often enough that he was wasted in his caretaking post. He had even agreed with her that it was not a permanent position, but still he had not said a word about being Administrator for the Care Village project. It was a local job, it would keep him in Kits Harbour; it looked as if he was determined to stick around.

By Tuesday Ella had got to the point of admitting that she missed Toby more than she would have thought possible. So it had been good tactics on his part to go away and leave her, even for a week. Presumably he was making progress with the tiresome business of disposing of the villa and arranging for the running of the holiday apartments. He might have telephoned, if only to confirm that he would be home as arranged.

'What flight is Uncle Toby on?' Harry asked.

'I don't know the number, only that he said he should be here in time to join us for supper.'

'Only there's been some trouble,' Harry said carefully.

'What sort of trouble?' Ella asked, most of her mind on the pastry for that night's meat pie.

'A hijacking.'

Ella put down her rolling pin. 'Where?'

'A Spanish airliner *en route* for London. It's been diverted to Beirut.'

'I don't believe it. I just don't believe that man could have got himself into *more* trouble.'

She was trembling, but she must control herself. Harry was already stiff with nerves and the others would be no better.

'We'll watch the News at six o'clock,' she said. 'And if he's not here by six-thirty I shall dish up and we'll eat without him.'

255

The trouble was, details were scanty. It was not known who the hijackers were or why they wanted to go to Beirut. The flight number was given, but since Ella did not even know whether Toby was flying by Iberia or British Airways that was not much use. The events were too recent for a helpline to have been set up, but there was a promise of one later.

'We'll eat,' Ella said. 'And I'll get through to the special number as soon as it's announced. Come on, no glum faces. Uncle Toby has survived worse than this and we're not even sure he's involved.'

'He's late,' Verity said flatly.

'Probably all the schedules have been thrown out,' Ella improvised. 'You know what it's like if one train or bus is late; just the same with aeroplanes.'

They hardly did justice to her good meat pie, but they did eat, mostly in silence. Verity made one comment which was far from helpful. 'Good job you didn't go with him. We might have been left with no one at all.'

'I keep telling you, Toby is a survivor. And there are no reports of anyone being hurt in this hijack. And I don't even believe he has been hijacked.'

'If he has I expect he'll knock the hijackers out and seize their guns and turn the plane round and fly home,' Jennifer provided. She was obviously rather taken with this version of events.

'I sincerely hope not,' Ella said. 'No heroics, that's what I'm praying for.'

They spent an edgy, nerve-wracking evening. The telephone rang twice, once with a message for Ella from Mrs Patel and once a long, inconsequential conversation between Verity and a school friend which stretched Ella's nerves to snapping point. She was on the point of beseeching Verity to put the telephone down when Harry called out, 'Mum, it's the nine o'clock News.'

They watched, but still there was nothing conclusive, just a few pictures of an aeroplane standing on a runway and, at last, a telephone number to call.

Ella rang it and explained the situation. No, she was not sure that her brother-in-law had been on the aircraft. On the other hand, he was due home that day and was already

256

extremely late. She was told that there was no record of a Toby Greville travelling on the hijacked aeroplane, but it was admitted that this was not conclusive. In other words, she could go on worrying until there was more definite news.

'That's all we can do,' she said, putting down the telephone. 'I know it's hard, but I think you should go to bed.'

'We won't be able to sleep,' Harry said.

'Go and wash and undress, then we'll decide whether to sit up or not.'

Harry and Jennifer dragged themselves reluctantly up the stairs.

'I'm too grown up to be sent to bed like a kid,' Verity said. 'And it's not ten o'clock yet.'

'Stay up if you like,' Ella said wearily. She was conscious of nothing more than a vast disbelief. She told herself that it was quite impossible for Toby to have been involved in yet another adventure. Of course, Verity was quite right in saying that it would have been a disaster for her to have been with him and yet that was what she longed for. To be with him to share his danger, to sustain him and be sustained by him.

She loved him. How could she have refused to admit it? Her foolish qualms, her silly pride had kept them apart, and now that there was a possibility of not seeing him again, not that she really believed it, not that she would admit there was any chance of that, she was bowed down by grief and remorse. What might have been. The bitterest words anyone could speak. She had refused to take Toby seriously and now she was tortured by her own inadequacy in the face of his constant love.

Harry and Jennifer were quarrelling over who had the right to use the bathroom first. Ella let them get on with it, too taken up with her unhappy thoughts to register the acrimonious sounds from upstairs.

Verity looked up, her head jerking. 'That's a taxi outside,' she said.

They sat frozen, looking at one another, and then they heard the gate creak and footsteps on the gravel path.

'I'll go,' Ella said.

By the time she got to the hall she knew it was Toby because she heard his key in the lock. As the door swung open she reached out to clutch his arm.

257

'You're all right,' she said inadequately. Behind her she could hear Harry and Jennifer tumbling down the stairs while Verity hovered in the doorway of the living room.

'You could say so. Sorry I'm so late. By the time I was set free all I could think of was getting hold of a taxi and putting space between myself and the airport.'

'So you *were* hijacked!' Harry exclaimed.

'Hijacked? No, of course I wasn't. Whatever made you think that?' He looked round their bemused faces. 'There really has been a hijacking?'

'You didn't even know,' Ella said limply. 'We've spent the most ghastly evening ...'

'So have I,' Toby said with feeling. 'Is there any food? I'm famished.'

'Yes, of course. I saved some meat pie for you. Come into the kitchen.'

They all trooped into the kitchen and Jennifer demanded, 'What happened? We thought you were being terribly, terribly brave and making the hijackers let everyone go.'

'Not me. If I'm ever hijacked I'll keep a very low profile.'

'So what did happen?' Ella asked, busy at the stove with Toby's belated meal.

'I was arrested for smuggling bloody Claudia's jewellery into the country.'

'Toby!' It was such an anticlimax that Ella could only stare at him in disbelief. 'But you had every right to bring her jewels home.'

'Try telling that to Customs & Excise when they think they're on to a good thing. Of course I told my story and they listened very politely, but I could tell they thought it was a pack of lies. I must admit it did look like a pretty good haul. Gold, diamonds, sapphires, the lot. I didn't know what was real and what was costume stuff so I just shoved it all into a red leather box that was on the dressing table, put it into my hand luggage and kept an extremely sharp eye on it. It never occurred to me to notify anyone about it. As far as I was concerned it was stuff that Claudia carried about with her and would have brought back to England just as I was doing.'

He looked with approval at the plate Ella put in front of him. 'That looks good.'

'Did they put you in prison?' Harry asked.

'Not quite, but I was certainly detained and searched and they went through my luggage with a fine toothcomb. I was held while they tried to get hold of the Spanish authorities to check my story, which wasn't easy because we were outside office hours by then. Same thing with the solicitors over here, but they did eventually come up with a home telephone number. That was when they started being less certain they'd caught an international jewel thief. It all took longer than you would believe possible.'

'I suppose it's quite funny, really,' Harry said. 'But we were very worried about you, Uncle Toby.' He gave an earsplitting yawn.

'Bed,' Ella said. 'And you, too, Jennifer.' She looked uncertainly at Verity.

'Yes, I'll go as well,' Verity said. 'Don't hit Uncle Toby with the rolling pin as soon as we're out of the way, will you?' .

'I won't do that,' Ella promised.

She sat down opposite Toby. 'I could have given you a glass of wine,' she said. 'I had a bottle all ready, but I forgot to open it.'

'You've been worried about me.'

'You could say that. Oh, while I remember, Sandra the Social came round, very put out because you'd forgotten about some Council meeting.'

'True, I did forget. I'll apologise tomorrow.'

'She was talking about the job you might get. You might have told me.'

'I was going to as soon as something definite materialised.'

'Will you take it?'

'If you can offer me an incentive to stay in this neighbourhood.'

Ella took his empty plate and went over to the stove again. 'Do you want rhubarb crumble?'

Toby followed her. 'Let's forget about the food. What I want is you. I always have, I always will. And the look on your face when I walked through the door tonight gave me the first bit of hope I've had since Piers died.'

Ella turned and clutched as much of him as she could reach. 'I do love you, I do!'

259

'Darling, why do you always attack me with kitchen utensils? Put that sticky spoon down and give me your full attention. I want to kiss you.'

Ella discarded the spoon and lifted her face. She knew that there were tears on her cheeks, but she was smiling, too. Toby's lips were warm on hers and then abruptly his breathing changed and he was holding her fiercely and kissing her with an intensity she wanted to match, to show him at last how desperately she had come to love him.

'That's more like it,' Toby said at last.

'I thought I'd lost you,' Ella whispered. 'I thought you'd been stolen away from me and I knew you'd do something foolish and brave and get yourself killed. I felt the second half of my life had been wiped out before it had even begun. I was *furious* with you.'

'But I hadn't done anything!'

'No, but you would have done if you'd been in that situation.'

'Tell you what, I'll have it drawn up in a marriage settlement – if hijacked, no heroics.' His hold on her tightened again. 'We are getting married, I take it?'

'Yes, please.'

Toby sighed. 'I know what's going to happen next, you're going to throw me out.'

'Darling, I can't take you upstairs, you must see that. And don't start dropping hints about the sofa bed because I'd only have one ear open for footsteps on the stairs the whole time.'

'A cup of coffee and a bit of a snog?'

'You have such an elegant way of putting things. Toby, I do love you. I would have come round to admitting it sooner or later, but today I had an awful jolt when I realised that "later" might have meant "too late".'

She shivered and Toby kissed her gently on the forehead. 'When I first came home, I expected too much, too soon. I was thinking of you as having parted with Piers at the time of the divorce, but his death was a second bereavement, wasn't it?'

'The circumstances were so sad. And I did love him once. Not the way I love you, more in a fairy-story kind of way which crumbled when reality touched it. I was horribly disillusioned, almost to the point where I felt I couldn't trust anyone again. But you ... there's something solid about you, Toby. I believe in you.'

'We'll build a great life together, Ella, darling Ella.'

Second time round, Ella thought, as she raised her mouth to his once more. Second time round, I'll know the score. No reservations. Toby is a man I can love for the rest of my life.

She had said she would hear footsteps on the stairs, but as she and Toby clung together she was blind and deaf as Jennifer crept back to the landing. At the top of the stairs Jennifer raised her thumb in a triumphant gesture to Harry and Verity.

Verity tried to look disapproving, but the truth was she was too pleased and relieved to reprove Jennifer for her inspired bit of spying. She put her finger to her lips to indicate the need for silence and the other two disappeared into their bedrooms. So it was going to be all right. Toby would be with them; lovely Uncle Toby; Ella was one of the few women Verity had ever seen who was worthy of him. She gave a jaw-breaking yawn. Not so much a happy ending, she thought as she crawled into bed; more, she hoped, a happy beginning.